JAMES P. HOGAN
ROCKETS, Redheads & REVOLUTION

ROCKETS, REDHEADS AND REVOLUTION

This is a work of fiction. All the characters and events portrayed in this book are fictional, and any resemblance to real people or incidents is purely coincidental.

Copyright © 1999 by James P. Hogan

All rights reserved, including the right to reproduce this book or portions thereof in any form.

A Baen Books Original

Baen Publishing Enterprises
P.O. Box 1403
Riverdale, NY 10471

ISBN: 0-671-57807-3

Cover art by David Mattingly

First printing, April 1999

Distributed by Simon & Schuster
1230 Avenue of the Americas
New York, NY 10020

Printed in the United States of America

TABLE OF CONTENTS

PUBLISHING HISTORY

"How They Got Me at Baycon" was first published in *Challenger*, 1995.

"Identity Crisis" was first published in the Ballantine-Del Rey *Stellar 7* anthology, August 1981.

"Leapfrog" was first published in the Bantam/Spectra anthology *What Might Have Been*, Volume 1, August 1989.

"Boom and Slump in Space" is reprinted from a newsletter of the British Libertarian Alliance in May 1990, and before that was published under the title "Paint Your Booster" in *New Destinies* Volume 8, Fall 1989.

"Last Ditch" was first published in *Analog*, December 1992.

"Zap Thy Neighbor" was first published in the Tor anthology *How To Save the World*, September 1995.

"Ozone Politics" was first published in *Omni*, June 1993.

"Fact-Free Science" was first published in *Analog*, April 1995.

"Out of Time" was first published as a stand-alone novella by Bantam Books, December 1993.

Madam Butterfly

Locally, in the valley far from Tokyo that she had left long ago, it was known as *yamatsumi-sou*, which means "flower of the mountain spirit." It was like a small lily, with tapering, yellow petals warmed on the upper surface by a blush of violet. According to legend, it was found only in those particular hills on the north side of Honshu—a visible expression of the deity whose name was Kyo, that had dwelt around the village of kimikaye-no-sato and protected its inhabitants since ancient times. When the violet was strong and vivid, it meant that Kyo was cheerful and in good health, and the future was secure. When the violet waned pale and cloudy, troubled times lay ahead. Right at this moment, Kyo was looking very sorry for himself indeed.

The old woman's name was Chifumi Shimoto. She hadn't seen a *yamatsumi-sou* since those long-gone childhood days that everyone remembers as the time when life was simple and carefree—before Japan became just a province in some vaster scheme that she didn't understand, and everyone found themselves affected to some degree or other by rules borrowed from foreigners with doubtful values and different ways. How it came to be growing in the yard enclosed

1

by the gaunt, gray concrete cliffs forming the rear of the Nagomi Building was anybody's guess.

She saw it when she came out with a bag of trash from the bins in the offices upstairs, where she cleaned after the day staff had gone home. It was clinging to life bravely in a patch of cracked asphalt behind the parked trucks, having barely escaped being crushed by a piece of steel pipe thrown down on one side, and smothered by a pile of rubble encroaching from the other. Although small, it looked already exhausted, grown to the limit that its meager niche could sustain. The yard trapped bad air and exhaust fumes, and at ground level was all but sunless. Leaking oil and grime hosed off the vehicles was turning what earth there was into sticky sludge. Kyo needed a better home if he was to survive.

Potted plants of various kinds adorned shelves and window ledges throughout the offices. When she had washed the cups and ashtrays from the desks and finished vacuuming between the blue-painted computer cabinets and consoles, Chifumi searched and found some empty pots beneath the sink in one of the kitchen areas. She filled one of the smaller pots with soil, using a spoon to take a little from each of many plants, then went back downstairs with it and outside to the yard. Kneeling on the rough ground, she carefully worked the flower with its roots loose from its precarious lodgement, transferred it to the pot that she had prepared, and carried it inside. Back upstairs, she fed it with fresh water and cleaned off its leaves. Finally, she placed it in the window of an office high up in the building, facing the sun. Whoever worked in that office had been away for several days. With luck, the flower would remain undisturbed for a while longer to gain strength and recover. Also, there were no other plants in the room. Perhaps, she thought to herself, that would make it all the more appreciated when the occupant returned.

She locked the cleaning materials and equipment back in the closet by the rear stairs, took the service elevator back down to the ground floor, and returned the keys to the security desk at the side entrance. The duty officer checked her pass and ID and the shopping bag containing groceries and some vegetables that she had bought on the way in, and then let her out to the lobby area where the cleaners from other floors were assembling. Five minutes later, the bus that would run them back to their abodes around the city drew up outside the door.

The offices in the part of the Nagomi Building that Chifumi had been assigned to had something to do with taxes and accounting. That was what all the trouble was supposed to be about between the federal authorities and others in faraway places among the stars. She heard things about freedom and individualism, and people wanting to live as they chose to, away from the government—which the young seemed to imagine they were the first ever to have thought of. It all sounded to her very much like the same, age-old story of who created the wealth and how it should be shared out. She had never understood it, and did so even less now. Surely there were enough stars in the sky for everyone.

She had a son, Icoro, out there somewhere, whom she hadn't seen for two years now; but messages from him reached her from time to time through friends. The last she had heard, he was well, but he hadn't said exactly where he was or what he was doing—in other words he didn't want to risk the wrong people finding out. That alone told her that whatever he was up to was irregular at best, very likely outright illegal, and quite possibly worse. She knew that there was fighting and people got killed—sometimes lots of them. She didn't ask why or how, or want to hear the details. She worried as a mother would, tried not to dwell on such matters, and when she found that she did anyway, she kept them to herself.

But as she walked away after the bus dropped her off, she felt more reassured than she had for a long time. The flower, she had decided, was a sign that Kyo still lived in the mountains and did not want to be forgotten. Kyo was a just god who had come to Earth long ago, but he still talked with the other sky-spirits who sent the rain and made the stars above kimikaye so much brighter. Chifumi had remembered Kyo and helped him. Now Kyo's friends among the stars would watch over her son.

Suzi's voice came from a console speaker on the bridge of the consolidator *Turner Maddox*, owned by Fast Forwarding Unincorporated, drifting two hundred fifty million miles from Earth in an outer region of the Asteroid Belt.

"Spider aligned at twelve hundred meters. Delta vee is fifteen meters per second, reducing." It maintained a note of professional detachment, but everyone had stopped what they were doing to follow the sequence unfolding on the image and status screens.

"No messing with this kid, man," Fuigerado, the duty radar tech, muttered next to Cassell. "He's going in fast."

Cassell grunted, too preoccupied with gauging the lineup and closing rate to form an intelligible reply. The view from the spider's nose camera showed the crate stern-on, rotating slowly between the three foreshortened, forward-pointing docking appendages that gave the bulb-ended, remote-operated freight retrieval module its name. Through the bridge observation port on Cassell's other side, all that was discernible directly of the maneuver being executed over ten miles away were two smudges of light moving against the starfield, and the flashing blue and red of the spider's visual beacon. As navigational dynamics chief, Cassell had the decision on switching control to the regular pilot standing by if the run-in looked like going outside the envelope. Too slow meant an extended chase downrange to attach to the crate, followed by a long, circuitous recovery back. Faster was better, but impact from an over-zealous failure to connect could kick a crate off on a rogue trajectory that would require even more time and energy to recover from. Time was money everywhere, while outside gravity wells, the cost of everything was measured not by the distance moved, but by the energy needed to move it there. A lot of hopeful recruits did just fine on the simulator only to flunk through nerves when it came to the real thing.

"Ten meters per second," Suzi's voice sang out.

The kid was bringing its speed down smoothly. The homing marker was dead-center in the graticule, lock-on confirming to green even as Cassell watched. He decided to give it longer.

The lunar surface was being transformed inside domed-over craters; greenhousing by humidifying its atmosphere was thawing out the freeze-dried planet, Mars; artificial space-structures traced orbits from inside that of Venus to as far out as the asteroids. It all added up to an enormous demand for materials, which meant boom-time prices.

With Terran federal authorities controlling all lunar extraction and regulating the authorized industries operating from the Belt, big profits were to be had from bootlegging primary asteroid materials direct into the Inner System. A lot of independent operators got themselves organized to go after a share. Many of these were small-scale affairs—a breakaway cult, minicorp, even a family group—who had pooled their assets to set up a minimum habitat and mining-extraction facility, typically equipped with a low-performance mass launcher. Powered by solar units operating at extreme range, such a launcher would be capable of sending payloads to nearby orbits in the Belt, but not of imparting the velocities needed to reach the Earth-Luna vicinity.

This was where ventures like Fast Forwarding Uninc. came into the picture. Equipped with high-capacity fusion-driven launchers, they consolidated incoming consignments from several small independents together into a single payload and sent it inward on a fast-transit trajectory to a rendezvous agreed on with the customer.

Consolidators also moved around a lot and carried defenses. The federal agencies put a lot of effort into protecting their monopolies. As is generally the case when fabulous profits stand to be made, the game could get very nasty and rough. Risk always comes proportional to the possible gain.

"Delta vee, two-point-five, reducing. Twenty-six seconds to contact."

Smooth, smooth—everything under control. It had been all along. Cassell could sense the sureness of touch on the controls as he watched the screen. He even got the feeling that the new arrival might have rushed the early approach on purpose, just to make them all a little nervous. His face softened with the hint of a grin.

As a final flourish, the vessels rotated into alignment and closed in a single, neatly integrated motion. The three latching indicators came on virtually simultaneously.

"Docking completed."

"Right on!" Fuigerado complimented.

Without wasting a moment, the spider fired its retros to begin slowing the crate down to matching velocity, and steered it onto an arc that brought it around sternwise behind the launcher, hanging half a mile off the *Maddox*'s starboard bow. It slid the crate into the next empty slot in the frame holding the load that was being consolidated, hung on while the locks engaged, and then detached.

Cassell went through to the communications room behind the bridge, then down to the operations control deck, where the remote console that the spider had been controlled from was located. The kid was getting up and stretching, Suzi next to him, Hank Bissen, the reserve pilot who had been standing by, still at his console opposite.

"You did pretty good," Cassell said.

"Thank you, sir." He knew damn well that he had, and smiled. It was the kind of smile that Cassell liked—open and direct, conveying simple, unassuming confidence; not the cockiness that took needless risks and got you into trouble.

"Your name's Shimoto. What is that, Japanese?"

"Yes."

"So, what should we call you?"

"My first name is Icoro. . . . Does it mean I have a job, Mr. Cassell?"

"You'd better believe it. Welcome to the team."

Nagai Horishagi leaned back wearily from the papers scattered across his desk in the Tariffs & Excise section of the Merylynch-Mubachi offices in the Tokyo Nagomi Building. It was his first day back after ten days in South America, and it looked as if he had been gone for a month. Even as he thought it, his secretary, Yosano, came through from the outer office with another wad. Nagai motioned in the direction of his In tray. He didn't meet her eyes or speak. Her movements betraying an awkwardness equal to his own, she deposited the papers and withdrew. Nagai stared down at the desk until he heard the door close; then he sighed, rose abruptly, and turned to stare out the window at the city. That was when he noticed the plant on the ledge.

It had bright green leaves, and flowers of pale

yellow with a touch of violet—one in full bloom, two more just opening. He stared at it, perplexed. Where on earth had it come from? He had no mind for flowers, as the rest of the office readily testified. And yet, as he looked at it, he had to admit that it seemed a happy little fellow. He reached out and touched one of the leaves. It felt cool and smooth. "Very well," he thought. "If you can do something to cheer this awful place up, you've earned your keep. I guess we'll let you stay."

All through the morning, he would pause intermittently and look back over his shoulder to gaze with a fresh surge of curiosity at the plant. And then, shortly before lunchtime, the answer came to him. Of course! Yosano had put it there. No wonder she had acted tensely. How could he have been so slow?

Before he went away, they had gotten involved in one of those affairs that a professional shouldn't succumb to, but which can happen to the best. But in their case it had uncovered real affection and become quite romantic. After years of living in an emotional isolation ward he had celebrated and exuberated, unable to believe his luck . . . and then blown the whole thing in a single night, getting drunk and disgracing himself by insulting everybody at that stupid annual dinner—even if they had deserved every word of it. He had agonized over the situation all the time while he was away, but really there was no choice. No working relationship needed this kind of strain. He had decided that she would have to be transferred.

But now this was her way of telling him that it didn't have to be that way. He was forgiven. Everything could be okay. And so it came about that he was able to summon up the courage to confront her just before she left for lunch and say, "Could we give it another try?"

She nodded eagerly. Nagai didn't think that he had

ever seen her look so delighted. He smiled too. But he didn't mention the plant. The game was to pretend that the plant had nothing to do with it. "Can I apologize for being such an ass?" he said instead.

Yosano giggled. "There's no need. I thought you were magnificent."

"Then how about dinner tonight?" he suggested.

"Of course."

Yosano remembered only later in the afternoon that she had agreed to meet the American that night. Well, too bad. The American would have to find somebody else. She would have to call him and tell him, of course—but not from the office, she decided. She would call his hotel as soon as she got home.

Steve Bryant hung up the phone in his room at the Shinjuku Prince and stared at it moodily.

"Well, goddamn!" he declared.

Weren't they the same the whole world over. He had already shaved, showered, and put on his pastel-blue suit, fresh from the hotel's cleaners. His first night to himself since he arrived in Japan, and he wasn't going to hit the town with that cute local number that he'd thought he had all lined up, after all. He poured himself another scotch, lit a cigarette, and leaned back against the wall at the head of the bed to consider his options.

Okay, then he'd just take off and scout the action in this town on his own, and see what showed up, he decided. And if nothing of any note did, he was going to get very drunk. Wasn't life just the same kind of bitch, too, the whole world over.

The bar was brightly lit and glittery, and starting to fill up for the evening. There was a low stage with a couple of dancers and a singer in a dress that was more suggestion than actuality. It was later than Alan Quentin had wanted to stay, and he could feel the drink going to his head. He had stopped by intending to have just one, maybe two, to unwind on his way back to the garage-size apartment that came with his year-long stint in Tokyo. Then he'd gotten talking to the salesman from Phoenix, here on his first visit, who had been stood up by his date.

On the stool next to him, Steve Bryant went on, "Can you imagine, Al, five thousand dollars for a box of old horseshoes and cooking pots that you could pick up in a yard-sale back home? Can you beat that?" American frontier nostalgia was the current rage in Japan.

"That's incredible," Al agreed.

"You could retire on what you'd get for a genuine Civil War Colt repeater."

"I'll remember to check the attic when I get back."

"You're from Mobile, right?"

"Montgomery."

"Oh, right. But that's still Alabama."

"Right."

Steve's attention was wandering. He let his gaze drift around the place, then leaned closer and touched Al lightly on the sleeve. "Fancy livening up the company? There's a couple of honeys at the other end that we could check out."

Al glanced away. "They're hostesses. Work here. Keep you buying them lemonades all night at ten dollars a shot. See the guy out back there who'd make a Sumo wrestler look anorexic? He'll tell you politely that it's time to leave if you don't like it. I'll pass, anyhow. I've had a rough day."

Steve sat back, tossed down the last of his drink, and stubbed his cigarette. His face wrinkled. "Suddenly this place doesn't grab me so much any more. What say we move on somewhere else?"

"Really, no. I only stopped by for a quick one. There's some urgent stuff that I have to get done by tomorrow, and—"

"Aw, come on. What kind of a welcome to some-one from home is this? It's all on me. I've had a great day."

The next bar around the corner was smaller, darker, just as busy. The music was from a real fifties juke-box. They found a table squeezed into a corner below the stairs. "So what do you do?" Steve asked.

"I'm an engineer—spacecraft hydraulic systems. We use a lot of Japanese components. I liaise with the parent companies here on testing and maintenance procedures."

"Sorry, but I don't have an intelligent question to ask about that."

"Don't worry about it."

Steve fell quiet for a few seconds and contemplated his drink. Suddenly he looked up. "Does that mean you're mathematical?"

Al frowned. "Some. Why?"

"Oh, just something I was reading on the plane over. It said that a butterfly flapping its wings in China can change the weather next week in Texas. Sounds kinda crazy. Does it make sense to you?"

Al nodded. "The Butterfly Effect. It's a bit of an extreme example, but what it's supposed to illustrate is the highly nonlinear dynamics of chaotic systems. Tiny changes in initial conditions can make the world of difference to the consequences."

He took in Steve's glassy stare and regarded him dubiously. "Do you really want me to go into it?"

Steve considered the proposition. "Nah, forget it." He caught the bartender's eye and signaled for two more. "How much do you think you'd get here for a genuine Stetson? Have a guess."

Al lost count of the places they visited after that, and had no idea what time he finally got back to his apartment. He woke up halfway through the morning feeling like death, and called in sick. He was no better by lunchtime, and so decided to make a day of it.

It so happened that among the items on Alan Quentin's desk that morning was a technical memorandum concerning structural bolts made from the alloy CYA-173/B. Tests had revealed that prolonged cyclic stressing at low temperatures could induce metal crystallization, resulting in a loss of shear-strength. These bolts should be replaced after 10,000 hours in space environments, not 30,000 as stipulated previously. Since CYA-173/B had been in use less than 18 months, relatively few instances of its use would be yet affected. However, any fittings that had been in place for more than a year—and particularly where exposed to vibrational stress—should be resecured with new bolts immediately.

Because Al wasn't there to do it, the information didn't get forwarded to his company in California that day. Hence, it was not included in that week's compendium of updates that the Engineering Support Group beamed out to its list of service centers, repair shops, maintenance & supply bases, and other users of the company's products, scattered across the Solar System.

Forty-eight hours after the updates that did get sent were received at GYO-3, a Federal Space Command base orbiting permanently above Ganymede, the largest satellite of Jupiter, the robot freighter *Hermit* departed on a nine-day haul to Callisto. In its main propulsion section, the *Hermit* carried four high-pressure centrifugal pumps, fastened to their mountings by CYA-173/B bolts. The *Hermit* had been ferrying assorted loads between the Jovian moons for over six months now, after trudging its way outward from the Belt for even longer before that. The bolts still holding the pumps were among the first of that type to have been used anywhere.

Fully loaded, the cargo cage combined the consignments from over fifty independents averaging a thousand tons of asteroid material each, and stretched the length of an old-time naval cruiser. The loads included concentrations of iron, nickel, magnesium, manganese, and other metals for which there would never be a shortage of customers eager to avoid federal taxes and tariffs. A good month's work for a team of ten working one of the nickel-iron asteroids would earn them a quarter of a million dollars. True, the costs tended to be high too, but the offworld banks offered generous extended credit with the rock pledged as collateral. This was another source of friction with the federal authorities, who claimed to own everything and didn't recognize titles that they hadn't issued themselves. But ten billion asteroids over a hundred meters in diameter was a lot to try and police. And the torroidal volume formed by the Belt contained two trillion times more space than the sphere bounded by the Moon's orbit.

Better money still could be made for hydrogen, nitrogen, carbon, and other light elements essential for biological processes and the manufacture of such things as plastics, which are not found on the Moon but occur in the carbonaceous chondrites. This type of asteroid contains typically up to five percent kerogen, a tarry hydrocarbon found in terrestrial oil shales, "condensed primordial soup"—a virtually perfect mix of all the basic substances necessary to support life. At near-Earth market rates, kerogen was practically priceless. And there was over a hundred million billion tons of it out there, even at five percent.

The driver, consisting of a triple-chamber fusion rocket and its fuel tanks, was attached at the tail end when the cage was ready to go. Now flight-readied, the assembled launcher hung fifty miles off the *Turner Maddox*'s beam. The search radars were sweeping long-range, and the defenses standing to at full alert. There's no way to hide the flash when a two-hundred-gigawatt fusion thruster fires—the perfect beacon to invite attention from a prowling federal strike force.

"We're clean," Fuigerado reported from his position on one side of the bridge. He didn't mean just within their own approach perimeter. The *Maddox's* warning system was networked with other defense grids in surrounding localities of the Belt. Against common threats, the independents worked together.

Cassell checked his screens to verify that the *Maddox's* complement of spiders, shuttles, maintenance pods, and other mobiles were all docked and accounted for, out of the blast zone. "Uprange clear," he confirmed.

Liam Doyle tipped his cap to the back of a head of red, tousled Irish hair and ran a final eye over the field and ignition status indicators. A lot more was at stake here than with just the routine retrieval of an incoming crate. The skipper liked to supervise outbound launches in person.

"Sequencing on-count at minus ten seconds," the Controller's voice said from the operations deck below.

"Send her off," Doyle pronounced.

"Slaving to auto. . . . Guidance on. . . . Plasma ignition."

White starfire lanced across twenty miles of space. The launcher kicked forward at five g's, moved ahead, its speed seeming deceptively slow for a few moments; then it pulled away and shrunk rapidly among the stars. On the bridge's main screen, the image jumped as the tracking camera upped magnification, showing the plume already foreshortened under the fearsome buildup of velocity. Nineteen minutes later and twenty thousand miles downrange, the driver would detach and fire a retro burn, separating the two modules. The cage would remain on course for the Inner System, while the driver turned in a decelerating curve that would eventually bring it back to rendezvous with the *Maddox*.

"We've got a good one," the Controller's voice informed everybody. Hoots and applause sounded through the open door from the communications room behind.

"Mr. Cassell, a bottle of the Bushmills, if you please," Doyle instructed.

"Aye, aye, Sir!"

Doyle turned to face the other chiefs who were present on the bridge. "And I've some more news for you to pass on, that this would be as good a time as any to mention," he told them. "It will be our last operation for a while. This can feels as if it's getting a bit creaky to me. You can tell your people that we'll be putting in for an overhaul and systems refit shortly, so they'll have a couple of months to unwind and blow some of their ill-gotten gains on whatever pleasures they can find that are to be had this side of Mars. Details will be posted in a couple of days." Approving murmurs greeted the announcement, which they toasted with one small shot of Irish mellow each.

Later, however, alone in his private cabin with Cassell, Doyle was less sanguine. "I didn't want to mention it in front of everybody, but I've been getting ominous messages from around the manor," he confided. "The *Bandit* has been very quiet lately."

Cassell took in the unsmiling set of the boss's face. The *Beltway Bandit* was another consolidator like the *Turner Maddox*: same business, same clients, same modus operandi. "How quiet?" he asked.

Doyle made a tossing-away motion. "Nothing." And that was very odd, for although accidents happened, and every now and again an unlucky or careless outfit was tracked down by federal patrols, disaster was never so quick and so total as to prevent some kind of distress message from being sent out.

"Are you saying it was the feds—they took it out?" Cassell asked.

"We don't know. If it was, they did it in a way that nobody's heard of before. That's the real reason why I'm standing us down for a while." He paused, looking at Cassell pointedly. "Some of the operators are saying that they're using insiders."

Cassell caught the implication. "You think Shimoto's one?" he said. "We could be next?"

"What do you think? He's with your section."

Cassell shrugged. "He's good at the job, mixes in well. Everybody likes him. We're operating standard security. It hasn't shown up anything."

"His kind of ability could come from a federal pilots' school," Doyle pointed out. "And a pilot would be able to get himself away in something once the strike was set up."

Cassell couldn't argue. "I'll make sure we keep a special eye on him during the R&R," he said.

"Yes, do that, why don't you?" Doyle agreed. "I want to be absolutely sure that we're clean when we resume operating."

Water.

With its unique molecular attributes and peculiar property of becoming lighter as it freezes, it could have been designed as the ideal solvent, catalyst, cleanser, as well as the midwife and cradle of life. Besides forming 90% of offworlders' bodies, it provided culture for the algae in their food farms, grew their plants and nurtured their animals, cooled their habitats, and shielded out radiation. The demand for water across the inner parts of the Solar System outstripped that for all other resources.

Callisto, second largest of the moons of Jupiter and almost the size of Mercury, is half ice—equivalent to forty times all the water that exists on Earth. Mining the ice crust of Callisto was a major activity that the Terran authorities operated exclusively to supply the official space-expansion program. One of the reasons for the Space Command's maintaining a permanent presence out at the Jovian moons was to protect the investment.

Enormous lasers carved skyscraper-size blocks from the ice field, which a fusion-powered electromagnetic launcher catapulted off the moon. Skimming around the rim of Jupiter's gravity well, they then used the giant planet as a slingshot to hurl them on their way downhill into the Inner System. As each block left the launch track on Callisto, high-power surface lasers directed from an array of sites downrange provided final course-correction by ablating the block's tail surface to create thrust. A crude way of improvising a rocket—but it worked just fine.

Or it had done all the time up until now, that is.

The robot freighter *Hermit*, arriving from Ganymede, was just on its final, stern-first approach into the surface base serving the launch installation as the next block out was starting to roll. One of the CYA-173/B bolts securing its high-pressure pumps sheared under the increased loading when power was increased to maximum to slow down the ship. The bolt head came off like a rifle bullet, disabling an actuator, which shut down engine number two. Impelled by the unbalanced thrust of the other two engines, the *Hermit* skewed off course, overshot the base area completely, and demolished one of the towers housing the course-correction lasers for the mass launcher just as the block lifted up above the horizon twenty miles away. As a result, two million tons of ice hove off toward Jupiter on a trajectory that wasn't quite what the computers said it ought to be. The error was actually quite slight. But it would be amplified in the whirl around Jupiter, and by the time the block reached the Asteroid Belt, would have grown to a misplacement in the order of tens of millions of miles.

If the cause of the accident was ever tracked down, Al Quentin wouldn't be around to be fired over it. He had started a small business of his own in Tokyo, importing Old-West memorabilia from home.

The *Turner Maddox* was back on station and accumulating crates for the first of a new series of consignments. Its drives had been overhauled, computers upgraded, and an improved plasma stabilization system fitted to the launch driver. But there was a strain in the atmosphere that had not been present in earlier times. Five more consolidators had disappeared, every one without trace.

It had to be the feds, but nobody knew how they were locating the collection points, or managed to attack so fast that nobody ever got a warning off. All the consolidators had adopted a stringent policy of moving and changing their operating locales constantly. They were deploying more sophisticated defenses and warning systems. They pooled information on suspected inside informers and undercover feds. They gave dispatch data for incoming consignments as separately encrypted instructions to each subscriber to avoid revealing where the trajectories would converge. Yet they were still missing something.

Cassell looked around the familiar confines of the operations deck. The retrieval crew were at their stations, with a crate from a new subscriber called Farlode Holdings on its way in. Icoro had graduated now and was standby pilot this time—he was okay, Doyle had decided after having him tailed for a period and commissioning a background check. A new newcomer, Ibrahim Ahmel, born in an offworld colony—he said—was about to try his first live retrieval. Not everyone had come back after the break, and taking on more new faces was another of the risks that they were having to live with. Hank

Bissen had quit, which was surprising. Cassell hadn't judged him as the kind who would let the feds drive him out. And then again, maybe he'd simply banked more money from the last few trips than Cassell thought.

The other major change was the outer screen of six autodrones toting needlebeams and railguns that Doyle had invested in, currently in position two thousand miles out, transforming the *Maddox* operation into a miniature flotilla. It brought home just how much this whole business was escalating. Cassell liked the old days better. What did that tell him about age creeping up? he asked himself.

Ibrahim was nervous. He had done okay on the simulator, but had an ultra-high self-image sensitivity that tended to wind him up. This was going to be a tense one. Cassell was glad to have Icoro there as standby, cool and relaxed behind a big, wide grin as always.

"Remember what you found on the sim, don't cut the turn too sharp as you run in," Suzi said from Ibrahim's far side. "It makes it easy to overshoot on the lineup, and you end up losing more time straightening it out downrange than you save."

Ibrahim nodded and looked across instinctively to Icoro for confirmation.

"She talks too much," Icoro said. "Just don't over worry. You're not going to lose anything. I'll cut right in if it starts to drift."

"How did you make out on your first time?" Ibrahim asked.

"I goofed most miserably," Icoro lied. Ibrahim looked reassured. Suzi caught Cassell's gaze and turned her eyes upward momentarily. Cassell just shrugged. A screen on each console showed a telescopic view of the crate, still over fifteen minutes away, being sent from one of the drones. The colors of the containers that it was carrying showed one to be holding metals, one light elements, a third silicates, and two kerogen.

"It's coming in nice and easy, rotation slow," Icoro commented. "Should be a piece of cake."

Suddenly the raucous hooting of the all-stations alert sounded. Doyle's voice barked from Suzi's console—he had taken to being present through all operations on this trip.

"We've got intruders coming in fast. Cassell to the bridge immediately!"

Ibrahim froze. Suzi and Icoro plunged into a frenzy of activity at their consoles. Cassell had no time to register anything more as he threw himself at the communications rail and hauled up to the next level. As he passed through the communications room, he heard one of the duty crew talking rapidly into a mike: "Emergency! Emergency! This is *Turner Maddox.* We have unidentified incoming objects, believed to be attacking. Location is . . ."

Seconds later, Cassell was beside Doyle on the bridge. Displays flashed and beeped everywhere. Fuigerado was calling numbers from the sector control report screen.

"How many of them," Cassell asked, breathless.

Doyle, concentrating on taking in the updates unfolding around him, didn't answer at once. He seemed less alarmed than his voice had conveyed a few moments before—if anything, puzzled now. Finally he said, "I'm not so sure it is 'them,' It looks more like only one . . ."

Cassell followed his eyes, scanned the numbers, and frowned. "One what? What the hell is it?"

"I'm damned if I know. The signature isn't like any ship or structure that I've ever seen."

"Range is twenty-five hundred miles," the Ordnance Officer advised. "Defenses are tracking. It's coming in at thirty miles a second."

"I've got an optical lock from Drone 3," Fuigerado

called out. "You're not gonna believe it." Doyle and Cassell moved over to him. "Have you ever seen an asteroid with corners?" Fuigerado said, gesturing.

It was long, rectangular and white, like a gigantic shoe box, tumbling end over end as it approached. Cassell's first fleeting thought was of a tombstone.

"Fifteen seconds from the perimeter," the OO called. "I need the order now."

"We have a spectral prelim," another voice said. "It's ice. Solid ice."

Cassell's first officer turned from the nav station. "Trajectory is on a dead intercept with the inbound Farlode crate. It's going to cream it."

"Do I shoot?" the OO entreated.

Doyle looked at him with a mixture of puzzlement and surprise. "Ah, to be sure, you can if you want to, Mike, but there's precious little difference it'll make. A railgun would be like bouncing popcorn off a tank to that thing. Your lasers might make a hole in a tin can, but that's solid ice."

They watched, mesmerized. On one screen, the miniature mountain hurtling in like a white wolf; on the other, the crate trotting on its way, an unsuspecting lamb. Maybe because of their inability to do anything, the impending calamity seemed mockingly brutal—obscene, somehow.

"That's somebody's millions about to be vaporized out there," Cassell said, more to relieve the air with something.

"And a percentage of it ours, too," Doyle added. Ever the pragmatist.

"Dead on for impact. It's less than ten seconds," the nav officer confirmed.

Those who could crowded around the starboard fore-quarter port. There wouldn't be more than a fraction of a second to see it unaided. Eyes scanned the starfield tensely. Then Cassell nudged Doyle's arm and pointed, at the same time announcing for the others' benefit, "Two o'clock, coming in high." Then there was a glimpse of something bright and pulsating—too brief and moving too fast for any shape to be discerned—streaking in like a star detached from the background coming out of nowhere . . .

And all of a sudden half the sky lit up in a flash that would have blinded them permanently if the ports hadn't been made of armored glass with a short-wave cutoff. Even so, all Cassell could see for the next ten minutes was after-image etched into his retina.

But even while he waited for his vision to recover, his mind reeled under the realization of what it meant. He had never heard of Farlode Holdings before. That inbound crate had been carrying something a lot more potent than ordinary metals, light elements, and kerogen. And a half hour from now, it would have been inside the cargo cage, just a short hop away from them.

So *that* was how the feds had been doing it!

The plant was a riot of bright green and yellow now, and the veins of violet were very bright. Chifumi nipped off a couple of wilted leaves with her fingers and watered the soil from the jar that she had brought from the kitchen behind the elevators. The accountant whose office it was seemed to be taking care of it, she was pleased to see. She would have to keep an eye on it for a while though, because he had not been in for several days. From the cards by his desk and the message of well-wishing that somebody had pinned on his wall, it seemed he was getting married. A framed picture had appeared next to the plant some time ago, of the accountant and the pretty girl that Chifumi had seen once or twice, who worked in the outer office. It seemed, then, that he was marrying his secretary.

Chifumi didn't know if that was a good thing or

not, but such things were accepted these days. Very likely the new wife would give up her job and have a family now, so she would no longer be his secretary, and the question wouldn't arise. Chifumi wondered if they would take *yamatsumi-sou* to their new home. It would be better for Kyo than being stuck alone in an office every night, she thought.

She finished her evening's work and went down to the lobby to wait for the arrival of the bus. While she sat on one of the seats, she took from her purse the letter that had come in from Icoro, which one of his friends from the university had printed out and delivered to her just as she was leaving.

My dearest and most-loved Mother, it began. *I hope that everything is well with you. I am doing very well myself, and have just wired off a sum to keep you comfortable for a while, which you should be hearing about shortly.*

Life out here where I am continues to be wonderfully interesting and exciting. I must tell you about the most amazing thing that happened just a couple of days ago. . . .

How They Got Me At Baycon

This volume is a follow-up to a similar collection of short fiction and essays of mine entitled *Minds, Machines, and Evolution,* that Bantam put out back in the eighties. At the time Lou Aronica of Bantam and I were considering the original project, several readers that I mentioned it to suggested including a biographical thread too, since all they ever got was the standard paragraph at the back of every book. Lou thought that was a good idea, and we incorporated a number of such pieces into *MM&E* accordingly. They were well received, so in putting together this later collection, Jim Baen and I decided to follow the same pattern.

By the end of *MM&E*, I was living in a town called Sonora in the Sierra Nevada foothills, about three hours' drive inland from San Francisco. The principal science fiction convention in that part of the world was the Bay Area Science Fiction Convention, "Baycon," held every year in San Jose. Cons provide a good break for writers showing symptoms of advanced cabin fever from being holed up alone with keyboards for too long, and whose verbal English has been reduced to ordering at the twenty-four-hour restaurant along the street and calling the phone company to find out what day it is. The additional attraction of a regular, local con is the feeling of being among familiar faces in a familiar setting, watching a familiar routine unfold. It's even nicer, of course, when you can do it as one of those special guests of the convention who get all their expenses paid.

But you can't expect that kind of treatment every time, of course. Others have to have their chance too, and the typical writer guest accepts making it to the privileged list in some years, and settling for a free membership in others. Well, by the second half of the eighties I had been Baycon's GOH, Special Writer Guest, Toastmaster, and everything else that qualified, and so this year I was happy to just enjoy the socializing in return for working a few panels. But when I checked into my room at the Red Lion Inn, a pleasant surprise was waiting. Standing in the bathroom was a large tub of ice containing an assortment of cans of my favorite beers and several bottles of wine, with a card attached to it that read: *Welcome back to Baycon, compliments of the committee.* It was their way of saying, "Sorry we can't cover your costs every year, but we're glad to have you back." Nice, I thought to myself.

Another thing that Baycon excelled at was parties. The organizers took the wise precaution of concentrating all the party rooms on one floor of the hotel, so there were no complaints from bewildered or panic-stricken regular guests, and the con people could get on with having a good time. It made the parties a lot easier to find, too. As the night wore on, they tended to flow out into the corridor and merge into one giant party that kept the hard-core partygoers happy and the security staff edgy through until dawn.

A fact of cons that authors become resigned to is being assailed by young, aspiring writers who seem to think that some of the mystique of being a pro will surely rub off if they get close to one and stay in proximity long enough. These are the people who bring notebooks to every panel on writing topics, show their expertise of the genre to be on a par with yours by citing books and authors that you've never heard of, and who could probably find allusions to symbolic metaphor in the Manhattan phone directory and debate the implied self-referential generalizations of a laundry list. The parties tend to be one of their favorite stalking grounds. Here, victims can be cornered off-duty, unable to invent urgent phone calls to be made to New York or to toss back a harried "Sorry, must get to a panel in two minutes," before retreating to the Green Room.

I say all this because it's expected—the kind of thing that authors tell each other in bars and agree how tedious it all is, to show that they're above finding gratification in such cheap ego trips—while all the time secretly reveling in it. The truth is that it's hard not to start coming on just a little bit when every word one utters is received with the raptness of a synod of bishops witnessing a theophany. It's even more true in a party setting when one is getting a little oiled oneself. Writers have an interest in communicating ideas, after all—otherwise they wouldn't be writers to begin with—and instant audience reaction is not something they get a chance to experience very often. All of which is a roundabout way of saying that given half a chance, they tend to talk a lot.

And so it was at Baycon. On the Saturday night of whatever the year in question, I was giving forth, probably on something that had to do with the Many Worlds Interpretation of quantum mechanics or the impact of electronic networks on totalitarian societies, to a group of studentish young men with intense expressions and wire-bound notebooks, when I was interrupted by a hesitant tap on the shoulder. It was one of the girls from the con staff, eighteen or so, I'd guess, quite pretty, and visibly nervous over what was probably her first stint on the committee. She asked me tremulously, "Did you get our present okay, in your room?"

I glanced at the intense faces of the group that had been belaboring me. It was a heaven-sent opportunity to lighten the atmosphere and get a little of my own back after all the heavy questions—and after a few straight Irish whiskies I needed to. I looked at her somewhat coolly, as if reluctant to make an issue over something. "Yes . . . I did."

She caught the tone and looked concerned. "Oh? . . . Was there something wrong?"

"Well, yes, as a matter of fact there was," I said. "Where was the long-legged kinky redhead?"

Her head gave a short, uncomprehending shake. "Long-legged kinky . . ." She faltered. "I'm sorry. I don't think I understand."

I emitted the kind of weary sigh that people make whose lives are a perpetual and predictable succession of evaporated computer bookings, wrongly ordered parts, and lost baggage. "Look," I said patiently. "I was quite specific with John"—John Mclaughlin was the con chairman that year—"as to the terms under which I would attend your convention. He agreed that two things would be provided for my personal enjoyment over the weekend: one, a tub full of booze, which I got—thank you very much; and two, a long-legged kinky redhead. But—" I spread my hands appealingly, "no redhead. Where's the long-legged kinky redhead?"

The girl blanched and shook her head helplessly. "I'm sorry. I don't know anything about it. I'll have to check. . . ."

And she fled.

I turned back, managing to keep a straight face,

and was rewarded by the sort of incredulous looks that you see in biker bars when a naked Schwarzenegger says, "I neet your clothes, your shoes, unt der motor zycle."

"This doesn't really happen, does it?" one of them whispered.

I gave them a pained, worldly look. "Come on, guys, let's get real. You don't think we do this just for the money and the prestige, do you? I mean, what else is life really all about?"

They exchanged looks that ranged from seasick wan through honest-envy green to agitated scarlatina, and muttered.

"Hey, guys, there's no other way. We gotta be writers."

"That's the way to live, man."

"I *knew* it had to be like that. . . ."

But I acted as if it were nothing and returned loftily to our previous track of quantum weirdness or whatever, and with the Bushmills flowing smoothly, I quickly forgot about the incident and the bit of fun I'd had out of it . . . until I realized that she was back. She drew me a little to one side, nodded in a conspiratorial kind of way, and murmured, "I think we can do something."

This time it was my jaw that dropped. But before I could say anything she lowered her voice and went on, "But the convention does have its reputation to think about, and there are family groups here. We do need to be a little discreet. So just stay here, and I'll be back in a few minutes when everything's fixed up." And with a smile and a wink, she disappeared again.

I'm not sure what the others and I talked about after that. I was completely on auto-mouth, wondering if, in fact, it was *I* who had been out of touch all these years. I suppose we English have something of a reputation too, and who could blame these zestful colonials for exercising a little prudent discretion in our direction also, until they got to know us better. I tried to recall all the attractive redheads that I'd seen around the con, wondering which one of them might have volunteered, and found myself scanning the vicinity with rising impatience. Probably nothing was going to happen at all. . . . But then, sure enough, our friend appeared around a corner of the corridor a few yards away and beckoned with a finger.

I looked at the guys and shrugged with what I hoped came across as man-of-the-world nonchalance. "Well, it's been nice talking. When it's time to go, you have to go, I guess. Enjoy the rest of the weekend, eh?" I walked away like John Wayne leaving the barroom, holstering a pair of smoking six-guns, but wondering inwardly how to handle this if they were serious.

And waiting around the corner, I found . . .

A redhead.

Tall, long-legged and slender, smiling lasciviously. And quite possibly very kinky.

He also had a big red mustache and a voice like Johnny Cash. "Hi," he greeted, thrusting out a hand. "My name's Mike. Glad ta meetcha."

And that was how the buggers got me at Baycon.

And since we're into the subject of things with a slightly kinky taint and conventions, this would be a good place for *Identity Crisis.*

Identity Crisis

"There he is!"

"Marty, Marty!"

"That's him!"

The group of young people who had been waiting around the main lobby of the Toronto Hilton converged in an excited flurry of brandished autograph books and pictures around the figure coming out of one of the elevators. Marty Hayes forced his five-foot-five body to stand firm in the face of the possible threat to his physical well-being and stared at them mournfully through his thick-rimmed spectacles with the hang-dog look that had made him famous. "Hey, easy does it, kids," he cautioned as he penned his name nervously across one of the books. "I can't stand being crowded. It plays hell with my claustrophobia."

"You don't have claustrophobia," a grinning, redheaded boy chided. "We know that's not for real."

"It's real," Marty said as he thrust a signed photograph back at a well-endowed blond girl who was gazing at him rapturously. "My younger brother used to have to put together my easy-to-make presents for me. That was how my inferiority complex started. I've had a morbid fear of Father Christmas ever since."

"We enjoyed the show last night," another girl said

as she passed him a pen. "Do you know when you'll be doing another week up here?"

"It depends on my doctor. He told me that I shouldn't take anything to excess, even moderation. I always had this feeling that too much health was bad for you."

"So when are you going back home to Los Angeles?" another inquired. "Will you be spending any extra time here now your run's through?"

"I have to go back tomorrow . . . I think. I'm not sure. I get depressed if I try and plan too far ahead. My doctor said he thought I ought to rest because he thought I had a heart condition. When I asked if I could have a second opinion, he said maybe it was a hernia." As Marty signed the last of the autographs, he caught sight of the broad, rotund figure of his manager, Abe Fennerwitz, standing outside the door of the coffee shop, his tanned scalp reflecting the light between the two patches of wrinkly hair that surmounted his ears. Abe was wearing a tartan jacket and chewing the unlit butt of a cigar. Marty gave an almost imperceptible nod to the hotel security man who was hovering discreetly in the background near the elevators.

The security man moved forward and began ushering the fans firmly but good-naturedly back into the center of the lobby. "Okay people—I guess we have to call it a day, huh? Mr. Hayes has a busy schedule this morning. It was nice seeing you all, but time's getting on."

"Thanks, Marty."

"It was nice talking to you."

"Come back to Canada soon."

Marty watched solemnly as they moved away through the main doors, then relaxed and strolled across the lobby to join Abe. "I only just woke up," he said. "Wow, a week like that takes it out of you. You had breakfast?"

Abe nodded. He waved in the direction of the main entrance. "You just get mugged?"

"They're okay. It's a pity you can't give 'em more time after they've hung around half the morning, but once they start they'll tie you up all day."

"As long as you're happy." Abe's brow creased into furrows, and his manner became more businesslike. "Look, Marty, we've got a problem with Karlson. I got a call from him personally about an hour ago. He's not gonna be able to make it here this afternoon to talk about the deal. He's got some family problems or something down in Texas, and he had to go there right away. He doesn't know how long it might take."

"Do you think he might have changed his mind or something?" Marty asked, sounding worried.

Abe shook his head. "Uh-uh. I think it's genuine enough. He was very upset and apologetic about it." He shrugged. "I guess we'll just have to set up a meeting again for some other time. He's due out on the West Coast sometime in the next two weeks. We can fix it for then. Don't worry about it. The deal will go through."

Marty sighed and tossed up his hands in resignation. "Oh, well, I suppose there's not much else we can do. So what else do we have fixed for today?"

"Nothing that I can't take care of on my own," Abe told him. "You've been burning it at both ends this week. It's time you put some credit back into your domestic account."

"What do you mean?" Marty asked.

Abe's expression brightened a shade, and he clapped Marty amiably on the shoulder. "Go get some breakfast, then go upstairs and pack your things, and then get the hell out of here. Take an extra day off and spend it with that pretty wife of yours. Have dinner out somewhere with her tonight and buy her some nice flowers from me. Charge 'em to the firm."

Marty frowned for a second and looked as if he

were about to object, then thought better of it. "Well . . . if you're sure that's okay, Abe. I guess it would sure . . ." He began nodding enthusiastically as he warmed to the idea. "That'd be just great! So . . . I'll see you again when?"

"I'll be back in L.A. tomorrow as scheduled. I'll get in touch."

"As long as you're sure it wouldn't—"

"Shut up, Marty. Just get the hell outa here."

A little over two hours later, Marty Hayes was looking down at the green and yellow checkerboard pattern of Nebraska from a Noram airlines hypersonic DC-16 streaking westward at one hundred fifty thousand feet; he was savoring the feeling of satisfaction and euphoria that comes with the knowledge that work is over for the time being, and the relaxation ahead has been well-earned. One of the drawbacks of being a celebrity was that whenever he traveled on business he had to go as himself, which meant having to endure the hassles of airports and taxicabs that had once been a bane in everyone's life. Whenever circumstances permitted, he preferred going Arabee, which took no time at all and required only a minimum of local moving around. But most of the time he was obliged to join the ranks of those who, for various reasons, either chose or were forced to use more traditional methods of travel. At least, he reflected philosophically, it meant that he was doing his bit to help keep the airlines in business.

If that was a drawback, it was minor compared to the pleasures that came with the success which life had bestowed in return. As a boy growing up on the West Side of New York, he had rapidly discovered his spastic lack of coordination in the gymnasium and on the athletic field, and that in class he could interchange French verbs with differential operators without altering the perceptible meaning of either. In all things practical he had proved an equally dismal failure, and it had seemed at times that Nature had selected him to be its visible, walking proof of the Second Law of Thermodynamics by increasing the entropy, suddenly and catastrophically, of everything he touched.

For many troubled years he had resented and fought against being laughed at, but later on the realization slowly dawned on him that people liked to laugh. It made them feel good. And when he laughed with them instead of being defensive, they liked having him around. He soon had lots of friends and went to lots of parties. People told him that he had talent. And so, eventually, humor had become his profession, and over the years he had cultivated and perfected his own unique brand. And then, two years previously, the girl of his dreams had appeared out of nowhere in the form of a reporter for a national women's magazine, sent on a special assignment to do a cover-story interview with him. For heaven-alone-knew what reason, she had fallen in love with him, and he and Alice were married five months later. Yes indeed, Marty Hayes thought to himself as he gazed contentedly down over the Midwest, after something of a precarious start, life hadn't treated him so badly at all.

Alice hadn't been at her office when he called just before leaving the hotel. The answering computer had advised him that she was out on an assignment and had not logged in a rerouting number. Marty fished his compad from his jacket pocket and tried calling her again, but received the same message. No doubt she was interviewing or something and didn't want calls coming in on her own unit, he presumed. He tried calling home but got the same response from the domestic computer there. Not to worry, he thought. He'd make it a surprise—a fitting prelude to a cozy dinner for two somewhere tonight. While he was still connected, he accessed the autochef and tapped in an instruction for a hot snack and some coffee to be ready when he arrived at home, then he cut the call, snapped shut the lid of the compad, and slipped the unit back into his pocket.

At the airport he was stopped by a couple who had recognized him and asked for his autograph. They had been married that morning and were on their way to Japan for a honeymoon. The encounter put Marty in an even more romantic frame of mind, and he hummed happily to himself as an aircab carried him above the Los Angeles suburbs toward his home in Newport Beach.

Marty set his suitcase down in the hallway, unslung his jacket from his shoulder, and draped it across the back of the chair standing at the foot of the stairs. He straightened up and looked around. The house was neat and tidy, and didn't appear to be very occupied. "Alice, surprise!" he called, just to be sure. "I'm back. Is anybody home?" There was no response. He went through into the kitchen, where a message on the screen of the monitor panel told him that his snack was ready and waiting. The time was not yet two o'clock, which would give him perhaps four hours to program an afternoon of music and relax with a good book before Alice came home. Or maybe he would call up the recordings of his Toronto performances from the Datanet and review them in privacy. Either way his afternoon sounded good. He began whistling tunelessly to himself as he walked out of the kitchen and went upstairs to freshen up.

Just as he was about to turn on the cold-water faucet in the bathroom, his eyes wandered downward to the bottom of the sink. He stopped whistling abruptly and stared. Around the drain, evidently deposited as the water ran away when the sink was last emptied, was a faint ring of black granules. Marty frowned at the residue for a few seconds while his mind refused to take in what it meant. It looked suspiciously like the shavings from a man's beard. He licked his lips nervously and tried to tell himself that he was overreacting. Alice probably just washed something in the sink, he decided. It wasn't what it looked like. But already his hand was moving to open the door of the wall-closet. He gulped hard and stood there, stunned. On the lowermost of the glass shelves inside, standing in a small cluster away from all the other, familiar things, were a safety razor, a can of foam, and a bottle of after-shave lotion. They weren't his.

"It's her brother from San Francisco," he muttered aloud to himself. "He showed up unexpectedly again. Or maybe one of the guys from back East is in town." But even as his mouth was mumbling its rationalizations, his feet were rushing him out into the passageway and along to the door of the guest-room. He flung it open and tore in. There was nothing—no bags by the bed or in the closet, no clothes in any of the drawers, and no clean linen beneath the counterpane. He came back out into the passageway, marched stiffly along to the door of the master bedroom, grasped the handle firmly, and entered.

A yawning pit opened up somewhere deep down in his stomach. The bed hadn't been made. It looked as if a whole football team had run amok in it. A man's blazer— dark brown with distinctive brass buttons and a lion's-head pin in the lapel—were thrown untidily across one of the chairs, and there was a crumpled white shirt underneath it on the seat. Draped over the blazer was a necktie with yellow and brown diagonal stripes, and a triangular motif offset to one side near the tip. A man's leather traveling bag stood by one of the walls behind a pair of tan leather shoes. And there were a few short, dark hairs on the pillows; Alice's was long and fair.

Five minutes later, dazed and bewildered, Marty came back downstairs, went into the kitchen, and consigned his snack directly from the autochef to the incinerator. Then he headed for the living room to pour a long, stiff drink with shaking hands, then slumped down into an armchair to read again the information that he had copied onto a scrap of paper from the hotel registration slip in the inside pocket of the brown blazer. It was from the Sheraton in Glendale, and confirmed that a Mr. Frank Vicenzo had a reservation from Friday the sixteenth, which was today, to Saturday the twenty-fourth. His room number was 494. There had been some other pieces of paper with various notes and phone numbers written on them, but they had meant nothing to Marty.

He downed half of his drink in one gulp and gnawed at his knuckle in an attempt to stop his body from shivering while he forced himself to think. His initial shock was giving way to anger, and he found himself growing impatient to confront them and mentally rehearsing what he would do. He would not humiliate himself in front of another man by allowing his hurt to show. A display of rage and indignation to see the expressions on their faces as they walked in . . . but what if Vicenzo were sneering and unrepentant or Alice unmoved? Perhaps he would show contempt by walking out in silent dignity and leave them to their shame. They might laugh at him instead. Slowly the cold, sickening realization came over him that he couldn't handle the situation . . . at least not here, today, like this. He needed more time to think it through, and they could come back at any minute. He had to talk to somebody to clear his head. After a few minutes of agonized pacing back and forth across the room, he picked up the compad from the coffee table and hammered in Abe's personal call-code. A few seconds went by.

Then the miniature screen came to life to reveal Abe's features.

"Yeah?" Abe's expression changed abruptly to one of recognition. "Marty, what gives? Hey, you look worried. Something up?"

"Lots . . ." Marty was surprised to hear his voice choking from somewhere near the back of his throat. "Abe, I've got problems. I need to talk to you."

Abe's face became serious. "What?"

"I can't go into it right now. Can you get back to L.A. tonight?"

"Tonight?" Abe frowned. "Well, I did have plans for seeing a coupla guys for dinner, but I could put it off. If it's really that—"

"It is. I wouldn't ask you if it wasn't important. I'm going to check into . . ." Marty thought for a moment. ". . . the Palm Ridge in Santa Monica tonight. Can you get an early evening flight and meet me there?" Abe never went Arabee.

"The Palm Ridge?" Abe looked surprised and confused. "You're supposed to be home tonight. What in hell—"

"I can't explain now. It's all a mess. Look, I've got to go. Can you be there?"

Abe hesitated, digested the urgency in Marty's voice, and nodded. "Okay. I'll try and make it there around eight. Are you sure you can't tell me what this is all about?"

"Not now," Marty told him. "Thanks a lot, Abe. I'll talk to you later."

Marty cut the connection and used the compad again to call an aircab. After that he rinsed and dried his glass, replaced it below the bar, and returned to the hallway just as the falling whine of an engine-note from outside told him that his cab had arrived. He slung his jacket over his shoulder, picked up his suitcase, and let himself out the front door.

❖   ❖   ❖

"Hell, I don't know what to say," Abe murmured awkwardly across a booth in the cocktail lounge of the Palm Ridge Hotel later that night. "Alice? . . ." He made a helpless gesture. "I'd never have believed it. It's easy to talk when it isn't you, so I'm not gonna say a goddamn thing. It happens. Most people survive. What else is there to say?"

"So what happens now?" Marty asked miserably.

Abe took a swig of beer and wiped his mouth with the back of his hand. "I'm not sure, but I think you were right to get out when you did. Sure, you could have stuck around and made a scene, but from a long-term point of view that wouldn't have been so smart. This way they don't know that you know, and it gives you time to get organized. Are you going to want out?"

The reality had by this time percolated through, and Marty could only nod morosely at his drink. "I wouldn't even want to live there any more, Abe," he said. "I had that house built for her, just the way she wanted . . . You know that." He shook his head disbelievingly. "In my own house. It doesn't make sense. If something was wrong, why didn't she talk about it? She always came across like she was on top of the world."

"It happens," Abe said again with a sigh. "Nothing's gonna change it." He studied his thumbnail for a second and used it to prise a piece of pretzel from his tooth. "What you have to do is snap out of feeling too sorry for yourself and start thinking about the practical side." Marty looked up but said nothing. Abe bunched his lips for a second, then spread his hands and explained. "I hate to say this, Marty, but you have to face facts. You're worth a lot of dollars these days, and in this kind of situation you could get burned bad no matter who's right or who's wrong. If you don't act smart, you could wind up getting ripped off on top of everything else."

"What are you saying?"

Abe looked solemn. "I know this is asking a lot, but I don't want you to do anything until we've got some hard facts and I've had a chance to talk to the lawyers. We have to know who this bum is, where he's from, how long he's been around, and all kinds of things like that. Right now it's your word against hers, and a compromise settlement could cost you an arm and both legs. For all we know, they might be fixing to set you up for just something like that." He paused while Marty grimaced at the thought, then went on. "Stay here tonight, go home tomorrow, and act natural, just as if nothing happened. It's tough, but you don't wanna let any of your hand show just yet. First thing on Monday I'll talk to the lawyers, and we'll see then how we play it from there. Believe me, I've seen this kind of situation before, and what I'm saying is for the best. Will you do that?"

Marty clenched his teeth, drew a long breath, and nodded resignedly. "Order us some more drinks, Abe," he said.

It was three AM when Marty eventually stumbled along to his room and fell into bed fully anesthetized. Even so he had a lousy night and woke up feeling lousier. He didn't call Alice to say what time he'd be back, and instructed his compad to reroute any incoming calls into Datanet storage for retrieval later.

Alice lowered her book a fraction and studied Marty quizzically over the top of it for the umpteenth time that evening. Marty pretended not to be conscious of her and kept his eyes riveted on the movie that he had called up onto the large wallscreen in the living room. The movie was about a political family and their intrigues back in the 1980s, or something like that. Marty wasn't all that interested. He had put it on to give himself something to look at

while he tormented himself with fantasies of the
person who had been in his home forty-eight hours
previously. Somehow Alice was managing to act calmly
and with composure, as if everything were normal.
It was inhuman.

"Marty, are you sure you're feeling all right?" she
asked again. He grunted. Alice waited for a moment,
then shook her head despairingly. "But you've hardly
said a word since you came home. You haven't told
me how the show went in Toronto or anything.
Something's the matter. Didn't it go too well?"

Marty forced himself to look at her. She looked fresh
and pretty in a loose orange blouse and white slacks,
her long waves of blond hair tumbling in a soft cas-
cade around her shoulders. The slacks were thin and
tight, emphasizing the curves of her hips and thighs
as she lounged back along the couch. Her pose made
her look sexy and him feel worse. Act natural, Abe had
advised. Right at that moment Abe was probably out
somewhere, sitting down to a T-bone steak. Marty felt
he could cheerfully have beaten Abe's brains to a pulp.
He tried to smile, but the effort fizzled out somewhere
on its way to his face. Instead he tossed up a hand
wearily and shifted his weight uncomfortably in his
chair. "Aw . . . things went okay. It was a rough week.
Maybe I've just had it. I'll get over it."

Alice waited for him to say more, but he lapsed
into silence again and looked back at the screen.
"Why don't you take a nice hot shower and get to
bed early and rest?" she suggested. "I'll be fine for
the evening reading this. It's quite good." An imp-
ish smile came onto her face. "I could wake you up
later."

Marty swallowed hard. What new adventures did
she want to relive? His imagination went into over-
drive, and he had to squeeze the arms of his chair
hard to keep control of himself. Act natural, he told
himself. It's important. "I dunno . . ." he mumbled.

"I don't feel all that good. Maybe I picked up a bug somewhere. I'll be okay."

"Then you really should get yourself to bed," Alice urged. "It's probably just nervous tension. How about it? A good night's sleep and you'll be as good as new in the morning."

"Just leave me alone!" Despite himself, Marty was unable to keep the harsh edge out of his voice. "I said I'll be okay." Hurt and indignation flashed in Alice's eyes. Marty slumped back and forced an apologetic tone. "I, er . . . I didn't mean it like that. It's okay . . . I'll be all right here."

Alice set her book down and looked at him for a few seconds. At last she gave an exasperated sigh. "I don't know what's got into you, Marty, but there doesn't seem to be much that I can do about it." She paused as if wondering whether or not to pursue the matter. Then she said, "I was going to wait until you got into a better mood, but you don't look as if you're going to. There's something I have to tell you." She swung her feet off the couch and sat up to look directly at him.

Marty went numb, unable to believe his ears. So calmly and dispassionately, she could bring it up like this? What kind of a woman was she? Had he been as completely blind as that? He lifted his chin an inch by way of reply and at the same time felt a gnawing, sinking feeling of dread taking hold deep inside. His mind was racing ahead and trying to decide how he would react, but nothing coherent would form in the confusion boiling in his head.

"I don't know if you knew, but the American Bioengineering Society is having its annual conference here next week," Alice said. "Margaret at the office wants me to cover it for a special-feature issue next month."

Marty blinked and shook his head uncomprehendingly. "So . . . what's the problem? Why ask me?"

"Because a lot of the functions and lectures will run late into the evening, and there will be social events even later after that," she replied. "To cover that kind of thing, you really have to be there all the time. So the office wants me to check in there for the duration." She smiled. "In other words, just when you get back, I have to take off, that's all. It's a shame, but I'll make it up. You don't mind, do you?"

Marty exhaled a long, quiet breath of relief. Things would probably be a lot better with her out of the way, he thought to himself. He nodded and did his best to look enthusiastic. "Sure, that's no problem at all. You go ahead. When does the meeting start?"

Alice bit her lip. "Well, actually . . . tomorrow. It runs through until next Saturday—the twenty-fourth. I'll be back that night. You can always call if you need me for anything. It's being held at the Sheraton Glendale."

It took a moment for what she had said to register. "Where?" Marty asked hoarsely.

"Glendale, the Sheraton. You know . . . the big place up behind the Rainbow Tower."

"You want to stay at the Sheraton Glendale next week?"

"Yes. That's where the conference is. What's wrong with that?"

"And you want to stay through to the twenty-fourth?"

Alice smile sheepishly. "Well, actually the office has already made the reservation. You don't mind, do you, Marty? Marty, you've turned as white as a ghost! I didn't think you'd feel that way about it, honestly. But I can't go and let them down now that it's this late, can I?"

Marty stared back at her with glazed eyes and shook his head woodenly. "No, I guess not," he heard himself say. There wasn't a lot else he could do.

That night he slept in the guest-room. He told

Alice it was because he had a temperature and a headache. His fans would have applauded.

"Coincidence, hell!" Marty retorted derisively over lunch at the Mardi Gras restaurant the next day. "It was the same hotel and the same dates. What do you take me for, Abe? Do you think I dreamed the rest or something?"

Abe looked up from a plate of spaghetti and meatballs. "Of course not. But the reason I said you had to play it cool was to get facts, not to start inventing fiction."

"Like hell it's fiction."

"You don't *know* that, Marty. You gotta admit that the gene-freaks are having a conference there next week. And it is the kind of assignment you'd expect Alice to get. And it's not unusual for people assigned to that kind of thing to be around for the duration. So what she said all adds up."

"It all adds up too much," Marty agreed scathingly. He stared at the shrubs growing in pots to one side of the table. "And to think I just stood there this morning like some kind of ass and watched her fly off in the cab. I even told her to have a good time! Can you beat that? What kind of guy stands there watching his wife walk out to go swinging for a week and tells her to have a good time? So help me, Abe, you'd better be right about this being for the best, or else I'm going to be looking around for a new manager."

Abe considered the statement stoically while he munched on a piece of garlic bread. "Did you call the Sheraton to see if she's booked in under her own name?" he asked.

Marty pulled a face. "What's the point?" he demanded. "I'm not going to get mixed up with playing games like that. Anyhow that wouldn't tell us a thing. Alice isn't stupid. She could have taken a room, sure, but never be there and just collect messages from the desk instead . . . something like that." He fiddled over his coffee with a packet of sugar. It burst and showered sugar everywhere but in the cup. "They've got it all set up. She's there with a legitimate cover, and Vicenzo breezes in, rents a room, and makes it a nice, cozy togetherness week for two. And you say act natural. Jesus, Abe, I swear that if you'd been there last night I would have strangled you."

"The evidence is all circumstantial," Abe said, ignoring the remark. "She's there because the conference is there and she's got a job to do. Like you say, she's probably got a reservation to keep things straight. So this Vicenzo jerk happens to be there too. So what? What have we got that would mean anything in court? Nothing. We still need facts."

"Christ, Abe, what more facts do you want? He was at the house, and they're staying at the same hotel together. Do you expect them to mail me a blue movie or something?"

"We don't *know* they're there *together*," Abe pointed out. "Okay, he was at the house, but we still don't know who he is or anything about him. If you started turning on the heat now he'd simply go to ground, and then you wouldn't have a goddamn thing you could prove. All you could do would be to file for a regular split, the settlement would be fifty-fifty, and she'd walk away clean with armfuls of your money. Do like I say and sit tight for now. Sooner or later they'll blow it, and then you'll have facts. That's when you move."

Marty fumed and pummeled his napkin into a ball. "Dammit, Abe, what facts are we going to get sitting here talking like this? The facts aren't here, they're there. Do you expect me to sit on my ass for a whole week while this is going on? You're out of your mind. Can't you get it into your head that I need to *do* something?"

Abe shrugged, his fork poised halfway to his mouth. "What can you do?"

Marty heaved a deep breath and glowered down at the table. Abe watched in silence while he finished the last of his meal. At last Marty looked up. "I'll go there," he declared. "That's the place to be to find out whether she's in with him or not, not here or anywhere else. And if he's there and not anywhere else, then that's the place to find out who the hell he is." He nodded decisively. "That's what I'm going to do. *I'll* check into the Sheraton too. Why don't we make it a real party?"

"Now, you're outa your mind," Abe said, looking alarmed. "I know it's a strain, but you don't have to flip all the way. Hasn't it occurred to you that your own wife just might recognize you? And with all the people that are gonna be at the Sheraton next week, she might see you before you see her. Then Vicenzo would be out of town inside an hour, and you'd never track him down. You don't even know what he looks like."

A strange light was creeping into Marty's eyes. "I didn't say I'd go as me," he replied. "Who says I can't go Arabee?"

Abe blinked at him. "What?"

"Arabee. I'll rent an Arabee and use that." Marty shrugged. "It's simple."

Abe frowned, started to say something, then changed his mind and thought about it. He fished a handkerchief from his pocket and dabbed perspiration off his head. "It might work," he conceded grudgingly. He returned the handkerchief to his pocket, picked up a toothpick, thought about it some more, and nodded. "Who knows? You might dig up something. What's to lose?"

"In fact I might just make it an outsize model and beat the hell out of the bum," Marty said, licking his lips and showing his teeth as he savored the thought.

"You get any damfool thought like that outa your head straight away," Abe told him in an alarmed voice. "This thing's complicated enough already as it is. You keep to one that's your own size, and that way you won't be likely to do anything stupid. If . . ." His voice trailed away as a new thought struck him. He sat back, cocked his head to one side, and looked at Marty thoughtfully.

"I wasn't really serious about that," Marty said, raising a hand. "But wouldn't . . . Why are you looking at me like that, Abe?"

"There's a problem with it," Abe said.

"What kind of problem?"

"You." Abe sat forward, spreading his hands palms-upward on the table, and explained. "You're unique. Your gestures, mannerisms, actions . . . they're like a signature. You've been perfecting them for twenty years. They're a part of you now. You use them unconsciously even when you're not on-stage. Alice would know you a mile off no matter what kind of Arabee you used."

"You're exaggerating," Marty said. "Not in the middle of all those people. And it's not as if she'd be looking for me, is it?"

"Maybe, but can we risk it?"

Marty threw out his hands helplessly. His voice rose. "I don't know, Abe. What other way is there? What I do know is that there's no way I'm going to sit on my ass in that house for a week and do nothing. Okay, so maybe she recognizes me. That's too bad." He thrust out his chin defiantly. "Yeah, I say we risk it. I say we have to risk it."

"Maybe we don't . . . at least not to that degree," Abe answered. There was a curious note in his voice. He looked at Marty thoughtfully again. "Maybe there is another way."

Marty eyed him suspiciously. "What other way?" he asked.

"Don't make it a 'he' Arabee at all," Abe said. "Make it a 'she.'"

Marty gaped across the table. "And you told me I was crazy?"

"No, I'm serious. Look, when you—"

"No way, Abe." Marty held up his hands protectively. "There's no way in this world that I'm—"

"Hear me out, willya?" Abe interrupted in an earnest voice. "Think about it. It makes a lotta sense. One, it would guarantee you stay outa trouble. Two, Alice would never make the connection in a million years. The idea was good, but it had risks. This way we get rid of the risks. It has to be a better deal."

Marty shook his head vigorously. "Abe, forget it."

"It's nothing to worry about," Abe insisted. "Freaks do it all the time for kicks. The Arabee people are used to it. They don't care. And you could be saving yourself thousands . . . hundreds of thousands. It has to be worth it."

"The answer is no," Marty told him firmly. "Definitely, finally, absolutely, no way, never. I won't do it. For the last time, forget it."

Unperturbed, Abe finished using the toothpick and tossed it into an ashtray. He brought his hands together on the table and interlaced his fingers in front of him. "Now let's go through this again and talk about it rationally," he suggested.

Late that afternoon Marty was standing in a corner of the reception foyer, as far from the desk as possible, of the Los Angeles area branch office of Remote Activated Biovehicles, Inc., or R.A.B., popularly known as "Arabee." He felt ridiculous in the false mustache, hat, and dark glasses that Abe had insisted on, and wanted to get the whole thing over with, but the customer talking in lowered tones to the clerk at the desk seemed to have sprouted roots there. The other clerk, who seemed unoccupied and was reading a paper a short distance back behind the counter, had mercifully refrained from pestering Marty with offers to be of assistance, but this didn't make Marty feel any less conspicuous and uncomfortable. He kept his back turned toward the desk and pretended to read the posters on the wall for what must have been the fifth time.

Technical matters had never been one of Marty's strengths, and he had never understood fully how the Arabees worked. To use a "Rentabody," you presented yourself at the nearest R.A.B. office, where you lay down on a couch with some kind of neural coupling device around your head. The next thing you knew, you were in another cubicle in New York, Tokyo, or wherever you wanted to be, "inside" another body that was yours for the duration of the trip. An Arabee was not regarded by law as a person, since it was cloned from synthetically produced DNA and did not contain a cerebral cortex or any of the higher mental faculties held to be essential ingredients of personality. It was, in effect, a remote-controlled biological robot, human in physical form and appearance only. All the information collected through its senses was relayed via an electronics package contained in the skull back to where your real body was, and somehow injected directly into your brain; at the same time the signals from your own voluntary nervous system, for example to control movement and speech, were relayed in the opposite direction to complete the loop. Thus you could move around, see, hear, feel, and talk through a body that was thousands of miles away in a way that was indistinguishable from actually being there, and be home in an instant. The method was not suitable for all purposes, of course, but many members of the business community and other classes of habitual globetrotters had found that the majority of their journeys were made simply to put bodies in places where they could assimilate or convey information, and it was much cheaper and faster to bring the information to the bodies instead. And as often happens, once money was involved, hearts and minds hadn't needed a lot of convincing.

At last the customer at the desk concluded his reading aloud of the Los Angeles area phone directory, or whatever he had been doing, and disappeared through one of the doors at the back of the foyer. Marty glanced around furtively to make sure that nobody else had come in, then braced himself and walked stiffly up to the desk. "May I help you, sir?" the clerk inquired.

Marty spread his elbows along the counter and leaned forward to speak without raising his voice. "Yes, er . . . my name is Green. I called earlier this afternoon about a reservation . . . You said it would be ready."

"One moment, Mr. Green." The clerk activated a terminal beside him and turned his head to inspect the information that appeared on the screen. "Ah, yes. Female, white, mid-thirties, class three-B figure and stature, red hair, green eyes. For collection right here and return next Saturday. Is that correct?" Marty winced inwardly and wished the clerk would keep his voice down. The other clerk, however, continued reading his newspaper in the background with no show of interest.

"That's correct," Marty replied. Somehow he was unable to raise more than a whisper. It made him feel like a spy in a bad movie divulging "ze plans." "Er . . . it should be for cash in advance. Nothing to sign. That right?" People didn't cheat with Arabees. True, you had one of their bodies, but then again they had yours.

The clerk checked the screen again. "That's fine, Mr. Green. It comes to five hundred fifty dollars."

"Okay. I've got it right . . . here." Marty reached into his coat and fumbled with the wad of twenties

in his inside pocket. The wad caught on a pen, breaking the rubber band around it, and exploded into a
cloud of fluttering bills when he wrenched it free.
The clerk collected together the ones that had fallen
on the counter and watched impassively while Marty
scrambled around scooping the rest up off the floor.
Marty straightened up hastily and thrust a fistful of
notes across, at the same time feeling his mustache
working loose. Unruffled, the clerk accepted them and
returned a plastic document wallet.

"If you'll go on through to cubicle nine, Mr. Green,
everything should be ready," he said. Marty snatched
the wallet with one hand, clapped the other to his
face, and fled through the door at the rear of the
foyer.

"That was Marty Hayes," the clerk at the back
murmured without looking up from his paper. "Why
didn't you get his autograph?"

"I know." The other shrugged. "What can you do?
There must be a weird party on somewhere tonight.
The guy who came in just ahead of him was into the
same thing."

Marty walked along a corridor flanked by doors on
either side and entered the one marked number nine.
The cubicle was small, containing just a padded couch
on one side and the usual bank of floor-to-ceiling
electronics and equipment panels on the other. He
ignored the sign inviting him to press the button
indicated if he needed instructions and sat down on
the edge of the couch. He took a deep breath, com-
posed a silent prayer for Abe to be smitten by
indescribable torments and biologically impossible
tribulations, then swung his feet up, lay back, and
allowed his head to sink into the support provided.

"Everything is ready," a pleasant voice informed
him from a speaker somewhere in the room. "Are you
set for departure?"

"Go ahead," Marty replied. A few seconds later the

biolink helmet swung away from its stowage position above his head and slid smoothly into place.

He was lounging back in an upholstered recliner in a small, cheerfully decorated cubicle with soothing music playing in the background. His hair felt too long, and his legs felt too bare. He looked down. He couldn't see his waist. His chest was sticking out too far behind the thin shirt of silky lilac material that he was wearing, and the legs protruding from the short pink skirt below that seemed . . . obscene somehow. He looked up again hastily and swallowed hard. He raised a hand in front of his face and stared disbelievingly at his slender fingers and tapering red nails.

And then he panicked.

He looked around frantically for some way of communicating to call the whole stupid thing off. There had to be a microphone somewhere, a screen . . . something. He stood up, tried to move, and catapulted himself across the cubicle when his heels wouldn't go down to the floor. To hell with this, to hell with Abe, to hell with . . . He clung to the wall and shook his head to clear it. No, there was no way out. He had to see this through. He straightened up cautiously and tottered back to put on the summer top-coat and pick up the pocketbook that were lying on a sidetable by the recliner. Abe would pay for this, he told himself grimly. How, he didn't know, but Abe would pay for every minute of this.

He took a moment to compose himself, then opened the door a fraction and stuck his head out. He was in a corridor similar to the one by which he had entered, but not the same one. A second later one of the doors opposite opened, and a tall blond woman looked out. They gaped at each other, horrified, and slammed the doors shut at the same instant.

Marty's breathing was coming erratically, and his blood was pounding. Pull yourself together, you turkey, he told himself. Nobody cares out there. They've all got their own problems. Get it into your head that nobody's interested. He calmed down, gritted his teeth, and turned again toward the door. The blonde was just disappearing through the swinging-door at the end of the corridor when he stepped out. He waited for a few seconds, then followed to find himself back in the reception foyer. Looking straight ahead and keeping his eyes averted from the desk, he minced across the foyer and walked out onto the plaza, where Abe was supposed to be waiting. Abe wasn't there.

He stopped, puzzled, and looked first one way, then the other. Abe was about ten yards away accosting the blonde. The blonde seemed to recoil in terror, and Marty caught snatches of a stream of obscenities that were most unbecoming for a lady. He closed his eyes and groaned to himself, then cupped a hand to his mouth.

"Abe, you asshole," he yelled. "That's not me. I'm here!"

Abe looked around, startled, glanced back at the blonde, and came scampering back along the side of the plaza. He grabbed Marty's arm and hustled him quickly away around a corner and out of sight of the astonished passers-by who had stopped to watch. A short distance farther on they slowed to a more normal pace.

"Get some style into the act," Abe hissed from the corner of his mouth. "You're walking like a gorilla."

"What do you expect, for crissake? I haven't exactly had a lot of time to practice. Honest to God, I'm gonna make you try this yourself sometime."

"Stop yelling and waving that pocketbook around like that. People will think we're married or something."

"Lay off, willya, Abe. I told you, I'll get the hang of it. Just gimme some time."

They walked on in silence for a short distance. "Did you get your reservation fixed at the Sheraton?" Abe asked.

"Yeah . . . all set. The hotel was all booked up for the conference, but they had a cancellation. I'm booked in as Phyllis Kronberg, Room seven-three-six."

"Phyllis!" Abe sniggered uncontrollably.

Marty came to a halt and glared at him malevolently. "What's funny?" There was an icy menace in the tone, of the kind that only a female larynx can produce.

Abe moved back a step warily. "Nothing . . . nothing at all." He glanced at his watch and looked around. "We have to get you some more clothes and whatever other junk you'll need for a week. Let's look around in there." He gestured toward a door of Jordan Marsh that opened onto the concourse. Marty marched up to the door and stopped. Abe lurched ahead and held it open dutifully.

An hour later Abe was standing outside the door of the fitting rooms in the Ladies' Dresswear department, clutching an armful of packages and stamping around impatiently. Marty emerged with a pile of dresses and other garments over his arm and dumped them on the wrapping table by the cashier's terminal. The assistant glanced back over her shoulder from where she was just finishing attending to another customer. "I'll be with you in one moment, madam," she called.

Abe put the packages down next to the clothes. "Did you figure out how it all goes together?" he asked in a low voice.

"I'll worry about the finer details later," Marty whispered. "Those look like they fit, which is the main thing." Abe was giving him a funny look. "What's wrong now?"

Abe looked over his shoulder self-consciously, and then waved a hand vaguely in the direction of Marty's chest. "You're all wrong there. They're not at the same level. You look like a Picasso with drapes."

"There's nothing you can do," Marty hissed back. "I tried. It's those straps and things. There's no way you can make 'em point the same way."

"There's gotta be. How do all the rest manage?"

"How the hell do I know? Maybe their mothers show 'em how." Marty looked around with a start and tried to smile when he realized that the assistant had come over to them and was waiting politely but not without a hint of curiosity.

"And how will madam be paying?" the assistant inquired as she began tallying the purchases.

Marty shot a venomous look at Abe. "Put them on my husband's account."

Abe grabbed his arm and drew him back a pace to whisper imploringly in his ear. "Be sensible about this, you jerk. How can I walk in here with you looking like that and charge a whole wardrobe to my account? I've got a reputation to think about. And suppose it got back to Joanne? How in hell would you expect me to explain that?"

"Don't give me that, Abe. Put it on the firm's tab."

"Why me?" Abe protested. "What about all the bread this is gonna save you?"

The assistant looked tactfully away and busied herself with wrapping the items.

"That's maybe, and only if this works," Marty retorted. "I'm doing all the work, aren't I? Don't tell me you're complaining about having to put a few lousy bucks into it. Are you telling me I'm not worth that much? To listen to you, anybody would think it was gonna hurt or something."

"Okay, okay." Abe motioned to Marty to shut up then felt inside his jacket for his billfold. "You should do just great," he murmured testily. "You're starting to think like a broad already."

❖   ❖   ❖

The main lobby of the Sheraton Glendale was crowded with regular hotel guests going about their business and groups of conference delegates talking and mingling between sessions. Marty was sitting at a table on a shallow terrace that formed an extension of one of the bars out into the lobby, sipping a martini while he thought about what he was going to do next.

After checking in, he had posed as an old school-friend of Alice's to inquire at the desk where he might find her. He was given room number 1248, which was not Vicenzo's. Since then Marty had called the room several times, intending to dismiss it as a wrong connection if anybody answered, but nobody had. Just what he had been expecting. He had toured the hotel and mixed with the attendees of the various conference functions, but he hadn't seen her anywhere, which seemed to indicate that she had to be in Vicenzo's room, 494. It would have been a simple matter to call there—neither Alice nor Vicenzo would have recognized his face—but for some reason he hadn't been able to do so. Perhaps subconsciously he was trying to put off the moment of truth.

"Do you think you'll enjoy the conference?"

Marty looked up in surprise when he heard the voice. A large, florid-faced man was sitting down in an empty chair on the other side of the table. He was wearing a lapel badge that said he was Dick Williams, and a thinly disguised leer that said that Dick Williams was scouting the territory. "Oh, you don't appear to have a name tag," Williams went on, as if he had just noticed. "I thought I saw you at one of the sessions earlier. I must have been mistaken." He looked at Marty expectantly. Presumably Marty was supposed to be curious and ask about the sessions.

"I guess you were," Marty said, and looked away.

"It's the American Bioengineering Society," Williams explained anyway. "It goes on all week. I'm here with an outfit called Calom-Freyn Biodynamics. You may have heard of us . . . we're the second largest in biotronics in the country. Over two billion a year turnover. I run the marketing side of it . . . international." He flipped a peanut into his mouth with his thumb in a way that was presumably meant to look cavalier and roguish. It didn't. He waited a second or two for a response, then took a more direct tack. "What brings you here . . . business, vacation, or what?"

"Oh, er . . . business," Marty said before he had really thought about it.

"Well, it's not all that bad a place. You here for the week?"

"Yes," Marty replied automatically. He began rummaging through the mess in the pocketbook on the chair next to him to find where he had put his cash so he could settle the tab and get out.

Williams was looking more interested. He slipped his left hand casually off the table and onto his lap. "Say, what do you know . . . we're both here for the week. You're very attractive, if you don't mind my saying so, and it is so refreshing to meet a girl who talks sense." Marty wondered what that was supposed to mean, since he hadn't said a damn thing. Williams hesitated for a moment, then added, "I, ah . . . I don't get to meet a lot of company since I got divorced. Er, maybe we could kinda . . . get to know one another just a little while we're here, know what I mean?" He winked meaningfully. Marty glared. Williams held up a hand and looked horrified. "Oh, don't get me wrong. I meant maybe we could get together for dinner or something . . . sometime in the week maybe."

"Maybe," Marty said, trying to squeeze all the interest out of his voice. Even as he spoke he knew he had said the wrong thing.

Williams smiled. "Say, you like the idea. Okay, we'll have to fix something up. I'm in Room eight-eight-six, just so that you know. What about you?"

Marty swore under his breath. His predicament resolved itself when another man, lean and swarthy, and with a crown of curly locks of oily-looking hair, swayed over to the table and sat down heavily in the chair next to Williams, at the same time clapping Williams heartily across the back. Williams didn't look too pleased about it. "Dick, you old son-of-a-bitch!" the newcomer roared. "So this is where you're hiding, huh? So what's new?" He turned his head toward Marty as if noticing him for the first time. "So aren't you gonna introduce me to your friend?" He shrugged a mock apology across the table and grinned. "I guess he's not. Hi. I'm Larry. Dick'll tell you lots of bad things about me if you let him, but they're not true." He nudged Williams in the ribs and laughed. "That right, Dick? They're not true, are they? You make 'em all up because I always make out and you never do, and you get jealous." He winked across at Marty. "It's okay. He knows I don't mean it. We're great buddies really. That right, Dick?"

Marty looked around frantically for an escape. Out in the lobby a tall, ruggedly handsome man with shoulders like those of a football player still wearing his pads under his suit was striding slowly and purposefully toward the main desk. With the loose throng of people around him, he stood out like a battleship plowing its course majestically through a gaggle of coal barges. "My husband just arrived," Marty said on impulse. "I have to go. It was nice talking to you." He stood up, slammed a five-dollar bill down on the table next to his tab, and hurried from the terrace. Halfway across the lobby he slowed down and glanced back. Williams and Larry were watching him curiously. He looked around again. The dark-haired man was at the main desk, signaling for the attention of one

of the clerks. Doing his best to look as if he belonged
there, Marty sidled up and stood next to him. From
close up the man was even more striking, with a face
formed from lean, solid planes, well-formed lips that
settled easily into a smile, and dark brown eyes that
danced elusively. Everything about him said that he
should have been in movies, but Marty couldn't place
him.

And then he spoke to the clerk in a firm, reso-
nant voice. "My name is Frank Vicenzo, Room four-
nine-four. You have an authorization for me to collect
messages for Mrs. A. Hayes. Is there anything?"

"Just a second, Mr. Vicenzo." The clerk checked
the pigeonholes behind the desk, took out some
message slips, and passed them across.

"Thank you." Vicenzo inspected the messages
briefly, then folded them and tucked them into an
inside pocket of the his suit, and walked away.

Marty almost died. Vicenzo was heading in the
direction of the elevators, which meant he had to be
going up to his room. And he had taken Alice's
messages. That meant Alice had to be there too.
Without really knowing what he was trying to accomplish or why, Marty tightened his grip on his pocketbook and hurried across the lobby after Vicenzo.
Williams and Larry were still watching him with
puzzled looks, but he didn't care about them any
longer.

He emerged on the fourth floor in a bay that
opened out to corridors leading to guest-rooms on
both sides. The wall of the corridor to the right
carried a sign indicating Rooms 452 to 498, and Marty
went that way. As he turned the corner into the
corridor his heart skipped a beat. Vicenzo was a short
distance in front of him, striding toward the far end,
where the higher room numbers were located. Marty
followed him breathlessly, finding that he almost had
to run to keep up. Vicenzo stopped outside 494 and

rapped twice on the door. He paused, evidently listening to something from inside which Marty couldn't hear, and then said in a loud voice, "It's me—Frank." He stepped back a pace to wait and looked casually back along the corridor. Marty turned toward the nearest door and started searching through his pocketbook as if he were looking for his key.

"It's never where you were sure you put it, is it?" Vicenzo called along the corridor. Marty looked up, startled. Vicenzo was smiling good-humoredly. Marty was too flustered to do anything but shake his head mutely and force the corners of his mouth to twitch upward. He was trying to smile. This wasn't real.

The door in front of Vicenzo opened. Vicenzo grinned at somebody inside and stepped through. The door closed. Instinctively Marty rushed up to it but came to his senses just in time to stop himself from pounding on it with his fists. With an effort he pulled himself together sufficiently to go back to his own room and down three straight Scotches one after the other. Then he called Abe.

Abe told Marty he was doing a good job and to keep working on it. Marty told Abe he was going to get drunk. He couldn't, Abe said. It didn't work with Arabees. Marty said that Abe didn't know what he was talking about; in fact Marty was beginning to feel drunk already. The power of suggestion, Abe said. Alcohol depressed the higher brain functions, and it couldn't work if the bloodstream with the alcohol was in one place, and the brain whose higher functions needed to be depressed was someplace else. Marty told Abe he was talking through his ass.

"You have to keep working at it," Abe insisted. "I just talked to Sam, and he says you gotta have witnesses. He's gonna show up there later on in the week and bring a photographer, but not until you've established the setup. I mean, for a start, have you actually seen her there yet?"

"No," Marty told him. "But she's checked in here, she hasn't been in her room, and that Adonis creep's collecting her messages. What else do you want?"

"You need to see her there, with him, and you need witnesses who'll say you saw them," Abe replied. "Keep at it, Marty. You're doing great. The sooner you can give us the setup, the sooner we can get Sam in and you out."

Marty thought it over after Abe had hung up. Alice was definitely there in the hotel now, it seemed, whether she had been earlier in the evening or not. Possibly she and Vicenzo had been out for the afternoon, which meant there was a good chance that they would be around from now on, maybe to have a drink or to get something to eat. One thing was certain—Marty wouldn't find them together if he stayed in his room. He showered, unpacked the undies that he had bought earlier, and after spending some time figuring out what went on top of what, finally fought his way into a new outfit. Then he went downstairs again to have a drink at one of the other bars.

The only vacant barstool was next to a thin man with a neatly trimmed ginger beard who soon started trying to make conversation. Marty told him in no uncertain terms to get lost, and for the next fifteen minutes they ignored each other. Then the man asked the bartender for his check and showed his room key as he signed it. The room number was 494. He signed his name, B.L. Tyson, and then left.

Marty sat there nonplused. What in hell was going on? If Tyson was booked into 494, then maybe he had opened the door for Vicenzo. But if Tyson and Vicenzo were sharing 494, where was Alice? Perhaps she was staying in her own room, 1248, after all. Marty decided he had to know the answer to that. He finished his drink, paid the check, and went to a house phone to call 1248. There was no reply.

He paced around for a while wondering what to

do. When he came into the main lobby, he noticed
that a night clerk had taken over at the desk from
the one who had been on duty earlier. This gave
Marty an idea. He walked up to the desk, inflated
his chest, and smiled across sweetly. "I have a small
problem," he crooned at the clerk. "Do you think you
could help me?"

The clerk's eyes widened with approval. "If I can,
ma'am. What's the problem?"

"I've been silly and locked my key up in my room.
Do you have a duplicate that I could borrow, by any
chance . . . just for a minute?"

"Which room is it?"

"Twelve-forty-eight. The name is Hayes—Mrs. A.
Hayes."

"Sure," the clerk replied. "I just need to see some
ID."

Marty pouted. "I thought you might say that. That's
the problem. All my papers and everything are in
there too. I really don't want to have to start calling people and bothering them this late at night." He
fluttered his eyelashes and lowered his voice to a
husky, seductive whisper. "Come on, you look like a
nice guy. You can trust me."

"Well . . . I don't know . . ." The clerk looked
worried. "It's against the rules. You could get me into
a lot of trouble."

"Who's going to tell anyone?" Marty said, winking.
"You don't even have to give it to me. You could leave
it lying on the desk there accidentally and be looking the other way. If anyone asks, I'll just say I took
it."

The clerk slipped the key quickly across the
counter. "Not more than five minutes," he murmured.

"You're really a sweetie," Marty whispered. "I knew
it."

He went up to the twelfth floor, found Room 1248,
and waited after tapping loudly several times. There

was no answer, and no sound of any kind from within. Marty took a long breath, pushed the key into the lock, let himself in, and switched on the light. The room had not been touched. There were no bags, clothes, or any signs of occupation. A sick, sinking feeling slowly took hold of him as the final glimmer of hope that he had been nursing without realizing it at last faded away. He turned out the light, closed the door, and went down to the lobby to return the key.

So what did it all mean? The only other place that Alice could be was in 494. But two men were also booked into that room. He stopped dead in his tracks halfway across the lobby and went cold as a new thought struck him. Two men and . . . ? Surely not. Not *that*. He found himself shaking. Anything could happen in California. He had said that to enough people himself. For the next few minutes he seemed to be in a haze, no knowing where he was going or what he was doing until he found himself coming out of an elevator on the fourth floor once again. He turned to the right and moved mechanically into the corridor to stand staring along toward where Room 494 was situated. He wasn't really sure why he had come back here or what he was going to do next, but somehow he had to know what was going on in that room.

A small group of men was standing around outside the door of one of the rooms near him, drinking beer from cans and talking loudly. The door was open, and the sound of lots of raised voices punctuated by shouts and laughs was coming from inside. It sounded like a party—probably being thrown by a bunch of the conference attendees. A couple of the men turned their heads to study him with interest as he moved closer to them to get a better view along the corridor.

"Hey, baby," one of them called. "Wanna come to

a party? Plenty of booze, lots of nice people. We're all pretty harmless." Somebody else guffawed.

"She ain't interested in ya, Benny," another man said. Then, louder, "Hey, I got class. How about just one drink?"

"Aw, she's too stuck-up."

"Just one drink. Don't take any notice of them. They've had too much already."

"Go crawl back under," Marty told them as he squeezed past to get farther along the corridor. At that moment the door of 494 opened ahead of him, and a man came out. Marty stopped and stared. It wasn't Vicenzo or Tyson but someone else, this time slim and distinguished-looking with graying hair and a three-piece suit. He stopped to fasten a button of his vest and straighten his necktie. Marty swallowed disbelievingly. And then Tyson came out. He said something to gray-hair, they laughed, and then began walking toward where Marty was standing rooted to the spot.

"She's some woman, all right," Tyson said to gray-hair as they passed him. "I don't know where she gets all the energy from."

"She often goes all night without a break," gray-hair replied.

"I can believe it."

They walked on by and stopped in front of the elevators. It was all Marty could do to stop himself from gibbering incoherently out loud. And then Vicenzo came out of 494, waving something over his head. "Tony," he called. "You forgot this . . . your watch." Gray-hair looked instinctively at his wrist. "Stay there or you'll miss the elevator," Vicenzo told him. "I'll bring it." He was walking briskly toward them as he spoke. As Vicenzo passed Marty, his eyes brightened with recognition. "Hi there, find your key?" he said, and walked on to where Tyson was holding open one of the elevator doors.

Marty turned around again and looked along toward Room 494. Vicenzo had left the door half open. This was his chance. Then somebody goosed him from behind—hard. He whirled around to find one of the party drunks grinning at him lewdly. Without stopping to think about it, he compressed his fist into a tight ball and delivered a straight, solid right to the jaw. Every ounce of the anger and frustration that had been building up for the past two days went into the punch. A sharp crack of teeth being snapped together sounded above the background murmur of voices.

"Holy Christ, a chick just slugged Benny!" a voice yelled behind him as he turned and rushed along the corridor.

"She's floored him!"

"Jesus, I felt it from here!"

He flung the door open wide and hurled himself through. There were men's clothes and papers everywhere, but no Alice. He rushed into the bathroom, tore aside the shower curtain, then came out again and began throwing open the doors of the closets.

"What's going on?" a powerful voice shouted from the door. Marty spun around. It was Vicenzo, looking mad. "Who are you? What in hell do you think you're doing in here?"

"Where is she?" Marty shrieked.

"Who, for God's sake?"

"You know who! Don't give me that garbage. I know what's going on." Marty snatched up the leather traveling case that he had found in the bedroom of his house and emptied the contents on the floor. Vicenzo stepped forward and tore it from his hands. Marty started opening the drawers of the vanity and hurling them onto one of the room's three beds.

"Stop that!" Vicenzo bellowed at him. "Are you crazy? There isn't anyone else here, I'm telling you." Marty pulled the covers off one of the beds, then wheeled around and started stripping another one. Vicenzo grabbed him and shook him roughly. "God-damn it, will you listen to me, you stupid woman! *There isn't anyone here!* What kind of nut are you?"

"She's here somewhere!" Marty screamed. "You know where she is!"

"Who, for Christ's sake?" Vicenzo bawled.

"My wife, that's who! I know all about you!"

Vicenzo released his grip and stared at Marty in total bewilderment. "Wife? *Your* wife?" He looked Marty up and down, blinked, and shook his head. "Oh, God! You . . . you really are nuts." He tried to smile reassuringly. "I'm sure we'll find her. Now why don't you just take it easy, sit down, and maybe—"

"Don't try any of that on me." Marty stormed across to an open closet and dragged out a dark brown blazer with distinctive brass buttons. He threw it in a heap on the floor. "See that? Do you think I haven't seen that before? And this!" A necktie with yellow and brown diagonal stripes followed the blazer. "Don't tell me they're not yours!"

"Of course they're mine!" Vicenzo yelled, losing his patience. "So they're mine, and they're in my room. What the hell's supposed to be wrong with that?"

"I found them in my house, that's what!" Marty shouted, pushing his face close to Vicenzo's and contorting it in fury. "You want to know what I'm doing in your room? I wanna know what *you* were doing in my house, with my wife!"

Vicenzo backed away and looked wary. "You're insane. I don't know who you are. I've never been near your house. I don't even know where your house is."

"You know where it is, all right. Or maybe too much sex affects your memory. Newport Beach, Twenty-seven Maple Drive, that's where. Now tell me you've never heard of it."

Vicenzo's eyes widened. "You're crazy," he gasped.

"Well?" Marty challenged. "Are you still telling me you don't know it?"

Vicenzo raised his hands helplessly. "Sure I do, but—"

"Aha! Now we're getting to the truth. So what were you doing there?"

"I . . . I . . ." Vicenzo shook his head. "I live there. That's *my* house!"

Marty gaped at him. "Now *you're* being crazy. D'you think I don't know where I live?"

"I don't know where *you* live, but I know where *I* live," Vicenzo said. "And that's where I live, with my husband."

"But . . . but . . ."

The charge from the atmosphere in the room evaporated suddenly, and they stood for a moment staring speechlessly at each other. Then Marty said in a small voice, "Alice?"

Vicenzo stared in astonishment. "Marty?"

He looked at her. She looked at him.

"What the hell are you doing in that?" they both asked together.

Marty sat down weakly on the edge of one of the beds and spread his hands wide. "I got home a day early . . . on Friday." He waved toward the clothes on the floor and the traveling bag lying to one side. "Those things were there—some guy's things . . . and there was a hotel registration that said he was staying here." He gestured down at himself. "So I . . . It was Abe's idea. We thought . . ."

Alice looked at him in amazement for a few seconds while the meaning of what he had said slowly sank in. Then she threw her head back and laughed. "Oh, Marty, you . . . *idiot*! You thought . . ." She shook her head. "Really, it's too funny for . . ." She began laughing again.

Marty looked at her sourly. "Well, I don't think it's

so goddamn funny. Would you mind telling me what the hell's going on here?"

Alice took a moment to calm herself. "It's very simple," she said. "You see, Margaret Sullivan, our editor-in-chief, had this idea about doing a story for women about what it's really like to be a man. She came up with this angle of having a couple of the girls renting male Arabees for a week and then writing up all the things that happened to them. I didn't tell you about it because . . . well, it's a bit strange, and, to be honest, you can be funny about things sometimes . . . and I did want to do it because it sounded like a lot of fun. We picked this week to do it so that we could use the conference as an excuse for being away from home. That's really all there is to tell."

"So who were those two other guys who were in here?" Marty asked.

"Nancy and Dianne from the office," Alice told him. "There are three of us doing it . . . sort of for moral support. We're all sharing this room. I did book another one in my own name, mainly in case you wanted to get in touch, but I'm not using it. It didn't seem a very good idea to have a man's body going in and out of my room all week. It's surprising how things like that can get around."

Marty was beginning to smile as he saw the funny side of it. "One more thing," he said. "What were you three talking about in here just before the others left?"

Alice thought for a moment. "Margaret Sullivan, I think," she replied. "We were saying what a human dynamo she is at the office. Sometimes she works right through until morning when she's got a tough deadline. Why? What made you ask that?"

Marty started to laugh. "It doesn't matter. I'll tell you some other time." He stood up and studied Alice with renewed curiosity. "It's amazing," he murmured.

Alice tilted her head thoughtfully to one side and ran a finger along his arm. "You know, you're quite cute," she remarked. They looked at each other, wondering who would dare to voice the thought first.

Marty looked around. "It, ah . . . it's a pity you're all sharing," he said at last.

Alice's eyes twinkled wickedly. "Well, I still have the other room up on the twelfth floor," she reminded him in an off-handed voice.

"True," Marty agreed, keeping his tone neutral.

"It would be deliciously . . . different," Alice said after a pause.

Marty thought about it. "And Margaret would want you to cover the subject thoroughly, wouldn't she?" he suggested.

"Oh, definitely. She's very thorough." Alice's six-foot-plus body started to giggle. She slipped her arm through his, and they moved toward the door. At the last second they remembered and switched their arms around the other way.

"Who knows?" Marty said as they stood waiting for an elevator. "We might want to try this again sometime."

"Who knows?" Alice agreed.

The elevator arrived, and the doors opened. Alice and Marty stepped in, clung tightly to each other, and began laughing again as the doors closed.

"Identity Crisis" first appeared in the seventh of Judy-Lynn Del Rey's *Stellar* anthologies (August 1981). A previous story based on the same premise, entitled "Till Death Us Do Part," had been included in *Stellar 6*. Our thought was to produce a series of "Rentabody" stories over the ensuing years, and then bring them all together into a single volume. Some readers sensed this and asked if they could expect to see more. As things turned out, it ended up as one of those projects that was just filed away. But who knows? It could be revived again one day.

Uprooting Again

One of the things that made Sonora an interesting place to live in was its population of individualists—the original "No-Name City," with lots of boots, vests, and wide-brim hats, covered-over sidewalks—but pickup trucks these days instead of horses. (How many people remember that the stagecoach full of French hookers that Lee Marvin hijacked in the movie *Paint Your Wagon* was heading for Sonora?) Some mining still went on in the area, and other traditional occupations included ranching and logging. But on top of that there was a population of transplanted ex-professionals from all walks who seemed to have woken up one morning and said, "To hell with this job. I'm going to do what *I* want to do!" . . . and they ended up in Sonora. We had a former UCLA psychologist running the bookstore, a SAC pilot who owned caves, an aerospace engineer running the health-food store, a biblical fundamentalist with a sandwich shop, and the hairdresser demonstrated twenty-board simultaneous chess in the ice-cream parlor. There was even a hard-drinking, hard-fighting, pot-smoking, fornicating Jehovah's Witness. And, of course, this strange English guy with an office over the hardware store, who wrote science fiction. No two of them seemed to share views or opinions on anything, and yet everyone tolerated everyone in a kind of way that said "Well, that's just the way the guy is." There was no concept of any norm that anyone "ought" to conform to. A microcosm, perhaps, of how the world could one day be.

I had been thinking for some time that I wanted to do a book on the subject of World War Two, the history of which had always interested me. A standard WW2 sf theme has been the alternate history where the war ended differently. The thought of churning out yet another of the same was unappealing. So, I turned things around to a storyline where time travelers from a very different postwar world alter the outcome into the history that we know. This was *The Proteus Operation*, my first book published with Bantam. It was also a lesson in the dangers of over-researching a book. I got so carried away in the politics of the prewar period, background to the Manhattan Project, biographies of Churchill, Roosevelt, Einstein, Teller, Szilard, and others, and various related issues, that six months went by between my writing the Prologue and commencing Chapter One. Our second son, Michael Robert, arrived just in time to get the dedication.

And, true to tradition, Jackie and I had another son, Edward Joseph, to coincide with the next book, *Endgame Enigma,* which added a bit of espionage-thriller flavor to an sf background and dealt with simulating a full-scale space colony on Earth, including how to camouflage the give-away of terrestrial gravity. Three sons in a row, after three daughters in a row, restored my faith in mathematics by showing that statistics do work in the end, provided one gives them long enough.

By this time, 1985, I had been a full-time writer for six years. One of the benefits of this situation was having the time and the freedom to read and think and talk about things that mattered to *me*, instead of—as it now became clearer had been so true of the past—playing the game of pretending that I cared about things that primarily served the interests of others. Preoccupation with such matters as liberty and rights had a lot to do with the writing of *The Mirror Maze*, my third book with Bantam, eventually published in 1989. Interestingly, it produced more excited responses from Eastern Europe and the former Soviet nations (maybe because the Russians are depicted in a Western novel as good guys for once, and end up cooperating with their Western counterparts to foil the real bad guys).

Life had by this time reached that settled, idyllic state where experience told that a change wasn't far off. When I was younger, growing up in London in the 1940s and '50s, my father had sometimes taken me to spend summers with his family in Ireland. He was from a village in County Cork, and at that time every farm in the vicinity, it seemed, belonged to some branch or other of Hogans. But never mind electricity—there was no running water in many of the houses in those parts then; the women carried the water in pails from springs in the fields, and milked cows straight into jugs to be set on the table for tea. As a teenager I used to go hiking and camping around western Ireland with bunch of pals from London, but after that pretty much forgot about the country until I found myself living in California in the late '80s with thoughts of moving back. And I realized that I had no idea how much, if anything had changed. Before uprooting the family and taking a Californian wife there, it seemed a good idea to find out. I decided that a reconnaissance visit was called for. Harry Harrison, the well known sf writer, and his wife, Joan, had lived there for a number of years, so one day I called from the States to ask questions and see how closely some of my impressions approached to reality. Harry said, "We can do a lot better than that. Why not come over and spend a week with us and check it out for yourself?" So I started putting arrangements in hand for an exploratory visit back the other way across the Atlantic.

In the meantime, further projects unfolded on the more immediate front. Lou Aronica, the publishing chief of Bantam-Spectra, and I had been talking on and off for some time about trying to mix Sherlock Holmes with James Bond. Holmes's intellectual puzzles were fascinating (although I've always thought his logic pretty shaky), but a bit tame for the modern reader. And while Bond brings in some excitement, he had to be the most inept secret agent ever conceived, spending all his time getting out of situations that no professional would ever have gotten into. The result was *The Infinity Gambit*, which dealt with a British former SAS counter-terrorism specialist turned freelance—an experiment in more mainstream writing, outside the sf genre.

This was about when I published with Ballantine again, also. *Giants' Star* had concluded the trilogy that began with *Inherit the Stars*, and in my own mind I was happy with the thought of leaving behind the world of those earlier books and going on to explore other things. Readers didn't quite see things that way, however, and Owen Lock, who had succeeded Judy-Lynn del Rey, ganged up with Eleanor Wood, my agent, in persuading me to add a fourth book to the series. I had no idea what direction it might take until Eleanor came up with the beginnings of an idea that eventually produced *Entoverse*. Although it all worked out fine in the end, I wanted it to be the last. The outline that I submitted to Owen ended: ". . . on the way back to Earth the ship blows up. Everyone of note is killed, and I can't be talked into writing a fifth in this series." Apparently

Owen, on reading it, grinned and said, "It's okay. Jim wouldn't do that to us." And of course, he was right.

Entoverse also combined another line of thought that had been going around in my head for some time. Years previously, when I was at lunch with a couple of editors in New York, one of them had asked if I thought I'd ever write a fantasy novel. I replied maybe, but if so it probably wouldn't be the kind of fantasy they had in mind. My view on the question that's always being asked about the difference between science fiction and fantasy is that sf might extrapolate the currently accepted principles of physics or incorporate them as a subset into something larger, but it doesn't violate them. With fantasy even this restriction goes away, which is to say that "magic" can happen. But since I'm not much into magic, how would I ever be likely to produce anything that qualifies as fantasy?

Well, one way would be to create an environment with laws of its own in which a world with weird effects could evolve, but supported by a substrate of everyday physics that the world inside it doesn't "see." An obvious approach was to make it a computer environment: the hardware runs according to regular physics, but supports an internal world governed by whatever rules the programmers write in for driving the system. The fun in developing this was the notion of information "quanta" in data space playing roles analogous to those of particles in ordinary space, and finding counterparts of mass, gravity, electromagnetism, and so on to afford the basis of a process via which constructs of sufficient complexity could eventually emerge to be capable of perceiving the world that had evolved with them. Making it work required a computer about the size of a planet, and a suitably mysterious candidate had been thoughtfully left behind by the aliens in *Giants'*

Star, together with the pieces for constructing a reason why anyone would want to build a computer that big.

My books were finding their way overseas also, and I got invited to conventions in Japan, Poland, Russia, Germany, and England, which offset any risk of life drifting toward monotony.

Many good stories arise simply from putting a character into an unusual situation and seeing what they make of it. In pondering this angle as a way to come up with the next book, I asked what would be the most unusual situation that somebody could find themselves in, and decided it would be waking up dead. (This kind of illogic starts to come naturally after a couple of years of living in Ireland.) Well, not literally "dead," obviously. But suppose that nobody recognized you, and everyone you knew insisted that the "you" you thought you were was dead? And that was how the trail began that led to *The Multiplex Man,* published in 1992, by Bantam again.

An idea of Virtual Reality was becoming popular by the early nineties. The alien civilization in the "Giants" series had taken VR to its ultimate by means of a direct neural I/O technology that bypassed the normal sensory system to produce total illusions indistinguishable from the real thing. How it worked was something I'd left to the reader to figure out as an exercise. *The Genesis Machine* had been written around a hypothetical account of the research and theoretical breakthroughs that led to the discovery of that great fable of science fiction, "hyperspace." In a similar kind of way, the background to *Realtime Interrupt* told the story of how various developments from corporate, academic, and government domains came together to yield a direct neural I/O interface capability, and the bizarre things that became possible as a consequence. Marvin Minsky, who had helped in the conceptual stages, got a walk-on part in the book.

Meanwhile, Owen Lock of Ballantine had been pressuring me again, this time for a sequel to *Code of the Lifemaker*, showing more about the aliens mentioned in the Prologue. After he had cajoled me into accepting a contract, he casually mentioned in a bar in Manhattan one night, "Oh, I finally got around to rereading *Code of the Lifemaker* last week. I'd forgotten: They all got wiped out about a million years ago, didn't they."

"Owen," I said, "that's what I've been trying to tell you. It makes it kind of tough to come up with a follow-up story about them."

"Oh well, you're a resourceful writer," was his response. "I'm sure you'll think of something." And he refused to discuss the matter further for the rest of the evening.

Now, to me, "sequel" implies a story that follows on from the one before and involves the same characters that the reader has come to know and wants to see more of. That meant it had to revolve around the central figures from "*Code*," whom we'd left out at Titan, solidly in the twenty-first century. On the other hand it had also to feature the aliens, who were extinct before humans existed. How to reconcile two such irreconcilables? I didn't want to resort to a cop-out like time travel, which hadn't been anticipated in any way in the first book; nor was I happy with something weak, along the lines of, "Well, actually they weren't *all* wiped out. . . ." and so on. Finally, a way out suggested itself, resulting in *The Immortality Option*, published in 1995. (Hint: A major help on this book was Hans Moravec of the Robotics Institute at Carnegie Mellon University. Hans has written a lot on uploading consciousness into computers or other non-organic hardware.)

I don't know if anyone else has noticed, but the

Atlantic is relativistic. Irrespective of what time a flight leaves the U.S., it invariably arrives on the other side at some ungodly hour of the morning, usually gray, overcast, and drizzling.

Such was the dawn when I disembarked at Shannon on the west coast of Ireland off a Pan Am flight from JFK, having changed planes the previous evening after a transcontinental haul from California. That was when I discovered that—according to local wisdom, because Pan Am competed on the New York run—Aer Lingus, the national Irish airline, didn't fly a connection to Dublin. "So how do I get there?" I groaned to the colleen at the information desk. All I wanted was a room and a bed. "No problem," she replied brightly. "The train from Limerick will get you there in a couple of hours."

"But we're not in Limerick," I pointed out.

"Ah yes, well, that's true enough. You have to get the bus."

By the time I collapsed into a taxi outside Heuston Station in Dublin, I was just able to mumble to the cabbie, "Get me to somewhere I can sleep—anywhere." I ended up at a guest house on Lansdowne Road, a block or so from the international rugby stadium of the same name. No recollection of checking in. Pillow. Bed. Blissful oblivion.

I was awakened late in the afternoon by a din of voices, drums, horns, and pipes out on the street. Civil insurrection? Brian Boru's army risen from the dead? I got dressed hurriedly and went down to the residents' lounge to find the beaming owner and his wife handing out glasses of whiskey to guests, friends, and family alike—indeed, seemingly anyone who cared to walk in off the street. Ireland had just beaten Bulgaria.

Thoughts of wet mornings, lurching buses, and gray Victorian railroad stations in the rain were soon forgotten. Not only was there running water, but a bathroom and shower in the room (Europeans haven't discovered water pressure yet, but that's another story), electricity, TV, and computer stores. I could get to like this place, I decided.

But that was before the saga of the house (again). We'll come to that part later.

Leapfrog

Fall had come to the northern hemisphere of Mars. At the north pole, the mean temperature had fallen to -125°C—cold enough to freeze carbon dioxide out of the thin Martian atmosphere and begin forming the annual covering that would lay over the permanent cap of water-ice until spring. In the southern polar regions, where winter had ended, the carbon dioxide was evaporating. Along the edge of the retreating fields of dry ice, strong winds were starting to raise dust. During the short but hot southern summer, with Mars making its closest approach to the sun, the resulting storms could envelop the planet.

Edmund Halloran watched the surface details creep across the large wallscreen at one end of the mess area of Yellow Section, Deck B, of the interplanetary transfer vessel *Mikhail Gorbachev*, wheeling in orbit at the end of its six-month voyage from Earth to bring the third settlement mission to the Red Planet. The other new arrivals sitting around him at the scratched and stained green-topped aluminum tables—where they had eaten their meals, played innumerable hands of cards, and talked, laughed, and exchanged reminiscences through the long voyage out—were also strangely quiet as they took in the view. Unlike the other views of Mars that they had studied and memorized, this was not being replayed from transmissions sent back from somewhere on the other side of millions of miles of space. This time it was really on the outside of the thin metal shell around them. Very soon, now, they would be leaving the snug cocoon with its reassuring routine and its company of familiar faces that they had come to know as home, to go down there. They had arrived.

The structure had lifted out from lunar orbit as a flotilla of three separate, identical craft, independently powered, each fabricated in the general form of a T, but with the bar curved as part of the arc of a circle, rather than straight. On entering the unpowered free-fall phase that would endure for most of the voyage, the three ships had maneuvered together and joined at their bases to become the equispaced spokes of a rotating Y, creating comfortable living conditions in the three inhabited zones at the extremities. The triplicated design meant that in the event of a major failure in any of the modules, everybody could get home again in the remaining two—or at a push, with a lot of overcrowding and at the cost of jettisoning everything not essential survival, even in a remaining one. The sections accommodated a total of 600 people, which represented a huge expansion of the existing population of 230 accrued from the previous missions. Some of the existing population had been distributed between a main base on Lunae Planum and a few outlying installations. The majority, however, were still up in Marsianskaya Mezhdunarodnaya Orbital 'Naya Stantsiya, or Mars International Orbiting Station," awaiting permanent accommodation on the surface. In the Russian Cyrillic alphabet this was shortened to MAPCMOC, yielding the satisfying descriptive transliteration MARSMOS in English, accepted as the standard international language.

The region coming into view now was an area roughly twenty degrees north of the equator. Halloran recognized the heavily cratered area of Lunae Planum and the irregular escarpment at its eastern edge, bounding the smoother volcanic plain of Chryse Planitia. Although he knew where to look, he could see no indication of the main base down there. He picked out the channels emerging from the escarpment, where volcanic heating had melted some of the underground ice that had existed in an earlier age, causing torrential floods to pour out across the expanse of Chryse, which lay about a kilometer lower.

An announcement from the overhead speakers broke his mood of reverie. "Attention please. The shuttle to MARSMOS is now ready for boarding. Arrivals holding disembarkation cards ninety-three through one hundred twenty should proceed through to the docking area. Ninety-three through one hundred twenty, to the docking port now."

Halloran rose and picked up his briefcase and a bag containing other items that he wanted to keep with him until the personal baggage caught up with them later. As he shuffled forward to join the flow of people converging toward the door, a voice spoke close behind him. "It looks as if we're on the same trip across, Ed." He looked around. Ibrahim and Anna, a young Egyptian couple, were next in line.

"I guess so," Halloran grunted. Ibrahim was an electronics technician, his wife a plant geneticist. They were both impatient to begin their new lives. Why two young people like these should be so eager and excited about coming to a four-thousand-mile ball of frozen deserts, Halloran couldn't imagine. Or maybe he couldn't remember.

"We'll be going straight down from the station." Ibrahim gestured toward Anna; she smiled a little shyly. "The doctors want her to adapt to surface conditions as soon as possible."

Anna's pregnancy had been confirmed early in the voyage. Although the baby wouldn't be the first to be born on Mars, it would be one of a very select few. The knowledge added considerably to Ibrahim's already exuberant pride of first fatherhood.

"It may be a while before I see you again, then, eh?" Halloran said. "But I wouldn't worry about not bumping into each other again. It's not as if there are that many places to get lost in down there yet."

"I hope it won't be too long," Ibrahim said. "It was good getting to know you. I enjoyed listening to your stories. Good luck with your job here."

"You too. And take good care of Anna there, d'you hear."

They moved out through the mess doorway, into a gray-walled corridor of doors separated by stretches of metal ribbing. Byacheslav, one of the Russian construction engineers, moved over to walk beside Halloran as they came to the stairway leading up to the next deck, where the antechamber to the docking port was located. He was one of the relatively few older members of the group—around Halloran's age.

"Well, Ed . . . it would be two years at least before you saw Earth again, even if you changed your mind today."

"I wasn't planning on changing my mind."

"It's a big slice out of what's left of life when you get to our end of it. No second thoughts?"

"Oh, things get easier once you're over the hump. What happens when you get over the top of any hill and start going down the other side? You pick up speed, right? The tough part's over. People just look at it the wrong way."

Byacheslav smiled. "Never thought about it that way. Maybe you're right."

"How about you?"

"Me? I'm going to be too busy to worry much about things like that. We're scheduled to begin excavating the steel plant within a month. Oh, and there was something else. . . ." Byacheslav reached inside his jacket, took a billfold from the inside pocket, and peeled out Unodollar tens and ones. "That's to settle our poker account—before I blow it all in the mess bar down at Mainbase."

Halloran took the money and stuffed it in his hip pocket. "Thanks. . . . You know, By, there was a time when I wouldn't have trusted a Russian as far as I could throw one of your earthmovers. It came with the trade."

"Well, you're in a different business now."

"I guess we all are."

They entered the antechamber, with its suiting-up room and two EVA airlocks on one side, and passed through the open doors of the docking port into the body of the shuttle. To align with the direction of the *Mikhail Gorbachev's* simulated gravity, the shuttle had docked with its roof entry-hatch mating to the port, which meant they had to enter down a ladder into the compartment forward of the passenger cabin. The seats were small and cramped, and Halloran and Byacheslav wedged themselves in about halfway to the back, next to a young Indonesian who was keeping up a continuous chatter with someone in the row behind.

"Do you know where you're going yet, Ed?" Byacheslav asked as they buckled themselves in.

"Probably a couple of weeks more up in orbit, until the new admin facility is ready down below," Halloran replied. "The director I'll be working for from MCM is supposed to be meeting me at MARSMOS. I should find out for sure then. I guess it depends on you construction people."

"Don't worry. We won't leave you stuck up here. . . ." Byacheslav looked at Halloran and raised his eyebrows. "So, one of the directors is meeting you personally, eh? And will they have a red carpet? If that's the kind

of reception an administrator gets, I think I'm starting to worry already. I can see how the whole place
will end up being run. That was what I came all this
distance to get away from. Hmm . . . maybe I've
changed my mind. Perhaps we will leave you up here."

Halloran's rugged, pink-hued face creased into a
grin. "I wouldn't get too carried away if I were you.
He's based up at MARSMOS most of the time, anyway. I'm just here to take care of resource-allocation
schedules. Nothing special. They used to call it being
a clerk."

"Now I think you're being too modest. There's a
lot more to it than scratching in ledgers with pens
these days. You have to know computer systems. And
in a situation like this, the function is crucial. You
can't tell me you're not good."

"Don't believe a word of it. It's just Uncle Sam's
way of retiring off old spy chiefs in a world that
doesn't need so many spies anymore."

Halloran sat back and gazed around the cabin. All
of the passengers were aboard and seated, and the
crew were securing the doors. The metaphoric umbil-
ical back to Earth was about to be broken. It had
been over thirty years ago when he joined the Agency.
Who would have thought, then, that two months after
turning fifty-five, he'd have found himself at a place
like this, starting with a new outfit all over again?

And of all outfits to have ended up with, one with
a name like Moscow-Chase-Manhattan Investments,
Inc., which controlled a development consortium
headed by the Aeroflot Corporation, the Volga-Hilton
Hotels group, and Nippon Trans-Pacific Enterprises.
Similar combinations of interests had opened up the
Moon to the point where its materials-processing and
manufacturing industries were mushrooming, with
regular transportation links in operation and constantly
being expanded, and tourism was starting to catch on.
If the U.S. space effort hadn't fallen apart in the

seventies and eighties, America could have had all of it, decades ahead of the Soviets. As it was, America was lucky to have come out of it, along with Europe and some of the other more developed nations, as junior partners. The Second Russian Revolution, they called it. Back to capitalism. Many people thought it was better that way.

In the case of Mars, of course, the big obstacle to its similar development was the planet's greater distance from Earth, with correspondingly longer flight times. But that problem would go away—and usher in a new era of manned exploration of the outer Solar System—when the race to develop a dependable, high-performance, pulsed nuclear propulsion system was won, which would bring the typical Mars round-trip down to somewhere around ten days. Although some unforeseen difficulties had been encountered, which had delayed development of such a drive well beyond the dates optimistically predicted in years gone by, the various groups working feverishly around the world were generally agreed that the goal was now in sight. That was the bonanza that MCM was betting on. Thirty years ago, Halloran would have declared flatly that such a coordination of Soviet and Western interests under a private initiative was impossible. Now he was part of it. Or about to be. . . .

He found himself wondering again if the Vusilov who would be meeting him could be the same Vusilov from bygone years. Possibly the KGB had its own retirement problems, too. But in any case, after all the months of wondering, it would be only a matter of minutes now before he found out.

The shuttle nudged itself away from the docking port, and Halloran experienced a strange series of sensations as it fell away from the *Mikhail Gorbachev*, shedding weight as it decoupled from the ship's rotational frame, and then accelerated into a curving trajectory that would carry it across to the MARSMOS satellite.

"MARSMOS has increased tenfold in size in the last six months," Byacheslav commented. "You'll probably have more places to discover there in the next couple of weeks than I'll have down on the surface."

"There'll need to be, with all these people showing up," Halloran said.

Even before the arrival of the manned missions, a series of unmanned flights had left all kinds of hardware parked in orbit around Mars. In a frenzy of activity to prepare for the arrival of the current mission, the construction teams from the first two had expanded the initial station into a bewildering Rube-Goldberg creation of spheres, cylinders, boxes, and domes, bristling with antennas, laser tubes, and microwave dishes, all tied together by a floating web of latticeworks and tethering cables. And the next ship from Earth, with another six hundred people, was only two months behind.

There was a brief period of free-fall, and then more disorienting feelings came and went as the shuttle reversed and decelerated to dock at MARSMOS. When Halloran unfastened his restraining straps, he found himself weightless, which meant that they were at the nonrotating section of the structure. Using handrails and guidelines, the newcomers steered themselves out through an aft side-door into an arrivals area where agents were waiting to give directions and answer questions.

After receiving an information package on getting around in MARSMOS, Halloran called Moscow-Chase-Manhattan's number and asked for Mr. Vusilov.

"Da?"

"Mr. Vusilov?"

"Speaking."

"This is Ed Halloran."

"Ah, Mr. Halloran! Excellent!" The voice sounded genial and exuberant. "So, you are arrived now, yes?"

"We docked about fifteen minutes ago. I've just cleared the reception formalities."

"And did you have a pleasant voyage, I trust?"

"It dragged a bit at times, but it was fine."

"Of course. So you are still liking the idea of working with us at MCM? No second regrets, yes?"

A reception agent murmured, "Make it brief, if you wouldn't mind, Mr. Halloran. There is a line waiting."

"None," Halloran said. "Er, I am holding up the line here. Maybe if I could come on through?"

"Yes, of course. What you do is ask directions to a transit elevator that will bring you out here to Red Square, which is a ring—a joke, you see, yes? This is where I am. It is the part of MARSMOS that rotates. First we have a drink of welcome to celebrate, which is the Russian tradition. You go to the south elevator point in Red Square, then find the Diplomatic Lounge. Our gentlemen's club here, comfortable by Martian standards—no hard hats or oily coverups. There, soon, I will be meeting you."

With no gravity to define a preferred direction, the geometry inside the free-fall section of MARSMOS was an Escherean nightmare of walls, planes, passages, and connecting shafts intersecting and going off in all directions, with figures floating between the various spaces and levels like fish drifting through an undersea labyrinth. Despite the map included in the information package, Halloran was hopelessly lost within minutes and had to ask directions three times to the elevator that would take him to the south terminal of Red Square. To reach it, he passed through a spin-decoupling gate, which took him into the slowly turning hub structure of the rotating section.

The elevator capsule ran along the outside of one of the structural supporting booms and was glass-walled on two sides. A panorama of the entire structure of MARSMOS changed perspective outside as the capsule moved outward, with the full disk of Mars sweeping by beyond, against its background of stars. It was his first close-up view of the planet that was real, seen directly with his own eyes, and not an electronically generated reproduction.

As the capsule descended outward and Halloran felt his body acquiring weight once again, he replayed in his mind the voice he had heard over the phone: the guttural, heavily accented tone, the hearty, wheezing joviality, the tortured English. It had sounded like *the* Vusilov, all right. Perhaps he had upset somebody higher up in the heap, Halloran thought—which Vusilov had had a tendency to do from time to time—and despite all the other changes, the old Russian penchant for sending troublemakers to faraway places hadn't gone away.

Direction had reestablished itself when he emerged at the rim. Halloran consulted his map again and found the Diplomatic Lounge located two levels farther down, in a complex of dining areas and social rooms collectively lumped together in a prize piece of technocratese as a "Communal Facilities Zone." But as he made his way down, austere painted metal walls and pressed aluminum floors gave way to patterned designs and carpeting, with mural decorations to add to the decor, and even some ornaments and potted plants. Finally he went through double doors into a vestibule with closets and hanging space, where he left his bags, and entered a spacious room with bookshelves and a bar tended by a white-jacketed steward on one side. On the other, vast windows looked out into space, showing Phobos as a lumpy, deformed crescent. Leather armchairs and couches were grouped around low tables with people scattered around, some talking, others alone, reading. The atmosphere was calm and restful, all very comfortable and far better than anything Halloran had expected.

And then one of the figures rose and advanced with a hand extended. He was short and stocky, with broad, solid shoulders, and dressed casually in a loose orange sweater and tan slacks. As he approached, a toothy grin broadened to split the familiar craggy, heavy-jowled face, with its bulbous, purple-veined nose—a face that had always made Halloran think of an old-time prizefighter—from one misshapen, cauli-flower ear to the other.

Vusilov chuckled delightedly at the expression on Halloran's face. "Ah-hah! But why the so-surprised look, Edmund Halloran? You think you could get rid of me so easy, surely not? It has been some years now, yes? It's often I am wondering how they figure out what to do with you, Halloran. . . . So, to Mars, welcome I say to you, and to Moscow-Manhattan."

They shook hands firmly. It was the first time they had done so, even though they had met on numerous occasions as adversaries. "I wondered if it was you, Sergei . . . from the name," Halloran said.

"As I knew you would."

"You knew who I was, of course."

"Of course. I've seen your file. It wouldn't have been customary for them to show you mine."

"Who'd have guessed we'd wind up like this?" Halloran said. "Times sure change. It all seems such a long time ago, now. But then, I guess, it was lit-erally another world."

"The axes are buried under the bridge," Vusilov pronounced. "And now, as the first thing, we must drink some toast. Come." He took Halloran's elbow and steered him across to the bar. The bartender, young, swarthy, with dark eyes and flat-combed hair, looked up inquiringly. "This is Alfredo," Vusilov said, gesturing with a sweep of his hand. "The best bar-tender on Mars."

"The only one, too," Alfredo said.

"Well, what of it? That also makes you the best."

"I thought there was a bar down in the main surface base," Halloran said.

"Pah!" Vusilov waved a hand. "That is just a workman's club. Dishwashing beer from serve-your-self machines. This is the only *bar*. Alfredo is the source of all that's worth knowing up here. If you want to know what goes on, ask Alfredo. Alfredo, I want you to meet Ed Halloran, a good friend of mine who is very old. He has now come here to work with us."

"Pleased to meet you, Ed," Alfredo said.

"Hi," Halloran responded.

"Now, you see, from the old days I remember the files we keep on everybody. Your favorite choice to be poisoned with is a scotch, yes?"

"That would do fine."

"I refuse absolutely. Today you are joining us here, so it must first be vodka. We have the best."

"Okay. Make it on ice, with a splash of lime."

"And my usual, Alfredo," Vusilov said. "Put them on MCM's account."

Alfredo turned away and began pouring the drinks. After a few seconds, Halloran asked Vusilov idly, "When was the last time?"

Vusilov's beady bright yes darted restlessly as he thought back. "In 2015, wasn't it? Vienna. Hah-hah! Yes, I remember." The Russian guffawed loudly and slapped the bar with the palm of his hand. "You paid a hundred thousand dollars to buy back the coding cartridge. But the truth, you never knew! It was worthless to us, anyway. We didn't have the key."

Halloran raised a restraining hand. "Now *wait* a minute. You may be the boss here, but I'm not gonna let you get away with that. We knew about the code. It was worth about as much as those hundred-dollar bills I passed you. Didn't your people ever check them out?"

"Hmph." The smile left Vusilov's face abruptly. "I

know nothing about that. My department, it was not."
Halloran got the impression that it was more a slight
detail that Vusilov had conveniently forgotten. Alfredo
placed two glasses on the bar. Vusilov picked them
up. "Come," he said. "There are two quiet chairs over
there, by the window. Never before do you see so
many stars, and so flammable, yes?"

"Don't change the subject," Halloran said as they
began crossing the lounge. "You have to admit that
we undid your whole operation in Bonn. When we
exposed Skater and he got sent back to Moscow, it
pulled the linchpin out of it."

Vusilov stopped and threw his head back to roar
with mirth, causing heads to look up all around the
room. "What, you still believe that? He was the decoy
you were *supposed* to find out about. We were inter-
cepting your communications."

"Hell, we knew that. We were feeding you garbage through that channel. That was how we kept
Reuthen's cover. He was the one you should have
been worrying about."

Vusilov blanched and stopped in midstride. "Reuthen? The interpreter? He was with you?"

"Sure. He was our key man. You never suspected?"

"You are being serious, I suppose?"

Halloran smiled in a satisfied kind of way. "Well,
I guess you'll never know, will you?" It was a pretty
tactless way to begin a relationship with his future
boss, he admitted to himself, but he hadn't been able
to resist it. Anyhow, what did career prospects matter at his age? Hell, it had been worth it.

Vusilov resumed walking, and after a few paces
stopped by a chair where a lean, balding man with
spectacles and a clipped mustache was reading what
looked like a technical report of some kind, in
French. "This is Léon, who you should know,"
Vusilov spoke stiffly, his joviality of a moment ago
now gone. "Léon is with the European group here,

who will build the launch base and make spaceships here."

"'Allo?" Léon said, looking up.

"Please meet Ed Halloran," Vusilov said. "He comes here to work with us at MCM."

"A pleasure, Monsieur 'alloran." Léon half-rose from his chair to shake hands.

"Mine, too," Halloran said.

"They work very hard on the race for the nuclear pulse drive back home," Vusilov went on. He seemed to have smoothed his feathers, and lowered his voice in a tone of mock confidentiality. "They think they will be first, and when they get it, they are already out here at Mars ahead of us all to go deep-space. Isn't it so, Léon, yes?"

The Frenchman shrugged. "Anything is possible. Who knows? I think we 'ave a good chance. Who else is there? Your prototype has problems. Rockwell and Kazak-Dynamik both admit it."

"Well, there is always the Chinese," Vusilov said, resuming his normal voice. He evidently meant it as a joke. For the past six months the Chinese had been constructing something large in lunar orbit, the purpose of which had not been revealed. It had provoked some speculation and a lot of unflattering satire and cartoons about their late-in-the-day start at imitating everyone else. "After all, what year is it of theirs? Isn't it the Year of the Monkey, yes?"

Vusilov started to laugh, but Léon cut him off with a warning shake of his head, and nodded to indicate an Oriental whom Halloran hadn't noticed before, sitting alone in an alcove on the far side of the room. He had a thin, droopy mustache and pointed beard, and was the only person in the room who was dressed formally, in a dark suit with necktie, which he wore with a black silk skullcap. He sat erect, reading from a book held high in front of his face, and showed no sign of having overheard.

Vusilov made a silent *Oh* with his mouth, in the manner of someone guilty of a faux pas, but at the same time raised his eyebrows in a way that said it didn't matter that much.

"Who's he?" Halloran murmured.

"The Chinese representative," Léon replied quietly.

"What are they doing here?"

"Who knows what they do anywhere?" Vusilov said. "We have many countries with persons at MARSMOS, whose reasons are a mystery. They do it for getting the prestige."

"That's why this is called the Diplomatic Lounge," Léon added.

"Anyway, we shall talk with you later, Léon," Vusilov said.

"I 'ope you enjoy your stay 'ere, Monsieur 'alloran."

Vusilov led the way over to the chairs that he had indicated from the bar, set one of the glasses down on the small table between them, and sat down with the other. Halloran took the other chair and picked up his drink. "So, here's to . . . ?" He looked at the Russian invitingly.

"Oh, a prosperous business future for us, I suppose. . . ." Vusilov's mood became troubled again. He eyed Halloran uncertainly as their glasses clinked.

But, just for the moment, Halloran was oblivious as he sipped his drink and savored the feeling of a new future beginning and old differences being forgotten. A portent of the new age dawning. . . .

Until Vusilov said, "What else did Reuthen do for you?"

"Hell, why get into this?"

"A matter of professional pride. You forget that the KGB was the number-one, ace, properly run operation—not sloppy-dash slipshoe outfit like yours."

"Oh, is that so? Then what about the general who defected in 2012, in Berlin? We snatched him from right under your noses. That was a classic."

"You mean Obarin?"

"Of course, Obarin."

Vusilov tried to muster a laugh, but it wasn't convincing. "That old fart! We *gave* him to you. He knew nothing. He was more use to us on your side than on ours."

"Come on, let's get real. He'd been a frontline man ever since he was a major in Afghanistan back in the eighties. He was a goldmine of information on weapons and tactics."

"All of it out of date. He was an incompetent in Afghanistan. It saved us having to pay his pension."

"Let's face it. You were all incompetents when it came to Afghanistan."

"Is that so, now? And are you so quickly forgetting a little place called Vietnam? It was we who sucked you into that mess, you know, like the speedsands."

"Baloney. It was our own delusion in the early fifties over global Communist conspiracy being masterminded from the Kremlin."

"Precisely! And where did the delusion come from, do you think? The misinformation-spreading was always one of our masterpiece arts, yes?"

They raised their glasses belligerently, looking at each other over the rims as they drank. Vusilov's mouth contorted irascibly. Clearly he was unwilling to let it go at that, yet at the same time he seemed to be having a problem over whether or not to voice what was going through his mind.

"It didn't do you a hell of a lot of good with China," Halloran said.

That did it. "But our greatest secret weapon of all, you never discovered." Halloran raised his eyebrows. Vusilov wagged a finger. "Oh, yes. Even today, you don't even suspect what it was. The Russian leaders we have today, they are young now, and even most of them forget."

"What are you talking about?" Halloran asked.

Vusilov gave a satisfied nod. "Ah, so, now I have got you curious, eh?" He paused to extract the most from the moment. Halloran waited. The Russian waved a hand suddenly. His voice took on a stronger note. "Look around you today, Ed Halloran, and tell me what do you see? Back on Earth, the Soviet space enterprises are supreme, and we are started already to colonize the Moon. And out here, you see we are the major presence in the nations who come to Mars . . . Yet, now look back at the way the world was when it ends the Great Patriotic War in 1945, and you see it is America that holds the oyster in its hand, yes?" Vusilov shrugged. "So where does it all go down the pipes? You had it made, guys. What happened?"

Halloran could only shake his head and sigh. "These things happen. What do you want me to say, Sergei? Okay, I agree that we blew it somehow, somewhere along the line. We've got a saying that every dog has its day—and so do nations. Look at history. We had ours, and now it's your turn. Congratulations."

Vusilov looked at him reproachfully. "You think that's all there is to it, that the power plant which the USA had become all just goes away, like the dog who had a lousy day? You do us a disservice. Wouldn't you grant us that perhaps, maybe, we might just have a little piece to do with what happens?"

Now it was Halloran's turn to laugh. "You're not trying to tell me it was your doing?"

"But that is exactly what I am telling you." Vusilov stared back at him unblinkingly.

Halloran's grin faded as he saw that the Russian was being quite serious. "What the hell are you talking about?" he demanded. "How?"

Vusilov snorted. "While for years your experts in universities are busy preaching our system and idolizing Marx, we are studying yours. What is it that makes the depressions, do you think?"

Halloran shrugged. "They're part of the boom-bust cycle. It's part of the price you pay with a market economy."

Vusilov shook his head, and his humor returned as he chuckled in the way of someone who had been suppressing a long-kept secret. "That's what most Americans say. But the joke is that most Americans don't understand how economies work. A depression, you see, is what happens when malinvestments liquidate. When the bubble goes bust, all the capital and labor and know-how that went in, nothing has any use for anymore, and so we have the depression."

Halloran nodded stonily. "Okay. So?"

"What you have been seeing ever since the one giant step for mankind is the depression in the American space program. It comes from the same reasons of which I have been telling you."

"I'm not sure I follow."

"It is nothing to do with any boom-bust bicycle that comes with capitalism. That was a fiction that we invented, and your 'experts' believed. In a truly free market, some decision makers might guess the wrong way, but they go out of business. It only takes a few who are smart to get it right, and the others will soon follow. The depression happens when *all* the businesspeoples make the same mistakes at the same time, which can only be because they all get the same wrong information. And there is only one way that can happen to the whole economy at once." Vusilov paused and looked at Halloran expectantly. Halloran shook his head. "Government!" Vusilov exclaimed. "They're the only ones who have the power to make the same mistakes happen everywhere."

Halloran didn't want to get into all that. "So what does that have to do with our space program fifty years later?" he asked.

Vusilov shrugged. "Think what I have been saying. What happened to your space program was a

depression, which is when wrong investments liquidate. And the only force that can cause it is when
government meddles into the business of people who
know what they're doing." He left it to Halloran to
make the connection.

Halloran frowned. "What, exactly, are you saying?"

"Well, you tell me. What was the biggest case of
where your government went muscling in and took
over directing the space program?"

"Do you mean Kennedy and Apollo?"

Vusilov nodded emphatically and brought his palm
down on the arm of his chair. "*Da!* Apollo! You've
got it!"

Halloran was taken aback. "But . . . that was a
success. It was magnificent."

"Yes, it was a success. And I give you, it *was*
magnificent. It did what Kennedy said. But what was
that? You stuck a flag in the Moon fine, very good.
And you concentrated your whole industry for years
on producing the Saturn V behemoth engine, which
ever since has no other use than to be a lawn orna-
ment at the Johnson Space Center. An expensive
gnome for the garden, yes?"

"Hey, there was more than that."

"Oh, really?" Vusilov looked interested. "What? You
tell me."

"Well . . ."

"Yes?"

"There was the spinoff . . . all kind of technologies.
Big scientific discoveries, surely . . ."

"But what about the other things that *didn't* happen because of it?" Vusilov persisted.

"What do you mean?"

"Think of all the other things that would have come
true if Apollo had never happened. In the late fifties,
the U.S. Air Force wanted to go for a spaceplane—
a two-man vehicle that would have pushed the
explored frontier to the fringes of space. We were

terrified of it. It would have led to a whole line that would have seen commercially viable hypersonic vehicles by the end of the sixties—New York to Tokyo in two or three hours, say, with the same payload and turnaround time of an old 747. That would have led to a low-cost, reusable surface-to-low-orbit shuttle in the seventies, permanently manned orbiting platforms in the eighties, with all the potential that would attract private capital, which gives us a natural jump-off point for the Moon, say, maybe in the mid-nineties, yes— all lightning-years ahead of anything we could have done."

Halloran raised a hand and nodded glumly. "Okay, okay." It was all true. What else could he say?

Vusilov nodded. "Yes, Apollo was magnificent. But it was all thirty years too soon. It got you your flag and your lawn pixie. But beyond that, it put government geniuses in charge of your whole space program. And what did that get you? Dead-end after Apollo. Then Skylab fell down. By the eighties you'd sunk everything in the original shuttle, which already had old-age. When that blew up there was nothing. The design was already obsolete, anyway."

Halloran nodded wearily. Now that it was all spelled out, there was nothing really to argue about. He raised his glass to drink, and as he did so, he saw that Vusilov's eyes were watching him and twinkling mischievously. "What's so funny?" he asked.

The Russian replied softly, in a curious voice, "Well, surely you don't imagine that all of that just . . . happened, do you?"

Halloran's brow knotted. "You're not saying it was *you* who brought it about?" Vusilov was nodding happily, thumping his hand on the arm of his chair again with the effort of containing himself. "But how? I mean, how could you possibly have manipulated U.S. government policy on such a scale? I don't believe it."

Vusilov brushed a tear from his eye with a knuckle. "It was like this. You see, we had been operating with centralized government control of everything under Stalin for decades, and we *knew* that it didn't work. It was hopeless. Everything they touched, they screwed up. By the time we got rid of him after the war, we knew we had to change the system. But America was racing so far in front that we would never catch up. What could we do? Our only hope was to try somehow to get America to put its space program under government control and let them wreck it, while we were getting ours together. . . . And we did!'

Halloran was looking dumbfounded. "You're not saying that . . ."

"Yes, yes!" Vusilov put a hand to his chest and wheezed helplessly. "We strapped a bundle of obsolete missile-boosters together and threw *Sputnik 1* into orbit; and then we scratched the Gagarin flight together on a shoelace and put him up, too. . . . And hysterical American public opinion and your wonderfully uninformed mass-media did the rest for us . . . ha-ha-ha! I can hear it now, Kennedy: '. . . *this nation should commit itself to achieving the goal, before this decade is out, of landing a man on the Moon and returning him safely to Earth.*' He fell for it. It was our masterstroke!"

Halloran sat staring at the Russian, thunderstruck. Vusilov leaned back in his chair, and as if finally unburdened of a secret that had been weighing him down for years, laughed uproariously in an outburst that echoed around the lounge. Halloran had had enough. "Okay, you've had your fun," he conceded. "Suppose we concentrate on the present, and where we're going from here."

Vusilov raised a hand. "Oh, but that isn't the end of it. You see, it made for you an even bigger catastrophe on a national scale, precisely *because* it succeeded so well."

Obviously Halloran was going to have to hear the rest. "Go on," he said resignedly.

"The U.S. economy could have absorbed the mistake of Apollo and recovered. But you didn't let it end there. It gave you a whole generation of lawmakers who saw the success and concluded that if central control and massive federal spending could get you to the Moon, then those things could achieve anything. And you went on to apply it beyond our wildest hopes—when Johnson announced the Great Society program and started socializing the USA. You didn't stop with bankrupting the space industries; you bankrupted the whole country. In Vietnam, at least you knew you'd gone wrong, and you learned something. But how can anyone argue with success?

"And what made it so hilarious for us was that you were doing it while we were busy dismantling the same constructions of meddling bureaucrats and incompetents in our country, because we knew they didn't work. That was the secret that the KGB was there to protect. That was why it was such a big organization."

Despite himself, Halloran couldn't contain his curiosity. "What discovery?" he asked. "What secret are you talking about?"

"*Capitalism!* Free enterprise, motivated by individualism. That was why our defense industries and our space activities were so secret. That was how they were organized. If America wanted to waste the efficiency of its private sector on producing laundry detergents and breakfast cereals, while destroying everything that was important by letting government run it, that was fine by us. But we did it the other way around."

Halloran was looking nonplussed. "That was the KGB's primary task?"

"Yes. And you never came close to finding out."

"We assumed it was to protect your military secrets—bombs, missiles, all that kind of thing."

"Bombs? We didn't have very many bombs, if you wish to know the truth."

"You didn't?"

"We didn't need them. Washington was devastating your economy more effectively than we could have done with thousands of megatons."

Halloran slumped back in his chair and stared at the Russian dazedly. "But why... how come we've never even heard a whisper of this?"

"Who knows why? The leaders we have now are all young. They only know what they see today. Only a few of us old-timers remember. Very likely, most of history was not as we believe."

Halloran drew in a long breath and exhaled shakily. "Jesus... I need another drink. How about you? This time it's scotch, no matter—" At that moment a voice from a loudspeaker concealed overhead interrupted him.

"Attention, please. An important news item that has just come in over the laser link from Earth. The People's Republic of China has announced the successful launch of a pulsed-nuclear-propelled space vehicle from lunar orbit, which is now en route for the planet Jupiter. The vessel is believed to be carrying a manned mission, but further details have not been released. A spokesman for the Chinese government gave the news at a press conference held in Beijing this morning. The Chinese premier, Xao-Lin-Huong, applauded the achievement as tangible proof of the inherent superiority of the Marxist political and economic system.

"In a response from Moscow amid public outcry and severe criticism from his party's opposition groups, the new Soviet premier, Mr. Oleg Zhocharin, pledged a reappraisal of the Soviet Union's own program, and hinted of a return to more orthodox principles. 'We have allowed ourselves to drift too far, for too long, into a path of indolence and decadence,'

Mr. Zhocharin said. '*But with strong leadership and sound government, I am confident that by concentrating the resources of our mighty nation on a common, inspiring goal, instead of continuing to allow them to dissipate themselves uselessly in a thousand contradictory directions, the slide can be reversed. To this end, I have decreed that the Soviet Union will, within ten years from today, send men out to the star system of Alpha Centauri and return them safely to Earth.*' Mr. Zhocharin also stated that . . ."

Excited murmurs broke out all around the lounge. Halloran looked back at Vusilov and saw that the Russian was sitting ashen-faced, his mouth gaping.

And then a shadow fell across the table. They looked up to see that the Chinese representative had risen from his chair in the alcove and stopped by their table on his way toward the door. His expression was impenetrable, but as Halloran stared up, he saw that the bright, glittering gray eyes were shining with inner laughter. The Chinese regarded them both for a second or two, his book closed loosely in his hand, and bowed his head politely. "Enjoy your day, gentlemen," he said.

And walking without haste in quiet dignity, he left the room.

"Leapfrog" was inspired by a talk I gave at a space conference in Chicago in 1989, celebrating the 20th anniversary of the first manned lunar landing. The event was generally a get-together of people from NASA and various contractors and universities involved with the space program, looking back on a job well done and sharing some nostalgia about where did all the good days go? So it was with some trepidation that I, a foreigner from a land remembered for certain distant acrimonies as well as more recent mutual cordiality, rose to put the suggestion to three-hundred-or-so Americans that in some ways the Apollo program might have been a bigger disaster than the Vietnam war. Mindful of the reputation of a place like Chicago, of all places, I had images of being thrown out bodily into some litter-strewn alley at the back of the building. To my gratification, however, I got a great ovation and was beset for the rest of the weekend by individuals coming up to declare, "You know, you hit it right on! Here, lemme getcha a drink."

The talk was based on an article called "Paint Your Booster," which Jim Baen had published in *New Destinies* (Vol 8, Fall '89). The version entitled "Boom

and Slump in Space" was reprinted in 1990 in a
newsletter of the British Libertarian Alliance, and later
in the *Prometheus* journal of the U.S. Libertarian
Futurist Society.

Boom and Slump in Space: What the American Space Effort Has Been and What It Could Have Been

Over twenty years have now gone by since the first footprint marked the surface of the Moon. Twenty years since the heady days of a decade when America took up a political challenge on behalf of its President.

The space program was—or at least was perceived to be—the measure in the world's eyes of America's continuing fitness to defend and lead the non-communist world; a symbol of its standing in the Cold War. And, as in any war, once the goal of victory had been set the only thing that mattered was achieving it. Other considerations were swept aside, and cost was no object.

The war was won. There were triumphant victory celebrations. The world applauded. In the heyday of it all, immediately after the Apollo 11 success, a Special Task Group created by Richard Nixon to chart NASA's future options came up with three alternative scenarios. First was a three-pronged program consisting of a fifty-man Earth-orbiting space station, a manned lunar base, and a Mars expedition by 1985. This program would have required as mere incidentals the development of both a reusable shuttle to service the space station, and a deep-space tug to supply the lunar base. Second, a less grandiose scheme called for just the space station and its shuttle, with no lunar program and a delayed Mars mission. And third—the bleakest that seemed possible to contemplate in the light of the reception accorded to the lunar landing—just the space station and shuttle, with no Mars mission at all. But it was to be a huge shuttle, with a fully reusable booster powered by air-breathing jet engines as well as heavy-lift rockets, and an orbiter the size of a 727 liner.

Heady days, indeed.

What actually happened is now history. The mood of the country had changed. America, having placed and won its bet, cashed in its chips, lost interest, and went home. The proposals were slammed from coast to coast. NASA's budget was so severely slashed that three of the remaining Apollo missions had to be scrapped. Eventually only the shuttle remained of all the things that had been dreamed of—and a severely cut-down version of it at that, probably saved only by a hastily contrived deal with the Air Force. The money for Skylab and the Apollo-Soyuz project was granted, but grudgingly, and then only because both would use left-over Apollo hardware. In the next five years NASA's staff declined by twenty-five percent.

A spectacular crash, of truly Wall Street 1929 proportions.

DEPRESSIONS CAUSED BY GOVERNMENT INTERVENTION

In fact, the similarity runs deeper than mere analogy. To see why, let's take a closer look at the phenomenon of the economic "crash," or "depression," and the things that bring one about.

There is a widely held notion that depressions are a part of a boom-bust business cycle which comes inevitably as part of the price one pays for a capitalist economy. I shall contend, however, that this is a Marxist propaganda myth embraced by belief systems that don't, or don't want to, understand how economics works.

In a market economy, where prices are set by supply and demand, interest rates provide an indicator of the investment climate and function as a natural regulator and stabilizer. Interest is simply a special name for a particular kind of price: the going rate for renting out surplus capital. It follows the same laws as any other price and, if allowed to find its own level, transmits information and exercises a stabilizing influence by adjusting the supply available from those competing to lend out capital to the demand of those wishing to borrow.

This isn't to say that economic life doesn't have its ups and downs, of course. But in the overall picture, ups are never occurring everywhere at the same time, and neither are downs. While some industries are in decline, letting people go and able to pay only marginal rates, others are expanding and competing for capital and labor, bidding up wages rates and paying higher prices to obtain the skills and resources that they need. The scene across the economic ocean is one of choppy waters, with the waves that fall in one place providing the momentum for others to rise elsewhere. Such localized fluctuations are normal features of the business scene and are not to be confused with the *general* depression: the across-the-board slump that sets in when it turns out that the entire business community has made wrong decisions all at the same time. When the whole ocean goes down at once, it means that someone, somewhere, has pulled the plug.

Like a naturally evolving, complex ecology—which it is—a freely interacting market is a superposition of

millions of feedback loops, compensating systems, and
error-correcting mechanisms, all adding up to a system
that is rugged, inherently self-stabilizing, and highly
resilient to serious disruption from internal causes.
Only external factors imposed upon the system as a
whole can affect everything, everywhere adversely.

Similarly, when the whole business community
makes wrong decisions at the same time, it's because
something outside has sent it the wrong signals. And
the only power that commands a force capable of
mis-directing the entire system of a nation is . . .
government.

In other words, what brings about general economic depressions is not some inexorcisable demon
residing deep in the workings of the market system,
but intervention in those workings by governments,
which are the only institutions that possess the force
necessary to do so. And the more massive the scale
of the intervention, the more severe the depression
will be when it comes.

The implications of Apollo begin to take on a new
significance in this light.

The way governments create depressions is by first
initiating inflationary booms, through the control
they've acquired over the money supply. The ability
to print money out of thin air means that assets of
real worth can be acquired in exchange for currency
of progressively diluted value, providing, in effect, an
invisible form of taxation. Another way of avoiding
political unpopularity by creating illusory prosperity
is to expand credit, which has the same effects as
increasing the money supply.

But such booms turn out to be temporary. The artificially created excesses of money and credit send the
same signals to the investment community as real capital accumulated through earnings and savings, the result
of which is to encourage malinvestment: the diversion
of capital, labor, and other resources into providing

goods for which no real demand exists. Eventually, malinvestments must liquidate. The prescription of continual credit expansion to postpone the reckoning has to be curtailed before it leads to hyper-inflation, and that's when the "bust" half of the cycle sets in. Wasteful projects are abandoned or scaled down to be salvaged as best they can be; inefficient enterprises die; prices fall, especially those of capital goods relative to consumer prices; and interest rates rise.

The bust is a natural period of adjustment following the malinvestment resulting from the manipulations that created the boom. Both the boom and the bust are not features of the free-market system at all, but the results of interfering with it.

Probably the best thing that government could do to help once it has created a post-inflationary depression is to stay out of it and let the market recover in its own way. In actuality, however, the inevitable response is to apply remedies that are seemingly purpose-designed to make things worse and not better—which was what turned the 1929 depression into a decade-long slump.

When the bust hits, demands go up from every side for the government to "do something," and a further round of intervention follows to put right what the previous round put wrong. And so the pattern for the future is set. As the patient gets sicker with every spoonful of medicine, the only response that the doctors can conceive is to increase the dose. The underlying premise that the treatment is in fact a cure and not the poison is never questioned.

THE WHOLE OF THE NATION'S AEROSPACE EFFORT

No one would doubt—would they?—that John F. Kennedy's announcement, on May 25, 1961, of the lunar-landing goal was first and foremost a *politically* motivated decision. Since Sputnik 1 in 1957, the Soviets had sent the first probe around the Moon, obtained the first views of the lunar farside, launched the first Venus probe, orbited the first animal, and finally the first man, Gagarin, a month before Kennedy's announcement. American prestige needed a big boost, and the experts had advised that the big boosters the Soviets already had would be sufficient to gain them every significant "first" this side of a manned lunar landing.

Hence, the American space industry became a political instrument, its business the nation's earner of political prestige. Other goals were subordinate. This constituted intervention on a massive scale into the more natural evolutionary path that the postwar development of aerospace technology would otherwise have followed.

I'm not saying that government has no place in the space program. Defense is a legitimate function of government—in an ideal world we wouldn't need it, maybe, but this is the real one, and we do—and clearly the fulfillment of that function in the modern world requires an active role in space. And traditionally, the U.S. Government has aided research into selected areas of scientific endeavor—for example through the setting up of NASA's predecessor, NACA, in 1915, which produced excellent returns for the aviation industry for a modest outlay.

But to direct virtually the whole of the nation's aerospace resources and effort, to channel all of its outwardly-directed energies and thinking for a whole decade into a single, politically inspired goal? . . . This goes beyond healthy involvement and becomes total domination which, if it sets in for long enough, carries the danger of stifling dissent and institutionalizing conformity to the point where nobody can conceive of any other way of doing things.

The way to get a wagon train safely through the mountains is to send dozens of scouts ahead in all directions. There might only be a single pass, but one of the scouts will find it and bring back the news. This is the kind of multiple approach that produces the inherent ruggedness of natural evolutionary systems and free-market economies. But when the wagon master, a council of elders, or a fire-and-brimstone preacher, acting on a hunch, signs written in the stars, faith in the Lord, or whatever, decrees which direction shall be taken, without any scouts being sent out, it's almost certain to be a wrong one.

Or in the economic case, a malinvestment. The boom that Apollo ushered in was evident: the ready money, unlimited credit, and instant prosperity. . . . And subsequently we saw the inevitable depression, when the malinvestment—eventually, as it had to—liquidated.

This isn't to belittle the technical and human achievements of Apollo, which were magnificent. But the truth was that, political prestige aside, nobody really needed it. The military had been making farfetched noises about national security needing a lunar outpost, but that was to attract attention and funds. Their true interest lay in long-range missiles, transatmospheric flight, and orbital observation. The foreseeable commercial potential at that stage was in communications, navigation, and earth-observation, again involving near-space. And despite the hype, the real scientific-information bonanzas of the sixties and seventies came from unmanned probes like Viking, Mariner, and Voyager for a tiny fraction of the costs of the manned-flight program. As Arthur Clarke has suggested, the whole thing happened thirty years too soon.

WHAT MIGHT HAVE BEEN

What alternative pattern might we have seen unfolding, then, if Apollo hadn't happened when it did, and in the way that it did?

Since the end of World War II, thinking and

developments in advanced aerospace technology had
been proceeding briskly but smoothly with the kind
of divergence that characterizes a healthy evolutionary
process. True, the U.S. had lagged in its development
of big boosters, mainly because of the Air Force's
commitment to preserving its fleets of manned bomb-
ers as the core of the deterrent policy, which relegated
ICBMs to second priority. The Soviets, with no viable
long-range bomber force to worry about, had no such
concern and forged ahead. It was *this one fact* that
gave them their string of space firsts from Sputnik
1 through to the Gagarin flight.

But by 1955, the U.S. had a number of missiles
under development with the potential of orbiting a
satellite: there were the Air Force's Atlas, Thor, and
Titan, the Army's Jupiter and Redstone, and the Navy's
Polaris. It has been persuasively argued that von
Braun's Army team at Huntsville, Alabama, could have
put a payload in orbit by the end of 1955 using the
Redstone if it hadn't been for inter-service infight-
ing and bureaucratic tangles—almost two years ahead
of Sputnik.

As things were, by 1958 the Air Force was pushing for what seemed a natural extension to the series
of rocket-plane flights that had culminated in the X-15,
and built up an investment of experience and the team
of crack pilots at Edwards AFB in California. The Air
Force plans envisaged a successor designated the
X-15B, which would have taken off like a rocket, gone
into orbit, and landed like an airplane, carrying a crew
of two—a familiar pattern, now being resurrected
many years later. Another, more ambitious, project was
the MOL—Manned Orbiting Laboratory, again with
a two-man crew, proposed initially for spy missions
and man-in-space research. And further, with a target date tentatively set as the late sixties, there was
the "Dyna-soar," a rocket-launched flying machine—
as opposed to a ballistic capsule—that would operate

up to 400,000 feet at twenty-one times the speed of sound—the kind of thing only now being talked about again in the form of the space plane. And NASA, formed in 1958 to promote civilian development of space, would initially have pioneered the kinds of unmanned scientific missions that turned out to be so productive.

We can only speculate about what might have followed if plans such as these had been realized instead of sacrificed to the moon god, and their progeny permitted to be born. Once the MOL was up, it's a safe bet that the Air Force would find good reasons for needing more of them. The Navy would want one because the Air Force has got one, and NASA would eventually want one, because the Air Force won't allow civilians inside the MOL. Then the Air Force will want a bigger one because the MOL is small and obsolete, and the Soviets are reported to be working on a better one.

If the Air Force had been allowed to mount its own manned program, it wouldn't have needed the shuttle, and NASA could have gone with the ESA-*Hermes*-like craft that it ended up proposing before politics made it grow again. And the major contractors, undistracted by constantly elbowing for places at a bottomless public trough, would probably be thinking along lines that will lead to TAV-like commercial transports, across-the-Pacific-in-two-hours and the turnaround time of a 747, once more sounding very much like things we're only beginning to hear talked about again today.

The picture this suggests is one of vigorous activity in near-Earth space, centered around a variety of orbiting stations and the vessels to supply them, extending through in the seventies and providing a natural jumping-off point for the moon and beyond. If the Soviets want to respond by bankrupting Siberia to send a hare with a Red Star there first, well let them. The Western tortoise will overhaul it soon enough, as soon as the time is right. Since there is no Holy Grail to focus effort and channel imagination, the conceivers and designers of different projects are free to pursue different solutions to their varying needs, resulting in a proliferation of vehicles large and small, manned and unmanned, reusable and expendable.

Such a pattern would have continued the curve of improving performance for aerospace vehicles that had been climbing fairly smoothly since the beginning of the century, instead of introducing a huge discontinuity that only a massive, forcibly public-funded venture could hope to bridge. And this is what effectively locked the private sector out. I don't mean the giant contractors, whose interests lay as much at the political end of the spectrum as those of the Pentagon or the huge bureaucracy that NASA became, but the independent entrepreneurs whose image is traditionally synonymous with American enterprise. By the end of the fifties, with the rough ground broken by the bulldozers of postwar defense-funded ventures, perhaps the time was about right for letting loose the kind of talent and ingenuity that brought the price of a barrel of oil down from four dollars to thirty-five cents, produced the Model-T Ford, and in more recent times the home computer. But in the climate of the massive diversion of the industry's supporting infrastructure and the cream of its expertise into a thirty-billion-dollar, single-purpose spectacular, such possibilities were literally unable to get off the ground.

There were some private ventures despite all the obstacles, such as SSI of Houston who launched the *Conestoga* rocket, Starstruck Inc. with its *Dolphin*, and PALS with the *Phoenix*, and more recently Amroc with its hybrid rocket motor. But such initiatives were systematically frustrated by NASA pricing practices that took advantage of forced public subsidy and effectively wrote off development overheads.

Another obstacle to private development has been a reluctance of investors to put up front-money in the face of skeptical expert reactions to such claims as that of MMI's "Space Van" that would orbit payloads for six hundred dollars per pound instead of the thousands of dollars that have come to be regarded as normal. But let's remember that the only experts available for would-be investors to seek advice from have all gained their experience and their world-view inside the same elephantine bureaucracy, where the rewards come not for doing things simply and cheaply, but for managing the most prestigious departments and the biggest budgets. I worked for Honeywell in the sixties, when computers that cost hundreds of thousands of dollars—when money was money—were less powerful than ones we buy in supermarkets today for our children. The same experts who scoff at the idea of six hundred dollars-per-pound into orbit would also have laughed at the idea of an Apple, a Commodore, or an IBM PC.

In the computer business, perhaps the last remaining area of genuine free-market opportunity, we take dazzling leaps in performance and plummeting costs for granted. But when it comes to space, we have built acceptance of the inescapability of Gargantuan budgets, political entanglement, and mammoth project management systems into our mindset of unconscious presumptions.

WHERE THE IRONY LIES

So much for the economic aspect of the post-Apollo depression. But at the deeper level there is a further irony that has to do with losing sight of the basic values of the way of life that Apollo came to symbolize.

America was founded on the principles of liberalism—in the original sense of the word, before it became a victim of contemporary doublespeak—which asserted the sovereignty of the individual, recognized basic rights and freedoms, and relegated the task of the state to the purely passive function of protecting them. Under such a system anyone is entitled to own property and trade it freely, to think and say what he likes, and to live his life in his own way to a degree consistent with the right of others to do the same, without its being forcibly subordinated to plans formulated for him by anyone else or by the state.

It's easy now, thirty years after McCarthy and the hysteria over the "missile gap," to see that Sputnik 1 did not signify a great overtaking of the Western way of life by the Soviet socialist utopia. Eisenhower saw it too and tried to downplay things to their proper proportions, but he miscalculated the reaction of the media, the public, and the world at large. It isn't really all that surprising that a totalitarian ruling elite, with the resources of a nation at its command, should be able to evoke an impressive performance in any single area of achievement that it selects as a demonstration. Building a pyramid isn't so difficult when the haulers-of-blocks don't have any say in the matter.

Very well, so the Soviets got a big booster first—but even that needed a lot of help from squabbling generals and bungling bureaucrats on our side. America had developed the greatest production and consumer economy the world had ever seen, an agricultural system whose productivity was becoming an embarrassment, and an average standard of living that exceeded that enjoyed by millionaires a hundred years previously, and more—all at the same time. The other guys were having to build walls and wire fences around their countries to keep the inhabitants of their workers' paradises from escaping.

Where the irony lies is that in seeking a tangible challenge to demonstrate the technological, scientific, and economic superiority of a free society, the planners turned to precisely the methods of centralized state-direction that their system was supposed to be superior to.

"We won. So our way is better," was the cry.

"Yes, but you had to use *our* way to do it!" was the retort that it invited.

The only debate was over *which way* the state should direct the program. The possibility that perhaps the state had its place, yes, but shouldn't be directing the overall form of the program at all was never entertained. As with doctors arguing over the dose, the premise that they were administering the right medicine was never questioned.

But the American economy was huge and robust. Even if Apollo was a long-term technological answer to a short-term political need, and even if it did represent something of a malinvestment, the effects could have been absorbed without undue damage. If we compare the cost with what the U.S. spends every year on such things as alcohol, cosmetics, or entertainments, it wasn't really so huge. The crowning irony is that its worst effect may have been due to the fact that it *succeeded!*

It's difficult to argue with success. Some of history's worst disasters have been brought about by taking a solution that has worked successfully in one area, and trying to apply it in another area where it isn't appropriate. And the greater its success in the past, the more persistently will its advocates continue trying to apply it even when it has long ago become obvious that it isn't working.

An example is the stupendous success of the physical sciences in the centuries following the European Renaissance, when the new methods of reason brought understanding to subjects that had been dominated by dogma and superstition for a thousand years. By the eighteenth century, apologists and enthusiasts for science saw scientific method as the panacea for all of humanity's problems. If science could unify astronomy and gravitation, heat and mechanics, optics and geometry, then surely science could accomplish anything. Poverty, injustice, inequality, oppression, and all of the other social problems that had plagued mankind since communal patterns of living first evolved, would all disappear in the scientifically planned, rational society.

Unfortunately, however (or is it?), people are less obliging and predictable than Newtonian particles, and tend to frustrate utopian grand designs by having ideas of their own about how they want to live. A society of individuals who were free to dissent and choose would never yield the kind of consensus that the various schools of early French and German socialism required on how to decide priorities and allocate resources. Hence, the institutions of a free society become obstacles to the plan and must be removed. And once the individual and his rights become subservient to the state's collectively imposed goals, society takes the first step down the slippery slope that leads towards the secret police, the Gestapo, the Gulag, and the concentration camp.

WHAT THE WORLD NEVER
HAD A CHANCE TO SEE

Apollo left a generation of administrators and legislators imbued with the conviction that if centralized government control and massive federal spending can land men on the Moon, then big government programs is the way to accomplish anything. Poverty, injustice, inequality, oppression, will all be cured by progressively larger doses of the same measures that have achieved just the opposite everywhere else they've been tried.

Yes, massive, state-directed programs can achieve results. They can produce bigger booster rockets, or build pyramids, or plant flags on the Moon with high

PR coverage at a cost that no one would pay freely—if that's what you want to do. But they don't solve social problems.

The real problem that I see was not so much the program itself—it represented a comparatively small proportion of the American GNP and was probably the kind of medicinal binge that the nation needed anyway—but the massive social programs inappropriately modeled on the rationale of Apollo afterward. The spectacle of government directing the nation to the successful conquest of the Moon became the model. The original ideals of a people free to direct their own lives with government functioning in a passive, protective capacity faded, and politics has become an arena of contest for access to the machinery of state to be used as a battering ram for coercing others. The only debate is over *whose* views the state's power should be used to impose upon everyone else. The notion that it doesn't exist for the purpose of imposing anyone's is forgotten.

As space came to be seen by the majority as posing such immense problems that only government could hope to tackle them, so society has turned increasingly to government for direction in the everyday aspects of living that were once the individual's own affair: to insure his health and security, to guarantee him a livelihood, to educate his children, to protect him from his errors, to compensate him for the consequences of his own foolishness, and to tell him what to think.

Yes, we got there first. But who won the race?

What lessons would younger Americans today have learned from growing up with, working in, and absorbing the value system of an independent, self-reliant, free-thinking people—government in its proper capacity, business corporations, scientists, and crazy individualists—charting their own expansion into space in their own way, according to their own needs, and for their own reasons? What the world never had a chance to see was a society free to evolve its own pattern of discovering, exploring, using, and adapting to the space environment.

For a true evolutionary pattern is just that: undirected. Only egocentric, Ptolemaic man could imagine that evolution was directed toward perfecting intelligence. Every eagle knows that it was directed toward perfecting flight, every elephant that it was to greater strength, every shark that it was to perfecting swimmers, and every eminent Victorian that it was to produce Victorians.

But in reality, evolution isn't directed *toward* anything. Evolution proceeds *away from*. Away from crude beginnings and on to better things that can lie in a thousand different directions. As the wagon train song says. "Where am I going, I don't know. Where am I heading, I ain't certain. All I know is I am on my way . . ."

But in that direction lies all that is truly new, exciting, revolutionary, and beyond the wildest dreams of even the most creative planners.

And *that*, maybe, would have shown the Soviets, and the world, something that was really worth knowing.

What *Really* Brought Down Communism?

Well, who knows? Maybe the collapse of the space effort really *was* a result of communist machinations aimed at bringing about the kind of future depicted in *Leapfrog*. So why didn't it happen? Because of the West's massive investment in deterrence and military preparedness over the last forty years? Don't believe a word of it. Never mind what you might have read about Reagan and "Star Wars"; or the inefficiencies of collective economics; or the inability of the Soviet rulers to censor information after people there got onto the Internet. Having risked wrath and mayhem by sticking a pin in the Apollo balloon, I might as well go the whole hog and let you into the secret of the *real* reason why the Soviet empire collapsed. It goes like this.

Sometime back around 1976, before I moved to the U.S., I was sitting around in a pub with a bunch of friends, putting the world's problems right, when one of them asked me what the answer to the trouble in Northern Ireland was. I replied that there wasn't one; and then, after thinking for a minute, added ". . . unless you find a way to separate the children from the adults for at least a generation." For as long as the hatreds and prejudices were programmed in at an early age, there would be no end to it. It was a roundabout way of saying that there was no practicable solution that I could see.

There's a part of every writer's mind that is always on the lookout for ideas that might form the basis for a story one day. For a long time afterwards I found a line of thought developing that asked, "How might a society develop that was descended from a first generation that had never been exposed to the social and psychological conditioning processes of conditioned human adults?" The outcome was *Voyage From Yesteryear*, published by Ballantine/Del Rey in 1982 (which also partly answers another question that writers are always being asked, namely, how long it takes to write a book).

Earth, well into the next century, is going through one of its periodical crises politically, and it looks as if this time they might really press the button for the Big One. If it happens, the only chance for our species to survive would be by preserving a sliver of itself elsewhere, which in practical terms means another star, since nothing closer is readily habitable. There isn't time to organize a manned expedition of such scope from scratch. However, a robot exploratory vessel is under construction to make the first crossing to the Centauri system, and with a crash program it would be possible to modify the designs to carry sets of human genetic data coded electronically. Additionally, a complement of incubator-nanny-tutor robots can be included, able to convert the electronic data back into chemistry and raise the ensuing offspring while others prepare surface habitats and supporting infrastructure, when a habitable world is discovered. By the time we meet the "Chironians," their culture is into its fifth generation. In the meantime, Earth went through a dodgy period but managed in the end to muddle through. The fun begins when a generation ship housing a population of thousands arrives to "reclaim" the colony on behalf of the repressive, authoritarian regime that emerged following the crisis period.

The *Mayflower II* brings with it all the proven apparatus for bringing a recalcitrant population to heel: authority, with its power structure and symbolism, to impress; commercial institutions with the promise of wealth and possessions, to tempt and ensnare; a religious presence, to awe and instill duty and obedience; and if all else fails, a military force to compel. But what happens when these methods encounter a population that has never been conditioned to respond?

Around about the mid-eighties, I received a letter notifying me that the story was being serialized in a Polish sf magazine, *Fantastyka*. (It appeared in Issues 3, 4, & 5, 1985.) They hadn't exactly "stolen" it, the publishers explained, but had credited zlotys to an account in my name there, so if I ever decided to take a holiday in Poland the expenses would be covered. (There was no exchange mechanism with Western currencies at that time, so no way of transferring the payment over.) Then the story found its way to countries of Eastern Europe, by all accounts to an enthusiastic reception. What they liked there, apparently, was the updated version of *satyagraha*— Gandhi's principle of resistance by nonviolent noncooperation to bring down an oppressive regime when they've got all the guns. And a couple of years later, they were all doing it. So there it is. *I claim the credit!*

In 1989, after communist rule and the Wall came tumbling down, the annual European sf convention was held at Krakow in southern Poland, and I was invited as one of the Western guests. On the way home, I spent a few days in Warsaw and at last was able to meet the people who had published that original magazine. "Well, fine," I told them. "Finally, I can draw out all that money that you stashed away for me back in '85." One of them remarked—too hastily—that "It *was* worth something when we put it in the bank"—there had been two years of ruinous inflation following the outgoing regime's policy of sabotaging everything in order to be able to prove that the new ideas wouldn't work. "Okay," I said, resignedly. "How much are we talking about?" The one with a calculator tapped away for a few seconds, looked embarrassed, and announced, "Eight dollars and forty-three cents." So after the U.S. had spent trillions on its B-52s, Trident submarines, NSA, CIA, and the rest—all of it ineffective—that was my tab for toppling the Soviet empire.

There's always an easy way if you only just look.

In fact, there may have been equally ridiculously easy alternatives, as the following story explores.

Last Ditch

It was Leonid Yevgenevich Konstantinov's ten-year-old son, Alexsandr, who first thought of the idea that would save the Soviet empire just when its final collapse seemed inevitable, and give it the weapon that would win the world.

Not that Alexsandr had anything quite so weighty and dramatic in mind at the time. He was simply exasperated at being checkmated by his father for the fifth time in a row as they sat playing chess on one of those interminable rainy Sunday afternoons.

"You need to think more about your pawn structure," Leonid said.

Alexsandr reacted with the uncanny ingenuity that boys his age everywhere display in the art of eliminating a problem without actually having to work at it.

"I'd rather use a time machine," he replied after considering the suggestion for a few moments.

His father frowned, not comprehending. "How?"

Alexsandr explained, "If I had a time machine, I'd get a copy of the best chess-playing program that there is and start it running on the biggest computer, and send the computer back a million years. Then, by today, it would have figured out every reply to every position, and I'd only have to look up the right move to win every time no matter what you did."

Leonid smiled dubiously. He wasn't sure offhand what a realistic estimate might be for all the possible moves that would make up all the possible games contained in the complete game-tree of chess. But he didn't think that a million years would come close, even for the most powerful of contemporary machines.

"How long would it have to run for, then?" Alexsandr asked.

Leonid shrugged. "A billion years, maybe," he replied. He really had no idea, but it sounded better.

A billion years is 365 billion days, not counting the effects of leap years and rainy weekends spent with actively disposed children. Therefore the work that a computer would normally take a billion years to get through would need only a day if the computer were able to run 365 billion times faster. And that, it occurred to Leonid when he was back at work the following day, was only a third of the time-acceleration that could be achieved with the highly secret laboratory prototype of RIACS.

Konstantinov was chief instrumentation engineer at the Institute of Advanced Physics on the outskirts of Novosibirsk, the Soviet Union's "science city" in the center of Siberia. "RIACS," standing for Resonantly Induced Artificial Curvature of Spacetime, had been developed in the course of ultra-classified research into gravity synthesization that the military had been conducting to find ways of confusing inertial guidance and navigation systems.

Essentially, the scientists had discovered that when protons were constrained to circulate at high speed inside a very small radius, at the same time interacting resonantly with externally applied electromagnetic fields, a zone of artificially deformed spacetime

could be created which mimicked the gravitational
effects of a large, highly concentrated mass—but in
a way that could be turned on and off or otherwise
manipulated at will. Theoretically, the mass-densities
that could be simulated in this way were astounding—close to the numbers normally thought of in
connection with black holes—but practical experimen-
tation on anything but a trivial scale was, to begin
with, ruled out by the catch that operating at anything more than a tiny fraction of maximum capability would have the unfortunate effect of pulping
every researcher in the vicinity and collapsing buildings for miles around. Then it was discovered that
the addition of an outer, counter-rotating system of
antiprotons produced a shielding effect that left the
inner intensity unaffected but neutralized the external
field, and the program suddenly took off. Soon the
scientists were able to create and study firsthand
conditions which up until then they had only been
able to simulate in computer models or speculate as
existing in remote and inaccessible regions of the
cosmos.

Even more extraordinary, when the roles of the
proton and antiproton recirculators were reversed, the
inner zone took on the characteristics of "negative
mass," which caused spacetime to curve the other way
from that induced by ordinary mass. The result was
to produce effects that were the opposite of those
encountered in the gravity wells surrounding dense
objects like neutron stars, where time slows down.
Inside the reverse-coupled RIACS, in other words,
time speeded up. And the amount by which it could
be made to do so was enormous indeed. This was
what caused Leonid Konstantinov to reflect that, in
principle, the RIACS could perform the same function as the time machine that his son, Alexsandr, had
mused about.

"It's a pity that the pinhole is just that," he said

to Dr. Yushenko, the head of Project Uzbek, as the gravitational physics program was officially designated, while they were discussing progress over lunch. "Pinhole" was the name given to the zone of highly deformed spacetime created within the inner recirculator: a deep and sudden change of geometry, but highly localized. "If it were possible to make it big enough to take a computer, we could have the ultimate chess analyzer."

Yushenko stopped, fork poised just as he had been about to take a bite of *beefshstek,* and stared at Konstantinov, intrigued.

"That's an interesting notion," he said. "I hadn't thought of anything like that. Quite ingenious. What made you think of it?"

"Oh, something that my son said yesterday. He wanted to send a computer back in a time machine so that he could beat me at chess. RIACS could do the same thing."

"How old is your son?"

"Ten . . . just."

"He must be a bright boy," Dr. Yushenko commented.

Which was the point that Konstantinov had been trying to make.

Yushenko found the notion amusing and mentioned it that afternoon to the director of the institute, Mikhail Drodzhkin, during a break in a meeting of the Appointments Committee. And Drodzhkin, although he didn't say so, *did* know, not of a RIACS big enough to take a computer, but of a computer small enough to run in the one they already had.

Another of the institute's secret programs was concerned with duplicating the production of molecular-scale processors and diffusion-array bulk memories from unpublicized Japanese research designs purloined through espionage. Hence Drodzhkin was one of the few people anywhere in the world who was aware that both technologies existed. The implications of combining them together were so startling that he booked a flight to Moscow the next day to bring the subject to the attention of Vasili Zladik, the Minister of Science. To illustrate the potential of what he had in mind, Drodzhkin used the same example of an unbeatable chess player that Yushenko had talked about.

"With a processor capable of examining positions at that speed, and a memory the size that we can make now, you've got a system that will analyze the complete game tree," he told Zladik across Zladik's office in the Central Committee Building. "From any position, it would be able to compute every path to every possible ending. Therefore it would always be able to steer the game along a path that leads to a win for itself. It would be invincible."

"A fascinating conjecture, Comrade Drodzhkin," Zladik agreed woodenly, completely missing the point. Games? The director had flown all the way from Novosibirsk at departmental expense to talk about games? Zladik was a political creature who had been made minister because of his reliability and party loyalty, not for outstanding brilliance in any field of science.

Drodzhkin accepted such a situation as normal and took nothing amiss. He added, smiling whimsically at what was intended to convey that he understood the depth and weight of the Great Man's problems, "It's a pity that we didn't have it sooner. It would have been the one thing that the West could never have matched. An invincible weapon!" Zladik jerked his head up and was staring at him fixedly, but Drodzhkin failed to notice and carried on in what was supposed to be a mildly joking manner, "All this preoccupation with tanks and megatonnage has been a waste of time—and in the end it got us nowhere, anyway. Shooting wars on any large scale belong to the past.

Being *cleverer* is what we should have concentrated on, not on being stronger."

Zladik thought for a few moments more, and then mustered his sternest expression of bureaucratic disapproval. "Such an attitude is completely contrary to the policy of the party, Comrade Drodzhkin," he rebuked stiffly. "Our official posture toward the Western democracies is one of détente, mutual understanding, and peaceful coexistence; not a continuation of the futile adversarial relationship that you seem to be advocating. I must consider this a severe lapse on your part."

Drodzhkin's reassignment as technical supervisor at an unheard-of meteorological station on the Taymyr peninsula in northernmost Siberia was arranged in less than a week. Zladik then made an appointment to see Yuri Grymokolov, the Soviet foreign minister, on what he claimed was a most important and highly confidential matter.

"It is a project that we conceived some years ago," Zladik said from the far side of the vast desk in Grymokolov's office at the Foreign Office on Smolensky Square. "But because of the technical uncertainties and the consequences that would have followed from false hopes being raised prematurely, I judged it best to keep a security blanket over it until we were quite sure."

Zladik spread his hands briefly. "Every possible game traces a path through a branching tree that must end in either a win for white, a win for black, or a draw. At the beginning of the game, white has a choice of twenty possible first moves: sixteen with pawns and four with knights. Similarly, black has twenty possible replies. Suppose that white opens by picking the first of the twenty moves available, and that black answers with the first of his twenty possible replies . . . and so on for all the billions of games that could follow from white's first possible move.

Now go back to the beginning and suppose that white plays, instead, his second possible move, and then go through the whole—"

"Thank you, but I am familiar with the rudiments of the game," Grymokolov interrupted. "I *did* have the benefit of a modicum of schooling."

Zladik subsided and nodded obsequiously. "Of course, Comrade Minister."

Nevertheless, Grymokolov had evidently taken the point. "You're saying that every outcome would be an open book to such a device," he said.

"Quite."

"It would be infallible? You could steer the game along a winning branch every time?"

"Yes. Exactly. In the past, the snag has always been that the number of variations becomes so large that no computer ever built could get through even a fraction of them in the estimated lifetime of the Solar System. But now we have one that can."

The foreign minister stared down at the mahogany expanse in silence for a while, then looked up.

"Who else knows about this?"

"About the entire scheme? Nobody. I was meticulous in keeping the various component activities strictly compartmentalized."

Three days later Zladik was committed to a psychiatric institution, certified as suffering from schizophrenic delusions and acute and psychological instability. The following morning, foreign minister Grymokolov gave a closed-door presentation to a specially convened meeting of the Secretary General and the inner council of the Politburo.

The outcome was a sudden and totally unexpected public offer by the Secretary General of the USSR to the United States President and other heads of the Western World: the Soviet Union would renounce its claims and scrap all of its weapons, nuclear, conventional, strategic and the rest, if the West would agree to do likewise—and let a single game of chess decide who would take the world. They announced simply that they had an unbeatable machine: *Kosmik Marx 1*, they called it. The West could put up people, computers, a mixture of both, against it. It wouldn't matter.

What could the West do? The tone of the challenge made it clear that whatever pundits and experts might be saying in their haste to write the Soviet empire off as a lost cause, it was still capable of causing plenty of mischief yet before it went under. The rest of the world, flatly refusing to resurrect all the fears that it had just put aside after almost half a century, left no doubt that it would rather be checkmated than cremated, and the President found himself with no real option but to accept.

The U.S. assembled a consortium of the best chess brains and programs that the West could muster. They drew first move and spent weeks debating before they announced their opening: P-K4.

In Moscow, chuckling technicians fed the move into the machine. The world waited breathlessly, while inside a tiny realm of almost infinitely accelerated time, whirling streams of binary digits computed and compared all possible continuations to their endpoints, arriving finally at the inference of flawless logic.

At last the printer clattered. The UN observers gathered round to announce the perfect opening reply to commence what would surely be the most momentous game ever played in history.

But there was one small thing which the analysts assembled by Grymokolov's department had overlooked in their haste: A fundamental principle of sound chess assumes that one's opponent will always play the best move available . . . and do so all the way through to the end.

Kosmik Marx 1 had resigned.

Sorry About That

We were sitting in a bar in Arklow, County Wicklow, not far from Harry Harrison's place, nursing a whiskey apiece, along with a Guinness chaser. "It's fine over here once you've made the adjustment," Harry said. "You have to allow for the Paddy Factor."

"What's that?" I asked him.

"Just part of the national makeup. They never quite get anything right. Always assume it'll cost twice what you think, and allow twice as long."

I was a bit puzzled. "Sorry, what are we talking about?"

"Anything—whatever you're trying to get done." Harry sipped his drink and reflected. "Then it'll have to be done all over again to get it right."

But Ireland exuded its own kind of charm with the touch of whimsy that was expected, and after a while Harry's words had wafted away on the wind. I brought Jackie over subsequently for a holiday, and we moved the family in 1988, to a town called Bray, on the coast about fifteen miles south of Dublin, conveniently situated between the metropolitan area to the north and the Wicklow Mountains to the south. This time we were going to do things sensibly for once, and just rent a house for a year at least, until we were sure that we wanted to make a long-term commitment. And then we saw one of those big, old, Irish houses, advertised in an auctioneer's window (they don't have realtors). "Let's go and look at it, just for fun," I said, echoing the words uttered in Sonora during a one-week trip to California that had ended up lasting eight years. But I felt safe now because I'd finally gotten the fixing-up-old-houses bug out of my system. We bought the house, of course—even though it needed a little work.

"A little." Killarney House had nine bedrooms and was shaped like the Queen Mary bent into a *U*. One of the wings was almost 200 years old and appeared as the original house on a map drawn at the time of the battle of Waterloo. Damp-proof courses were not laid at the foundation level, even in the days when the later parts came to be built. Moisture rose in the lower walls like the filling of a fruit flan. The previous owners ran a photography business, and one whole upstairs section was filled with pipes, tubes, tanks, and bathtubs like a moonshine mass-production plant. Half the electrics must have come from sales of Faraday leftovers. . . . But it had "atmosphere" and "potential." One of the drawbacks of being a writer—or, I suspect, of any other profession considered as manifesting an "artistic" bent—is that it exercises and develops the imagination. You don't see what's in front of your eyes. It's obscured by visions of "what could be."

Reality starts percolating through with the realization of a signed contract and the first serious estimates of the work needed to sort everything out. That was when we got our first glimmerings that things here didn't work quite the way they did in the U.S. The previous owners were still there, doing their laundry, three days after the closing date, while we were moving in. So were their children and half their furniture. So was an electrician—stripping power sockets and fixtures off the walls. They presumed we "wouldn't mind" if they left an enormous assortment of electrical equipment, plumbing, and heaps of junk in one of the outbuildings "until we find somewhere to put it." The only problem was, the outbuilding was falling down, and we'd already scheduled that by tomorrow it wouldn't be there—at which the outgoing parties seemed quite indignant and put out.

Then, closer inspection revealed that the map included with the deeds didn't match what we assumed we'd bought. According to the boundaries as specified, we owned the driveway of the house next door. And even more disconcerting, a builder who had bought part of the original estate for a development on the other side owned our drive, which was several hundred feet long, curving up from the road through trees. The attitude of the lawyer who had handled the transaction (at a fee that would keep his wine cellar from running dry for a while), part of whose job was to check all this, was not exactly inspiring. "Ah, as long as you can still get in and out, what does it matter?" he said when we pointed it out. "The Land Registry must have made some kind of mistake, that's all." The thought of maybe doing something to rectify it was evidently beyond human nature to conceive. No, things didn't work the way they did in the U.S. (In fact, there was no mistake. The previous owner had concluded a private agreement signing over the neighbor's driveway—a fact which he had neglected to mention or file with the Land Registry, but done nothing about recovering title to his own driveway. Hence, the property was landlocked, owning no access to a public highway. But that all surfaced later, when the builder wanted $12,000 to sell us our own driveway back.)

The native-born and those who have been in Ireland long enough to know who's who and how the system works can get good work done at a fair price.

But for the new, the naive, and the unwary, a sure kiss-of-death is the well-meaning friend who says, "Don't be wasting your money on those big contractors with their high rates and the taxes and all, and all. I know a fella who'll do you a good job. . . ." And here we were, fresh from California with its codes, laws, and regulations, all designed for the protection of brain-dead and blind amputees at a convention of pickpockets, used to a country where—laugh if you will—the old work ethic still counts for a lot, and there's genuine pride in seeing customers satisfied. Lambs, to the abattoir.

So it was that the very next day a couple of trucks arrived with "yer man" and his crew, wielding sledgehammers, jackhammers, pickaxes, crowbars, to be followed shortly by a backhoe and bulldozer. Scaffolding went up, and house started coming down with alarming dispatch, day by day coming more to take on an appearance more often associated with intensive attention by heavy siege artillery. I soon realized that this was going to be more than a one- or two-month undertaking. After the upheaval and disruption of moving from California, I was getting behind on my workload. So, deciding first things had to come first, I left Jackie in charge and gallantly went off and got myself a flat to think and write in while the demolition proceeded. Hence, it was she who got the first uneasy inklings of Harry Harrison's Paddy Factor possibly in evidence.

Such as when one of the workers, after an ornamental table that he had climbed on in his boots to reach a high spot collapsed in pieces underneath him, went back into the dining room to fetch another. Or when a battery of hot water pipes that had been set in concrete from one end of the house to the other leaked and turned the sunken lounge at the rear into literally just that. Or the new section of roof that channeled rainfall behind the wall to produce a waterfall inside the house—picturesque had it been over a pool, possibly, but it happened to be in my workshop. Then there was the paneled door that was hung upside down, its handle three feet from the top, the window glass fitted without putty, heating pipes that just ended beneath the floor without connecting to anything, and the surplus paint that was disposed of by being poured down newly installed drains. "Oh, sorry about that," got to be about as routine as "Have a nice day," in California. The locals that we remonstrated to in the pub seemed to find nothing especially remarkable in all this, matter-of-factly according it the same inevitability as sex scandals among the clergy, or having four seasons a day irrespective of the time of year. A gardener appeared at the door one day to ask if we had anyone to take care of the acre or so of lawns, flower beds, and shrubs. After making a round with Jackie he announced that he could start that afternoon and asked for twenty-five pounds (about $40) for weedkiller and chemicals. That was the last she saw of him. "Ah yes, that would be Willy," Mary said when Jackie talked to her in town. "He tries that whenever someone new moves into any of the big houses."

Meanwhile, I was having adventures of my own with the flat.

One evening a spurious alarm started sounding somewhere farther along the street. As it became progressively more annoying, and nobody seemed available or disposed to do anything, I called the Fire Department intending to inquire if they had authority to enter and do something in a situation like that. I got a taped recording inviting me to leave a message. The Fire Department!

A writer, of course, needs a phone. When I placed the order, the phone company said it would take ten days. Three weeks later, the figure had shrunk to two weeks. In the course of calling their sales department to chase things, I remarked that Americans can get a phone in the next day. The woman that I was talking to started arguing that, "Yes, but then everything in America is so much more expensive than over here," which was not only irrelevant, but utterly untrue. Had she been there? No, it turned out. The fact that I had lived in the U.S. for eleven years, raised three sons there, owned two houses, rented several apartments, bought seven cars, traveled in just about every state . . . counted for nothing. So where did she get this idea from? It went like this. She had spent a weekend in Paris and spent 600 pounds, which she'd never do in a weekend in Ireland. Hence, "other places" are more expensive. America was "another place." Ergo, triumphant completion of syllogism: America is more expensive than Ireland. Really. She was quite serious, absolutely adamant, and nothing would change it. I gave up and got back to the subject. "When will I get my phone?"

This time I actually got a date. "May 21."

Suspicious, I asked how certain this was. She admitted that she didn't know. "But call us on the 20th and we should know for sure." So I did, and this time talked to a man. He agreed that it might be tomorrow, but on pressing admitted that it might just as easily be another week. When I started to get impatient he said—honestly: "I'll get the installation engineer in your area to ring you. What's your number?"

"HE CAN'T RING ME! I DON'T HAVE A PHONE! THAT'S WHAT WE'RE TALKING ABOUT!"

"Oh, right. Sorry about that. Well, I'll give you his number."

"What's the point? Nobody knows anything. Will he be able to tell me whether or not I might get a phone between now and the next ice age?"

"Probably not. There's only an answering machine on that number anyway."

"Where's the engineer?"

"Out installing the phones, of course. If he was there to answer the number all day, nobody would ever get a phone at all, would they?"

Later, when I was giving out in the pub, somebody drew my attention to an item in the *Irish Times* to the effect that Telecom Eireann (official name of the Speed of Light Telephone Company) have announced a rebate scheme for customers experiencing unduly long installation delays. Intrigued, I called the next day to ask what this is all about and was told that if the installation time goes over the target time for the area in question, we get twenty pounds off the first bill. So what's the target time for Bray? 25 days. "Ahah! I've been waiting 6 weeks. How do I put in a claim?" But alas, it wasn't to be. The offer only applies to orders placed after May 23. Mine went back to the middle of April. So—and where else on Earth could this be true? —the reason I failed to qualify for a slow-service rebate was, I'd been waiting *too long!*

One day the water supply to the flat shut down. There were no road works in the vicinity, so no immediate reason of that nature (a rare occurrence, since Dublin Gas had been lunaforming the entire city and its environs for almost a year, laying new natural gas lines, then digging them up again because they leaked—but I digress). The neighbors on either side had no problems. Then, in a flash of that inexplicable intuition which only the home-born can display, somebody linked it with a large, empty house on the next street that was for sale. Sure enough, when we checked, the realtor (auctioneer) had had his maintenance man turn off the water main the same evening that my supply was lost. When we persuaded him to turn it on again, mine was restored too. So somehow, for reasons that will forever remain shrouded in the forgotten past, my water line came from a house on the next street. A plumber was sent to locate the connection to fit an independent line, but was unable to find it in the maze of pipes, valves, and water tanks that the building had sprouted over the years. So I just got him to turn the main supply on again, and so it remains to this day.

Meanwhile, back at the house, the initial frenzy of activity was giving way to a creeping lethargy. The tea-breaks were getting longer, physical motion slowing, shifting down through the gears practically visibly as one watched, like a wasp doused with hair lacquer. The realization dawned that they had reached their Parkinsonian limit of competence in every direction and were unable to put the rest of the place back together again. Whole days went when nobody showed up, except, maybe, for one of the "lads" with a paintpot, who wandered around dabbing at whatever took his fancy, stretching things out to stay on the payroll. The rest of them, it turned out, had started another job elsewhere.

Okay, I was out of my depth. It was time to bring in professional help. When we purchased the house we had, as was normal, engaged the services of a "surveyor" to go over the property and report on the general condition. And, to be fair, the surveyor that we'd hired had pretty much called all the essential items that needed attention. I contacted him again with an account of our woes, conceded that this wasn't my field, and asked if he would be willing to find a reliable contractor to finish the work, and supervise costs and quality on our behalf. "Sure, I can do that for you, no problem," he told me. No cowboys, I emphasized. The object was to do it right. "Absolutely." He drew up specifications, put out tenders, and from prior experience personally recommended one of the contractors who responded. At last we were in safe hands. Several days later a truck drew up bringing the crew.

One evening I was telling the story to Tom Collins, an Irish writer that I'd gotten to know in Sandycove, a few miles along the coast from Bray, who has written extensively on the troubles in the North. Tom listened and remarked distantly, "Then We Moved to Rossenara."

"What?"

He explained that it was the title of a book by Richard Condon of *The Manchurian Candidate* fame. Condon had moved to Ireland in the seventies and acquired a big, old house in need of repair in Kilkenny, to the south. His experiences had been much the same, prompting the book and eventually driving Condon to despair and capitulation. He was now back in the States.

"I'm glad you mentioned it," I told Tom. "Eleanor Wood, my agent, and I have been talking about possibly doing a book on this too. It sounds as if I ought to read Condon's."

"You won't find a copy," Tom replied. "The Irish trade unions have had it banned over here."

And so it turned out to be. I couldn't obtain it in the bookstores or any of the libraries. Checking Condon's other titles revealed that we had both published with Penguin, Arrow Books, and Grafton in England, but when I contacted the editors, none of them had handled that particular one. Finally, I wrote to Richard Condon in Dallas describing the situation and my thoughts about writing a book, but expressing fear that he might have beaten me to it. How could I get to read his? Condon sent me a copy of the Australian paperback with a letter that began: "*Dear Mr. Hogan, There can never be enough books about the Irish construction industry. . . .*"

Dublin Gas corporation had extended its piped natural gas to Bray and were offering a fifty percent discount for the first three years to attract new customers. Killarney House used propane gas from a tank, and with its voluminous halls and high-ceilinged rooms was like Carlsbad Caverns to heat, so this seemed a deal worth looking into. Seventeen phone calls and three broken appointments later, I still hadn't managed to get an assessor to come out to Bray to give us an estimate on the conversion. In exasperation I called the corporation again and demanded to speak to the general manager. "He's out at a conference for the next three days," the receptionist informed me. "Would you like to speak to one of our sales executives?"

"No, I've tried that. It doesn't do any good. None of them ever get back to me."

"Sorry about that. You couldn't speak to them anyway, today. They're all at the conference too."

"What's this conference about?" I asked curiously.

"It's a seminar on effective marketing."

Finally, I did get one out to assess the job. "Two thousand pounds," he announced to my astonishment and horror. It transpired that the figure was based on digging up the long driveway and running a pipe all the way out to the road. But at the rear of Killarney House there was a kitchen garden and small lawn with the boundary wall barely fifty feet away. Over the wall was a development of new houses. "Look," I said, pointing. "There has to be a gas line into those houses. Why couldn't you run a connection under the wall?" He agreed it sounded plausible but didn't have a map with him, so promised to go away and check. Several weeks and innumerable phone calls later, I managed to raise him again.

"You were right," he told me. "In fact, the house just over the other side of that wall is on gas."

"How much are we talking about, then?"

"Two hundred pounds."

"Done."

The first I knew of the operation actually commencing was a commotion of voices some weeks later, coming from the far side of the kitchen-garden-lawn wall. On peering over, I found the irate owner of the neighboring house confronting a crew of Dublin Gas workers. It appeared that in commencing the work they had demolished one of her gate piers. That was between her and them, and I left them to it. But in the day or two that followed, lo and behold a trench appeared under the wall, grew along by the lawn and across the gravel drive outside the kitchen; a pipe duly found its way therein, rising three feet above the ground when it reached the wall of the house; the trench was filled in, and a meter affixed to the top of the pipe. And there, all operations ceased.

"What's all this?" I asked when papers were produced to be signed.

"Your gas connection, as ordered."

"But it doesn't go anywhere."

"We only take it as far as the meter. What happens on the other side of it is something you have to organize."

"How do I do that?"

"We have a list of approved contractors that you can get in touch with. You'll need to talk to our marketing department."

Months later, three contractors had appeared, made notes and measurements, gone away to cogitate, and never been heard from again, probably because the burner on the furnace had to be changed, and the furnace was German. I had taken it upon myself to get the correct part from Germany and was still corresponding with the manufacturer when the first bill came in from Dublin Gas. It not only covered the connection fee, but included an amount for gas consumed—with actual readings.

"Ah, well, it's an estimated figure, you see," I was told when I called to query it. "Our man couldn't get in when he came to read the meter."

"He doesn't need to get in. The meter's right there on the outside wall."

"Oh, then it must be a mistake. We'll correct it on the next bill. Sorry about that."

Needless to say, there was no correction on the next bill. In fact, it showed was more phantom gas used. I wrote and protested. Next month, no avail. Then we received a final demand, with notification that if it wasn't settled within seven days we would be disconnected. I called and asked them to let me know in advance when someone would be coming out, so I could have somebody there from the local paper to photograph how they did it.

The surveyor, in the meantime, had been working a scam. Ostensibly brought in to conduct dealings on our behalf with the contractor, it turned out that he himself *was* the contractor. The tender had been a fraud; the person presented as the contractor submitting it was simply a hired journeyman. In short, it was out-and-out misrepresentation and conflict of interests, the surveyor effectively paying himself behind his back, while cranking up all the prices in the process—and then expecting a fee on top of it all for representing our interests. It all came to light thanks to Vincent, a sharp-eyed neighbor who happened to be a professor of civil engineering at University College Dublin, and who noticed that all was not as it should have been. At our invitation Vincent went over all the work that the tender had covered, then brought in an independent surveyor—a Londoner this time—to corroborate his findings.

The details of the corners that had been cut, work charged for but not performed, outrageous price gouging, would fill the rest of this book. The original surveyor denied all, failed to respond to detailed breakdowns of what was amiss, and so, of course, things ended up as a lawsuit. And since he'd been caught with his hand in the till, no defense to offer, no friendly witnesses, he agreed, finally, to settle out of court.

Which he did. With a dud check. (What? You mean that a lawyer accepted a personal check from someone admitting to theft and fraud? Yes—I said things here don't happen the way they do in the U.S.)

So we got an injunction not against his business, which he could have folded, but against his house. And for once things did work out right—in the end. It took five years, during which everything imaginable seemed to conspire to impede the process at some crucial juncture. The Post Office went on strike, preventing documents from being delivered. The banks went on strike. Even, at one point, the law courts(!) were on strike. By the time he coughed up, "For Sale" signs had been erected in his front yard and the local sheriff given orders to evict him for obstructing justice—by pulling the signs down again. And since he'd defaulted, all legal costs—ours included—devolved upon him also, all with accumulated interest.

By this time we were getting to know our way around a little better. One of the key men in the local network was Billy, who worked as a plumber for the urban council, and turned out to be a magician. Whatever kind of work was needed, whether it be roofing, decorating, electrical, or fixing the sewer lines, Billy had a "mate." All of Billy's mates did good, solid work and charged reasonable prices. Killarney House gradually came together and transformed into a comfortable home.

We didn't keep it, however. For one thing, Jackie's mother, who had been living with us, moved back to the States. We decided that a smaller place would suit us better, perhaps enabling us to keep a residence in the U.S. and spend time there as well, to avoid getting out of touch. A well known Irish songwriter who has six children bought it. Despite all its problems we developed a distinct fondness for Killarney House, and it's gratifying to see it still being used as the kind of family home that it deserves to be. (At the time of sale, it was still using propane gas from the tank.)

We seem to be accepted now as of a rare breed of foreigners who proved themselves through an ordeal of fire that few see through to the end. "It's nice to see somebody going after one of those villains for a change," is the kind of approving comment we get typically in the local pubs. I bumped into Willy, the gardener, again some time later, too, in a pub, and extracted the twenty-five pounds that he'd conned from Jackie.

"I suppose if you're one of Billy's mates, I owe it you back, anyway," he said a bit sheepishly as he peeled off the notes.

It's really not so difficult once they see that you know now how the system works.

AIDS Heresy and the New Bishops

Science is supposed to be concerned with objective truth—the way things are, that lie beyond the power of human action or desires to influence. Facts alone determine what is believed, and the consequences, good or bad, fall where they may. Politics is concerned with those things that are within human ability to change, and beliefs are encouraged that advance political agendas. All too often in this case, truth is left to fall where it may.

When the hysteria over AIDS broke out in the early eighties, I was living in the Mother Lode country in the Sierra Nevada foothills of northern California. Since I had long dismissed the mass media as a credible source of information on anything that mattered, I didn't take a lot of notice. A close friend and drinking buddy of mine at that time was a former Air Force physicist who helped with several books that I worked on there. Out of curiosity, we checked the actual figures from official sources such as various city and state health departments. The number of cases for the whole of California turned out to be somewhere between 1100 and 1200, and these were

151

confined pretty much totally to a couple of well defined parts of San Francisco and Los Angeles associated with drugs and other ways of life that I wasn't into. So this was the great "epidemic" that we'd been hearing about? Ah, but we didn't understand, people told us. This was being spread by a new virus that was 100% lethal and about to explode out into the population at large. You could catch it from sex, toilet seats, your dentist, from breathing the air, and once you did there was no defense. The species could be staring at extinction.

But I didn't buy this line either. I can't really offer a rationally packaged explanation of why. Part of it was that although AIDS had been around for some years, it was still clearly confined overwhelmingly to the original risk groups to which the term had first been applied. If it was going to "explode" out into the general population, there should have been unmistakable signs of it happening by now. There weren't. And another large part, I suppose, was that scaring the public had become such a lucrative and politically fruitful industry that the more horrific the situation was made to sound, the more skeptically I reacted. All the claims contradicted what my own eyes and ears told me. Nobody that I knew had it. Nobody that I knew knew anybody who had it. But "everybody knew" it was everywhere. Now, I don't doubt that when the Black Death hit Europe or smallpox reached the Americas, people knew they had an epidemic. When you need a billion-dollar propaganda industry to convince you there's a problem, you don't have a major problem.

So I got on with life and largely forgot about the issue until I visited the University of California, Berkeley, to meet Peter Duesberg, a professor of molecular and cell biology, whom a mutual friend had urged me to contact. Talking to Duesberg and some of his colleagues, both then and on later occasions,

left me stupefied and led me to take a new interest
in the subject. This has persisted over the years since
and involved contacts with others not only across the
U.S., but as far removed as England, Germany,
Australia, and South Africa. We like to think that the
days of the Inquisition are over. Well, here's what can
happen to politically incorrect science when it gets
in the way of a bandwagon being propelled by *lots*
of money—and to a scientist who ignores it and
attempts simply to point at what the facts seem to
be trying to say.

The first popular misunderstanding to clear up is
that "AIDS" is not something new that appeared
suddenly around 1980. It's a collection of old diseases
that have been around for as long as medical history,
that began showing up in clusters at greater than the
average incidence. An example was *Pneumocystis
carinnii*, a rare type of pneumonia caused by a normally benign microbe that inhabits the lungs of just
about every human being on the planet; it becomes
pathogenic typically in cancer patients whose immune
systems are suppressed by chemotherapy. And, indeed,
the presence of other opportunistic infections such
as esophagal yeast infections confirmed immunosuppression in all of these early cases. Many of them also
suffered from a hitherto rare blood-vessel tumor
known as Kaposi's sarcoma. All this came as a surprise to medical authorities, since the cases were
concentrated among males aged 20 to 40, usually
considered a healthy age group, and led them to
classify the conditions together as a syndrome presumed to have some single underlying cause. The
victims were almost exclusively homosexuals, which
led to a suspicion of an infectious agent, with sexual
practices as the main mode of transmission. This
seemed to be confirmed when other diseases associated with immune deficiency, such as TB among
drug abusers, and various infections experienced by

hemophiliacs and transfusion recipients, were included in the same general category too, which by this time was officially designated Acquired Immune Deficiency Syndrome, or "AIDS."

Subsequently, the agent responsible was stated to be a newly discovered virus of the kind known as "retroviruses," later given the name Human Immunodeficiency Virus, or HIV. The AIDS diseases were opportunistic infections that struck following infection by HIV, which was said to destroy "T-helper cells," a subset of white blood cells which respond to the presence of invading microbes and stimulate other cells into producing the appropriate antibodies against them. This incapacitated the immune system and left the victim vulnerable.

And there you have the basic paradigm that still pretty much describes the official line today. This virus that nobody had heard of before—the technology to detect it didn't exist until the eighties—could lurk anywhere, and no vaccine existed to protect against it. Then it was found in association with various other kinds of sickness in Africa, giving rise to speculations that it might have originated there, and the media gloried in depictions of a global pandemic sweeping across continents out of control. Once smitten there was no cure, and progression to exceptionally unpleasant forms of physical devastation and eventual death was inevitable and irreversible.

While bad news for some, this came at a propitious time for a huge, overfunded and largely out-of-work army within the biomedical establishment, which, it just so happened, had been set up, equipped, trained, and on the lookout for exactly such an emergency. Following the elimination of polio in the fifties and early sixties, the medical schools had been churning out virologists eager for more Nobel Prizes. New federal departments to monitor and report on infectious diseases stood waiting to be utilized. But the war on cancer had failed to find a viral cause, and all these forces in need of an epidemic converged in a crusade to unravel the workings of the deadly new virus and produce a vaccine against it. No other virus was ever so intensively studied. Published papers soon numbered thousands, and jobs were secure as federal expenditures grew to billions of dollars annually. Neither was the largess confined to just the medical-scientific community and its controlling bureaucracies. As HIV came to be automatically equated with AIDS, anyone testing positive qualified as a disaster victim eligible for treatment at public expense, which meant lucrative consultation and testing fees, and treatment with some of the most profitable drugs that the pharmaceuticals industry has ever marketed. And beyond that, with no vaccine available, the sole means of prevention lay in checking the spread of HIV. This meant funding for another growth sector of promotional agencies, advisory centers, educational campaigns, as well as support groups and counselors to minister to afflicted victims and their families. While many were meeting harrowing ends, others had never had it so good. Researchers who would otherwise have spent their lives peering through microscopes and cleaning Petri dishes became millionaires setting up companies to produce HIV kits and drawing royalties for the tests performed. Former dropouts were achieving political visibility and living comfortably as organizers of programs financed by government grants and drug-company handouts. It was a time for action, not thought; spreading the word, not asking questions. Besides, who would want to mess with this golden goose?

And then in the late eighties, Peter Duesberg published a paper suggesting that AIDS might not be caused by HIV at all—nor by any other virus, come to that. In fact, he didn't even think that "AIDS" was infectious!

What he saw was different groups of people getting

sick in different ways for different reasons that had
to do with the particular risks that those groups had
always faced. No common cause tying them all together had ever been convincingly demonstrated;
indeed, why such conditions as dementia and wasting disease should have been considered at all was
something of a mystery, since they are not results of
immunosuppression. Drug users were ruining their
immune systems with the substances they were putting into their bodies, getting TB and pneumonia from
unsterile needles and street drugs, and wasting as a
consequence of the insomnia and malnutrition that
typically go with the lifestyle; homosexuals were
getting sarcomas from the practically universal use of
nitrite inhalants, and yeast infections from the sup-
pression of protective bacteria by overdosing on
antibiotics used prophylactically; hemophiliacs were
immune-suppressed by the repeated infusion of foreign protein; blood recipients were already sick for
varying reasons; people being treated with the "antiviral" drug AZT were being poisoned; Africans were
suffering from totally different diseases long characteristic of poverty in tropical environments; and a few
individuals were left who got sick for reasons that
would never be explained. The only difference in
recent years was that some of those groups had gotten
bigger. The increases matched closely the epidemic
in drug use that had grown since the late sixties and
early seventies, and Duesberg proposed drugs as the
primary cause of the rises that were being seen.

Although Duesberg is highly qualified in this field,
the observations that he was making really didn't
demand doctorate knowledge or rarefied heights of
intellect to understand. For a start, years after their
appearances, the various "AIDS" diseases remained
obstinately confined to the original risk groups, and
the victims were still over 90% male. This isn't the
pattern of an infectious disease, which spreads and

affects everybody, male and female alike. For a new disease loose in a defenseless population, the spread would be exponential. And this was what had been predicted in the early days, but it just hadn't happened. While the media continued to terrify the public with a world of their own creation, planet Earth was getting along okay. Heterosexuals who didn't use drugs weren't getting AIDS; for the U.S., subtracting the known risk groups leaves about 500 per year—fewer than the fatalities from contaminated tap water. The spouses and partners of AIDS victims weren't catching it. Prostitutes who didn't do drugs weren't getting it, and customers of prostitutes weren't getting it. In short, these had all the characteristics of textbook non-infectious diseases.

It is an elementary principle of science and medicine that correlation alone is no proof of cause. If A is reported as generally occurring with B, there are four possible explanations: (1) A causes B; (2) B causes A; (3) something else causes both A and B; (4) the correlation is just coincidence or has been artificially exaggerated, e.g. by biased collecting of data. There's no justification in jumping to a conclusion like (1) until the other three have been rigorously eliminated.

In the haste to find an infectious agent, Duesberg maintained, the role of HIV had been interpreted the wrong way round. Far from being a common cause of the various conditions called "AIDS," HIV itself was an opportunistic infection that made itself known in the final stages of immune-system deterioration brought about in other ways. In a sense, AIDS caused HIV. Hence, it acted as a "marker" of high-risk groups, but was not in itself responsible for the health problems that those groups were experiencing. The high correlation between HIV and AIDS that was constantly being alluded to was an artifact of the way in which AIDS was defined:

HIV + indicator disease = AIDS

Indicator disease without HIV = Indicator disease.

So if you've got all the symptoms of TB, and you test positive for HIV, you've got AIDS. But if you have a condition that's clinically indistinguishable and don't test positive for HIV, you've got TB.

And that, of course, would have made the problem scientifically and medically trivial.

When a scientific theory fails in its predictions, it is either modified or abandoned. Science welcomes informed criticism and is always ready to reexamine its conclusions in the light of new evidence or an alternative argument. The object, after all, is to find out what's true. But it seemed that what was going on here wasn't science. Duesberg was met by a chorus of outrage and ridicule, delivered with a level of vehemence that is seldom seen among professional circles. Instead of willingness to reconsider, he was met by stratagems designed to conceal or deny that the predictions were failing. This is the kind of reaction typical of politics, not science, usually referred to euphemistically as "damage control."

For example, statistics for new AIDS cases were always quoted as cumulative figures that could only get bigger, contrasting with the normal practice with other diseases of reporting annual figures, where any decline is clear at a glance. And despite the media's ongoing stridency about an epidemic out of control, the actual figures from the Centers for Disease Control (CDC), for every category, *were* declining, and had been since a peak around 1988. And this was in spite of repeated redefinitions to cover more diseases, so that what wasn't AIDS one day became AIDS the next, causing more cases to be diagnosed. This happened five times from 1982 to 1993, with the result that the first nine months of 1993 showed as an overall rise of 5% what would otherwise—i.e. by the 1992 definition—have been a 33% drop. Currently (1997) the number of indicator diseases is

29. One of the new categories to be added was cervical cancer. (Militant femininists had been protesting that men received too much of the relief appropriations for AIDS victims.) Nobody was catching anything new, but the headlines blared heterosexual women as the fastest-growing AIDS group. Meanwhile, a concerted campaign across the schools and campuses was doing its part to terrorize young people over the ravages of teenage AIDS. Again, actual figures tell a different story. The number of cases in New York City reported by the CDC for ages 13-19 from 1981 to the end of June 1992 were 872. When homosexuals, intravenous drug users, and hemophiliacs are eliminated, the number left not involving these risks (or not admitting to them) reduces to a grand total of 16 in an 11 year period. (Yes, sixteen. You did read that right.)

Viral diseases strike typically after an incubation period of days or weeks, which is the time in which the virus can replicate before the body develops an immunity. When this didn't happen for AIDS, the notion of a "slow" virus was introduced, which would delay the onset of symptoms for months. When a year passed with no sign of an epidemic, it was upped to five years; when nothing happened then either, to ten. Now we're being told ten to fifteen. Inventions to explain failed predictions are invariably a sign of a theory in trouble.

(Note: This is not the same as a virus going dormant, as can happen with some types of herpes, and reactivating later, such as in times of stress. In these cases, the most pronounced disease symptoms occur at the time of primary infection, before immunity is established; subsequent outbreaks are less severe—immunity is present, but reduced—and when they do occur, the virus is abundant and active. This does not describe AIDS. A long delay before any appearance of sickness is characteristic of the cumulative buildup of a toxic cause, like lung cancer from smoking or liver cirrhosis from alcohol excess.)

So against all this, on what grounds was AIDS said to be infectious in the first place? Just about the only argument, when you strip it down, seems to be the correlation—that AIDS occurs in geographic and risk-related clusters. This is not exactly compelling. Victims of airplane crashes and Montezuma's revenge are found in clusters too, but nobody takes that as evidence that they catch their condition from each other. It all becomes even more curious when you examine the credentials of the postulated transmitting agent, HIV.

One of the major advances in medicine during the last century was the development of scientific procedures to determine if a particular disease is infectious—carried by some microbe that's being passed around—and if so, to identify the microbe; or else a result of some factor in the environment, such as a dietary deficiency, a local genetic trait, a toxin. The prime criteria for making this distinction, dating from the last century and long adopted universally, are known as Koch's Postulates. There are four of them, and when all are met, the case is considered proved beyond reasonable doubt that the disease is infectious and caused by the suspected agent. HIV as the cause of AIDS fails every one.

(1) *The microbe must be found in all cases of the disease.*

By the CDC's own statistics, for 25% of the cases diagnosed in the U.S. the presence of HIV has been inferred presumptively, without actual testing. And anyway, by 1993, over 4000 cases of people dying of AIDS diseases were admitted to be HIV-free. The most recent redefinition includes a category in which AIDS can be diagnosed without a positive test for HIV. (How this can be so while at the same time HIV is insisted to be the cause of AIDS is a good question.

The required logic is beyond my abilities.) The World Health Organization's clinical case-definition for AIDS in Africa (adopted in 1985) is not based on an HIV test but on combined symptoms of chronic diarrhea, prolonged fever, body-weight loss, and a persistent cough, none of which are new or uncommon on the African continent. Subsequent testing of sample groups diagnosed as having AIDS has given negative results in the order of 50%. Why diseases totally different from those listed in America and Europe, now not even required to show any HIV status, should be called the same thing is another good question.

(2) *The microbe must be isolated from the host and grown in a pure culture.*

This is to ensure that the disease was caused by the suspect germ and not by something unidentified in a mixture of substances. The tissues and body fluids of a patient with a genuine viral disease will have so many viruses pouring out of infected cells that it is a straightforward matter—standard undergraduate exercise—to separate a pure sample and compare the result with known cataloged types. There have been numerous claims of isolating HIV, but closer examination shows them to be based on liberal stretchings of what the word has always been understood to mean. For example, using chemical stimulants to shock a fragment of defective RNA to express itself in a cell culture removed from any active immune system is a very different thing from demonstrating active viral infection. Despite the billions spent, no isolation of HIV has been achieved which meets the standards that virology normally requires.

(3) *The microbe must be capable of reproducing the original disease when introduced into a susceptible host.*

This asks to see that the disease can be reproduced

by injecting the allegedly causative microbe into an uninfected, otherwise healthy host. It does not mean that the microbe must cause the disease every time (otherwise everyone would be sick all the time).

Two ways in which this can condition can be tested are: injection into laboratory animals; accidental infection of humans. (Deliberate infection of humans would be unethical). Chimpanzees have been injected since 1983 and developed antibodies, showing that the virus "takes," but none has developed AIDS symptoms. There have been a few vaguely described claims of health workers catching AIDS from needle sticks and other HIV exposure, but nothing conclusively documented. For comparison, the figure for hepatitis infections is 1500 per year. Hence, even if the case for AIDS were proved, hepatitis is hundreds of times more virulent. Yet we don't have a panic about it.

(4) *The microbe must be found present in the host so infected.*

This is irrelevant in the case of AIDS, since (3) has never been met.

The typical response to this violating of a basic principle that has served well for a century is either to ignore it or say that HIV is so complex that it renders Koch's Postulates obsolete. But Koch's Postulates are simply a formalization of common-sense logic, not a statement about microbes. The laws of logic don't become obsolete, any more than mathematics. And if the established criteria for infectiousness are thrown away, then by what alternative standard is HIV supposed to be judged infectious? Just clusterings of like symptoms? Simple correlations with no proof of any cause-effect relationship? That's called superstition, not science. It puts medicine back two hundred years.

So how did HIV come to be singled out as the

cause to begin with? The answer seems to be, at a press conference. In April, 1984, the Secretary of Health and Human Services, Margaret Heckler, sponsored a huge event and introduced the NIH researcher Robert Gallo to the press corps as the discoverer of the (then called HTLV-III) virus, which was declared to be the probable cause of AIDS. This came before publication of any papers in the scientific journals, violating the normal protocol of giving other scientists an opportunity to review such findings before they were made public. No doubt coincidentally, the American claim to fame came just in time to preempt the French researcher Luc Montagnier of the Pasteur Institute in Paris, who had already published in the literature his discovery of what later turned out to be the same virus. From that point on, official policy was set in stone. All investigation of alternatives was dropped, and federal funding went only to research that reflected the approved line. This did not make for an atmosphere of dissent among career-minded scientists, who, had they been politically free to do so, might have pointed out that even if the cause of AIDS were indeed a virus, the hypothesis of its being HIV raised some distinctly problematical questions.

Proponents of the HIV dogma assert repeatedly that "the evidence for HIV is overwhelming." When they are asked to produce it or cite some reference, the usual response is ridicule or some ad hominem attack imputing motives. But never a simple statement of facts. Nobody, to my knowledge, has ever provided a definitive answer to the simple question, "Where is the study that proves HIV causes AIDS?" It's just something that "everybody knows" is true. Yet despite the tens of thousands of papers written, nobody can produce one that says why.

Sometimes, reference is made to four papers that Gallo published in *Science* after the press conference, deemed to have settled the issue before any outside scientists had seen them. But even if the methods described are accepted as demonstrating true viral isolation—which has been strongly disputed—they show a presence of HIV in less than half of the patients with opportunistic infections, and less than a third with Kaposi's sarcoma—the two most characteristic AIDS diseases. This is "overwhelming" evidence? It falls short of the standards that would normally be expected of a term-end dissertation, never mind mobilizing the federal resources of the United States and shutting down all investigation of alternatives.

And the case gets even shakier than that.

Viruses make you sick by killing cells. When viruses are actively replicating at a rate sufficient to cause disease, either because immunity hasn't developed yet or because the immune system is too defective to contain them, there's no difficulty in isolating them from the affected tissues. With influenza, a third of the lung cells are infected; with hepatitis, just about all of the liver cells. In the case of AIDS, typically 1 in 1000 T-cells shows any sign of HIV, even for terminally ill cases—and even then, no distinction is made of inactive or defective viruses, or totally nonfunctional viral fragments. But even if every one were a lethally infected cell, the body's replacement rate is thirty times higher. This simply doesn't add up to damage on a scale capable of causing disease.

HIV belongs to a class of viruses known as "retroviruses," which survive by encoding their RNA sequences into the chromosomal DNA of the host cell (the reverse of the normal direction of information flow in cell replication, which is DNA to RNA to protein, hence the name). When that part of the host chromosome comes to be transcribed, the cell's protein-manufacturing machinery makes a new retrovirus, which leaves by budding off through the cell membrane. The retrovirus, therefore, leaves the cell intact and functioning, and survives by slipping a copy of itself from time to time into the cell's normal production run. This strategy is completely different from that of the more prevalent "lytic" viruses, which take over the cell machinery totally to mass-produce themselves until the cell is exhausted, at which point they rupture the membrane, killing the cell, and move on, much in the style of locusts. This is what gives the immune system problems, and in the process causes colds, flu, polio, rabies, measles, mumps, yellow fever, and so on.

But a retrovirus produces so few copies of itself that it's easy meat for an immune system battle-trained at dealing with lytic viruses. For this reason, the main mode of transmission for a retrovirus is from mother to child, meaning that the host organism needs to live to reproductive maturity. A retrovirus that killed its host wouldn't be reproductively viable. Many human retroviruses have been studied, and all are harmless.

(Some rare animal cancers arise from specific genes inserted retrovirally into the host DNA. But in these cases tumors form rapidly and predictably soon after infection—completely unlike the situation with AIDS. And a cancer is due to cells proliferating wildly—just the opposite of killing them.)

HIV conforms to the retroviral pattern and is genetically unremarkable. It doesn't kill T-cells, even in cultures raised away from a body ("in vitro"), with no immune system to suppress it. Indeed, HIV for research is propagated in immortal lines of the very cell which, to cause AIDS, HIV is supposed to kill!—and in concentrations far higher than have ever been observed in any human, with or without AIDS. Separated from its host environment it promptly falls to pieces, which has led some researchers, looking skeptically at the assortment of RNA fragments, bits of protein, and other debris from which its existence is inferred, to question if there is really any such entity at all. (*Q*. If so, then what's replicating in those culture dishes? *A*. It has never been shown conclusively that anything introduced from the outside is replicating. Artificially stimulating "something" into expressing itself—it could be a strip of "provirus" code carried in the culture-cell's DNA—is a long way from demonstrating an active, pathogenic virus from a human body.)

For the same reason, HIV is almost impossible to transmit sexually, requiring something like 1000 different contacts, compared to 4 for genuine STDs (which is neither here nor there if it's harmless anyway). Hence, far from being the ferocious cell-killer painted by the media, HIV turns out to be a dud.

Most people carry traces of just about every microbe found in their normal habitat around with them all the time. The reason they're not sick all the time is that their immune system keeps the microbes inactive or down to numbers that can't cause damage. An immune system that has become dysfunctional to the point where it can't even keep HIV in check is in trouble. On their way downhill, depending on the kind of risk they're exposed to, every AIDS group has its own way of accumulating a cocktail of just about everything that's going around—unsterile street drugs; shared needles; promiscuity; accumulated serum from multiple donors. By the time HIV starts to register too, as well as everything else, you're right down in the lowest 5% grade. And those are the people who typically get AIDS. Hence, HIV's role as a marker of a risk group that collects microbes.

If HIV is virtually undetectable even in its alleged terminal victims, how do you test for it? You don't; you test for the antibody. That is, the body's own defense equipment—that you either acquired from your mother, learned to make yourself at some time earlier in life when you encountered the virus, or were tricked into making by a vaccine. In other words, your way of making yourself immune. Is this starting to sound a little bit strange?

Actually, testing for the antibody to a suspected pathogen can make sense, given the right circumstances. *If* a person is showing clinical symptoms—say, fever, with a rash, sweating, shaking, delirium—that are known to be caused by that pathogen, (perhaps by satisfying Koch's postulates), *and* a test has been shown independently to identify an antibody specific to it, *then* testing for the antibody in the presence of the observed symptoms can be a convenient and dependable way of confirming the suspected disease. But none of this is true of HIV. It has never been shown to cause anything, nor has a likely explanation even been advanced as to how it could. And the only way of showing that an antibody test is specific to a virus is to compare its results with a "gold standard" known to measure the virus and nothing else. Establishing a standard requires isolating the virus from clinical patients in the true, traditional sense, and for HIV that has never been done. What, then, if anything, does the "HIV test" mean?

A genuinely useful antibody test can confirm that an *observed sickness* is due to the virus thought to be the culprit. A positive HIV result from somebody who is completely symptom-free, on the other hand, means either that the antibody has been carried from birth without the virus ever having been encountered, or that the virus has been successfully neutralized to the point of invisibility. So in this context, "HIV positive" means HIV-immune. Interpreting it as a prediction that somebody will die years hence from some unspecifiable disease makes about as much sense as diagnosing smallpox in a perfectly healthy person from the presence of antibodies acquired through childhood vaccination.

The test can mean a lot of other things too. The most common, known as ELISA, was developed for

blood screening. Now, when you're looking for contaminated blood, you *want* a test that's oversensitive—
where anything suspect will ding the bell. If the
positive is false, after all, you merely throw away a
pint of blood. But if a false negative gets through, the
consequences could be catastrophic. (Whether or not
what you're screening for is a real hazard isn't the
issue here.) But the same test started being used for
diagnosis. And when people are being told that a
positive result means certainty of developing a disease that's inevitably fatal, that's a very different thing
indeed.

Here are some of the other things that can give
a positive result, which even doctors that I've talked
to weren't aware of: prior pregnancy; alcoholism;
certain cancers; malaria antibodies; leprosy antibodies;
flu vaccination; heating of blood sample; prolonged
storage of the sample; numerous other viruses; various parasitic diseases; hepatitis B antibodies; rheu-
matoid arthritis. The WHO performed 50 million
antibody tests in Russia over a two-year period and
found 50,000 positive results. Attempts to confirm
these yielded around 300, of which 50 or so were
actual AIDS cases.

African AIDS affects both sexes equally and is fre-
quently cited as a heterosexually transmitted epidemic
and foretaste of what's in store for the rest of the
world. The actual diseases are very different from those
reported in New York and San Francisco, however—
the same that have afflicted those parts of Africa
through history. Today they're called AIDS on account
of correlation with positive HIV results. But we've
already noted that lots of factors endemic to those
regions—malaria, leprosy, parasitical infections—can
test positive. Nevertheless, it is decreed that all positives shall be interpreted as due to HIV, making every
instance automatically an AIDS statistic. Further, every
case of "AIDS" thus diagnosed that is not a homosexual

or drug abuser is presumed to have been acquired through heterosexual transmission. It isn't difficult to discern an epidemic in such circumstances. People in desperate need of better nutrition and sanitation, energy-intensive industrial technologies, and capital investment are instead distributed condoms.

Over 90% of the inhabitants of Southeast Asia carry the hepatitis B antibody. And we all "know," because the newspapers say so, that an AIDS epidemic is ravaging Thailand. The figure for actual disease cases in this region populated by tens of millions was around 700 in 1991, and by 1993 had grown to 1500 or so. Perhaps what the papers meant was an epidemic of AIDS testing. Just like the inquisitors of old, the more assiduously the witch hunters apply their techniques and their instruments, sure enough they find more witches.

In the cuckoo land of HIV "science" anything becomes possible. To combat the effects of an agent declared soon after its discovery as being inevitably lethal after a dormancy of 10-15 years (?), HIV positives, sick and symptom-free alike, were put on the drug AZT, which billed as "antiviral." Well, it is, I suppose, in the same sense that napalm or Liquid Plumber is antiviral—it kills everything. AZT was developed in the 1960s as a chemotherapy for leukemia but never released because of its toxicity. It's a DNA chain terminator, which means it stops the molecule from copying. It kills every cell that tries to reproduce. The idea for cancer treatment is that a short, shock program of maybe two or three weeks will kill the tumor while only half killing the patient, and then you get him off it as quickly as possible. You *can't* take something like that four times a day indefinitely and expect to live. (Although some people don't metabolize it but pass it straight through; hence the few long-term AZT survivors that are pointed at to show how benign it is).

Chemotherapies are notoriously immunosuppressive. The "side effects" look just like AIDS. Yet this is the treatment of choice. Nobody says it actually cures or stops AIDS, but the recipients have been told that they're due to die anyway—which could possibly be one of the most ghastly self-fulfilling prophecies in modern medical history. The claim is that it brings some temporary respite, based on results of a few trials in which the augurs of biochemistry saw signs of short-term improvement—although bad data were knowingly included, and other commentators have dismissed the trials as worthless. In any case, it is known that a body subjected to this kind of toxic assault can mobilize last-ditch emergency defenses for a while, even when terminal. A sick chicken might run around the yard for a few seconds when you cut its head off, but that isn't a sign that the treatment has done it any good.

In the fifteen years or so up to the late eighties, the life expectancy of hemophiliacs doubled. This was because improved clotting factor—the substance they can't make for themselves—meant fewer transfusions. The cumulative burden of constantly infused foreign proteins eventually wears down an immune system and opens the way for infections. Many also acquired HIV, but the death rates of those testing positive and negative were about the same. Then, from around the late eighties, the mortality of the HIV positives from conditions diagnosed as AIDS rose significantly, and a widely publicized study cited this as proof that their AIDS was due to HIV. What it didn't take into account, however, was that only the HIV positives were put on AZT. Nobody was giving AZT to the HIV negatives. Peter Duesberg believes that AZT and other "antivirals" are responsible for over half the AIDS being reported today.

The latest diagnostic disease indicator, "viral load," is an indirect measure divorced from any actual symptoms at all, based on the "polymerase chain reaction" method of amplifying formerly undetectable amounts of molecular material by copying them in enormous numbers. But errors are amplified by the same amount. The mathematical basis of the model has been shown to be fatally flawed and based on wrong assumptions. The inventor of the PCR method, Nobel Prize winner Kary Mullis, has dismissed its application in this way as totally worthless.

And the AZT story of hastily rushing into print to claim miracle cures based on selective anecdotal reporting and uncompleted trials performed without controls seems to be in the process of being repeated with the new drug "cocktails" based on protease inhibitors. Researchers who have worked with PIs all their professional lives state flatly that they are incapable of doing what the highly publicized claims say they do. Their efficacy is assessed by measuring the reduction of the number designated "viral load," which has never been shown to correspond to anything defining sickness in the real, physical world. As a "control," the viral load of those given cocktails is compared with the former level when they received AZT. A reduction is taken as meaning that the cocktails have reduced sickness. On the same basis you could claim that chewing gum stops cancer because fewer smokers who switch go on to develop it.

Although the mainstream media don't report it, a growing number of scientific and medical professionals are coming around to Duesberg's position or somewhere close to it. Many, especially in times of uncertainty over careers and funding, keep a low profile and refrain from public comment. When you see what happened to Duesberg, you can see why. One of the pioneers in retroviral research—the first to map a retroviral genome, seven-time recipient of the NIH Outstanding Investigator award, and tapped for a Nobel Prize—he was subjected to vilification, abused at conferences, and his funding cut off to the point that he can no longer afford a secretary. In two years, he had seventeen applications for funding for research on alternative AIDS hypotheses turned down. Publication in the scientific literature has been denied— even the right of reply to personal attacks carried in the journal *Nature*, violating the most fundamental of scientific traditions. His scheduled appearances on talk shows have been repeatedly canceled at the last moment upon intervention by officials from the NIH and CDC.

Duesberg is accused of irresponsibility on the grounds that his views threaten confidence in public health-care programs based on the HIV dogma. But scientific truth doesn't depend on perceived consequences. Public policy should follow science. Attempting to impose the reverse becomes Lyshenkoism.

In any case, what do those programs have that should command any confidence? After all these years they have failed to save a life or produce a vaccine. (And if they did, to whom would it be given? The function of a vaccine is to stimulate the production of antibodies, and HIV positives have them already.) No believable mechanism has been put forward as to how HIV kills T-cells. And billions of dollars continue to be spent every year on trying to unravel the mysteries of how HIV can make you sick without being present, and how an antibody can neutralize the virus but not suppress the disease. Scientific principles that have stood well for a hundred years are arbitrarily discarded to enable what's offered as logic to hang together at all, and the best that can be done at the end of it is to prescribe a treatment that's lethal even if the disease is not. Yet no looking into alternatives is permitted; all dissenting views are repressed. This is not the way of science, but of a fanatical religion putting down heresy.

The real victim, perhaps not terminally ill but

looking somewhat jaded at the moment, is intellectual honesty and scientific rigor. Maybe in its growth from infancy, Science too has to learn how to make antibodies to protect itself from opportunistic infection and dogmatism. And in the longer term it seems that it can. Today, everybody remembers Galileo. How many can name the bishops who refused to look through his telescope?

Evolution Revisited

A characteristic of good science, we're told, is the ability and readiness to change one's mind when the circumstances seem to call for it. One day, when my agent, Eleanor Wood, Jim Baen, and I were still considering a reissue of *Minds, Machines and Evolution*, I called Jim and said that if we decided to go ahead, maybe we should leave out "The Revealed Word of God." Jim asked why. I explained that the assured zealousness with which I had pressed the Darwinist case when I wrote the piece back in the mid-eighties was somewhat embarrassing to read now. A decade later, I was less sure. Jim was interested and curious to know why. So, he thought, would quite a lot of other people be. Instead of taking it out, he suggested leaving it as it was and saying something about the reasons for having second thoughts, and then elaborating further on them in a piece to be written for this volume. So here it is.

To be clear at the outset, I'm not arguing about whether or not evolution happens. Life today is clearly very different from that of long ago. What I am beginning to doubt is the orthodox account we're given of how it happens—specifically, the mechanism of random mutation and natural selection as the driving force responsible. I'm not even saying that selection doesn't happen. It demonstrably does, and it has its results—but within limits, as plant and animal breeders know well. When domesticated animals return to the wild state, the most specialized are quickly eliminated and the survivors revert to the wild type. Selection is overwhelmingly a conservative force, preserving existing types by culling population and diluting away variations to prevent the kinds of extremes that human breeders encourage. The fossil record shows periodic epochs of profuse radiation and diversity of life forms appearing and subsequently being thinned down as the unfit, or the unfortunate, proceed to die out. (For a discussion of the relative merits, see David Raup, *Extinction: Bad Genes or Bad Luck?* W.W. Norton, 1991.) But this is exactly the opposite of the gradual increase of variety from a few ancestral types that the theory of diversification via natural selection predicts.

The effects of genetic mutations are nearly always harmful, but occasionally they do slightly improve an organism's ability to survive and reproduce. And this one fact, although it has never been observed to produce a single new species, is the basis for attributing to the process the innovative and creative power to build, starting from molecules, all of the wonder and diversity that makes up the living world. An example proclaimed in practically all the textbooks as proof of the principle in action is the case of the British peppered moth, which tends to settle on the bark of trees. Where trees in industrial areas became darkened by pollution the dominant coloring of the moth population shifted from light to dark, whereas in untainted rural regions it remained light—in both cases affording better camouflage against predatory birds. Nothing genetically new was created. All that took place was a pretty basic demonstration of population dynamics involving the differential survival of variations already present. Yet this is held as proving the ability of the same process to shape birds and insects out of microbes, and turn fish into mammals and mammals into us—the best proof we can come up with after a hundred and fifty years.

More and more scientists, biologists, geneticists are coming to the conclusion that pure chance cannot be the explanation of it all. The improbabilities involved are simply too vast, the numbers too huge. The complexity of the molecular apparatus being uncovered in even a single biological cell stupefies the imagination. In *Evolution: A Theory in Crisis* (Adler & Adler, 1985), Michael Denton, an Australian molecular biologist, describes the cell as an immense automated factory, larger than a city when viewed from the scale of the machinery inside, made up of endless branching corridors and conduits interconnecting manufacturing galleries and control centers supporting processes that exhibit all of the features of our own most advanced production systems: artificial languages and decoding systems; data and program memory systems; control and regulation of part and component assembly; error fail-safe checking and proof reading for quality control—the whole capable of replicating its entire structure within a few hours. The astronomer Fred Hoyle, in his 1983 book *The Intelligent Universe*, puts the odds against chance processes forming just the 200 enzymes used in human metabolism as a number having forty pages of zeros.

Crucial to the idea of evolution by natural selection is the doctrine of gradualism—the accumulation of micromutations over long periods of time. Darwin had little doubt that now investigators knew what to look for, evidence for slow change would be found in abundance. The fact is, after a century and more of intensive searching, it simply isn't there. Species, genera, families appear suddenly in the fossil record, fully differentiated and specialized, and what's remarkable after that is their stability. The anticipated intermediate forms don't exist. Instead of gradual transition, the scheme of animal and plant classification shows the hierarchical pattern characteristic of discontinuous systems like atomic structures or methods of human transportation. It doesn't exhibit the overlapping bands that mark continuous change, as seen for example, in the progressive changes of climate and vegetation from equator to poles.

Instances where a progressive change can be traced for some distance through the fossil record involve relatively minor morphological transitions. One of the best known is the sequence leading from the doglike *Eohippus*, placed at sixty million years ago, to the modern horse. But although a great deal is made of it, the series shows variation on a theme rather than innovation, making it more an abnormal extension of microevolution than a demonstration of something genetically significant. The traditional view is that such sequences prove the reality of a general principle, of which only a few limited traces have been preserved or so far been discovered. It is possible, however, to interpret their rarity differently by reading it directly for what it says: that what is exceptional about such sequences is not that they were preserved but that they occurred at all; that in general nature cannot be arranged in orderly sequences, and the occasional instances where a trend is discernible were comparatively trivial. Such a suspicion is reinforced by the fact that the handful of plausibly convincing sequences that are known involve little in the way of real change, which emphasizes by making all the more conspicuous the absence of intermediates in major evolutionary transformations. If sixty million years and ten genera separate *Eohippus* from the horse, and yet their differences are relatively trivial, how many uncountable myriads of forms ought there to have been connecting such diverse forms as, say, land mammals with whales or mollusks with arthropods? Indeed, Darwin himself imagined them as an "infinitude." Yet all traces of such enormous numbers have vanished, leaving only records of a few comparatively minor details that appeared along the way. Once again, this is precisely the opposite of what a gradualist theory predicts.

Living things exist as clusters of distinct, related kinds: fishes, insects, mammals, birds—islands of viability scattered across a vast ocean of disfunctional forms that are not found either in the world today or the fossil record of the past where they were expected. The leaps needed to cross these gulfs defy explanation by any form of gradualist doctrine. Better teeth are no good without an improved jaw to hold them; having the jaw won't help without stronger muscles to close it; stronger muscles can't function without more efficient circulation and respiration systems, and so on. Everything needs to change together. Accumulating gradual changes caused by random gene mutations runs into the same problem as trying to turn a washing machine into a refrigerator by altering one part at a time: the intermediate forms aren't viable, which means they can't leave descendants to inherit anything. On the other hand, postulating sufficient simultaneous changes to preserve viability requires coincidence to a degree indistinguishable from miracles.

Speculations along these lines in the nineteenth century gave rise to what were known as "hopeful monster" theories, in effect postulating, in desperation, that at some time a reptile laid an egg and a bird came out. (And if it did, what would it mate with?) In addressing the same problem, some scientists have come perilously close to resurrecting the idea today. "Punctuated equilibrium" models, for instance, acknowledge the evident stability of species and absence of transitional forms by having evolution occur in spurts separated by long periods of quiescence. But this is really a restatement of the facts, squeezing the impossibilities into timescales too small to leave traces but coming no closer to explaining them.

The 1970s brought hopes that the rapidly advancing new science of molecular biology would provide the picture that the fossil record had failed to deliver. Instead, it revealed greater inexplicable complexity, making the situation worse, not better, to the degree that molecular biologists are today among the leading critics of the conventional theory. Or they maintain a deafening silence in explanations of how Darwinian theory can account for the molecular basis of life. Michael Behe, an associate professor of biochemistry, in his book *Darwin's Black Box* (The Free Press, 1996), which has been creating quite a furor, describes the scientific community as paralyzed in the face of the complexity that has been uncovered inside the cell. No one at Harvard, the National Institutes of Health, no member of the National Academy of Sciences, nor any Nobel prize winner, he writes, has hazarded a guess at how the cellular cilium, vision, blood clotting, energy metabolism, or the immune response could have developed in a Darwinian fashion. In a survey that he conducted of thirty biochemistry textbooks, out of a total of 151,000 index entries, just 138 were to evolution. Thirteen of the texts contained no reference to evolution at all.

So what's this—Hogan going creationist? No, but this is just the false dichotomy that much of the world would see, and why many scientists with doubts don't air them publicly. Showing that a radio isn't driven by clockwork doesn't mean that it must therefore operate by magic. The concept of evolution was not something new that came with Darwin. Like so many ideas, it can be traced back to ancient Greece. What

Darwin did was offer for the first time an explanation of how evolution could work in a way that was free of supernatural underpinnings. This had great relevance to the political situation at the time.

The traditional aristocracy, with power rooted in the authority of religion, was being challenged by the newly arrived merchant and industrialist class. Every political system brings with it a dependent priesthood to justify and validate the order of things by appeals to moral argument, revelation, manifest destiny, or whatever. In this case it was the claim of rationality, pressed by the mechanistic, materialistic scientific forces of the day. The scientific revolution of the sixteenth and seventeenth centuries had replaced God as Overseer of the heavens and physical world with mechanical processes and mathematical law. A rationalist alternative to divine intervention to explain the origin of life would complete the undermining of the old authority. The teaching of everything specially created for a purpose, in its place, had justified the feudal order but it didn't suit new ambitions.

Darwinism also gave apparent scientific endorsement to social and economic doctrines that favored the shifting power structure. The suggestion of survival and territorial expansion being the natural reward for superiority and aggressively pursued excellence was exactly what those prospering from empire and laissez-faire wanted to hear after a century of being lambasted by moralists and pleaders for equality and charity. God's role was changed from umpire of the game to writer of the rules, which while admittedly harsh, humanity was powerless to change—and no doubt with patience, sacrifice, and observance of virtue and duty, the underlying wisdom would one day be revealed. There were few interests of influence who would argue with that.

Even the ruling houses of the old order, which at first sight might seem to have been threatened, were better served by going along with it. By and large they had made theirs and were willing to let the upstarts take the reins in return for being left alone to enjoy their social lives and estates in peace and comfort. The real threat to their existence came not from the rising newly rich, who shared the same values, aspired after the same successes, and with whom a understanding could always be reached, but from increasingly restless elements at the base of the social pyramid, with no stakes to lose or any interest in compromises. This was where the gradualist aspect of Darwin's theory had its most important impact.

At the time of his early observations and famous voyage aboard *H.M.S. Beagle*, Darwin was struck most of all by the signs of sudden and catastrophic change that he saw everywhere in the geological record. *What, then,* he wrote in his journal, *has exterminated so many species and whole genera? The mind, at first, is irresistibly hurried into the belief of some great catastrophe; but thus, to destroy animals . . . we must shake the entire framework of the globe.* But shaking the entire globe, surely, was inconceivable. By the time Darwin published his work twenty years later, he had come around to the idea of slow, gradual transitions operating over immense periods of time.

Essentially, what Darwin did was adapt to biology the "uniformitarianist" doctrine that the lawyer-turned-geologist Charles Lyell had succeeded in getting accepted as the governing principle that had shaped the Earth's surface. In this, Lyell and his school won out over the "catastrophist" school championed by the French naturalist Georges Cuvier, who read the past primarily in terms of immense periodic upheavals of the kind that Darwin had perceived originally.

Gradualism held that the forces operating in the past had been the same in kind and degree as those observed today. By measuring the rates of such processes as erosion and sedimentation and estimating how long they would have needed to work to produce the results observed, the enormous timescales were arrived at that have come to be assigned to the geological record. And Darwinian evolution, likewise based on the gradual accumulation of small changes, to be believable, also required immense timescales.

This debate took place at a time when memories of the French and American revolutions were fresh in the minds of the European ruling class. Napoleon's armies had carried the idea of popular uprising against traditional aristocracy everywhere from Catholic Spain to Tsarist Russia, and virtually all the European nations were seeing violent political movements advocating socialism. It was a time, in other words, when the reigning power structure was terrified by the thought that cataclysmic upheaval might be shown to be the natural mechanism for bringing about change. By contrast, the suggestion of slow, orderly progression as God's instrument of change—so slow that individuals shouldn't expect major changes of their situation even in a lifetime—justified opposition to radicalism and defending the status quo.

All this makes it easy to suspect that the eagerness with which the theory was accepted and alternatives speedily disposed of owed more to its political, economic, and philosophical expedience than to scientific merit and the hard evidence available to support it. Survival of the fittest provided the religion of moral justification for capitalism just as Lyshenko's inheritance of improvement through ceaseless striving later did for communism. And the same remains largely true today. Selection is the only mechanism available that explains evolution in naturalistic, materialistic terms. For those who rule out supernatural or non-uniformitarianist causes a priori, or who look for nature's model to justify society's ways—the intellectual successors to Herbert Spencer, John Huxley, David Ricardo—there is no other choice. Tenacious defense—not testing—of the theory on principle becomes the only alternative to admitting to not having one. The belief structure comes first and is unquestionable; evidence is molded to fit. Everything *must* have some selective advantage for being the way it is—and with ingenuity a plausible-sounding candidate can always be found. Anything and its opposite can be pressed into service to achieve the same effect—"survival"; but no method exists for assessing "fitness" independently to predict survivability, against which the actuality can be compared. Thus, we have a system capable of explaining anything, absolutely anything—but only after the event. Ironically, just as with creationism.

Having mentioned creationists once or twice, I should put in a word that I think is due in their defense against what I would term "humanist fundamentalism." By this I mean the convention that limits the terms of debate in advance by defining words in such a way as to exclude unwelcome theories from the argument.

If "evolution" is taken to mean the emergence over time of more complex forms from simpler ones, either gradually or in jumps, and "creationism" in the broad sense is the belief that life requires a creator, there is no necessary conflict between the two. Indeed, numerous individuals with impeccable scientific qualifications have concluded that evolution without a guiding intelligence of some kind at work behind it just isn't credible. The main reason why Michael Behe's book (above) caused such a stir was that he makes no bones about coming out into the open and saying so. But when "evolution" is allowed to mean only change brought about by mechanistic, naturalistic forces, and "creationism" is equated with "Biblical literalism" and then attacked for interpreting everything through its own belief structure, the real agendas being advanced are political and ideological, with science left foundering somewhere in the background. Not everyone would agree, of course. For many, "science" means endeavoring to construct a mechanical, materialistic explanation of the universe, "by definition." So here we go again. But the interesting question then is, where does this leave "science" if the faith that such an explanation exists should happen to be wrong? Excluded, it would seem, by its own definition from any knowledge of the perhaps only truth that ultimately matters. In the one case, firm belief, and in the other, willingness to concede, didn't seem to impair the scientific insights of such as Isaac Newton and Albert Einstein.

A good discussion of the legal, political, and ideological wars being waged under false scientific colors is presented in *Darwin on Trial* (Regnery Gateway, 1991), by Phillip Johnson, a professor of law at the University of California, Berkeley. What qualifications does a law professor have for getting involved in disputes about evolution? Well, when it comes to assessing evidence and the quality of arguments, maybe quite a lot.

Surely, if it means anything, the true spirit of science lies in avoiding bias and prejudice to the best of one's ability and letting the evidence lead where it may. Rejecting such possibilities as intelligent design on principle is being as dogmatic as any fundamentalist. When huge emotional investments have been stacked on what the answers are required to be, the objectivity and open-mindedness of genuine inquiry become impossible, and science has ceased to operate.

Just because one doesn't buy the creationist interpretation, it doesn't mean they can't have some valid points. Certainly, you can never know if you've never bothered to read what they have to say. I have, and to my own admitted surprise I found some of their evidence for a young Earth to be pretty persuasive. Not as young as the few thousand years that the literalists insist on, to be sure, but certainly younger than the billions conventionally assigned at present. In other words, I wouldn't be surprised if the future has a few surprises in store in the form of some drastic revising downwards of estimates of Earth's age.

Evolutionary theory is full of tautologies and circular reasoning. Its basic mechanism is explained as survival of the fittest, where "fittest" means whatever survives. An ordering of fossils dictated by the assumption of an ancestral lineage is taken as proof that the lineage is real. And so it is with the huge timescales of the various geological strata being used to date the fossils found in them. These ages were arrived at in the first place by *assuming* the uniformitarian principle to be true, and estimating how long the processes seen today would take to lay down rocks to the depths that are found. The biologists were happy to accept this uncritically since their own theory too—of natural selection—required huge time spans to be credible. Later, when it was found that certain "index fossils" appeared typically in association with certain strata, their occurrence was used to estimate the ages of newly explored rocks. Again, the logic is circular. The suspect was in the building at noon, when the jewels went missing; we know they were taken at noon because that's when the suspect was there.

Already, I can hear a muttering chorus of, "Radioisotope dating corroborations. What about them, then?" And that was very much my own first reaction too. But when I began looking deeper into the subject, it turned out to be a lot less infallible and reliable than textbooks and fiction writers (including myself) tend to depict. In principle, yes, the ratios of radioactive isotopes and decay products provide a means of measuring the running times of steadily ticking clocks that are unaffected by external physical factors such as heat, pressure, sunlight, chemistry, and so on. The difficulties come from the ease with which the results can be contaminated.

One way of picturing the decay of radioactive atoms is as a bunch of green grapes changing into black grapes—either a different isotope of the same atom, or a different type of atom—at a steady rate. "Steady" means that half of the number of green grapes left at any particular time will change within a fixed period characteristic of the substance. This is the well known "half life," which can be (for different types of atom) anything from a tiny fraction of a second to millions of years. If we know the rate, then measuring the fraction of green grapes that has changed into black ones will tell how long the process has been going on. This is how it works in theory. However, if some other agency were to carry away some of the green grapes initially present, the proportion of black grapes would be greater relative to the remaining greens than it ought, and the indicated age would be too high. The same would follow if black grapes were added from some source other than their decay from green grapes. Conversely, adding extraneous greens or removing a portion of the blacks would give age that were too low. And with more than one such process taking place at the same time, things would get more complicated still.

Unfortunately, this kind of situation tends to be the norm rather than the exception in the reality that exists outside test tubes, textbooks, and fiction writers' imaginations. In nature, things don't happen in isolation from the rest of the world, but in rocks, soils, oceans, living systems, where chemical exchanges replace one kind of atom with another, and differential melting, dissolution, and other selective transportation mechanisms that separate substances out are operating all the time. Decay products can be gases, which easily escape and are lost. Other processes cause absorption from the air, for example oxidation and respiration. Major changes in climate or volcanic activity can alter the atmospheric composition from the standard assumed. One of the major agents, both of introducing contaminants and removing genuine indicator substances, is water, which finds its way virtually everywhere.

As a consequence, dating tests typically return not a single, clean result but scatterings of figures that can span wild extremes. Obviously nonsensical ones can be dismissed on sight. Plants growing by an airport absorbed excess "old" carbon from the carbon dioxide of aircraft exhausts and dated at 10,000 years. Tissues from freshly killed seals gave readings of 1,300 years. Lava flows from volcanic eruptions historically recorded as taking place 900 to 1000 years ago gave ages of 210,000 to 230,000 years. Moon rocks gave readings covering the range from thousands of years to twenty-five billion—more than the officially ascribed age of the universe. But what do you do when there's no obvious second source to turn to as a check—for example, when the remains of mammoths, trees associated with them, and their mouth and stomach contents give dates disagreeing by thousands of years?

The only thing you can do is ask what makes sense in terms of the prevailing theory. This means, essentially, picking out what fits and rejecting what doesn't as "bad data." But in that case, how can the resulting match be pointed to as a test of the theory? We have a massive case of circularity again. When I talked to one or two professionals to ask if that was a fair assessment of the present state of things they hummed and hawed a bit, but in the end agreed that, "Well, yep, that's pretty much the way it is."

The normal procedure when submitting a sample to a dating lab is to indicate the range of results considered acceptable. When Britain's Science and Engineering Research Council ran a trial in which samples of known ages were submitted blind to 38 major dating laboratories around the world, only seven returned dates that were deemed satisfactory. A stunning 81% of the figures returned were dead wrong (Charles Ginenthal, *The Extinction of the Mammoth*, Ivy Press, Forest Hills, New York, 1997). Now, I don't want to belittle the efforts or question the sincerity of workers in the field, but until we're further along the road to resolving some of these uncertainties, how much confidence can we really have in figures selected for their conformity with preconceived expectations?

All of which brings us back to the question of the Earth perhaps being younger than conventionally taught, and evidence for events having taken place more recently and over much shorter periods of time than uniformitarian geological and evolutionary theory says. Some examples:

- Polystrate fossils: typically trees, extending through deposits supposed to have taken millions of years to form, e.g. coal seams separated by layers of shales and limestone.

- A baleen whale in California preserved in sedimentary rocks vertically. Unless a result of the most astounding balancing act in history, this didn't happen by burial through slow deposition and accumulation over ages.

- Clastic dikes: intrusions of clastic rocks (rocks formed from pieces of previously existing rock, e.g. sandstones) from below into hardened layers such as limestone or granite above. For this to have happened the sandstone must still have been soft and fluid, not hardened as it would have been if laid down far earlier as uniformitarian theory requires.

- Top layers of buried strata showing no traces of soil formation or the activities of climate and living things such as worms, roots, bacteria, as would occur with exposure on the surface for significant periods. Implication is that they were covered rapidly to considerable depth.

• And yet, surface imprints such as ripple marks, animal tracks are preserved against erosion long enough for rock formation to occur. Again, this suggests rapid burial.

(Those curious to read what the other side has to say on the subject might try *The Young Earth* by John D. Morris, Creation-Life Publishers, Colorado Springs, 1994. The sections on geology raise what strike me as some excellent points, although be aware that elsewhere the author does accept a literal 6-day creation and a 6,000-year-old Earth.)

The very richness of many fossil beds itself speaks against the uniformitarian doctrine of slow, gradual burial, for fossils don't normally form under such conditions. Either on land or in the oceans, dead animals are quickly eaten and scattered by scavengers, and the remains decomposed by bacterial and chemical action. Even bones and ivory are far from as permanent as many imagine. Fossils are preserved when burial and insulation from destruction and decay takes place quickly. Now, a few unfortunate specimens or even groups of local animal populations might fall into tar pits or crevasses, be overwhelmed by mud slides or avalanches, or meet with mishaps in any one of a hundred other ways that could preserve a record down through the ages. But what are we to make of the bones of millions of animals ranging from mastodons, caribou, horses, camels, rhinoceros, bears, and deer, smashed and broken, mixed with the splintered remains of countless trees, covering a band stretching across northern Europe, Siberia, Alaska, Canada, in some places forming islands in the Arctic Ocean hundreds of feet high? Or entire forests of trees sixty feet high preserved from their bases to their tops? Or valleys excavated by flash floods, and layers built

up by successive lava flows, showing after a few years
the same characteristics as other formations that were
supposed to have taken millions of years? Books filled
with such instances were being written a hundred and
fifty years ago. Darwin himself, as we've noted, made
many such observations in his earlier research. But
since uniformitarianism triumphed it has all been
ignored or explained away by arguments contrived for
the purpose. Because it doesn't fit with the theory.

We're back to catastrophism again. And interestingly, with the discovery of the iridium layer and
suggestion of a comet impact causing the demise of
the dinosaurs, and now similar events being proposed
to account for other sudden mass extinctions, the
notion of vast cataclysms marking the real changes
in Earth's history is becoming respectable again. For
more from the creationists, Steven Austin's *Catas-
trophes in Earth History* (ICR, El Cajon, CA, 1984)
provides a fascinating collection of instances—no
scriptural interpretations this time, just a 318-page
compilation of geological evidence. Some astronomers are beginning to question the dogma of an end-
lessly repeating Newtonian clockwork Solar System,
and are developing models of a precarious and
turbulent heavenly sphere, like life itself lulled into
delusions of serenity between sudden onsets of violent surprises.

My own belief, if it isn't obvious already, is that
the final story will eventually come together along
such catastrophist lines. It's consistent with the sudden appearance of species in the fossil record, though
not (necessarily) for the reason Biblical literalists
maintain. Think how the record of Africa, say, would
appear thousands or millions of years from now if a
planet-wide cataclysm were to occur now—just a
snapshot of the forms existing now. And it accords
with Darwinism to the extent of agreeing that evolution happens, though not at present offering a

workable explanation of how. But then, for my money, neither does natural selection.

It seems to be the custom near the end of every century for a spate of books to appear claiming that everything worth discovering has been discovered, and the only work left for science is polishing up the details and rounding off a few constants to more decimal places. I can think of few things more laughable and take it as a sure prediction of major revolutions in our thinking lying just around the corner. Demanding an explanation of something as complex as life at our current state of knowledge is probably as unrealistic as expecting a medieval artisan to make sense of electronics. Whatever the shorter-term inconveniences, it seems to me that science would benefit in the long run by being candid and saying, when appropriate, "We don't know." For one thing, it would regain a lot of the respect and credibility that science has been losing in some quarters. But more importantly, it would acknowledge that there are more fascinating and exciting things to be learned yet than we have begun even to scratch the surface of, perhaps flying beyond our wildest imaginings. And at times like this, with the dreary environmentalist myths that people are being force-fed via the schools and the media, that wouldn't be at all a bad thing to be reminded of, either.

Zap Thy Neighbor

Mervyn Taub, editor-in-chief of the *San Francisco Daily Clamor*, turned his broad but gangling six-foot frame back from the window of his office overlooking the intersection of Geary and Market Streets, and nodded a balding dome fringed by mutinous tufts of red hair above the ears.

"Intolerance!" he pronounced sonorously, making it sound like a revelation of the final secret that the universe had guarded obstinately to the end. "That's what's at the bottom of every problem left in the world. Nobody's hungry these days; everyone has somewhere to live; there's plenty of affordable everything. Science has solved all that it can solve. The problems left now are all social. And I just wanted you to know, Gary, that I'm proud to have somebody on the staff of this paper who not only has the guts to tell the biggest of them like it is, but names the names of the worst offenders too. This could do a lot for your promotion prospects."

Gary Summers was due to die sometime that day, and hence found it difficult to work up a lot of enthusiasm. Merv had a tendency to get carried away at times, and without meaning to seem insensitive could overlook things like that.

Taub raised a copy of the morning issue of the *Clamor*, folded back at an inside page to reveal an article with the head: A°°HOLES I DON'T NEED IN MY LIFE: *Some People That It Would Be Nice to Start a Day Without*, over Gary Summers's byline.

"Intolerant people," he went on. "The ones who find it impossible to leave everyone else alone to just be what they want. They're the ones who are screwing everything up for the rest of us." Taub raised a finger for a moment, posing as if addressing a shareholders' meeting or a political campaign rally. "And I agree we've put up with them for long enough! It's time we made it plain that we're not going to let them get away with it any longer. This article of yours could be the beginning of a general tightening up of permissiveness to this kind of thing that's long overdue. I had a thought this morning that the *Clamor* could launch a public-awareness campaign based on the theme. What do you think, Gary? How about 'HELP STAMP OUT INTOLERANCE' as a bumper sticker?"

For a moment Summers thought he could feel himself pitching forward out of the chair right then, but it was illusory, probably caused by autosuggestion. The official descriptions said that deactivation happened too instantaneously for any impression to register at all—and was perfectly painless. His still-dazed non-sequitur of an answer was because he had not been really listening.

"It was never supposed to be serious. . . . Casey and I were out hitting the bars, and we had a couple too many. We only sent it in as a gag . . . but Casey appended the wrong destination code. It got slotted into "Night Priority, Immediate," instead of being held under "File Editorial." When I got here this morning it was already out. . . ."

The intercom on Taub's desk buzzed before Summers could ramble further. Taub moved from the window and flipped a switch. "Yes, what is it?"

The voice of Emily, his secretary, answered from the outer office. "Just a reminder that you've got lunch fixed with Morton Leland. Reception have just been through. He's here now and on his way up."

"Oh, right, I'd forgotten about that. Thanks, Emily. Gary and I are just about through." Taub looked across at Summers, showed his palms, and shrugged.

"I need to be getting along, anyway," Summers mumbled, straightening up in the chair and preparing to rise.

Morton Leland owned a left-liberal monthly magazine that held every evil to have been caused by capitalism, called for democracy within the ranks to choose military officers, and advocated world government as the solution to everything. The two men loathed one another's politics with a passion, invoked plagues and poxes upon the opposite house constantly—and had lunch together at least once a month.

Taub's face darkened as he flipped the intercom off. "The man's a public menace with that damn socialist rag of his," he muttered. "Give him his way, and half the country would be locked up in work camps for not agreeing with him. No concept of simply letting other people live how they want." He produced a pocket compad from his jacket and pointed at the red button set prominently in the lower right corner of the rectangular array below the miniature screen. "Do you know, Gary, there are days when some of the garbage that he publishes makes me so mad that for ten cents I could cheerfully punch his number in and . . ." He cut himself short, his face frozen in an awkward smile that was half grimace as he remembered that this was not the most tactful of subjects to be talking to Summers about today. An incoming call extricated him.

"Hello? Mervyn Taub here."

Summers began moving toward the door. "Well, I guess I'll be on my way, then."

"Owen! Say, what's up? Oh, excuse me just a second." Taub clapped a hand over the mouthpiece of the phone. "Hey, Gary, you didn't think I was just gonna let you walk off like that, did you? I mean, it's been a long time now." He shrugged apologetically. "I only wish there was something I could do, but you know how it is. . . . So, ah, well, all the best, eh?"

"Thanks." Summers opened the door to let himself out.

Taub returned his attention to the phone. "Hi, Owen. How are things? Got something for us? I was just thinking yesterday . . . Wait just another sec. Oh, Gary." Summers paused and looked back. "I hope you didn't take me too seriously a minute ago—you know, about Mort. The guy can be a bit trying at times, but we wouldn't wanna do anything really bad to the old buzzard. It was just a joke, understand?"

"That's okay," Summers said.

"And if you could get any outstanding expenses in—you know, just to leave things clean and tidy before . . . Well, I'd sure appreciate it."

"Yeah. Right."

"You still there, Owen? Okay, where were we? . . ."

Emily was gone from her desk when Summers emerged into the outer office, closing Taub's door behind him. He was halfway across the room when the scrawny, hook-nosed figure of Morton Leland appeared through the open doorway from the corridor. He had a bristly white beard, contrasting with florid, knobbly features, and was wearing a lightweight tan jacket with pink shirt and bootlace tie.

"Is Taub through there?" he asked Summers, indicating the closed door with a nod.

"Yes, but he's on a call right now."

"I was supposed to meet him for lunch."

"His secretary was here a moment ago. She can't have gone far. She'll be back shortly."

"Yes, I know Emily. . . ." Leland peered more closely. "I know you. You're Gary Summers, aren't you?"

"That's right."

"You wrote that piece this morning that said all the things we've been dying to read for years. Congratulations on your courage, my boy! Too bad you won't be around much longer to enjoy the praise that you've earned. But rest assured, there will be plenty of it—if that's any consolation." Leland moved a step closer. His voice fell and took on a harsher note. "The only one missing from it was that snake in there that you work for. Can't imagine how a person of your obvious intelligence ends up writing for a fascist propaganda swamp like this. Greed and corruption is all that the people who that man in there toadies to understand and worship. Give him his way, and half the country would be reduced to cheap labor for the industrial plantation." He pulled back a sleeve to uncover a communicator wristset. "Do you know, I must confess there have been days when for ten cents—"

The inner door opened, and Taub came out. His face creased like a rubber bendy-doll's into a smiling picture of bonhomie and delight. Leland's mouth split into a wide, toothy grin.

"*Mort*, you old son of a gun! How've you been keeping?" They shook hands vigorously.

"Not bad, Merv, not bad. And you're not looking too bad yourself. . . ."

Summers hesitated, but neither took any notice of him. He went out into the corridor and walked away toward the elevators.

The amazing thing was that it was almost lunchtime, and still, nothing had happened. Summers made a half-hearted attempt to finish a piece that he had been working on, but it was becoming increasingly difficult for him to concentrate, and he gave up. He retrieved his expense records with a view to clearing them as Taub had requested, but as he stared at the figures on the screen, a sudden upsurge of rebelliousness overcame him. "Screw 'em all," he muttered, and erased the whole file. He was still sitting and staring morosely at the wall of his work cubicle when a tone from the comterminal announced an incoming call.

The face that appeared on the screen was a man's, white-haired, heavy jowled, and twisted with suppressed fury. The eyes blazed righteousness that could be felt radiating from the phosphor. Summers recognized him as the Texas TV evangelist Elias Broad, "Sword of the Lord," whom Summers's article had described (actually in one of Casey's contributions) as showing ". . . the compassion of a Rottweiler and about as much considered reason as a feeding frenzy of barracudas."

A hand in the foreground brandished a Bay Area communications directory open at one of the "S" pages. Summers was unable to make out the print, but a bright red ring had been scrawled around what was euphemistically termed the "Remote Deactivation Code" listed against one of the entries, alongside the regular calling numbers. A finger of Broad's other hand pointed to the circled item, while his voice trumpeted from beyond.

"Don't start having any ideas about getting away with this, boy, because you're not. We've got your number right here! *Nobody* takes the name of this defender of the Lord in vain. I just wanted to see you sweat a little before the divine retribution." The page was whisked aside and replaced by Elias Broad's glowering visage once again, framed behind a giant-size finger wagging accusingly.

"You're gonna burn in hell before today's out, know that? The Lord talked to me this morning, and he wants me to tell you what he said. Said them things you wrote were mean and full of spite, and that doesn't incline him to feel very kindly about you at all. See, he really wants us all to be charitable the way the Book says, but you think that means being nice to people who don't see things the right way. The unforgiving must be taught a lesson, and I am the instrument of his vengeance." The finger disappeared, and Broad's face enlarged as he leaned forward. "Did you ever stand close to an open furnace? Can you feel them flames lickin' around you already, eh? Gonna burn today, hee-hee!"

Summers licked his lips dryly. "All I really said was that it's a good thing that human fathers don't treat their children the way the all-wise, all-merciful one does His. And I didn't even say it. I got it from Mark Twain."

Broad studied him calculatingly for a second. "The Lord also asked me to tell you that in his infinite forgiveness, he might be willing to arrange a half-off remission. One small check wired through to the account of my humble church today is all it needs. Minimum's a thousand."

Summers tossed his hands up hopelessly. "Where am I supposed to get a thousand bucks from, just like that? It's a lot of money."

"For fifty percent off eternity? It works out at nothing at all," Broad retorted. "Anyhow, it won't be any use where you're going."

"But I don't have any. I got divorced six months ago. She cleaned me out."

"Don't you have a house? All you have to do is tap on the equity a little."

"It's an apartment, rented—along with the furniture."

"Got no car? There's gotta be something you can put up as collateral."

"The bank owns my shirt already."

"How about insurance policies, credit-card limits?

The Catholics are pretty good with emergency loans if you can come up with a good line."

Summers blinked, wondering for a moment if he had missed something. "Well . . . if that's the case, how about your church? Couldn't we work out some kind of credit?"

Broad looked incredulous. "What do you think this is, a charity operation that I'm a-running? The Lord has entrusted me with his *business* here! And he's telling me right now that he'll give you until five o'clock to figure out something." The hand reappeared in the foreground, this time holding a portable communicator, with an index finger extended toward the red button. "Then it's curtains. Too bad you never learned goodwill and tolerance. We've got your number, boy. Have a nice day." The screen went blank.

Summers realized that he had broken out into a sweat. He brought up a hand and switched his own wristset to chronometer mode. The screen displayed 12:17. Even as he stared at them, the digits changed to 12:18. He had a feeling of time flying uncontrollably, like a smooth ice-slope rushing past beneath a falling mountaineer. Irresistibly, his eyes came to rest on the red button set prominently in the lower right corner of the rectangular array below the miniature screen and stared at it in fearful fascination. The answer was obvious. In all these years he had never considered such an option seriously, preferring—in what he now conceded readily to have been naive idealism—to believe that there had to be better ways of dealing with life's differences, which he would discover in the course of time with a little bit of work, and some patience and perseverance. But he hadn't made these insane rules of modern living. What choice was he left with?

He reached out and lifted the East Texas communications directory from one of the shelves beside the desk, opened it at the pages headed "BR," and began running a finger down the columns. He found the name halfway down the third page: BROAD, REVEREND ELIAS J.; *Church of the Golden Fleece,* Fort Worth, followed by a regular calling number and fax number. And there right after it, staring him in the face, was Broad's Remote Deactivation Code: XXX-7951-26995-43WV-7KW. All that Summers had to do was enter the RDC into his wristset—or any other personal communications device, press the red activation button, and follow with "YYY" when the screen requested confirmation. It really was a simple as that. And yet the enormity of even contemplating something so drastic overwhelmed him.

Well, actually, it wasn't quite as simple as that. As a safeguard against the whole thing getting out of hand, and to provide some curb over individual pettiness and impetuosity, the same RDC would need to be entered from at least five different personal-coded sources within a one-hour period to be effective. That meant that Summers would need to find allies, and that was generally no easy task. The ensuing tangles of suspicion and intrigue over who was secretly ganging up on whom tended to escalate into impossible complications, and the majority of people were—understandably—only too happy to stay clear of the whole business by attending to their own affairs and leaving others to theirs without censure or interference. It was different for somebody like Elias Broad, with a devoted band of followers marching in step for the cause. Summers had not missed the significance of his ". . . *we've* got your number . . ."

He was still staring at the directory and wondering whether to try it, and if so, whom to start with, when Casey came into the cubicle through the gap in the partition. "Say, Gary, you're still here! That's great. I was getting worried. Look, about that twenty I lent you last night. Do you think we could kinda . . . Well, you know, while you're still walking around. I mean, it's not as if it's gonna do you any good, having it in your pocket."

But Summers wasn't paying attention. Here, as if Providence were sending him a signal, was an obvious person to recruit if anyone was. He looked up at Casey with the intense, presageful expression of somebody about to bare his soul. Casey caught the vibe and frowned suspiciously.

"What?"

"I've never said this to anyone before, Casey. I've always been the kind of guy who tries to stay out of trouble—you know, mind my own business, let other people minds theirs, always look for friendly ways to sort out problems. But this thing this morning is something else. You can't just sit here and wait for it to happen. If they're not giving you any choice, then eventually you have to defend yourself. Know what I'm talking about?"

Casey looked at him uncertainly. "What do you mean?"

Summers gestured at the directory still lying open on his desk. "Elias Broad just called. He's mad as hell, got himself some co-sponsors, and they're going to key my number in at five o'clock. But that gives me an out, doesn't it, Casey? If I can get some seconders and go for him first. All we have to do is find three more—"

Casey stepped back and raised both hands in front of him protectively. "Now *wa-it* a minute, Gary. What's this 'we' I'm hearing all of a sudden? Not me. This is *your* show, pardner. I'm sitting this one out."

"How can you say that, Casey? I seem to remember you as having a lot to do with it last night. In fact, the worst parts about Broad were your doing in the first place. And who was the genius who appended the wrong destination code?"

Casey looked pained. "Believe me I sympathize, Gary. But it wouldn't do you any good. We pissed *everybody* off, man, not just born-again Broad. Even if you do zap him, you'll never work the whole list before one of the others gets you. My life's complicated enough already. I don't need freaks looking my number up all the way from here to New Jersey."

Summers sat back heavily in his chair and slammed the directory shut. "Well, thanks for being a pal when I needed it. I really feel sorry that you've got complications. If that's how it is, why don't you just go and take care of them, huh?"

"That's what I figured. Only I've got this lunch date with that blonde in Classifieds, but I'm a bit short." Casey grinned sheepishly, at least having the decency to look moderately embarrassed. "Er, do you think I could have that twenty . . . please?"

Two o'clock came, and Summers was suffering from nothing worse than strained nerves. After a lot of thought, he had come to the conclusion that there had to be more to remote "deactivation" than the public at large were aware of—some inner angle that only a privileged few knew about. Surely, he reasoned, the people who controlled the system wouldn't leave themselves as vulnerable as everyone else. If anyone could tell him how the system really worked, it would be his ex-brother-in-law, Ted, who worked for the Effectuations section of the Justice Department, which administered the system. They had gotten along well together through the years of Summers's marriage, played golf, gone fishing, and fixed cars together, and Ted accepted the eventual split affably and nonjudgmentally as being none of his business.

Summers found him in the photo lab in the basement of the Federal Regional Building, located in the Financial District, and explained his problem. He concluded:

"I just find it impossible to believe that there isn't a way out of this, Ted. Nobody who thought up an idea like this would turn it loose without taking some kind of insurance. It'd be like firing off germ bombs without a vaccine for your own side. I just can't see anyone doing it the way we're all told. There has to be more to the story."

Ted showed a pair of empty palms while shaking his thinning, moonlike head. "Believe me, Gary, I'd help you if I could. But honestly, there's nothing I can do. There aren't any exceptions. The device self-assembles from nano-components that enter the brain via blood vessels from mandatory food additives. It's smart enough to find the right, key neural nexus to build itself around, which it disrupts on receipt of its unique transmitted code. That's really about all I can tell you. For the details you'd need to talk to one of the techs, or maybe read up on it . . ." Ted reflected on that for a second and added as an afterthought, rubbing his nose with a knuckle, "but then, I guess you don't have that much time left for reading, eh?"

Summers slumped back in the chair despairingly. "I just can't believe this is happening. I mean, am I really that bad? I've never hurt anyone. Yet every-one I talk to acts like it's nothing. You'd think they'd at least try to sound as if they cared. Were people always this way?"

Ted took a pipe from his shirt pocket and began filling it from a tin tobacco box that he took from his desk nearby. "Oh, don't take it to heart, Gary. It's just a front they put up because they can't change anything. Would it make you feel better to know what a nicer place the world is generally these days? 'Deactivation' sounds so impersonal. We prefer, 'Tech-nologically Assisted Encouragement of Amiability and Courtesy.' Crazies were everywhere before RDCs were introduced: harassing people on the streets, closing down bookstores, dictating what movies you could watch, lobbying against everything, infesting City Hall, practically running the campuses. Now you don't hear from them so much—until somebody like you goes out asking for trouble." Ted struck a match, held it to the bowl of his pipe, and puffed several times. "I haven't seen the *Clamor* today. Out of curiosity, who else did you manage to upset apart from Elias Broad?"

Summers exhaled a weary sigh. "Oh . . . just about everyone there is: environmentalists, technarchs; anarchists, statists; lifers, choicers; militant gays, militant anti-gays . . . You name it." Ted groaned and shook his head. Summers tossed up his hands. "Casey and I did it as a catch-all. The ones who worry me the most are the psycho-feminists. I mean, to show that they're against racism and sexism they were telling women to punch in white-male RDCs at random, even before we wrote this. It beats me why I'm still sitting here talking to you, on account of them alone."

"Who did you name, specifically?" Ted asked, looking across the room. "Melda Grushenstein?"

As the leader of a strident new activist movement across the Bay in Berkeley that had been getting a lot of coverage recently, she was the obvious first guess. The group wanted physics to be formulated differently because they held that terms like "force," "action," "thrust," and "power" carried masculine aggressiveness connotations. Besides calling for a random RDC blitz, they also demanded penile muzzling for single males over the age of eighteen.

Summers nodded heavily. "I think we said that she and her bunch need to worry about harassment from men about as much as Dracula needs protection at a convention of hemophiliacs."

"Well, I think I can set your mind at rest on that score, anyway," Ted said. "Melda's car went off the freeway and hit the base of an overpass early this morning. She won't be punching in your number or anyone else's."

Summers stared at him in astonishment. "You're kidding!"

Ted shook his head. "It was on the news. She had a couple of her diesel dikes with her. The police figure that whichever one was driving must have had a coronary or something." His eyes had a strange, half-amused twinkle. "Maybe it's your lucky day, eh?"

Summers shrugged in a resigned way that said in the long run it wouldn't make any difference. "But that's only one of them, Ted. Then there's that neo-Nazi nut down in LA who calls himself Siegfried—the one who has morons in jackboots marching up and down, and says concentration camps should replace welfare."

Ted waved a hand dismissively. "Oh, he's making too many enemies all over the place. He won't last long."

"But he's sure-as-hell likely to last longer than *me*," Summers protested, jabbing a thumb at his own chest. "He's having another flag-waving rally this afternoon and says he's destined to follow in the steps of Hitler. We said we hope he does, and quick—all the way."

Ted sighed and puffed a cloud of smoke regretfully. "You're right. A guy like him isn't gonna just let something like that go by. They're all the same, these bigots: if you've seen one, you've seen 'em all. Gee, I only wish I could help ya." He pulled his pipe from his mouth and stared at it thoughtfully for a few seconds. Then he looked up. "I guess that means we won't be teeing off at eight on Saturday after all—and just when I was looking forward to trying out that new set of clubs, too. This has really messed up my weekend, Gary. I guess I'll just have to give Phil a call tonight and see how he's fixed."

Dr. Meckelberg was pale and thin-lipped, with an angular face that accentuated the bone lines, hair stacked in stiff gray waves, and intense, colorless eyes peering through steel-rimmed glasses. He had just finished seeing patients when Summers arrived at the Embarcadero Hospital, and as good luck would have it, had a few spare minutes to talk without an appointment. There was probably no hope of even preparing for surgery at such short notice, but it was now three-thirty and Summers was past being rational. It turned out, however, that no solution was to be found in that direction, anyway.

"Ziss question I haff been asked before, unt it iss der insurmountable obstacle zat you face, I'm afraid, Mr. Summers," Meckelberg told him across the desk of his office in the Neurology Department. "Der nanochip matrix forms itself inextricably into der interstices of der primary cerebral terminal ganglion. To take zem apart again, it vould be like separating ze vite parts out of der scrambled ekks unt leaving der yellow." He flashed a smile of silver-capped teeth, and the light glinted off his lenses. "Unt if ve try to remove all, you end up just ze same, anyvays."

Summers swallowed. "So, that's it? . . . There's nothing you can do?"

"*Nein*. Not possible, vat you ask. For you, all iss kaput."

"Oh." Summers stared numbly at the pen turning idly between the talon-like fingers above the desk.

Meckelberg tilted his head, pursed his lips for a moment, and shrugged. "Or maybe der luck today, you are haffing. Since ziss morning der Nazi in LA you are vorrying about, but him it iss who goes kaput."

Summers looked up with a start. "What do you mean, him? I don't understand."

Meckelberg looked surprised. "Ach so, you don't hear about it, *nein*?"

"Hear what? I don't know what you're talking about."

"Today, der marching rally mit der flags unt der

seig heils he vas supposed to be haffing, *ja?* I make der time between surgeries to vatch on der television, but all ve get is der ball-game from Chicago instead. Zen ve find Siegfried haff der stroke late ziss morning, unt iss rushed to der hospital. Vat happens to him aftervard, I don't know."

Summers was shaking his head disbelievingly. "Two in the same day? My luck doesn't work like that. This isn't real."

Meckelberg raised his voice to call through the open office door to the nurse outside. "Joyce, iss it true vat I say about der Nazi? Vat happens to him after zey take him avay? Do you hear any more vile I am operatink?"

Joyce appeared on the far side of the doorway. "Storm trooper Siegfried? He's out of it: DOA. I guess he made Valhalla."

Meckelberg spread his hands. "Him, it seems you do not need to vorry yourself over. Unt to show zat my sympathies are viss you, Mr. Summers, if you don't make it past tonight, zen I von't bill you for der consultation. Vat you zink? Iss a gutt deal zat I make for you, *ja?*"

Summers walked the streets back toward the offices of the *Daily Clamor* in a daze. First Grushenstein, then Siegfried. Coincidences like that didn't happen. Yet the clock outside the Bank of America HQ building read 4:07, and still nothing had happened to Summers.

Surely not.

Was it possible that it had really worked this way around all along? His mind boggled at the implications. . . . Or was he inventing the explanation in his mind through some instinctive defense mechanism, creating an illusion of hope where there was no hope? He didn't feel that he was any longer capable of judging. There was only one way to test it out. His pace quickened as he came onto Market Street and turned west.

He sat in his cubicle back on the third floor of the *Clamor* building, rubbing his moist palms on his thighs and vainly trying to coax some moisture into his mouth. The lines of text showing on the screen were just to make it look as if he were doing something—he hadn't even registered which file he had loaded. His eyes were fixed on the numbers showing in the time-of-day box at the end of the header line, in the top right-hand corner of the display.

4:56

He had never understood relativity—nor really thought about trying to, for physics was not his subject—but he knew it had something to do with time running at different speeds. How could anyone ever have believed that time always ran at the same speed? He remembered that when he was a boy, a whole morning seemed to last forever and what happened after lunch was another world away. As people got older, time ran faster until there was never enough of it to get anything finished anymore. Then, at times like this, it could stand still.

4:57

He was feeling nauseous. The phone rang. He lifted the receiver momentarily, then put it down again to cut the call. An old saying came to mind about watched pots never boiling. Seemingly, watched digits never changed, either.

Maybe it just took some people—depending on their circumstances, or just plain whether they thought about it enough—longer than others to figure the deactivation business out. Very likely, some people never did. So had Merv known all along? And Leland? Maybe, maybe not. There really wasn't any way to tell. Summers tried to ask himself how he would react—if it turned out he was right. Very probably, he'd just smile, make bad jokes, and keep it to himself too.

Then he realized with a start that despite the moment his mind had wandered, and the display was showing 4:59. His hands tightened on the armrests of his chair. The tensing of his jaw made his teeth ache.

4:59 . . . 5:00 . . .

His shirt was soaking, his breath coming in short gasps. Knots were tying themselves in his stomach. A miniature preview of eternity. Then:

5:01

He had resolved to allow five full minutes past the hour, but he could wait no longer. He picked up the phone and called the number in Fort Worth that he had already looked up.

A woman's voice answered, "Police Department."

"Emergency dispatcher, please."

With barely a delay, a man answered. "This is Emergency."

"Hello, look I hope this isn't an awkward time to be calling, but I have a question that's urgent. My name is Gary Summers. I'm with the *San Francisco Daily Clamor.* We have reason to believe that there may have been a recent incident involving the Reverend Elias Broad, who's well known in your city. Could you confirm if you've had any report, please?"

There was a short pause. Then the voice spoke again, sounding incredulous. "I don't believe this! Are they giving you guys crystal balls or something, out in California? We only got it ourselves less than a minute ago."

"Then you can confirm it's true? What are the details?"

"We don't know yet. Heart attack, something like that. The ambulance has only just left. It's on its way there now."

Summers almost dropped the phone in his excitement. "Let me try just one more hunch," he said. "By any chance, did you get any other calls at about the same time . . . several, maybe?"

"No, I can't say that we . . . Wait a second. What's going on over there? Well, I'll be darned! You're right—there's one coming in right now, from the other side of the city. . . . Now, would *you* mind telling *me* just what's going on around here?"

Summers was unable to stifle a guffaw of relief. "It doesn't matter. Just an item that I wanted to verify. I'm tying up an emergency line. You have a good evening, officer."

He hung up and looked around him, feeling the last shreds of tension falling away like dead leaves, and a swelling, intoxicating sense of well-being surging up inside to take its place. He sat back, thumped the rests of his chair repeatedly with both hands, leaned his head back, and sent a delirious, *"Yeeaaahhh!"* up to the ceiling. Then he sat forward to the phone once more, checked his personal directory, and called Ted's number.

"Photo Lab. Ted speaking."

"Hi, Ted. This is Gary."

"I was just leaving. What's up?"

"You were holding out on me. I think I've figured this thing out."

"You have, huh?" Ted didn't sound overly surprised. His voice fell to a confidential murmur. "Well, for Christ's sake don't go spreading it around. It works better than God ever did. The world's a much better place than it used to be."

"There's one thing I don't understand, though. It's the people who try to zap you who zap themselves. But how does the system know who they are? Their numbers aren't entered."

"It doesn't matter," Ted replied. "The numbers don't mean anything. If somebody presses a button for real, it simply fires any deactivator that's within a two-foot radius."

Summers frowned. "That could be a bit dangerous, though, Ted. I mean, what if somebody's just having a bad day. I almost tried going for Elias Broad myself earlier today—I might have done it, too, if I'd gotten some seconders."

"Did you try finding any?"

"Just one."

"Any luck?"

"Not really."

"See, people who don't want to do that to anybody stay around. That's why it's set up that way. But you'd still have been okay, even if you had found another four. The computer gives you three chances. Try it more times than that, and it decides you're a bad guy."

"Well, I just wanted to tell you not to bother calling Phil. I'll be there at eight sharp on Saturday. You'd better be in good form, Ted, because I'm feeling just great."

"Who are you trying to kid? I could lick you with a shovel."

"We'll see. Want to make it twenty?"

"Twenty. You're on."

"See you Saturday, Ted."

"Take care. And don't go upsetting any more people, okay?"

Summers was humming to himself as he walked along the sidewalk away from the office, when Casey caught up with him, ashen-faced and breathless, and grabbed him by the sleeve. "Gary, you've got to help me. I'm in trouble."

"Why, what's up?"

"That eco-freak woman who we said has got more boobs than IQ points—I just got a call from one of the believers. They've found out that I was the co-writer on it, and they're gonna do my number."

Summers fought hard to look concerned. "Gee,

that's too bad. I wish there was something I could do."

"You said it earlier today," Casey gibbered. "All we have to do is find three more people who—"

"Hey, now, *wa-it* a minute, Casey. How did you suddenly figure me into this? I'm doing okay as things are. Why rock the boat?"

"You don't seem to understand. This time tomorrow I might not be here."

"That's true." Summers looked contemplatively into the distance for a few seconds, as if weighing his options. "I guess you won't be dating the blonde in Classifieds, then. Want me to take care of it for you?"

Casey shook his head wildly. "Hey, I'm not hearing this. How long have we been buddies, Gary? And this is what I get? If things were the other way around, do you think . . ." His voice trailed away lamely.

"Yeah?" Summers challenged.

"Well, that was different. You're on borrowed time anyway."

Summers shook his head. "Sorry, no dice. I'm going for a beer. I'd ask you along, but if you're gonna just keep on about your problems all night, it'll spoil the evening. If I don't see you around, well . . . something else would have happened eventually, anyway."

"You can't do this, Gary. Okay, maybe I was a bit hasty this afternoon. But if it was the other way around, I'd give a guy a break. Do you think I'd . . ." Casey's voice faded in the crowded sidewalk behind as Summers strolled on his way, whistling silently to himself, enjoying the city and watching the evening diners, shoppers, and people just out on the town.

"Excuse me, *sir!*" the man coming out of a doorway exclaimed, smiling apologetically as he bumped an Oriental walking on the sidewalk.

"Thank you, ma'am," the black going into a restaurant acknowledged as the woman ahead of him waited, holding the door.

"You're welcome."

Farther along the street, two men arrived simultaneously at a waiting cab.

"Go ahead, please," one invited.

"I'm not in a hurry. You take it," the other insisted.

"Why don't we share?"

Ted was right. The world was a nicer place these days. Summers had never really noticed it before. And people seemed to enjoy it.

There were still those who would mess things up if given the chance, of course. But for some strange reason they were a lot fewer than they used to be, and they tended not to be around for very long.

It was a fine evening, with the air balmy and the sky clear. A good evening for a steak and a bottle of burgundy to wash it down, Summers thought. If he'd thought a bit quicker, he could probably have talked Casey into giving him the twenty back.

Ozone Politics:
They Call This Science?

> *Every age has its peculiar folly: some
> scheme, project, or phantasy into which it
> plunges, spurred on by the love of gain, the
> necessity of excitement, or the mere force
> of imitation.*
>
> —CHARLES MACKAY,
> "Extraordinary Popular Delusions and
> the Madness of Crowds," 1841.

Earlier centuries saw witch hunting hysteria, the
Crusades, gold stampedes, and the South Sea Bubble.
Periodically, it seems, societies are seized by collective delusions that take on lives of their own, where
all facts are swept aside that fail to conform to the
expectations of what has become a self-sustaining
reality. Today we have the environmentalist mania
reaching a crescendo over ozone.

Manmade chlorofluorocarbons, or CFCs, we're told,
are eating away the ozone layer that shields us from
ultraviolet radiation, and if we don't stop using them
now, deaths from skin cancer in the U.S. alone will
rise by hundreds of thousands in the next half century.

As a result, over 80 nations are about to railroad through legislation to ban one of most beneficial substances ever discovered, at a cost that the public doesn't seem to comprehend, but which will be staggering. It could mean having to replace virtually all of today's refrigeration and air conditioning equipment with more expensive types running on substitutes that are toxic, corrosive, flammable if sparked, less efficient, and generally reminiscent of the things that people heaved sighs of relief to get rid of in the 1930s.

And the domestic side will be only a small part. The food industry that we take for granted depends on refrigerated warehouses, trains, trucks, and ships. So do supplies of drugs, medicines, and blood from hospitals. Whole regions of the sunbelt states have prospered during the last forty years because of the better living and working environments made possible by air conditioning. And to developing nations that rely totally on modern food-preservation methods to support their populations, the effects will be devastating.

Now, I'd have to agree that the alternative of seeing the planet seared by lethal levels of radiation would make a pretty good justification for whatever drastic action is necessary to prevent it. The only problem is, there isn't one piece of solid, scientifically validated evidence to support the contention. The decisions being made are political, driven by media-friendly pressure groups wielding a power over public perceptions that is totally out of proportion to any scientific competence that they possess.

But when you ask the people who do have the competence to know, scientists who have specialized in the study of atmosphere and climate for years, a very different story emerges.

What they're saying, essentially, is that the whole notion of the ozone layer as something fixed and finite, to be eroded away at a faster or slower rate like shoe leather, is all wrong to begin with—it's simply not a depletable resource; that even if it were, the process by which CFCs are supposed to deplete it is highly speculative and has never actually been observed to take place; and even if it did, the effect would be trivial compared to what happens naturally. In short, there's no good reason for believing that human activity is having any significant effect at all.

To see why, let's start with the basics and take seashores as an analogy.

Waves breaking along the coastline continually generate a belt of surf. The surf decomposes again, back into the ocean from where it came. The two processes are linked: big waves on stormy days create more surf; the more surf there is to decay, the higher the rate at which it does so. The result is a balance between the rates of creation and destruction. Calmer days will see a general thinning of the surfline, and possibly "holes" in the more sheltered spots—but obviously the surf isn't something that can run out. Its supply is inexhaustible for as long as oceans and shores exist.

In the same kind of way, ozone is all the time being created in the upper atmosphere—by sunshine, out of oxygen. A normal molecule of oxygen gas consists of two oxygen atoms joined together. High-energy ultraviolet radiation, known as UV-C, can split one of these molecules apart (a process known as "photodissociation") into two free oxygen atoms. These can then attach to another molecule to form a three-atom species, which is ozone—produced mainly in the tropics above 30 kilometers altitude, where the ultraviolet flux is strongest. The ozone sinks and moves poleward to accumulate in lower-level reservoirs extending from 17 to 30 kilometers—the so-called ozone "layer."

Ozone is destroyed by chemical recombination back into normal oxygen, by reaction with nitrogen dioxide (produced by high-altitude cosmic rays), and also through ultraviolet dissociation by the same UV-C that creates ozone, and also by a less energetic band known as UV-B, which is not absorbed in the higher regions. Every dissociation of an oxygen or ozone molecule absorbs an incoming UV photon, and that is what gives this part of the atmosphere its ultraviolet screening ability.

Its height and thickness are not constant, but adjust automatically to accomodate variations in the incoming ultraviolet flux. When UV is stronger, it penetrates deeper before being absorbed; with weaker UV, penetration is less. Even if all the ozone were to suddenly vanish, there would still be 17 to 30 kilometers of hitherto untouched, oxygen-rich atmosphere below, that would become available as a resource for new ozone creation, and the entire screening mechanism would promptly regenerate. As Robert Pease, professor emeritus of physical climatology at the University of California, Riverside, says, "Ozone in the atmosphere is not in finite supply." In other words, as in the case of surf with oceans and shores, it is inexhaustible for as long as sunshine and air continue to exist.

If ozone were depleting, UV intensity at the Earth's surface would be increasing. In fact, actual measurements show that it has been *decreasing*—by as much as 8% in some places over the last decade.

Ordinarily, a scientific hypothesis that failed in its most elementary prediction would be dumped right there. But as Dr. Dixy Lee Ray, former governor of Washington state, chairman of the Atomic Energy Commission, and a scientist with the U.S. Bureau of Oceans and the University of Washington, put it when I asked where the depletion idea came from, "Scientists are capable of developing their own strange fixations, just like anyone else."

Even though the physics makes it difficult to see

how, the notion of something manmade destroying the ozone layer has always fascinated an apocalyptic few, who have been seeking possible candidates for over forty years. According to Hugh Ellsaesser, retired and now guest scientist at the Atmospheric and Geophysical Sciences Division of the Lawrence Livermore National Laboratory, "There has been a small but concerted program to build the possibility of man destroying the ozone layer into a dire threat requiring governmental controls since the time of CIAP." (Climatic Impact Assessment Program on the super sonic transport, conducted in the early '70s.)

In the 1950s it was A-bomb testing, in the '60s the SST, in '70s spacecraft launches and various chemicals from pesticides to fertilizers. All of these claims were later discredited, and for a while the controversy died out. Then, in 1985–1986, banner headlines blared that a huge ozone hole had been discovered in the Antarctic. This, it was proclaimed, at last confirmed the depletion threat, the latest version of which had been around for just under a decade.

In 1974, two chemists, Rowland and Molina, at the University of California, Irvine, hypothesized that ozone might be attacked by CFCs—which had come into widespread use during the previous twenty years. Basically, they suggested that the same chemical inertness that makes CFCs noncorrosive, nontoxic, and ideal as a refrigerant would enable them to diffuse intact to the upper atmosphere. There, they would be dissociated by high-energy ultraviolet and release free atoms of chlorine. Chlorine will combine with one of the three oxygen atoms of an ozone molecule to produce chlorine monoxide and a normal two-atom oxygen, thereby destroying the ozone molecule. The model becomes more insidious by postulating an additional chain of catalytic reactions via which the chlorine monoxide can be recycled back into free chlorine, hence evoking the specter of a single chlorine atom running amok in the stratosphere, gobbling up ozone molecules like Pac Man.

Scary, vivid, sensational: perfect for activists seeking a cause, politicians in need of visibility, just what the media revel in. Unfortunately, however, it doesn't fit with a few vital facts. And if you claim to be talking about science, that's kind of important.

First, CFCs don't rise in significant amounts to where they need to be for UV-C photons to break them up. Because ozone absorbs heat directly from the sun's rays, the stratosphere exhibits a reverse temperature structure, or thermal "inversion"—it gets warmer with altitude, rather than cooler. As Robert Pease points out, "This barrier greatly inhibits vertical air movements and the interchange of gases across the tropopause [the boundary between the lower atmosphere and the stratosphere], including CFCs. In the stratosphere, CFC gases decline rapidly and drop to only 2% of surface values by 30 kilometers of altitude. At the same time, less than 2% of the UV-C penetrates this deeply." Hence the number of CFC splittings is vastly lower than the original hypothesis assumes, for same reason that there aren't many marriages between Eskimos and Australian aborigines: the partners that need to come together don't mix very much.

For the UV photons that do make it, there are 136 million oxygen molecules for them to collide with for every CFC—and every such reaction will *create* ozone, not destroy it. So even if we allow the big CFC molecule three times the chance of a small oxygen molecule of being hit, then 45 million ozone molecules will still be created for every CFC molecule that's broken up. Hardly a convincing disaster scenario, is it?

Ah, but what about the catalytic effect, whereby one chlorine atom can eat up thousands of ozone molecules? Doesn't that change the picture?

Not really. The catalysis argument depends on encounters between chlorine monoxide and free oxygen atoms. But the chances are much higher that a wandering free oxygen atom will find a molecule of normal oxygen rather than one of chlorine monoxide. So once again, probability favors ozone creation over ozone destruction.

At least 192 chemical reactions occur between substances in the upper stratosphere, along with 48 different, identifiable photochemical processes, all linked through complex feedback mechanisms that are only partly understood. Selecting a few reactions brought about in a laboratory and claiming that this is what happens in the stratosphere (where it has never been measured) might be a way of getting to a predetermined conclusion. But it isn't science.

But surely it's been demonstrated! Hasn't 1000 times more chlorine been measured over the Antarctic than models say ought to be there?

Yes. High concentrations of *chlorine*—or to be exact, chlorine monoxide. But all chlorine atoms are identical. There is absolutely nothing to link the chlorine found over the Antarctic with CFCs from the other end of the world. What the purveyors of that story omitted to mention was that the measuring station at McMurdo Sound is located 15 kilometers downwind from Mount Erebus, an active volcano currently venting 100 to 200 tons of chlorine every day, and which in 1983 averaged 1000 tons per day. Mightn't that just have more to do with it than refrigerators in New York or air conditioners in Atlanta?

World CFC production is currently about 1.1 million tons annually, 750,000 tons of which is chlorine. Twenty times as much comes from the passive outgassing of volcanoes. This can rise by a factor of ten with a single large eruption—for example that of Tambora in 1815, which pumped a *minimum* of 211 million tons straight into the atmosphere. Where are the records of all the cataclysmic effects that should presumably have followed from the consequent ozone depletion?

And on an even greater scale, 300 million tons of chlorine are contained in spray blown off the oceans every year. A single thunderstorm in the Amazon region can transport 200 million tons of air per hour into the stratosphere, containing 3 million tons of water vapor. On average, 44,000 thunderstorms occur daily, mostly in the tropics. Even if we concede to the depletion theory and allow this mechanism to transport CFCs also, compared to what gets there naturally the whiff of chlorine produced by all of human industry (and we're only talking about the *leakage* from it, when all's said and done) is a snow-flake in a blizzard.

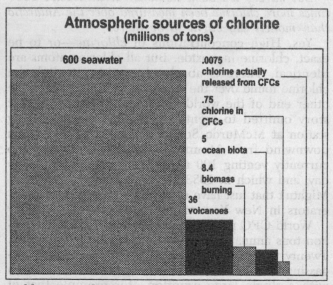

Chlorine in the atmosphere from natural processes compared to that contained in CFCs.

Despite all that, isn't it still true that a hole has appeared in the last ten years and is getting bigger? What about that, then?

In 1985 a sharp, unpredicted decline was reported in the mean depth of ozone over Halley Bay, Antarctica. Although the phenomenon was limited to altitudes between 12 and 23 kilometers and the interior of a seasonal circulation of the polar jet stream known as the "polar vortex," it was all that the ozone-doomsday pushers needed. Without waiting for any scientific evaluation or consensus, they decided that this was the confirmation that the Rowland-Molina conjecture had been waiting for. The ominous term "Ozone Hole" was coined by a media machine well rehearsed in environmentalist politics, and anything that the scientific community had to say has been drowned out in the furor that has been going on ever since.

Missing from the press and TV accounts, for instance, is that an unexpectedly low value in the Antarctic winter-spring ozone level was reported by the British scientist, Gordon Dobson, in 1956—when CFCs were barely in use. In a forty-year history of ozone research written in 1968, he notes: "One of the most interesting results . . . which came out of the IGY [International Geophysical Year] was the discovery of the peculiar annual variation of ozone at Halley Bay." His first thought was that the result might have been due to faulty equipment or operator error. But when such possibilities had been eliminated, and the same thing happened the following year, he concluded: "It was clear that the winter vortex over the South Pole was maintained late into the spring and that this kept the ozone values low. When it suddenly broke up in November both the ozone values and the stratosphere temperatures suddenly rose." A year after that, in 1958, a similar drop was reported by French scientists at the Antarctic observatory at Dumont d'Urville— larger than that causing all the hysteria today.

These measurements were on the edge of observational capability, especially in an environment such as the Antarctic, and most scientists regarded them with caution. After the 1985 "discovery," NASA reanalyzed their satellite data and found that they had been routinely throwing out low Antarctic ozone readings as "unreliable."

The real cause is slowly being unraveled, and while some correlation is evident with volcanic eruptions and sunspot cycles, the dominant factor appears to be the extreme Antarctic winter conditions, as Dobson originally suspected. The poleward transportation of ozone from its primary creation zones over the tropics does not penetrate into the winter vortex, where chemical depletion can't be replaced because of the lack of sunshine. Note that this is a localized minimum relative to the surrounding high-latitude reservoir regions, where global ozone is thickest. As Hugh Ellsaesser observes, "The ozone hole . . . leads only to spring values of ultraviolet flux over Antarctica a factor of two less than those experienced every summer in North Dakota."

But isn't it getting bigger every year? And aren't the latest readings showing ozone depletion elsewhere too?

In April, 1991, EPA Administrator William Reilly announced that the ozone layer over North America was thinning twice as fast as expected, and produced the figures for soaring deaths from skin cancer. This was based on readings from NASA's *Nimbus*-7 satellite. I talked to Dr. S. Fred Singer of the Washington-based Science and Environmental Policy Project, who developed the principle of UV backscatter that the ozone monitoring instrument aboard *Nimbus*-7 employs. "You simply cannot tell from one sunspot cycle," was his comment. "The data are too noisy. Scientists need at least one more cycle of satellite observations before they can establish a trend." In other words, the trend exists in the eye of the determined beholder, not in any facts that he beholds.

February this year saw a repeat performance when a NASA research aircraft detected high values of chlorine monoxide in the northern stratosphere. Not of CFCs; nor was there any evidence that ozone itself was actually being depleted. Nor any mention that the Pinatubo volcano was active at the time. Yet almost as if on cue, the U.S. Senate passed an amendment only two days later calling for an accelerated phaseout of CFCs. (It's interesting to note that NASA's budget was coming up for review at the time. After getting their increase they have since conceded that perhaps the fears were premature, and the Great American Ultraviolet Catastrophe isn't going to happen after all.)

But apart from all that, yes, world mean total ozone declined about five percent from 1979 to 1986. So what? From 1962 to 1979 it increased by five and a half percent. And since 1986 it has been increasing again (although that part is left out of the story that the public gets). On shorter timescales it changes naturally all the time and from place to place, hence surface ultraviolet intensity is not constant and never was. It varies with latitude, i.e. how far north or south from the equator you are, with the seasons, and with solar activity. And it does so in amounts that are far greater than those causing all the fuss.

The whole doomsday case boils down to claiming that if something isn't done to curb CFCs, ultraviolet radiation will increase by 10% over the next 20 years. But from the poles to the equator it increases naturally by a whopping factor of fifty, or 5000%, anyway!—equivalent to 1% for every six miles. Or to put it another way, a family moving house from New York to Philadelphia would experience the same increase as is predicted by the worst-case depletion scenarios. Alternatively, they could live 1500 feet higher in elevation—say, by moving to their summer cabin in the Catskills.

Superposed on this is a minimum 25% swing from summer to winter, and on top of that a 10 to 12 year pattern that follows the sunspot cycle. Finally there are irregular fluctuations caused by the effects of volcanic eruptions, electrical storms, and the like on atmospheric chemistry. Expecting to find some "natural" level, that shouldn't be deviated from, in all this is like trying to define sea level in a typhoon.

Skin cancer is increasing, nevertheless, though. Something must be causing it.

An increasing rate of UV-induced skin cancers means that more people are receiving more exposure than they ought to. It doesn't follow that the intensity of ultraviolet is increasing, as it would if ozone were being depleted (in fact it's decreasing, as we saw earlier). Other considerations explain the facts far better, such as that sun worship has become a fad among light-skinned people only in the last couple of generations; or the migrations in comparatively recent times of peoples into habitats for which they are not adapted, for instance the white population of Australia (Native Australians have experienced no skin cancer increase).

Deaths from drowning increase as you get nearer the equator—not because the water becomes more lethal, but because human behavior changes: not many people go swimming in the Arctic. Nevertheless, when it comes to skin cancer the National Academy of Sciences has decided that only variation of UV matters, and from the measured ozone thinning from poles to equator and the change in zenith angle of the sun, determined that a 1% decrease in ozone equates to a 2% rise in skin cancer.

How you make a disaster scenario out of this is to ignore the decline in surface UV actually measured over the last 15 years, ignore the reversal that shows ozone to have been increasing again since 1986, and extend the 1979-86 slope as if it were going to continue for the next forty years. Then, take the above formula as established fact and apply it to the entire U.S. population. Witness: According to the NAS report (1975), approximately 600,000 new cases of skin cancer occur annually. So, by the above, a 1% ozone decrease gives 12,000 more skin cancers. Projecting the 5% ozone swing from the early '80s through the next four decades gives 25%, hence a 50% rise in skin cancer, which works out at 300,000 new cases in the year 2030 AD, or 7.5 million over the full period. Since the mortality rate is around 2.5%, this gives the EPA's "200,000 extra deaths in the United States alone." *Voila:* instant catastrophe.

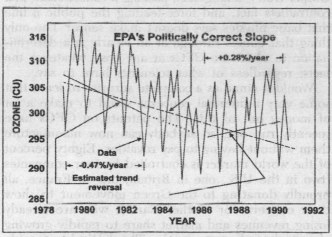

EPA's depletion trend as sold to the public, compared to what actually happens. The extrapolation ignores the obvious reversal following the solar minimum in 1985. Source: "Global average ozone change from November 1978 to May 1990," J.R. Herman and others, Journal of Geophysical Research.

As if this weren't flaky enough, it is known that the lethal variety of skin cancer has little to do with UV exposure, anyway. The cancers that *are* caused by radiation are recognizable by their correlation with latitude and length of exposure to the sun, and are relatively easily treated. The malignant melanoma form, which does kill, affects places like the soles of the feet and underarm as well as exposed areas, and there is more of it in Sweden than in Spain. It is increasing significantly, and as far as I'm aware the reasons why are not known.

So, what's going on? What are publicly funded institutions that claim to be speaking science doing, waving readings known to be worthless (Garbage In, Gospel Out?), faking data, pushing a cancer scare that contradicts fact, and force-feeding the public a line that basic physics says doesn't make sense? The only thing that comes through at all clearly is a determination to eliminate CFCs at any cost, whatever the facts, regardless of what scientists have to say.

Would it come as a complete surprise to learn that some very influential concerns stand to make a lot of money out of this? The patents on CFCs have recently run out, so anybody can now manufacture them without having to pay royalties. Eighty percent of the world market is controlled by four companies (two in the U.S., one in Britain, one in France, all proudly donating to the Green movement to show their concern for Mother Earth), who are already losing revenues and market share to rapidly growing chemicals industries in the Third World, notably Brazil, South Korea, and Taiwan. They also hold the patents on the only substitutes in sight, which will restore monopoly privileges once again if CFCs are outlawed. Mere coincidence? As Mark Twain said, "Maybe so. I dunno."

Ultraviolet light has many beneficial effects as well as detrimental. For all anyone knows, the increase that's being talked about could result in more over-all good than harm. But research proposals to explore that side of things are turned down, while doomsayers line up for grants running into hundreds of millions. UN departments that nobody ever heard of and activists with social-engineering ambitions could end up wielding the power of global police. The race is on between chemicals manufacturers to come up with a better CFC substitute, while equipment suppliers will be busy for years. Politicians are posturing as champions to save the world, and the media are having a ball.

As Bob Holzknecht, who runs an automobile air company in Florida, and who has been involved with the CFC industry for over twenty years observes, "Nobody's interested in reality. Everyone who knows anything stands to gain. The public will end up paying through the nose, as always, but the public is unor-ganized and uninformed."

Good science will be the victim too, of course. For a while, anyway. But science has a way of winning in the end. Today's superstitions can spread a million times faster than anything dreamed of by the doom prophets in days of old. But the same technologies which make that possible can prove equally effective in putting them speedily to rest, too.

The above article appeared in *Omni* magazine in June, 1993. When editor Keith Ferrell commissioned it, we agreed to stay out of the politics and focus on the scientific arguments as to why the ozone scare is flaky.

Since writing it, I've come across a number of references to medical studies indicating that the "sunblocks" that have become all the rage since the UV hysteria started might not be such a good idea. (I spend much of most years in Florida and wouldn't touch them.) The problem is that while the wavelengths that burn might be blocked out, clearly others get through—otherwise you wouldn't tan. It appears that it's the latter—the ones that the blocks let through—that cause the damage that leads to skin cancers. So the net effect is to switch off the body's warning mechanism while leaving the risk undiminished. No, worse than that—increasing the risk, since those signals that used to tell people to cover up and get in the shade for a day or two aren't being generated.

In days when people traveled slowly, they had weeks to adjust to varying climate, or months as the seasons progressed. Today, when I look out across a swimming pool or a beach and see all those white bodies fresh off planes, soaking up hundreds of times the UV that they're accustomed to, with their alarm systems blissfully deactivated, I wonder if we're not asking for an epidemic of chronic skin problems around twenty years from now. When it happens, what's the betting it will be blamed on the great ozone depletion in the eighties that was cured by banning CFCs?

Like the wagon trains mentioned in the earlier article on space, the trouble with federally imposed programs is that if they're wrong, the same mistakes get inflicted on everybody, very often with no other standard for comparison to indicate that a mistake has been made. I can think of few stronger arguments for insisting on local autonomy in formulating health care and similar policies. A country like the United States provides an ideal natural laboratory for leaving different authorities free to find out what works and what doesn't, automatically containing the damage from ill-conceived decisions.

The following article, which appeared in *Analog* in April 1995, talks about some other areas where it seems to me good science is being trampled by politics.

Fact-free Science

Beliefs don't have to be true to be effective. One result of government's influencing—either by direct funding with tax dollars, or through support of the institutions that in turn promote the research—what gets presented to the public as science, is conflict between the motives of those who call the tunes, and what science is supposed to be all about. Policymakers and the bureaucrats who serve them are interested in promoting beliefs that will advance their political agendas. What makes a belief acceptable are its perceived consequences. Science is concerned with what's true. Facts decide what is believed, and the consequences—good or bad, which is a separate issue—fall where they will.

At least, that's how it would work in an ideal world. But with who gets supported, and who does not, coming to depend more on official approval, what we seem to be getting instead is the unchallenged spread, as science, of politically correct dogmas that appear to fly in the face of a few elementary and readily verifiable, inconvenient facts.

Take, for instance, the commonly heard assertion that "no level of radiation is safe." In other words, any exposure to ionizing radiation, however small, is damaging to health. Yet at the levels encountered ordinarily—i.e. excluding bomb victims and patients subjected to massive medical doses, usually as a last resort in terminal situations—no conclusive results are actually observed at all. Low-level effects are inferred by taking a known high-level point where the effect is measurable, and assuming that it connects to the zero-point (zero dose, therefore zero effect) as a straight line. From this presumed relationship it is possible to read off as an act of faith the pro-rata effects that small doses ought to have, if one accepts the straight-line assumption. This is a bit like saying that since a temperature of 1000°C is lethal, 1 degree kills 1/1000th of a person, and therefore raising the temperatures of all the classrooms in American schools by two degrees will kill so-many million children. Yet this is just the kind of model that the figures the media are so fond of blaring are based on. Research that has been known to the health and radiation physics community for many years indicates, however, that it is wrong.

Trying to emulate the labors of Hercules would cause most of us to drop dead from exhaustion. Nevertheless, jogging a few miles a week makes lots of people feel good and keeps them in shape. A dip in the boilers of a power plant would be decidedly damaging to one's health, but soaking in a hot tub is relaxing. Things that get lethal when taken to extremes are often beneficial in small quantities.

This has long been acknowledged for chemical and biological toxins. Trace amounts of germicides can *increase* fermentation of bacteria. Too-small doses of antibiotics will stimulate growth of dormant bacteria that they are supposed to kill. A moderate amount of exercise keeps the immune system fit and in good tone, no less than muscles. The phenomenon is known as "hormesis," from the Greek *hormo*, meaning "to stimulate."

For over a decade, evidence has been mounting that hormesis holds true also for ionizing radiation. Not that sunbathing during a nuclear strike is good for you; but low levels aren't as bad as many would have us believe.

In the early eighties, Professor T.D. Luckey, a biochemist at the University of Missouri, published a study[1] of over 1200 experiments dating back to the turn of the century on the effects of low-level radiation on biota ranging from viruses, bacteria, and fungi through various plants and animals up to vertebrates. He found that, by all the criteria normally used to judge the well-being of living things, modest increases above the natural background make life better: they grow bigger and faster; they live longer; they get sick less often and recover sooner; they produce more offspring, more of which survive.

And the same appears to be true also of humans[2,3,5]. The state that the EPA found as having the highest average level of radon in the home, Iowa, also has below-average cancer incidence.[4] The mountain states, with double the radiation background of the U.S. as a whole (cosmic rays are stronger at higher altitudes, and the rocks in those states have a high radioactive content), show a cancer rate way below Iowa's. The negative correlation—more radiation, less cancer—holds for the U.S. in general and extends worldwide.[5] The waters of such European spas as Lourdes, Bath, and Bad Gastein, known for their beneficial health effects since Roman times, are all found to have high radioactivity levels. British data on over 10,000 UK Atomic Energy Authority workers show cancer mortality to be 22% below the national average, while for Canada the figure is 33%[6]. (Imagine the hysteria if those numbers happened to be the other way around.)

This state of affairs is represented not by a straight line, but by a *J*-shaped curve sloping upward to the right. Dose increases to the right; the damage that results is measured vertically. The leftmost tip of the J represents the point of no dose/no effect. ("No dose" means nothing above background. There's some natural background everywhere. You can't get away from it.) At first the curve goes down, meaning that the "damage" is negative, which is what we've been saying. It reaches an optimum at the bottom, and then turns upward—we're still better off than with no dose at all, but the beneficial effect is lessening. It disappears where the curve crosses its starting level again, and beyond that we experience progressively greater discomfort, distress, and, eventually, death.

So what optimum dose should our local health-food store recommend? Recent work reported from Japan[7] puts it roughly at two thousandths of a "rem," or two "millirems," per day. That's about a tenth of a dental X-ray, or one coast-to-coast jet flight, or a year's worth of standing beside a nuclear plant. For comparison, the crossover where the net effect becomes harmful is at around two rems per day; 50 (note, we're talking rems now, not millirems) causes chronic radiation sickness, and 100 is lethal.

On this basis, if regulatory authorities set their exposure limits too low, i.e. to the left of where the J bottoms out, then reducing levels to comply with them can actually make things worse. In a study of homes across 1,729 U.S. counties [8], Bernard Cohen, professor of physics and radiation health at the University of Pittsburgh, has found a correlation between radon levels and lung cancer mortality almost as high as that for cigarette smoking. Except, it's in the opposite direction: As radon goes up, cancer goes down.

Perhaps tablets for those who don't get enough regular exposure wouldn't be a bad idea. Or a good way to use radioactive waste might be to bury it underneath radon-deficient homes. And perhaps cereal manufacturers should be required to state on their boxes the percentage of the daily dietary requirement that a portion of their product contributes. After all, if radiation is essential for health in minimum, regular amounts, it meets the accepted definition of a vitamin!

Another area in which what "everybody knows" to be true seems to be strangely out of kilter with a few basic facts is the controversy over ozone. The June 1993 issue of *Omni* carried an article of mine on the subject, in which I said that the bottom-line test, after all the modeling and involved arguments over atmospheric chemistry were said and done with, was the ultraviolet light reaching the Earth's surface. If stratospheric ozone were under relentless chemical attack in the way that we're told, the measured UV ought to be increasing. People who have measured it say it isn't.

In 1988, Joseph Scotto of the National Cancer Institute published data from eight U.S. ground stations showing that UV-B (the wavelength band affected by ozone) decreased by amounts ranging from 2 to 7 percent during the period 1974-1985[9]. A similar politically wrong trend was recorded over 15 years by the Fraunhofer Institute of Atmospheric Sciences in Bavaria, Germany[10].

The response? Scotto's study was ignored by the international news media. He was denied funding to attend international conferences to present his findings, and the ground stations were closed down. The costs of accepting the depletion theory as true will run into billions of dollars, but apparently we can't afford a few thousand to collect the data most fundamental to testing it. In Washington, scientists who objected were attacked by environmentalist pressure groups, and former Princeton physics professor William Happer, who opposed the present administration and wanted to set up an extended instrumentation

network, was dismissed from his post as research
director at the Department of Energy. The retiring
head of the German program was replaced by a
depletionist who refused to publish the institute's
accumulated data and terminated further measurements, apparently on the grounds that future policy
would be to rely on computer models instead[11].
(Garbage In, Gospel Out?)

Critics jeered, and the depletion lobby was not
happy. Then, after a lengthy silence, a paper appeared
in *Science,* claiming that upward trends in UV-B had
been shown to be linked to ozone depletion[12]. So,
suddenly, all of the foregoing was wrong. The party
line had been right all along. Depletion was real after
all.

The study showed plots of ozone above Toronto
declining steadily through 1989-1993, and UV increasing in step over the same period. But Dr. Arthur
Robinson, a biochemist at the Oregon Institute for
Science and Medicine (a privately funded organization that accepts no public money), noticed something
curious: Although the whole point was supposed to
be the discovery of a correlation between decreasing
ozone and increasing UV-B, nowhere in the study was
there a graph relating these two quantities one to the
other[13]. Neither were there any numbers that would
enable such a graph to be constructed. Robinson
enlarged the published plots and performed his own
analysis. And the reason why no consequential trend
line was shown, he discovered, was that there was no
trend.

For the first four years, the ozone and UV-B rose
and fell together: completely opposite to what the
paper claimed to show. The result wouldn't have
surprised depletion skeptics, however, who never
accepted that UV has to go up as ozone goes down,
in the first place. Rather, since UV creates ozone out
of oxygen in the upper atmosphere, more UV getting

through means that more ozone is being made up there. Hence, all else being equal, both quantities should change together with the seasonal variations and fluctuations of the sun. And the 1989-1992 pattern shows just that.

But all else isn't always equal. Ozone worldwide fell through the second half of 1992 to reach an extraordinarily low level in 1993. Satellite maps for this period show the diffusion through the stratosphere of huge plumes of sulfur dioxide from the Mt. Pinatubo volcano eruption in 1991. This would extend to global dimensions the depletion chemistry usually restricted to polar ice clouds (and responsible for the notorious Antarctic "hole"—replacement can't occur in the winter months because there's no sun).

So the low 1993 ozone was not caused by unusually low solar activity. Solar activity was normal, which of course gave above-normal UV intensity with the chemically thinned ozone cover. This one-time event was then stretched out to create an illusory trend beginning in 1989. In fact, it was produced from just four high readings out of more than 300 data points[14].

Logically, this would be like proving to the landlord that there's damp rising in the house by waiting for a flood and then averaging the effect back over four years. If the lawyers catch onto this one, it could open up a whole new world of liability actions.

People once thought that the skies turned about them. Then, early astronomers noticed that the "planets" (Greek: "wanderer") moved against the background of stars, sometimes pulling ahead of the herd, sometimes falling behind. They accounted for these anomalies by superposing smaller circles, or "epicycles," on the main circles. More accurate observations added epicycles to the epicycles, until by the Middle Ages the motions had become so complicated that no law of forces devisable by the human mind could accommodate them. The system could explain anything, but only after the facts were known. Then Copernicus put the sun in the center, and suddenly all was simple. Kepler and Newton took it from there, and the predictive science of modern astronomy quickly followed.

The HIV virus must be one of the most bewildering objects to challenge comprehension. And that's odd in itself, for as biological entities go, viruses are rather simple.

In the early eighties, clusters of certain known diseases were appearing with above-average incidence. For reasons that remain obscure it was decided that they were all due to a breakdown of the immune system, although only about 60% would normally be thought of as involving immunosuppression. Viruses were much in vogue at the time, which immediately prompted searches in that direction for a cause. In 1984 the Health and Human Services secretary announced that HIV had been identified as the AIDS virus, and promised a vaccine within two years. Viral diseases are infectious, and with no countermeasures available, a sexually transmitted epidemic "exploding" through the population at large was direly predicted.

But the epidemic didn't happen. AIDS diseases remained overwhelmingly confined to the same, readily identifiable, behavior-related risk groups, and within those groups over 90% of the victims were male[15,16]. That isn't the pattern of infectious diseases, which spread and tend to be distributed equally. But instead of questioning the theory, the official response was a redefinition of AIDS to cover more previously known diseases; hence, what wasn't AIDS one day became AIDS the next, causing bigger numbers to be diagnosed. This happened five times from 1982 to 1993. As a result, the first nine months of 1993 showed as a 5% rise what would otherwise (i.e. by the 1992 definition) have been a 33% drop[17]. One of the new categories was cervical cancer—so now women were affected more equally too.

Viruses make you sick by killing cells. Flu infects 30% of the lung cells, and hepatitis almost every cell of the liver. Yet with even terminal AIDS patients, only 1 in 1000, on average, of the immune system's T-cells show HIV. In fact, HIV is so difficult to find that the "AIDS test" doesn't test for the virus at all, but for the antibody. So "HIV positive" really means HIV-immune. This turns nearly two hundred years of medicine on its head. For any other disease, presence of the antibody is taken as indicating that the body has acquired resistance, not that it is susceptible and requires preemptive treatment.

To explain this, it was postulated that HIV doesn't kill T-cells directly, but by somehow tricking the immune system into attacking itself. But tens of thousands of HIV positives continued walking around quite healthily. Why weren't *their* immune systems committing hari kiri? Ah, yes, well . . .

Because HIV on its own isn't enough. It requires an unspecified "cofactor," you see. Or maybe cofactors. Others decided that it was a "slow" virus with a ten-month latency, which was why the expected epidemic was being slow. But no other virus works that way. Infectious agents reproduce if they get a hold, and take effect within days or weeks. Sickness after long latencies is characteristic of the cumulative buildup of a toxin. When the ten month prediction didn't happen either, its proponents changed it to five years. Five years went by and the world didn't end, so they upped it to ten.

Then it was admitted that not only could you have HIV without getting AIDS, but thousands of cases existed of AIDS with no HIV—surely making it the most extraordinary causative agent ever discovered. Nobody ever heard of polio without polio viruses. The self-contradiction was conjured away by giving it a different name and claiming that it doesn't happen. So now, if you have all the symptoms that would qualify unhesitatingly as AIDS if you checked HIV positive, but as it happens you don't, then you're suffering from idiopathic-CD4-lymphocytopenia, which is obscurese for HIV-free AIDS.

Currently, two billion dollars per year are being spent to unravel the paradox of how the HIV antibody fails to confer immunity while neutralizing the virus; no mechanism has been found for how HIV kills T-cells; and no vaccine is in sight. The viricentric theory fails every prediction, and always another epicycle is added to explain why. But the "paradoxes" disappear if Peter Duesberg has been right all along, and HIV doesn't cause AIDS at all[18].

Professor Duesberg, of the Department of Molecular & Cell Biology, U.C. Berkeley, has been saying since the mid-eighties that not only is AIDS nonviral, it's not even infectious. Drugs, behavior, and other environmental factors, he maintains, are what is ruining the victims' immune systems. Like virtually all other "retroviruses," HIV is a harmless passenger that can be passed around and become a marker of a risk group, but it's not responsible for the group's health problems. This has not made Duesberg popular with the establishment. He has been vilified, lost his funding, and been denied publication and even the right of reply. Some refuse to consider his arguments because they find the social consequences unacceptable—as if that could change a scientific truth.

He's usually described as a rebel, but really his position is classically conservative: like Copernicus, making the simplest interpretation of what the facts seem to say. Or perhaps Giordano Bruno, who dared make pretty much the same case while it was still politically incorrect. Today, it's Copernicus who is most remembered. Bruno was burned at the stake.

These days, we've done away with racks and stakes,

at least. But the mentalities who would bring them back again still seem to be around. Some scientists that I talk to tell me that almost everyone in the business is running scared at the prospect of funding being cut off in response to some politically inadmissible statement, or a career being otherwise jeopardized. Dissenters are refused even the most basic funds to test their theories, while conformists to the party line are rewarded with millions, which makes it very easy to sell out and lose sight of objectivity. In the opinion of some, science would be better in the long run if all government support were ended except for research essential to national defense. As Mark Twain once said, maybe so, I dunno.

But it doesn't sound much like the way science was supposed to be.

REFERENCES

(1) T.D. Luckey, *Hormesis With Ionizing Radiation*, (222 pp.) CRC Publishing Co., Boca Raton, FL., 1980.

(2) T.D. Luckey, letter to *Nuclear News*, December, 1981.

(3) J. Fremlin, "Radiation Hormesis," *The Atom* (London), April, 1989.

(4) EPA statement dated October 15, 1989, reported in *Access to Energy*, December, 1989 (Box 1250, Cave Junction, OR 97523).

(5) T.D. Luckey, *Radiation Hormesis*, (306 pp.) CRC Publishing, December, 1992.

(6) *Nuclear Issues*, vol 15, no. 12 (1993), pp 2-3.

(7) K. Sakamoto, reported by T.D. Luckey, *Health Physics Society's Newsletter*, May, 1991.

(8) B.L. Cohen, *Health Physics*, vol 57, p. 897 (1989).

(9) Joseph Scotto et al. "Biologically Effective Ultraviolet Radiation: Surface Measurements in the

United States, 1974-1985," *Science,* Vol 239 (Feb 12) pp. 762-764.

(10) Stuart A. Penkett, "Ultraviolet Levels Down, Not Up," *Nature,* Vol 341 (Sep 28, 1989), pp.282-284.

(11) Rogelio A. Maduro & Ralf Schaurhammer, *The Holes in the Ozone Scare,* (345pp.) 21st Century Science Associates, 1992 (P.O. Box 16285, Washington, D.C., 20041).

(12) James Kerr & Thomas McElroy, "Evidence for Large Upward Trends of Ultraviolet-B Radiation Linked to Ozone Depletion," *Science,* November, 1993.

(13) A. Robinson, *Access to Energy,* January, 1994.

(14) S. Fred Singer, "Shaky Science Scarier than Ozone Fiction," *Insight,* March 28, 1994, pp. 31-34.

(15) World Health Organization, 1992, WHO Report No. 32: *AIDS Surveillance in Europe (Situation by 31st December, 1991).*

(16) Centers for Disease Control, 1992, *HIV/AIDS Surveillance, Year-end edition.* U.S. Department of Health & Human Services, Atlanta, Ga.

(17) Robert Root-Bernstein, "Good (Hidden) News About the AIDS Epidemic," *Wall Street Journal,* December 2, 1993.

(18) For a full discussion of Duesberg's case and his response to the various claims cited abnove, see P. H. Duesberg, "AIDS Aquired by Drug Consumption and Other Noncontagious Risk Factors," *Pharmac. Ther.* Vol. 55, pp. 201-277, 1992.

Out of Time

1

Beep ... Beep ... Beep ... Beep ... Beep ...
"All right, goddammit."

Beep ... Beep ... Beep ... The infuriating electronic yelps continued relentlessly. Joe Kopeksky groped in the darkness and stabbed a button at random among the mess of incomprehensibility that the Malaysian instruction leaflet said was the digital calculator/clock/radio/tape-player/coffee-maker's "Control Functionality Console." A girl screaming adenoid problems as she drowned in a torrent of hard-rock pounding added to the din, tearing away the last shreds of sleep. Kopeksky pressed another button, any button. Merciful silence.

Technology's answer to the hysterical, yappy dog, he reflected sourly. The chill of mid-November in New York seeping in from the streets outside touched his face. There was something unnatural about having to get up on mornings like this—why else would people need to invent gadgets to make them do it? Kopeksky had a theory that people were like pizzas. Ovens were supposed to be preheated before you put the pizza in. It should be the same with days. Days ought to be preheated before people walked out into them.

Beep . . . Beep . . . Beep. . . .

"Hi to any listeners out there that we might be getting through to, who are wondering if there's any let-up in sight to the crazy things that have been happening all over the city for the last few—"

Hiss, squelch, bubble-bubble . . .

Snarling, Kopeksky swung his legs out of the bed and sat up, knocking over the bedside lamp as he fumbled for the switch, and quietened the beeping, babbling, digital ensemble with a savage swipe at the thoughtfully provided panic button that turned everything off.

Peace, once again. The apartment greeted him familiarly as he had left it, like a dog that had lain without moving all night: single bedroom; lounge with kitchen/dining area; bathroom/shower off the tiny hall inside the front door; den with overfilled shelves of books, files, boxes relating to cases he was working on, and hand-scrawled charts and reminders on the few empty spaces of wall. Kopeksky had a habit of turning information into charts. You could add new information just where it belonged and see how it related to the rest—like having the map of a city instead of having to memorize directions.

All in all, not as much as some had to show after fifty-three years of fighting the terminal disease known as life, he thought to himself, looking around and yawning. But not bad at five-fifty a month in the West Side upper forties; and it was clean and more-or-less orderly in a lazy kind of way that focused on essentials without worrying too much about making impressions. A lot like Kopeksky's thinking.

Now that he was awake, he regretted having cut off the radio announcer so abruptly. The strange disruptions of time that had been affecting New York for days were affecting transmission frequencies, causing

havoc with radio and TV reception. He checked the
time being shown by the digital chronometer on his
wrist, with its innumerable other arcane functions that
he had given up bothering with. *Tuesday, November
14*, the calendar part of the readout said. *7:12 A.M.*
Or was it? The display on the now-sulkily-silent bedside Wurlitzer said 7:09. He checked with the silver-
plated windup pocket watch that he had placed beside
the lamp on going to bed. It was a memento from
his father, and his father's father before that, which
he had retrieved from a lower drawer in the bedroom
chest and taken to carrying with him in the last few
days as a last attempt to preserve some datum of reference. Its hands were reading, clearly and incontest-
ably, with the solid assurance of the age from which
it had come: 7:19. Kopeksky sighed, shook his head,
heaved the two hundred pounds that he kept saying
he'd have to do something about getting into better
shape some day reluctantly to its feet, and headed
through to the lounge.

In normal circumstances he thought he was more-
or-less orderly. But Japlin's report, which he had
brought home from the City Bureau of Criminal
Investigation to read the night before, was still
untouched by the armchair where he had left it, and
the phone and utility bills stood unopened in the rack
on the table. And when he ate in, he never left the
dishes until next morning like this, he reflected as
he set up the coffee maker (old fashioned, low-tech
kind, with one on-off switch and a red light to tell
you which position it was at).

This time-glitch business was affecting everything.
There used to be time enough to get things done.
Now, what in hell was happening to it? Clocks all over
the city running at different rates. He'd never heard
the like of it. Nothing made any sense.

He tried the TV for an update on the latest situation, but was unable to get any channel. Then he

called the Bureau, and, surprisingly, got through on the third attempt. Mike Quinn was on duty in the Day Room that morning.

"Mike, Joe Kopeksky. How's it going?"

"How long do you have, Joe? Hysteria City. It's the usual."

"Got anything for me?"

"Ellis wants you in a meeting at nine sharp, whatever that means. He's got a visitor coming—Doctor Grauss, from out of town. That's all I know."

"What time do you have there, Mike."

"Clock on the wall here says . . . 7:11."

Kopeksky's digital wrist set was showing 7:19, which meant that the windup back in the bedroom would be at about 7:25. "Well, that gives me almost two hours. Time for another coffee, anyhow."

"Wouldn't be so sure," Quinn replied. "We've just heard it from the top floor that whatever else the rest of the city's doing, the Bureau is resetting to Washington EST at eight o'clock. And right now EST's running at seven twenty-five, which says you've got closer to an hour and a half."

Kopeksky sighed. "Okay, I'm on my way."

He hung up and went through to turn on the shower while the coffee was brewing. It was interesting to note that amid the chaos of different timekeeping devices getting out of synchrony all over the city, the one piece that agreed with the broadcast standard from Washington was his grandfather's old windup, with its snap case, Roman dial, and silver chain. That had to say something significant. Just at this moment, though, Kopeksky had no idea what. After drying himself and dressing, he reset the digital chronometer to tally with the windup. Clocks ought to be made of clockwork, he told himself. That's what the word means.

2

Kopeksky was almost killed on Broadway by a horn-blaring Lincoln charging the line of crossing pedestrians, and again by a cab on Seventh. The sidewalks were practically as dangerous, with running, briefcase-flailing commuters and people rushing in and out of subway entrances, and every public phone booth seemed to be occupied by a yelling figure gesticulating wildly in the air. No two clocks that Kopeksky saw anywhere said the same thing. Sidewalk vendors were already selling watches hand carried from Grand Central and set to Grand Central time, which much of Midtown had apparently adopted as a standard. Kopeksky found it to be eleven minutes behind his windup, which, if nothing had changed since he talked to Quinn, was in step with the rest of the country's EST. Nope, he told himself as he hurried on. It wasn't going to be one of "those" days, after all. There had never been a day like this one was looking to be.

He reached headquarters by ten minutes before nine and stopped by at the Day Room to check on the latest. NBC had retuned a channel to a frequency that worked, and a group of Bureau people were taking in the news from a portable on Quinn's desk. Kopeksky helped himself to his second morning coffee from the pot on the corner table and moved over to join them. "What gives?" he asked.

"They've just given out a time check as 8:15," Alice, one of the records clerks, replied.

"The airports are closed," Quinn said without looking away from the screen. "Incoming traffic's screwed up trying to synch to the tower times and frequencies. It was still the other side of eight o'clock at JFK, just a few minutes ago." He shook his head. "Oh man, oh man. This is wild, wild, wild."

Kopeksky listened to the newscaster. Apparently the retuned channel was being picked up in a few places around the city, but that was by no means true universally. "But I assure you that we're working on it, folks. The latest opinion from our experts here is that it's probably a glitch in the computers somewhere." Kopeksky felt the same kind of reassurance that he did when he listened to TV evangelists or presidential candidates. He took another mouthful of coffee, turned away, and left to make his way up to Ellis's office on the fifteenth floor.

Ellis Wade had arrived steerage through the ranks, not first class, courtesy of any social connections or college degree, which put him at odds with the Bureau's new management style and image. His natural taciturn and laconic disposition did not effectively project the new-age analytical openness that the PR firm hired from Madison Avenue had decided was appropriate to business-school forensics and computer-aided impartiality, and their efforts to enlighten him only deepened the cynicism and suspicion that made him the kind of chief that Kopeksky could live with. The same qualities also made him the only kind of chief that could live with Kopeksky. He was short, but broad and solidly built, with straight, close-cropped, steel-gray hair, tanned and fleshy, heavy-jowled features, and a bear-trap mouth that writhed, pursed, stretched, and compressed itself ceaselessly when he wasn't talking—which was most of the time.

The man sitting to one side of Wade's desk when Kopeksky entered and hung his hat on the stand inside the door at once put Kopeksky in mind of his schoolboy imaginings of a Martian: small, but with a disproportionately large and rounded cranium, mildly pink and almost bald, and peering intently through circular lenses that magnified his ocular movements into erratic sweeping motions that suggested the data-input scannings of an intelligent, wide-eyed octopoid. He was wearing a heavy jacket of plain, light-blue tweed and a misshapen maroon tie.

Wade introduced him as Dr. Ernst Grauss, from the National Academy of Sciences, Washington, D.C.

"He's been sent to help people here look into this crazy business that's been going on with the clocks," Wade explained. "He deals in . . ." His voice trailed off as he realized that he didn't really know what Grauss dealt in.

"Der physics theoretical it iss, in vich I specialize," Grauss supplied, and by way of elaboration presented Kopeksky with a reprint of a scientific paper that he had authored, entitled *Higher Dimensional Unifications of Quantum Relativity*.

"A scientist," Wade offered, his tone conveying that the title meant as much to him as Kopeksky's expression was registering. Kopeksky sat down in the empty chair in front of the desk and stared back with an okay-let's-hear-it look.

Wade tossed out a hand indifferently to indicate the wall behind him, the rest of the building beyond, and the city outside that in general. "It's all a mess. First they told us it was just something affecting a few TV stations. Then people started getting time checks that didn't add up, so it was the phone company computers, too. Now nothing anywhere makes sense. I just came up from Communications. They're having trouble getting through to anybody by radio now. The latest is that JFK, La Guardia, and Newark have shut down operations. All their frequencies are out."

Kopeksky nodded. "I know. I heard on the way up."

The sounds of a door opening and closing came from the corridor outside, then hurrying footsteps accompanied by jabbering voices, fading rapidly. The phone range on Wade's desk. He picked it up irascibly. "Yeah, Wade? . . . I said I'd be busy. I'm busy. . . . It is, huh? Okay, fifteen minutes. . . . I just said, fifteen minutes." He hung up and looked back at Kopeksky.

"It's as if the time you thought you had suddenly isn't there any more. Nothing's getting done. Everything's a rush. Nobody's finishing anything."

"Tell me about it," Kopeksky muttered, crushing his empty paper cup in a palm.

Wade made a gesture that could have meant anything. "Well, here's something I bet you haven't thought of. Has it occurred to you that the reason why there suddenly doesn't seem to be enough time any more could be that someone, somewhere is stealing it?"

Kopeksky stopped in the act of pitching crumpled cup toward the trash bin and stared speechlessly. "Stealing it?" he repeated. "Someone is stealing time?" Wade nodded heavily, in a way that said it wasn't he who had dreamed this up, and then waved a hand in Grauss's direction. Evidently he himself had said all he was prepared to on the subject.

Grauss wiped his glasses on a pocket handkerchief, then replaced them and brought them to bear on Kopeksky as if making sure that he had his target clearly in the sights before beginning.

"Vor many years now, der scientific vorld hass perplexed itself been by der unpredictabilities unt strangenesses at . . ." he waved a hand in the air, searching for a word . . . "untermicroscopic, ja?—levels below der atomic—vich are called quantum uncertainty." He barely moved his mouth as he spoke, which with his accent caused his voice to come out as a hiss. "But ve find ven computing eigenfunction connectives across many complex planes, dat der solutions produce conjugate loci vich converge to yield definitions off orthogonal spaces. Unt der quantum reconciliations ve find at ze intersections, unt so obliges us to conclude dat der existence is real. So far is gutt, ja? . . ."

Kopeksky just stared, glassy eyed. "I think what he's trying to say is that the 'other dimensions' that people have been talking about for years really exist," Wade threw in. His tone made it clear that *he* wasn't saying so. He was just saying that whatever bunch Grauss was from were saying so. Wade's accountability ended right there.

"Ja, ja!" Grauss nodded several times, excitedly. "Ve haff der universe mitt other dimensions vat ve don't see, but vich can intersect along der complex vectorspaces. Unt vy not, ve ask ourselffs, cannot ziss other universe vich iss here but vat ve can't see, haff its own inhappitants too, who also master der sciences unt der physics, maybe more so zan ve do here?"

"Another guy from NAS called Langlon last night," Wade told Kopeksky. David Langlon was Wade's chief at the Bureau. "They've got a theory down there that we've somehow collided with aliens who exist in another dimension." Kopeksky nodded, having to his surprise extracted more-or-less that much himself. Wade shrugged. "The way it looks is that time has suddenly started disappearing from the New York area. So one thought is that these guys in the other dimension might be stealing it." Wade showed his palms in a gesture that said it made as much sense as anything else that had been going on lately. The phone rang again. Wade snatched it up, barked "Later," into it, and banged it back down.

Kopeksky jerked his head back at Grauss for some justification. The scientist went on, "Vy, in our vorld, ve spend der lifetimes vorking, vorking, always vorking? Iss to get rich unt make more der money, ja? Unt then, vat is it ve vant to do viss all der money? Ve vant it to spend vat little life iss left doing der things ve vanted ven ve vass younger peoples, unt never had der *time!* You see, dat iss vot ve really vant all along, not der moneys at all. Vat ve vant iss der *time.*" He spread his hand briefly, as if the rest should have been too obvious to need spelling out.

"But vy spend der lifetime chasing der money around unt around, vich you then haff to use to buy ze time? Iff you possess der capability unt der technology zat iss advanced enough, vy not you simply take der time direct?" Grauss looked from one to the other and concluded, "Unt ziss iss vat, dese aliens, ve conjecturize zey do."

Even after more years than he cared to remember of doing a job that he believed could leave no capacity remotely close to experiencing surprise any more, Kopeksky had to strain hard to keep his composure. Finally he looked back at Wade and protested, "What in hell does this have to do with us? We don't know anything about outer space dimensions and quantum . . . whatevers. It's for—"

Wade had expected it and cut him off with a wave. "I know, Joe, I know. But save it. It's not gonna do any good. The situation has been classified a national emergency, which means following up any line that might turn up a solution. It sounds strictly scientific to me too, but somebody somewhere has decided it qualifies as larceny, which also makes it a law-enforcement matter."

Kopeksky shook his head helplessly for a second before he could manage words. "Larceny? . . . Where are we supposed to look for the merchandise? Show me the list of it. I mean, what the hell kind of larceny is this? It's crazy."

"Well, of course it's crazy," Wade agreed. "Why else would the Bureau have gotten mixed up in it? Anyhow, that's your assignment: Find out who's stealing the stuff and what can be done about it. Okay? It's straight down the line from Langlon."

Kopeksky sat back heavily in the chair. "That's it? You're sure you don't want anything else? I mean, do you need it before lunch, or would afterward be okay?"

"For now, go and do some head-scratching and see

what kind of a strategy you can come up with. We'll get together and go over it this afternoon," Wade answered, unperturbed.

"But what kind of help can I expect to get on it?" Kopeksky demanded. "What kind of resources? Who are the contacts? Don't I even get some idea of that to take back to the office?"

Wade was looking at his watch. "Gee, is that the time already? Oh yeah, that's right. They reset to EST. I've got another appointment waiting already."

Grauss rose to his feet, revealing a gangling frame that seemed to be all limbs, giving Kopeksky the feeling that it might be about to come apart at the joints inside his clothes. "I must der train to Hartvord catch, unt den from zere fly der plane pack to Vashinkton," he announced. "A pleasure to be meetink you it hass peen, Mr. Kopinsky."

Wade spread his hands apologetically. "Sorry, Joe. It looks like there isn't time."

Deena Rosenberry, Kopeksky's junior partner, rummaged about in the confusion of billfold, checkbook, notes, envelopes, clippings, pens, and make-up paraphernalia filling the bulging purse that she always placed at arm's length on the floor by her desk, and which Kopeksky was certain contained everything she owned.

She was a good six inches taller than he, lean bodied and long limbed, and uncoordinated to the verge of creating a new art form. And yet, she was shapely of body and graced with potentially fine looks—if she'd only learn how to go the right way about helping them a little, and to pick the right clothes. The pointed chin, high cheekbones, and straight, narrow nose that was a shade too long made her face heart-shaped in front and interestingly angular from the side; but her hair, full-bodied and dark, was somehow always too stern when she tied it up, and fell all over the place in riotous disarray when she wore it loose. Today she had on a dark green skirt that was too old for her mid-thirties, with a mauve top that was too young, and a jacket that went with neither. The brown leather walking shoes were good quality, practical for her kind of work, eminently sensible for New York in winter—and should have been banned as an offense against public decency for any woman under forty-five.

Eventually she retrieved two laundry tickets from one of the purse's innumerable pockets and pouches, and transferred them to a pocket in her jacket. "A couple of sweaters that I meant to pick up on the way in, but I ran out of time," she explained. To anybody who wasn't used to her, it would have sounded as if she hadn't heard a word that Kopeksky had been saying. But then she went on with barely a pause to hint of any change of continuation, "It is November 14, right?"

"It was the last I heard . . . unless things have gotten really fouled up out there," Kopeksky replied from where he was sitting on the other side of the office that they shared three floors down from Wade's. He was sprawled back in his chair with his feet on the desk and hands propping his chin, contemplating his shoes. That was the other thing: her mind seemed to share her body's proclivity for doing several disconnected things at once—and somehow disentangling them all successfully in the end, no matter how disconcerting it was to anyone watching.

"I mean, it isn't April first or something," Deena said, pushing the purse back to its place. "This isn't somebody's idea of a crazy joke?"

"Oh, it's crazy all right. But that strudel wasn't joking. And maybe it's true. . . . What else has anyone got to explain what's going on out there, all over the city?"

Deena moved piles of files and typescripts to clear

some space amid the layers of documents that covered her desk like geological strata. Somehow, a page of notes on the story that Kopeksky had related, heavily underscored in places and adorned with query marks and aside thoughts captured in circles, had materialized in the midst of it all while the search for the laundry tickets was in progress.

"What did he mean by a technology that's advanced enough?" Deena asked, checking over what she had written. "Is he talking about these aliens having some kind of machine that sucks time out of our universe like . . . like a vacuum cleaner, and then spews it out in theirs—like a siphon or something?"

"You tell me."

"But if that's so, then what is anyone supposed to do? The way I remember it, the whole thing about other dimensions is that they're at right angles to everything you can think of, which means you can't even imagine them, let alone affect what happens in them."

"Well, they seem able to affect what happens with us," Kopeksky pointed out, "so why not the other way around?" He moved his feet off the desk, stretched himself back, and clasped his hands behind his head to stare up at the ceiling. "As if we didn't have it bad enough here already. People getting hernias and heart attacks chasing to airports to catch planes, and worrying about filing taxes on time. . . . I mean, who are these aliens? Do they live in fancy villas or something, get to watch a movie and finish the books they put down, play golf, take in a ball game, stop by at their friends', and still have plenty of time to go fishing with the grandchildren? Is that what they're at? . . . And doing it all on *our* time—time that they've stolen from us? Well, hell, I don't like it. There has to be something that someone can do."

"Like what?" Deena invited, and then went on without missing a beat, "Oh, yes. I've been trying a number all morning, and it's busy—I mean not right now, but all the time. Can you tell me if there's some kind of fault?" She was holding a memo pad and had picked up the phone.

"Well, let's take things right back to the beginning," Kopeksky said. "What do you do when you suspect that something is being stolen? You mark it somehow, okay? Or watch it, or maybe you set up a stakeout. . . ." He pulled a face. "Nah. Nothing like that's gonna work. How do you start?"

"Oh, really? . . . Them too, eh. So what do you have right now?" Deena scribbled something on a slip of paper. "Okay." She put down the phone and looked over at Kopeksky. "See, all those things depend on some kind of information getting back to you about the actions of whoever you're out to nail. But with what Grauss is talking about, there isn't any way that it can. What we've got is a communications problem." She indicated the piece of paper that she had written on and changed the subject like a stage impersonator switching hats. "It isn't just the phone company's time checks, either. The clock at the exchange I just talked to is at 10:14 right now. Calls have been coming through in what to them is less time than we're seeing, and that's why they're jammed."

Kopeksky looked at his old windup. It read 10:53. The digital watch that he had set to EST time at 7:25 when he talked to Quinn immediately after getting up was now three minutes behind at 10:50. Out of curiosity he called down to the Day Room to inquire if they still had the channel from NBC. They did. What time was NBC giving? 10:22. So the telephone exchange was eight minutes behind NBC, which was thirty-one minutes behind EST (assuming Kopeksky's windup was still reading EST), but the digital watch had dropped three minutes behind the windup since he synchronized them both early that morning. He noted the figures down, but didn't even try thinking about what they could mean.

"Well, if Ellis says it's an emergency and to try all approaches, why don't we try what the scientists down in Washington won't be trying?" Deena suggested. "If we're talking about contacting places that you can't normally contact, let's talk to some psychics."

"Psychics," Kopeksky repeated, looking at her. His tone asked why not the Tooth Fairy and the Easter Bunny, too, while they were at it?

"I know it's weird idea," Deena said, "but the whole thing is weird already. Besides, if there really is something to these aliens that Grauss is talking about, then maybe there's something to psychics too, after all." She shrugged. "Anyhow, we won't find out any other way. And it is somewhere to start. Got any better ideas?"

Kopeksky thought about it. "It might give us a new angle on what time is, if nothing else," he conceded finally. "Aren't they supposed to have oddball notions about things like that, as well as catching ghosts and talking to dead grandmothers?" He warmed more to the idea as he thought it over. "You could be right. Maybe that's what we need—some new angles on what time really is. What other kinds of people know anything about it? . . . Philosophers are into stuff like that, aren't they? Better put them down if we're talking about making a list of experts."

"Mathematicians," Deena said. "There must be dozens of them in the colleges and universities around the city."

"Astronomers," Kopeksky said. "That's an obvious one."

"Maybe a religious expert or two?" Deena suggested. "If we're looking for unusual angles. . . ."

Kopeksky gave a what-the-hell shrug and nodded. "Why not one of them Eastern Yogi-Bears? You know, the guys who stand on their heads and think about navels. Aren't they supposed to fly around in astral dimensions or something?" At that moment his phone rang. It was Ruth, Wade's secretary, letting him know that Wade had rushed off on something urgent and wouldn't be able to see him that afternoon.

"Looks like we've got the afternoon clear," Kopeksky told Deena as he replaced the receiver. "Okay, we'll spend the rest of today going through contact lists and making calls, and tomorrow we can start interviewing. First we need to start with some research. That's your department. Okay, let's get to it. There's work to do."

Deena surveyed the devastation of her workplace. "Joe, where does all this mess come from?" she sighed. "Eskimos may have a hundred different words for it, but I'm snowed. Where does the time go?"

Kopeksky shrugged and picked at a tooth with a thumbnail. "File a lost property report," he suggested.

3

By next morning, the various official measures that had been introduced to bring some order to the situation had shown mixed results, since nobody could agree whose official measures to go by. Government departments had been instructed to follow EST time as broadcast from Washington. But that was of little benefit, since after setting to the EST standard, offices in different places would then fall behind it at different rates, which in any case turned out not to be constant. Typically the lag was 14 minutes per (EST) hour at the Defense Department on Varick Street, 12 minutes at NASA on Broadway, 8 minutes at City Hall, and 7 minutes at the Justice Department. Meanwhile, NBC was sticking to a half-daily update schedule of its own that meant losing 3 hours out of every 12, but Grand Central Station had fallen into line with the power companies, who were having to run their generators faster to compensate for delivered frequencies falling by up to twenty percent. At JFK, the situation had improved overnight after the shutdown and reversion to caretaker operations only. Whereas the previous morning's chaos there had been caused by a time discrepancy of over thirty percent— one of the greatest measured anywhere—now it was less than ten.

At 11:45 sharp by his pocket windup, Joe Kopeksky arrived for his final appointment that morning at a converted Upper-East-Side block of pricey apartments on a corner overlooking the Park, that contained the town residence of Inigo, "The Extraordinary," Zama. Psychic, clairvoyant, medium, telepath, foreteller of the future, gazer across distance, and seer into realms unknown; the man for whom, the flap copy on the latest collection of his feats and revelations to hit the bestseller lists proclaimed, "the Universe holds no secrets."

"Where did you say you were from, Mr. Kopalsky?" he inquired as the woman who had answered the door showed his visitor in. It was a large, bay-fronted room with heavy drapes and leafy-embroidered furniture finished with tassels and raised cord welts. A white marble fireplace set between Ionic columns and surmounted by a huge, gilt-framed mirror divided the wall opposite the window. An oval mahogany table standing below a chandelier dominated the center of the room, and a marble-topped stand in the window bay supported a fish tank. On all sides were shelves and cabinets carrying a varied collection of books, antique European ornaments, and curios.

"It's Kopeksky," Kopeksky said. "City Bureau of Criminal Investigation. We talked on the phone yesterday. Today is Wednesday."

Zama had a balding head fringed by hair that was turning white, and a matching mustache that he curled at the ends and waxed, making him look like the Monopoly man without a hat. His eyes had an unnatural glint to them, due either to the unearthly powers that dwelt within or to reflectively tinted contacts, and he was wearing a silk robe carrying an elaborate oriental design of pointy leaves, birds, and dragons. He dismissed the secretary, whom he addressed as Sonia, and moved around the center table toward the open area before the fireplace, stopping on the way to gaze at the fish tank by the window. The fish swimming around looked to Kopeksky like gray cigars with rounded tails resembling duck's feet at one end, and gloomy faces trailing overgrown warts at the other.

"A species of catfish that inhabits muddy waters where the visibility is practically nonexistent," Zama commented. "Nevertheless, it manages to 'see' quite well by sensing changes that obstacles and other creatures produce in the electric field surrounding it. A perfectly natural phenomenon, but beyond the comprehension of other fish not equipped to share its abilities. An interesting analogy to the powers that lie beyond our own everyday human senses, wouldn't you agree?"

"Can they talk to pigeons?" Kopeksky asked.

Zama blinked. "I beg your pardon?"

"I'm interested in communicating with places that are out of this world. People tell me that's what you do."

"It is one of numerous fields that appear separate on this plane, but which stem from the same nexus of association manifolds in the higher ether," Zama said. "The kind of assistance that I normally offer to police departments is in locating missing persons or objects. The precedent is well established, you know."

"We're not exactly talking about persons or objects," Kopeksky started to explain; but as if not hearing, Zama steered him to the large table in the center of the room and picked up a silver chain of finely formed links, attached to a multi-faceted crystal sphere. The sphere was elongated on one side and tapered to a point, like a pendulum bob.

"This is a technique that extends back through adepts over many centuries," Zama said. "Science has never been able to explain it."

"That's great, and I'm sure there are guys in other departments who—"

"Do you have a dime and a penny?"

"A what?"

"Some loose change. I haven't dressed yet, and I'm not carrying any in my robe."

"Probably. Let me see. . . ." Kopeksky felt in his right-hand pants pocket and produced an assortment of coins. Zama selected a dime and a one-cent piece, and placed them on the table about eight inches apart.

"Every object possesses a characteristic aura, which is an induced disturbance of the permeative-vibrational field that flows everywhere from the galactic poles," he explained, suspending the chain above the dime. "An individual who is sensitive to the fluctuations unconsciously translates the received impressions into muscular actions, which the pendulum amplifies and makes visible." As Kopeksky watched, the crystal bob swung to and fro in a pattern that quickly became circular. "Note, clockwise: the signature of nickel and other silver metals," Zama said. Then he moved the pendulum over to the cent. "But cupric and ferrous alloys produce a linear response." The bob obliged by swinging backward and forward. "It is also effective in discriminating most other minerals, as well as colors, drugs, plants . . ."

"How about places?" Kopeksky said again.

"Ah, you mean spirit communications," Zama said, nodding. "You are in need of information from the deceased. Yes, I have some experience of that."

Kopeksky shook his head. "Dead guys don't have

anything to tell me. I'm talking about aliens in other dimensions."

Zama frowned for a moment and turned away from the table. "Please understand that my work demands a broader terminology than that which suffices for the more restricted, orthodox sciences," he said. "There are many structures of existential continuum containing energy-information equivalents capable of being orthorotated into our own reality sphere. The parametric probes necessary to establish an identification may take time, and my time is in high demand and expensive." He glanced back at Kopeksky in the gilt-framed mirror above the fireplace. "I, er, take it that you are here officially . . . on Bureau business?" In other words were they talking a taxpayer-funded checkbook?

Kopeksky decided that he wasn't going to learn much about communicating with aliens. "Forget about it. Let's talk about time," he suggested instead. "Isn't that something you're into? What can you tell me about that?"

"Time, Mr. Kopeksky?" Zama swung around and voiced the word imperiously, as if there were more contained in the term than they could cover if they had all week.

"What clocks tell. . . . The stuff there's never enough of when you've got a plane to catch."

Zama made a sweeping gesture toward the window. "The fabric of it is rending apart as we speak. You know what's going on out there. It's the nuclear power plants that are doing it—so-called scientists meddling with forces they don't understand."

Kopeksky nodded sharply. "Exactly: what's going on out there. That's what I'm interested in! We know that somehow time is messing up. But what *is* time?"

Zama turned his palms upward contemptuously. "To me it doesn't exist. It is a fabrication. A necessary construct of lesser developed psyches that are not yet capable of comprehending the totality So they must apprehend piece by piece, in infinitesimal slices. But for me, the future lies as a map to be read. Would you like to see a demonstration of elementary precognition, Mr. . . . Kopeksky?" Zama picked up a wooden box from a shelf and opened its lid to reveal a pair of dice.

"Isn't that the kind of thing that magicians do at kids' parties?" Kopeksky queried.

Zama snapped the box shut and tossed it back down on the shelf. "I'm sorry, I thought that you had come here to discuss something serious," he said in a pained voice. "Those are mere entertainers."

"I know *they* are," Kopeksky agreed. "But if you've got the real thing, I'd have thought there'd be more point in using it for something that matters. For instance, who can you tell me about, somewhere in those offices out there right now, maybe, that shouldn't try driving home tonight? Or who oughta call in a contractor about the roof instead of going up a ladder and trying to fix it themselves? Know the kinda thing I mean?"

"Regrettable, but inevitable." Zama showed his hands and sighed. "Grief has always been with us. It sounds callous, I know, but really, what would be the true worth of averting one individual's tragedy in this complex web we call life, that involves billions? I could devote twenty-four hours a day of the rest of my life to such noble causes, and it wouldn't add up to making a scrap of difference that would matter. No, Mr. Kopeksky, I must conserve my energies for more important works."

"You mean like finding dimes with pendulums?"

"That was just a trivial illustration," Zama said, sounding irritable. He moved forward, away from the fireplace. "But the same technique can find deposits of valuable ores, oil fields . . . You see, benefits that will affect millions of people. Not many people know how much money the major companies are investing in this kind of thing nowadays."

That was probably true, Kopeksky reflected. He sure-as-hell didn't know. It could have been nothing, and Zama wouldn't have lied. "You mean it still works, right down through all that rock?" He sounded impressed.

"Oh, absolutely," Zama assured him loftily, moving forward again and sounding on firmer ground. "Space, matter, and distance are no objects."

Kopeksky gestured down at the top of the mahogany table, where he had covered the two coins with a handkerchief from his other pocket. "Then obviously this wouldn't be any problem. I'm sure you're right, but you know how unimaginative policemen are. Just to satisfy my personal curiosity, can you still tell which one of these is the dime?"

Zama stopped and looked down uncertainly. "You expect me to waste my time on parlor tricks?" He was trapped, and his voice betrayed it.

"It would be too bad if I had to go back and report a failure, wouldn't it?" Kopeksky answered with a shrug. "Especially with all those lost people and objects they've got on the files back there."

Zama extended his arm to hold the pendulum over one end of the handkerchief. He hesitated, then moved the pendulum to the other end. Kopeksky's mouth twitched, and after a second or two the bob began tracing a circle.

"That's it?" Kopeksky inquired, cocking an eyebrow. Zama nodded stiffly. Kopeksky turned back the end of the handkerchief. Sure enough, the coin lying there was a dime. He nodded approvingly. "Not bad."

Zama moved the pendulum back to the other end, where it promptly changed its motion to a straight line. "And there is the penny," he pronounced, his former self-assurance now restored. "As I said earlier, just a trivial illustration. But it proves the principle, you see."

"You mean about the permeative-vibrational field that flows from the galactic poles? That was what you called it, right?"

Zama's eyebrows raised a fraction in surprise. He nodded. "Precisely."

Kopeksky lifted the remainder of the handkerchief to reveal a second dime. He shook his head sadly and clicked his tongue. "Oh dear. Well, I guess nothing in life is perfect, eh? Maybe you just need to work on it a little more before you file for the patent."

Zama glared down at the evidence, his waxed mustaches bristling. "Interference," he pronounced. "The B Line subway goes right under here. The metal of the rails interferes with the reading."

"Yeah," Kopeksky said, gathering up his things and heading for the door. "They dig 'em real fast these days."

4

"They were all yo-yos," Kopeksky told Deena across the booth when they met in a deli on Lexington to compare notes forty (windup) minutes later. "I learned about birthday-party tricks and electric fish. Might as well have stayed home and read fortune cookies. How'd it go with the philosophers?"

Deena shuffled among the notebooks and papers littering the tabletop between her coffee mug and plate with its half-eaten pastrami-on-rye. The purse that accompanied her everywhere was on the seat next to her, and a nylon carry-bag, bulging with reference books, had appeared alongside it.

"I talked to Morton Bridley at Columbia, Schumann at Fordham, Arnold Cuppenheim at NYU . . ." she turned a page, scanned over the scrawl on the one beneath, then delved among some loose papers covering the sugar bowl, "and a guy called Chaim

Mendelwitz from the Jewish Theological Seminary, that one of them recommended. Gellsard from Rockefeller had to rush off in a panic about something, but I did get to see a another guy there called . . . Hunter, was it? . . . Oh, yes, here we are: Herman Hunter."

"So what have we got?" Kopeksky grunted. On days like this it was easy to feel inadequate.

Deena took another bite from her sandwich and then searched around again, finally retrieving a wad of handwritten sheets from beneath her coffee mug. "One of the earliest mentions of time as a discrete concept is in Aristotle's *The Categories*. He listed it as one of them."

" 'Them' what? Categories?"

"Yes."

"He was some Greek, right?

"Fourth century B.C."

"Okay, so what's a category?"

"Nobody seems to know. Kant and Hegel use the term too, but they're all different. Russell described them as being 'in no way useful to philosophy as representing any clear idea,' so maybe it doesn't matter. But in his *Physics*, Aristotle says it's 'motion that admits of numeration.' That means motion that can be counted in numbers."

"Why? What's so special about numbers?" Kopeksky asked.

"It isn't clear," Deena answered. "It seems like Aristotle just had this thing about numbers. He wondered if time could exist without there being souls around, since he figured there couldn't be anything to count unless there was somebody to count it. And that proves time couldn't have been created."

Kopeksky stared at her fixedly while he poked at his teeth with a pick. "Uh-huh."

Deena picked up the next sheet. "But Plato didn't agree. According to him, the creator wanted to make an image of the eternal gods. But that wasn't possible—

for it to be eternal, I mean, I guess because that's what
gods are—so it had to move."

"What did?"

"The universe. That's what the creator was creating."

"Oh. Okay."

"And that's where time came from. Without days
and nights we wouldn't have thought of numbers. In
other words God made the sun so that animals could
learn arithmetic . . ." Deena caught the expression on
Kopeksky's face and hastily switched to another section
of her notes.

"Saint Augustine also thought that time came out
of nothing. See, he worried about why the world
wasn't created sooner. And the answer he came up
with was that there couldn't have been any 'sooner.'
So, time had to have been created at the same time
everything else was."

"Brilliant."

"But there were some parts of his system that he
had problems with."

"Really?"

"Yes. First, he figured that only the present really
is. But he had no doubt that the past and the future
really exist too. So here was an apparent contradiction."

"Did he come up with a brilliant answer for this
one too?"

"Of course. He was a saint."

"What was it, then?"

"The past still exists as what you remember, and
the future exists already as what you expect to happen. So really there are only a present of things past,
a present of things present, and a present of things
future. And that explains it: they only exist now, and
they're all real."

Kopeksky's face registered a conviction that fell
somewhere short of total. "What if what I expect
doesn't get to happen," he asked. "Is it still real?"

"Er . . . it doesn't say."

"Scratch one saint. Who's next?"

"Spinoza didn't think time was real at all, and so any emotions that have to do with the future or past are contrary to reason. Only ignorance makes us think we can change the future."

"If we buy that, we might as well turn in our badges. What else?"

Deena separated some insurance papers from among her notes and stuffed them into the top of the purse beside her. "Schopenhauer claimed that the world is all an objectification of will. The aim of existence is total surrender of the will, in which all phenomena that are manifestations of it will be abolished. That includes time and space, which constitute the universal form of this manifestation. Thus there will be no will: no idea, no world. The only certainty is nothingness."

Kopeksky bit the end off his pickle and considered the proposition. "What does that mean?"

"I don't know. . . . Hegel didn't believe in space and time either, because they involve separateness and multiplicity, and only the whole can be real. . . . Hume defined it as one of seven kinds of philosophical relations, but then he got kind of tangled up over whether we see the causes of things, or only the results of causes. . . . Kant thought it was real but subjective: it exists in your head, not in the world you're looking at."

"How'd he figure that?"

"It kind of came out of a general theory he had about perceptions being due to two parts: the part of what you think you see that's really out there, and the part that you add to it inside. Like, if you wear red glasses, you see a red world. But the red that you see is something you carry around with you. The space and time that we think is part of the universe are really orderings that we impose on it because of the way our minds work."

Kopeksky thought about it. "So how come we've all got the same color lenses?" he challenged. "Why does everybody see the roof on top of the house instead of the other way round?"

Deena nodded as she searched under the papers for her pen. "A lot of other philosophers asked the same thing."

"So what did he tell them?"

"He didn't have to. They only got around to asking about it after he was dead."

Kopeksky sat back in his seat and stirred his coffee for a while. Deena began tidying her notes back into some semblance of order. "Out of curiosity, what did all these guys manage to agree about?" he ventured finally.

"Not much."

Kopeksky nodded in a way that said it was what he had expected. "Well, I guess we had to try."

"So where do we go now?" Deena asked.

He raised his cup and drank moodily. "Back to basics and start at the scene of the crime. Or in this case, scenes. Some of the biggest time lags we heard about were at the airports, before they closed, the TV networks, the phone company, and the utilities. We talk to them and see what we can dig up there."

"That's what I figured." Deena rummaged in her purse again and found a notebook. "I've already got us some leads in those places."

"Fine. Then I'll finish working the list we've already got," Kopeksky said. He shrugged and produced the check, which he had kept out of harm's way in his breast pocket. "Might as well see it through now." His tone said that he didn't expect to get much out of it.

"Who've you got next?" Deena asked.

"The priest." Kopeksky's mouth moved expressionlessly. "Why not? What the hell, it can't get any nuttier."

5

Kopeksky found the church of St. Vitus in The Fields hidden between a pile of sooty-windowed offices and the rear of a warehouse in the jumble of streets that dated from the beginnings of New York City, before planners discovered right angles, on the Lower East Side below the Manhattan Bridge. Its unassuming frontage of weathered stone stood sandwiched between soaring perpendicularities of concrete and glass, looking as if year by year it yielded a little more to the encroaching city, and one day would be squeezed out of existence entirely.

A housekeeper with gray hair and a robust smile answered the door to the presbytery, which was situated behind the church along a narrow passage fenced from the street by iron railings. She took Kopeksky's coat and hat, stated that it was "a grand day for November, especially at this time of year," and showed him upstairs to the study of Father Bernard Moynihan.

It was a warm and cozy room, with oak paneled walls and a deep maroon carpet. Solidly made bookshelves extended to the ceiling on either side of a leather-topped desk angled across one corner by the window, and two armchairs faced a cheerfully blazing fire. Moynihan himself, in shirtsleeves, was standing before the hearth, warming his back, when Kopeksky entered. Kopeksky put him at fiftyish. He was a good five-ten in height and hefty, with florid, craggy features and iron-gray hair combed straight back. As the housekeeper moved around to add more smokeless briquettes to the fire, he came forward a pace and brought his hands around to rub them together in front of him.

"Mr. Kopeksky, who has the job of picking up the pieces when we fail at ours." He motioned with his head to indicate the clock on the mantelpiece behind him. "And right on time. That seems to be quite an achievement these days, from what we've been hearing." The brogue was soft and diluted by years of living this side of the water—but definitely present.

Kopeksky pulled out the pocket windup and compared it. They matched to the minute. "I'll be darned," he said. "It's the first time that's happened."

"Ah, is that a fact, now?" Moynihan answered. "Then this must be the first time you've been near a place with any sanity in it for days." A hint of humor around the mouth, Kopeksky saw, and more about the eyes. Not a flake, he decided. Flakes took themselves too seriously to be able to afford any concession to humor.

"Is that what it's all about, then?" he replied. "Sanity?"

"Ah, sure ye've only to look at the places it's happening in and ask yourself what it is they've got in common. But first things first. Will you take a cup of tea, Mr. Kopeksky?"

"Any chance of coffee?"

"Certainly, if you prefer. But I'm not talking about the tea bag floating in bathwater that they try fobbing you off with over here. It's the real stuff I'm meaning, made boiling in a pot the way God meant it to be. One of the only two good things that ever came out of England." The priest's eyes were clear and alert, and gave the impression of already having absorbed all there was of Kopeksky to be divined outwardly.

"Okay, I'll try it," Kopeksky conceded.

"A pot of tea for two if you would, please, Ann," Moynihan said as the housekeeper moved toward the door.

"And biscuits, is it?" she inquired.

"Cookies," Moynihan translated.

Kopeksky shook his head. "Not for me." Ann went out, closing the door behind her.

"Please." Moynihan waved Kopeksky to one of the armchairs and settled himself down in the other. The fire felt warm and relaxing after the drab dampness of the day outside.

"Some fields," Kopeksky said, referring obscurely to the fact that the church could have been called something more appropriate to Lower Manhattan. It was a test to see if he was dealing with somebody who caught on quickly.

"Oh, I think it was a name that somebody brought with them from the old country a long time ago now," Moynihan told him. "There might have been some truth in it then, too."

Kopeksky grunted. "So what was the other good thing that came out of England?"

"Oh, this stodgy thing of theirs that they call reasonableness and common sense. Not a bad idea, I suppose. They tried to import it, you know, but it didn't grow. In Ireland it's an exotic—not suited to the climate or the soil."

"You sound like you know something about plants," Kopeksky commented.

"A little," Moynihan agreed. "In the years of my wilder youth I spent some time in missionary work, mainly in Africa, which of course entailed dabbling in all kinds of biology. But my main interest was in entomology rather than botany."

"That's bugs, right?"

Moynihan nodded. "I started out as a medical man—insect-borne diseases. But then one day I got to thinking, what's the use of saving lives if it isn't so that people can learn to live them better? And that was the side of things that seemed to be in need of the most help." Kopeksky nodded that he both understood and agreed. Moynihan glanced across. "Insects are still what you might call a hobby of mine, though. In fact I keep a colony of termites in the basement here. Fascinating, the habits of the social insects. . . . Would you like me to show them to you?"

Kopeksky held up a hand apologetically. "It sounds great, Father, but I gotta take a rain check. Maybe another time."

"Of course. You're doubtless caught up in all that bedlam that's going on out there. Then tell me how I can help."

Kopeksky had by now come to the conclusion that he wasn't going to find any sudden illumination as to the true nature of time, and that even if he did, it wouldn't get him anywhere. However, he still hadn't given up on the notion that the way to reach Grauss's aliens might be through some unsuspected means that could have been staring them in the face all along.

"When people pray, does it work?" he asked.

Moynihan lifted his head and looked at him with undisguised surprise for a few seconds. "Well now, there's a question that I wasn't expecting from one the likes of yourself," he declared.

"They do it all over, and they have been for thousands of years," Kopeksky went on. "That's enough to say to me that there could be something to it."

" 'Twould be a fine way I'd be wasting my life if there wasn't," Moynihan commented.

"But is there really anybody on the other end of the line?" Kopeksky persisted. "Or is it something that you trigger inside yourself?"

The tea arrived. Moynihan stroked his chin and regarded Kopeksky long and thoughtfully while Ann arranged cups and saucers, milk jug, and a sugar bowl on a side table between the two chairs, along with a silver pot covered by a padded cozy. Then she retired, closing the door again. Moynihan leaned over to pick up the pot and poured for both of them. "The tea goes in first. Then you can add enough milk to make it whatever strength you fancy. I just take a splash meself, with no more than half a spoon of sugar so you don't lose the flavor of the tea. 'Tis no good at all unless the spoon can stand up in it, in my opinion."

Kopeksky followed his example and tried a sip. It was hot, strong, and even the small drop filled his mouth with a taste that made everything he'd tried before insipid. "Not bad," he pronounced. "I could get used to this."

"I'll let you have a small box to take home and experiment with," Moynihan said. He stared into the fire, set his own cup down, and looked across at Kopeksky again. "To get back to your question, how many times did Christ tell us that God's kingdom is within? But that's the one place where people refuse to look. The Buddha told them to reject external ministrations as the means of deliverance and find their own eightfold way to proper thought. Confucius taught inner integrity as the only basis for a moral society." He made a brief open-handed gesture. "The one thing that all the true religions of the world have ever said is the same. But people insist on demanding outside powers to help them. Therefore that's what we must be." Frank and direct, with no beating about the bush. It was also an assessment of Kopeksky and a statement of presumption that Kopeksky understood. The priest wrinkled his nose and rubbed it with a knuckle. "It's a strange kind of question to be coming from a policeman, if you don't mind me saying so."

Which was as good a way as any of asking what this was all about. Kopeksky nodded, having expected it. "This business that's jumbling up time all over the city. Some scientists have got a theory that it could be due to the activities of some kind of other intelligences, in a dimension that we don't interact with directly." He deliberately avoided any mention of "stealing." For one thing, Grauss had shown no evidence to warrant such an interpretation; for another, this whole thing was zany enough already without straining Moynihan's credulity further. Moynihan, however, accepted the suggestion with surprising matter-of-factness and had evidently seen where Kopeksky's line of thinking was leading, without need of any lengthy explanation.

"A strange matter to be involving people like yourselves in," Moynihan remarked. "Are these intelligences considered to be violating the law?"

"You know how it is with bureaucrats."

Moynihan sighed and inclined his head. "I'm afraid that my limited abilities are only good for trying to communicate something to members of our own species in these familiar dimensions," he said. "The Church doesn't presume to extend its dictates to other beings in other realities that it has no knowledge of. Apparently the same notions of self-restraint don't apply to secular legislators. Ah, well . . ." He shook his head regretfully. "I'm sorry, Mr. Kopeksky, but I don't think I can supply what you're looking for."

Kopeksky had already concluded as much. But it was something to have been listened to and taken seriously. He realized that without its feeling the least bit unnatural, he had divulged more to Moynihan than to anyone else he had spoken to since the thing began. Maybe there was more to priests than he had realized, he thought to himself. They talked more about the bizarre behavior of the city's clocks over a second cup of tea and were equally lost for the beginnings of an idea of what could be done about it. Finally Kopeksky rose and announced that he had to be on his way. As had by now become habit, he compared his watch with the clock on the mantelpiece again. The two were still in agreement. He added a note of the fact to the other figures that he had been collecting since the previous morning, and left.

The first thing he encountered on emerging was

an electronics shop that had managed to get three
channels showing on the TVs in the window, all
showing gabbling heads and different times. As he
walked on, he thought back to the place that he had
just left, with its calm, dependability, and image of
unpretentious integrity. An island of sanity in a world
that was coming closer to literally not knowing what
day it was. Just as Moynihan had said.

6

When Kopeksky got back, the Bureau had just
updated itself from 3:27 local to 4:00 p.m. EST. It
had thus lost thirty-three minutes in the process, and
everyone was flying around in a frenzy. Wade didn't
have time to talk to anybody, nothing in the Day
Room was making any sense, and Deena was still out
chasing leads. He went on up to their office on the
twelfth floor, got himself a coffee, and sat down at
his desk to see once more if he could make anything
out of the figures that he had been gathering.

The most affected locations, as measured by the
rate at which their time fell behind the standard being
maintained outside the area, seemed to be the telephone exchanges, TV centers, several of the larger
data-processing bureaus, the City University computer
center on the West Side, an automated machining
plant in Queens, and the physics faculty at Columbia University. And at all of them the situation had
been getting worse over the last two days, with two
exceptions that stood out notably: the improvement
at JFK since it ceased operating; and the reduced lag
that the telephone exchanges experienced during the
nights.

Kopeksky spread the sheets of paper out and stared
at them, clasping his coffee mug in front of him
between the fingers of both hands. The only thing

that came to mind immediately about the places he had flagged with asterisks was that they were all fairly heavy users of computer systems of some kind or another. . . . Or were they? Did TV centers do much computing? He didn't know. And the power companies were high in the ranking there, but he wasn't sure how much computing went on in connection with generating electricity. Something to check. He wrote the word *Computers?* in large letters on his scratchpad and circled it in red, then sat for a while contemplating it, waiting for it to tell him something. It didn't. . . . But there had to be something significant in the fact that the two cases he knew about of the trend reversing had both occurred after a substantial drop in activity.

He picked up the phone and called JFK International, hitting lucky by getting through on the second try. A couple of minutes later he was through to a Marty Fasseroe, the engineer in charge of maintenance for most of the airport's computer facilities. Kopeksky explained who he was, why he was calling, and obtained some more figures for his collection from the records in Fasseroe's log. Then he asked, "Is the problem connected with the computers somehow? Have they been acting up in any way?"

There was a pause, indicating that Kopeksky had scored a hit on something. Then Fasseroe replied, "Not what you'd call acting up, exactly. But . . ."

"There is something that's not right?" Kopeksky prompted.

"The timings and disk synchs are all out. It's as if the internal clocks are even more screwed up than what's going on outside. Programs run correctly, but they take longer than they should—sometimes as much as twenty-five percent. At least, that's how it was when we were trying to run normally. Since we suspended operations, it's down to about five, maybe six percent."

"Are you shut down completely? The computers, I mean?"

"Not completely. We're still running some routine monitoring and logging operations. But we don't have any traffic to deal with now, and regional ATC is being handled outside the affected area. So all the heavy stuff is down, yes."

Kopeksky added the information to his notes. "Okay," he pronounced. And then, routinely, "Anything else unusual?"

"Well, yeah, there was one other funny thing—up until early yesterday, that is. Inside the machines . . ."

"You mean the computers?"

"Yes. In the processor and memory cabinets—the guts of where it all happens—for a while we were getting this kind of . . . red haze. Everything in there turned red . . . you know, like in a photographer's dark room. And when you stuck a flashlight in there to look, the light from that turned red too. Nobody here ever saw anything like it."

"But it's not there now?" Kopeksky checked.

"No. It went away soon after we reverted to standby operations. I know I've never seen anything like it before."

"Well, thanks, Mr. Fasseroe. It's been a big help. If anything else strange happens, would you let me know?"

"Sure, I'd be happy to."

Kopeksky gave his direct number and cleared down. Then he tried calling Fasseroe's counterparts at Newark and La Guardia to see if the patterns they had experienced there were in any way similar, but he was unable to get through in either case. He did get an operator at the local Manhattan exchange, however, who after an initially rancorous response since she was harassed and not in a mood for dealing with kooks and their questions that day, put him through to a supervisor at the engineering section.

Kopeksky asked his by-now-routine questions about what time standard the company was using, how often they reset to it, and how much they drifted away in between doing so. It turned out that currently the exchange computers were running slow by about 23%. Then he said, "Just one more thing. Out of curiosity, is there anything unusual going on inside the boxes? Maybe things turning red in there—what could be described as a red light, or 'haze'?"

"How did you know about that?" the supervisor asked. He sounded suspicious.

"Just a hunch," Kopeksky replied. "The airports had it too, before they closed down. Nobody there knows what it was, either. Does it suggest anything to you?"

"One guy here thinks it's black holes. The radiation field generated from time falling into submicroscopic black holes. He's into some strange things, though—you know, science fiction and stuff."

"Does he have any ideas what to do about it?" Kopeksky asked.

"We don't know. He figured the whole world is going to disappear down the same drain, and got so drunk we had to send him home. I could give you his number but I don't think it'd do you much good. He's out of it until tomorrow. Or we all go down the tubes. Whichever happens first."

"No, but thanks anyhow. Would you let me know if anything else unusual happens. . . ."

Kopeksky spent the remainder of the afternoon compiling a list of further locations and calling them, including the Stock Exchange, Weather Bureau, computer centers of the major banks and several hospitals, and a number of scientific research centers. He found he could carry on into the evening past normal working hours because in many cases the clocks at the places he was calling were still indicating late afternoon. But when Kopeksky checked, the people there agreed with him that it was dark outside—which according to their clocks it shouldn't have been. Hence it seemed that even at the same location the time according to an artificial timekeeping device could be one thing while that given by the sun was another. When Kopeksky called down to the Day Room to check the situation at Bureau HQ itself, he was informed that the sun had been observed to set six minutes before the clocks that had been reset to EST less than an hour earlier said it should have done.

So now a further layer of complication seemed to be adding itself. Not only was synchronization being lost between different places around the city; if the evidence in front of him was to be believed, different means of measuring time at the same place weren't even staying in step with each other!

He sat back wearily and looked at the litter on his desk, which be now was beginning to resemble Deena's. Lots of numbers. Still no pattern to them. He didn't think like a computer. What he needed was a picture.

He went down to the library and checked out a large-scale wall map of the New York area, then brought it back up and fixed it to the wall between his desk and Deena's. Then he called out for a pepperoni-salami pizza and salad to keep him going through the evening, rolled up his sleeves, and commenced the task of figuring out a system for turning his figures into some kind of a chart that would, hopefully, reveal something meaningful.

It was 9:25 according to his pocket windup when Deena called (also 9:21 by the digital watch on his other wrist, 9:02 by the Bureau clock on the wall, which had been reset to EST at 6:00 that evening, and 8:26 according to the channel showing on the portable TV that he'd set up in a corner of the office, which had just been restored after a retuning of the transmitter). Her usual routine for getting ahold of him in the evenings was to call first his apartment, followed by his three favorite neighborhood restaurant-bars. That she had gone on to try the office next said that it was something urgent.

"The astronomers couldn't really help. But I think I've found a scientist that you ought to talk to," she told Kopeksky when he answered.

"You mean there's a sane one?" he said.

"Well, he talks English and he seems to make sense."

"Where are you? And what the hell are you doing still out knocking on doors at this time? Did your landlady throw you out or something?"

"I'm at a place called Scicomp—that's short for Scientific Computing Institute. It's a fairly new place on the East Side, just as you come off the Queensboro Bridge. It's computer city in here. They take on research contracts for all kinds of scientific work that needs big computing—you know, the heavy stuff. They're into, oh . . ." Kopeksky could picture her delving into a pile of notes while she wedged the phone on a shoulder, "things like cosmology, particle physics, big economic models, engineering simulations, reality modeling. . . . The place is packed with specialized equipment that you don't see everywhere: Crays, Connection Machines, pipeline processors, super graphics."

Whatever they were. "Okay, I get the idea," Kopeksky said. "So what gives?"

"Well, I don't know how many words Eskimos have for 'panic,' but that's what it is here. We thought that the phone exchanges and TV centers were being hit the hardest, but this place is even worse. What time do you have back there right now, Joe?"

Kopeksky looked at his windup again. "Nine twenty-six."

"Right. And I just called NBC to check there.

They're showing 8:30." That was close enough to the channel showing on Kopeksky's TV, which was from a different network.

"Okay," he acknowledged.

"But here inside Scicomp it's only 7:21. We're over an hour behind the networks, even. I haven't come across anywhere like this. Everything's going crazy here."

"How did you find out about it?"

"It was a lead I got from somebody I talked to at an IBM site I was at. The computer people around town seem to be getting a better feel for the pattern of whatever's going on. It looks like a lot of installations are affected. And the airports and the phone companies use them a lot. I'm beginning to think that this whole things might have something to do with computers somehow."

Which was also the direction that Kopeksky's thinking had been heading in. "So who's this guy I should talk to?" he asked.

"His name is Dr. Graham Erringer. He's a physicist here, running simulations of, what was it? . . . Oh yes, here we are. *Electromagnetic Pinch Filaments in the Pre-Gravitational Plasma Universe.*" Deena paused. "Er, I guess that's what he does," she said to fill the silence that greeted her from the other end of the line.

"And he knows what's going on?" Kopeksky said finally.

"He's intrigued by what Grauss had to say, anyhow. And the engineers here have downed the machine he was working on, so he's got plenty of time now. Like I said, he seems to make sense. I think we should talk to him, Joe."

"Okay, see if you can set something up here at the Bureau for first thing tomorrow morning. . . . Oh, and Deena?"

"Yes?"

"Ask them if they've been finding anything unusual inside them computers, willya—maybe like a red light, or a funny red hazy effect."

Deena's voice took on a note of surprise. "Why, yes, they have. We were just talking about it. That was why they stopped Erringer's machine. How did you know about that?"

"Hey, kid," Kopeksky said, leaning back in his chair and feeling pleased, "don't think you're the only genius in the Bureau. I know a little bit about researching cases too, you know."

After he hung up, Kopeksky stared at the figures that he had noted and asked himself why things should be in a panic where Deena was, where it was still only 7:21. On the face of it, oughtn't she to have *more* time available, not less? It was all a case of whose time they decided was correct, he supposed. As far as he was concerned it was late evening, and he had accomplished a lot. If they agreed that his time was correct—in other words the aliens had been taking time from Scicomp, where Deena was, which was what the theory said—then she would have to adjust her clock to his, which meant she'd suddenly find that it was half after nine with a whole chunk of the evening gone and nothing to show for it. If, on the other hand, he were to adjust to her, he'd find himself back with a whole evening ahead, but with his work still done. Yes, he told himself, when you got around to looking at it that way, that part of it did seem to add up.

But why should the aliens take time from there rather than time from someplace else? Why would they prefer a TV center's time to the Bureau's time, say . . . but less so at night? All very strange. Kopeksky poured himself another coffee and studied the figures again. He had begun marking them on a transparent overlay covering the map on the wall. He hoped that Dr. Erringer would be able to make more out of what they meant than he could just at this moment.

7

The next morning there was a note from Ellis Wade on Kopeksky's desk, along with a copy of a fax from Grauss, who was apparently now at the Fermi National Accelerator Laboratory near Chicago. From what Kopeksky could make of it, Grauss had come up with a theory that the energy consumed in particle-pair creations could somehow be used to send signals to the aliens who were helping themselves to New York's time. The powers at Washington had considered anything worth a try, and sent Grauss to Fermilab to guide the scientists there in setting up a suitable experiment. There was also an apologetic message from Dr. Erringer, saying that he would be late. Kopeksky showed Deena the chart that he had been developing and let her take over the task of adding the remaining figures, while he went up to the fifteenth floor to see what more Wade could tell him about the latest from Grauss.

He found Wade sitting dazedly at his desk, and his secretary, Ruth, cowering inarticulately in a corner while a lean, hawk-faced man in a black suit delivered a harangue, at the same time stabbing a finger at an open Bible that he was holding. With him were two women, also in black, their hair tied up in buns and held by white mesh bonnets.

"Can you not see that this is a repeat of the warning that was given to us with Babel? Man built him a tower, thinking that it could gain him the heavens, but God confused him with many tongues. And now, again, we seek machines to go where only the righteous may ascend, and God confuses us with many times. It was foretold here in Matthew 'Can ye not discern the signs of *the times?*'!"

"Who are they?" Kopeksky muttered at Ruth from the door.

"How do I know?" she returned desperately. "What are they even doing in the building?"

The man's voice reverberated stridently across the office. "Hear the revelation of St. John: 'The devil is come down unto you, having great wrath, because he knoweth that he hath but a short *time*.' "

Then Wade noticed for the first time that Kopeksky was there. A look of relief flooded into his face and his mouth started to open. Kopeksky felt for the doorknob behind him and backed out, raising a hand protectively. "Sorry, Ellis. I just remembered something downstairs that can't wait. Talk to you later when you're not so busy, huh?" He walked away rapidly, declining to wait for an elevator and taking the stairs instead.

Opinions around the water fountain were that the time-dilation anomaly would spread around the world within a month, and the only way out would be a reversion to pre-industrial living. The Bureau's Finance & Commerce section was inundated with a rash of insurance scams involving the advance purchase of cover in one part of the city against incidents that had already happened in another, and international stock trading was in chaos. By the time Kopeksky got back to his own office Erringer had arrived and was showing a lot of interest in the chart. Except that it was now "charts": Erringer and Deena had moved a table over to the wall below the map and were busy with colored marker pens, copying the figures from Kopeksky's original onto a series of separate overlays.

"What's this?" Kopeksky asked them as he ambled in.

Deena turned to gesture, but knocked a stack of papers off the corner of the table. "It's Graham's suggestion," she said over her shoulder as she stooped to collect them together. "We're grouping the data into twelve-hour time frames. The way the pattern changes might tell us something."

"Not a bad idea," Kopeksky agreed. A similar thought had occurred to him, too, the night before, but it had been too late then to do anything about it.

"Oh." Deena straightened up and put the papers on her desk. "This is Graham Erringer that I mentioned, from Scicomp. Dr. Erringer, that is. . . . And this is Joe Kopeksky."

The two men shook hands. Erringer was tall and athletically built, with a ruddy, healthy complexion, shaggy blond hair, and easygoing features that smiled easily. Kopeksky guessed him to be around thirty-five. He was wearing a tan sport jacket with a patterned V-neck sweater and light blue, open-neck shirt.

"I'm sorry I was late, Mr. Kopeksky," he said. "We had another crisis this morning. And we're constantly running out of time over there—but you already know that, of course."

"It's happening all over," Kopeksky said.

Erringer turned to look at the wall map again. "This is very interesting. It's the first time I've seen a systematic compilation of the whole picture." He raised a hand briefly. "I hope you don't mind my intruding like this. Sorting the data by time seemed the obvious next step, and I couldn't contain my curiosity. We haven't interfered with your original."

"That's okay," Kopeksky said. "It's the next thing I was thinking of trying, anyhow."

Erringer gestured at the new charts that Deena was working on. "The points are still a bit thin, but it's already evident that there's a pattern there. We're adding in some more figures that I brought with me, mainly pertaining to computer installations."

"Do you figure this whole thing has got something to do with computers?" Kopeksky asked.

"Possibly. Sites with large facilities certainly seem to show longer time lags," Erringer replied.

"Like Scicomp."

"One of the longest so far."

"And you had that funny red haze inside the boxes there."

"Yes," Erringer said. "That was why the engineers shut down the machine that I was using—to investigate the haze. Other installations have been reporting the same thing, as I presume you already know. That must be how you came to be aware of it."

Kopeksky nodded. "Does anyone have any idea what it is?"

Erringer turned to sit against the edge of the table below the map. "From the measurements I've seen, the time loss isn't simply one number that applies to the whole of a place—" he motioned with an arm at the room around them "—such as this building. The rates can be different, even at two points quite close to each other—say two different kinds of clocks in the same room."

That was what Kopeksky himself had observed with his two watches, and from the lack of correlations between sunset times and clock times at various locations. He nodded.

Erringer went on, "The greatest lags of all seem to occur inside the cabinets of large processor and memory arrays—in some cases we've looked at, more than thirty-five percent. But at the same time, the clocks in the room outside the cabinets might be losing at only, say, six or seven percent." Erringer gave an apologetic smile, as if for something too farfetched to treat seriously. "Well, what it looks like to me is a localized red shift. Time inside the cubicle is slowing down sufficiently to produce a visible lengthening of the wavelengths of the light in there. Are you familiar with red shift?"

"Losing time is effectively the same as saying it's running slower," Deena threw in from where she was tiptoed on a chair, fixing the first of the revised overlays onto the map. "When time runs slower, light gets redder. Colors are due to frequencies, which depend on time. So when it changes, they all shift."

"Quite," Erringer said, nodding.

Kopeksky thought for a moment. "So is that why the radio and TV channels keep having to be retuned?"

Erringer nodded again. "Exactly."

They were getting some information at last, even if it didn't explain everything yet. Might as well throw everything in while they were at it, Kopeksky decided. "So what about this guy Grauss's idea that we've got aliens stealing it?" he said. "Does that make sense to you?"

Erringer hesitated. "I don't quite see the factual support that says just because it seems to be disappearing, someone is taking it deliberately," he replied. "With all due respect to a professional colleague, my answer would be—" The phone rang and interrupted.

"Excuse me." Kopeksky muttered, picking it up. Then, louder, "This is Kopeksky."

"Joe, Harry here in the Day Room. We've got a visitor down here asking for you: a Father Moynihan. Want me to send him up?"

Kopeksky's eyebrows lifted in surprise. "Sure. I'll meet him at the elevators."

"He's on his way."

"Who is it?" Deena asked from where she was still standing on the chair. She let a corner of the transparency slip before it was pinned and almost lost her balance trying to catch it. Erringer stepped in deftly and saved the situation.

"The priest from yesterday," Kopeksky told her.

"What does he want?"

"Good question. You okay?"

"Sure." Deena stepped back down to the floor, kicking a box of thumbtacks off the chair in the process.

"Back in a few minutes," Kopeksky said.

So Erringer thought that Grauss was rushing into a blind alley, Kopeksky thought to himself as he walked out into the corridor of banging doors and scurrying figures. He wondered how much luck Grauss would have persuading the Fermilab scientists to go along with his experiment if they felt the same way.

Moynihan was in uniform this time, with a black raincoat, white dog collar, and carrying a furled umbrella. In his other hand he was carrying a leather bag from which he produced a package in white plastic wrapping. "I'm after forgetting to give you the tea that I promised yesterday," he explained. "It so happened that I was passing this way, so I thought I might as well drop it in. Punjana—one of me favorites."

"Er, thanks." Kopeksky took the package. "Tea first. Half a spoon of sugar, just a splash of milk. Right?"

"Grand man, you've got it. Oh, and I wondered if you might be interested in these." Moynihan dug into the bag and began pulling out a stack of books two or three at a time. "I picked out some works on mystical experiences. I can't be sure that what I said about our own product offering applies to all brands, you understand. For all I know, there might be others who've stumbled on things that could point a way to contacting these aliens of yours. Anyhow, for what help they might be, you're welcome to borrow them."

"We'll check it out, anyway," Kopeksky said, taking the books. After the trouble that the priest had gone to, he didn't want to say that the case for aliens appeared to be receding.

"And I remembered how interested you were that the clocks at St. Vitus agreed with that silver pocket watch that you were carrying, and I saw how you were noting down the times of everything," Moynihan went on, feeling inside the bag again. "So I did a little bit of extra research for you meself, that I thought might be useful." He drew out a black notebook and opened it to reveal several columns of neatly penned number. "These are the corresponding figures for the rest of our churches and other establishments around and about. It was a great excuse to call all me colleagues last night and catch up on the gossip."

Kopeksky grinned appreciatively. "You went to a lot of trouble."

"Ah, not at all, at all, at all."

Nevertheless, Kopeksky felt that he could hardly just say thanks and send Moynihan on his way—at least, not without offering a cup of tea. "Everything helps," he acknowledged. "How would you like to see what we're doing with it?"

"Well, if it wouldn't be interrupting the good work? . . ."

"Nah, that's okay. The office is this way." They began walking back along the corridor. Nobody had said anything about this business being secret, Kopeksky reflected. Anyhow, if the official aim was to try and attract the attention of aliens who didn't even know they existed, how could secrecy be an issue?

They joined Deena and Erringer in the office. Kopeksky introduced Moynihan and explained what was going on. Erringer accepted Moynihan's notebook eagerly and began transferring the figures from it to the several overlays now covering the map, one for each half-day period for the last two and a half days. "This is interesting," Erringer commented. "They're all like oases in the middle of it. Hardly affected at all."

"Islands of sanity," Moynihan said. "Aren't I after telling you the same thing yesterday?"

"True," Kopeksky agreed.

"And then there are these other kind of islands where we have things going to the other extreme, such as at Scicomp," Erringer said, pointing. "Where the time lags are greatest. Look—again, distinctly localized."

"Ah." Moynihan stepped forward to peer at the chart with interest.

"A lot of them seem to be places that have got big computers," Kopeksky commented.

"Is that a fact?" Moynihan lifted the top overlay to study the one beneath, and then the next one beneath that.

"Actually, I think it might not be quite as simple as that," Erringer cautioned. "See here, the TV centers don't use what you'd call excessive computing, but they're high up there. Same with the phone exchanges—they're scattered around a lot, not as big as you might think. Same thing with the utilities."

"What, then?" Kopeksky asked him.

"It looks as if it has something to do with electrical activity, which of course includes computers," Erringer said. "But exactly what, at this stage it's difficult to say. We'd need to analyze what's going on at these high-dilation centers and see what kind of correlations we get." He rubbed his chin between thumb and forefinger and ran his eye over the map again. "Regular patterns of fast switching seem to come into it. But I think it has to do with power densities as well. . . . Maybe some kind of more complex relationship that involves the two."

"What can you make out of that?" Deena asked him.

"Right at this moment, not a hell of a lot more than that," Erringer confessed.

Moynihan had gone back to the earliest of the charts and was turning slowly through the sequence again, studying each intently and muttering an occasional "Ah, yes," and "There we are," to himself. The others fell silent and waited curiously. Finally Moynihan stepped back and looked at them.

"Now, I don't know too much meself about computers and the like, you understand," he said. "But

I do know a little about the characteristic spreading pattern of an epidemic when I see one. Look, there are your primary infection sources there, there, and here. And you can see the secondary centers and the growth over the ensuing two days. The spread has stopped at the airports following the closures." Moynihan made an open-handed gesture that said they could make what they liked out of it, but those were the facts. "Never mind aliens," he said. "It's bugs ye should be looking for, if you want my opinion on the matter."

"Bugs? You mean software bugs are real?" Deena shook her head hopelessly. "This is getting insaner."

Before anyone could say more, the phone rang again. This time Deena answered. "It's for you," she said, holding the phone out to Erringer. "Somebody from Scicomp."

He took the phone and acknowledged. His expression grew serious as he listened. Finally he said "I'll be right back," and hung up.

Nobody bothered asking the obvious. "Things are getting worse back there," Erringer told them. "The red haze is spreading out into the building. Also they're finding problems with the structure all of a sudden. We may have to close the place down entirely, which would be ruinous. I have to get back and see what we can do."

"Mind if I come along?" Kopeksky said.

"Sure, if you want. Do you have any ideas?"

"No."

"You'd better carry on with the map, now that it looks like we might be getting us somewhere," Kopeksky said to Deena. "Get some help from one of the techs downstairs—somebody who knows about, what was it? . . ." He looked at Erringer. "Fast electrical switching patterns and power densities? That was what you said, right?"

"Right." Erringer nodded.

"Will do," Deena confirmed.

"And I have to be heading on me way," Moynihan said. "I'm glad I was able to help."

"Maybe more than you think," Kopeksky answered. "Sorry to have to break it up like this. We didn't even get to make any tea."

"Perhaps another time," Moynihan said, checking that he had his bag and his umbrella. "My turn to take the rain check, I gather."

Kopeksky looked at Erringer again. "Anything else, Doc?"

"No. I guess that's it."

"Then let's go."

The cabs they tried hailing were all full and burning rubber—an all-yellow Indianapolis 500. But then one screeched to a stop right in front of Bureau HQ to disgorge a fat man in a fawn coat who practically threw a twenty at the cabbie and scampered away into the entrance next door without stopping to wait for change. "They're doing it all over," the cabbie chuckled, tucking the bill away as Kopeksky climbed in. "Whatever's going on in this city, it's one of the best things that ever happened. Your pleasure, gentlemen?" Erringer gave the address and got in beside Kopeksky.

"So what are pinch filaments in the pre-gravitational universe?" Kopeksky asked as the cab moved off.

"You don't forget much." Erringer said. He made it a compliment.

"Aw, in this job you're pestering people all the time with questions," Kopeksky replied. "It doesn't help make friends if you have to keep asking them over again."

"What got you into this line of work?"

"I never could stay away from trouble. So I figured that if I was going to be around it anyway, I might as well get paid for it."

Erringer nodded. "That makes sense, I guess."

They edged out onto Ninth and were almost hit by a Toyota van running the red light. "So what are these filaments?" Kopeksky asked again.

"Oh . . . Basically we're pretty certain now that what people have been told for years about the Big Bang origin of the universe is all wrong. It never happened. There isn't enough mass for gravity to have formed galaxies in the fifteen billion years since the universe is supposed to have formed, and there are larger-scale structures out there that go back way, way farther than that. My line of work involves compression of an initially diffuse, primordial plasma medium into extended filaments by electromagnetic forces, which are trillions of times stronger than gravity. Gravitational collapse only came later."

"Oh," Kopeksky said.

"It's basically an optimistic view, because it leads to a picture of an evolving universe, not one that's degenerating to a heat death. In fact, just the opposite."

"You mean it's winding up, not running down?" Kopeksky said. Despite the technicalities, he'd heard enough bits of the subject to follow the essentials of what Erringer was saying.

"Exactly. We're evolving away from equilibrium, creating bigger temperature differences that increase energy flows. Extrapolation of the second law to a universal scale simply isn't valid." Erringer waited a couple of seconds, then decided it was time to change the subject. "I imagine you must meet all kinds of people," he said, switching back to Kopeksky's work again.

"You can say that again. Most of them are mean, dumb, or crazy. But there are a few okay ones too, who make up for it."

"That priest who was back at the office," Erringer

said. "Father Moynihan. He seems like an interesting person."

"Oh, sure. You don't get a lot like that."

"How does he come to know so much about diseases?"

"He worked in Africa years ago. Medical missionary. His specialty was diseases you get from bugs. Says he still keeps bugs in his basement today, kinda like a hobby."

"Interesting." There was another short pause. Kopeksky pretended not to notice Erringer's quick glance sideways at him. "That woman you work with, er . . ."

"Deena?"

"Right. She's quite an interesting person too. Very intelligent, compared to many that you meet. She seems to know something about practically everything."

"Deena's a good partner," Kopeksky said. "We've worked together for four years. I wouldn't trade."

"Is she, er, you know, married . . . anything like that?" Erringer tried with abysmal lack of success to make his voice nonchalant.

Kopeksky's eyebrows shot upward. "No, nothing like that," he replied. "I've never known a freer spirit." Was he detecting some personal attraction here?

" 'Free spirit,' " Erringer repeated, sitting back. "Yes, that's a good way to put it. "She does have this charming spontaneity about her, don't you think?"

Kopeksky turned his face away to gaze out at the perpetual still-life study of Manhattan's cross-town traffic. Charming spontaneity. He'd never heard it put that way before. "Yep, I guess you could call it that," he agreed. His face split into a craggy smirk. Maybe Erringer was right, and the universe wasn't such a bad place after all.

8

The scene outside the Scientific Computing Institute on East 59th Street had the look of a national emergency. Several fire trucks with uncoiled hoses and ladders extended were drawn up in front of the building, but their crews stood around uncertainly since there wasn't any fire to tackle. They had no doubt been called because of the eerie red glow showing through several of the second and third floor windows, Kopeksky guessed as he and Erringer got out of the cab. There were also police cruisers parked haphazardly all over the street, which had been closed for two blocks, and a couple of military vehicles from which soldiers in National Guard uniforms were unloading boxes and reels of cable. On the far side, a crowd of what Kopeksky took to be Scicomp employees were standing watching, having presumably been evacuated from the building.

Kopeksky followed Erringer over to some people who looked like management, talking and gesticulating with a group of police and Guard officers. While Erringer hurried forward to join them, Kopeksky stood back and ran an eye over the Scicomp building again. He could see the fluorescent tubes on the ceilings in the rooms that seemed to be affected the most. The light that they were putting out was red, not the normal white. And through the large glass doors of the entrance at ground level he could see that the light in the reception area was also tinted, but not to the same degree as higher up. There was something odd about the figures visible in there—something about the way they moved. Their postures and attitudes as they gestured to and fro at each other, went in and out of doors, and crossed the vestibule floor, all told of haste and agitation inside; but there was a strange floating quality to the way they went about it all, as if the whole scene were curiously unreal. And then Kopeksky realized why. The slow-down factor of time in there had grown big enough to see. The people that he was looking at were literally living in a different time.

He moved over to one of the patrolmen standing nearby and flashed his ID. "Kopeksky, City Bureau. What's the score here?"

"I'm not too sure," the patrolman answered. "All I know is it's a big computer center of some kind. From what I hear of it, the time glitches that have been happening all over really freaked. That's what's making the spooky red up there."

"Why the Army?"

"None of the phones are working. They're running field sets inside." The cop shook his head wonderingly. "It's time to go home, man. This doesn't happen in Wyoming."

Then Erringer came back over, accompanied by a man in a check overcoat. Erringer introduced him as Chuck Milliken, an engineer from a firm of architectural consultants who had been involved with the construction of the building. They had been called in to help investigate the structural problems that were the latest thing to have been reported. The problems seemed to be appearing in the places where the time dilation was greatest.

"It's worst down in the basement, where we've got a trio of new supercomputers hooked together doing comprehensive climatic modeling," Erringer told Kopeksky. "That was where the haze began spreading first, and then all the disk drives started seizing up. External communications are out all over the building. The Guard are trying army field telephones with local frequency shifters to talk to the outside—in case it gets worse at other places too, and they have to set up an emergency net for the whole city. Anyhow, let's go inside and take a look."

"You're sure it's healthy in there?" Kopeksky asked dubiously.

Erringer managed a grin despite the strain of the moment. "Oh, sure. The effect is purely perceptual. Come on, follow me."

They crossed the street, and the policemen standing a short distance back from the entrance parted to let them through. As the three approached the glass doors, the light inside gradually lost its pinkish hue and the moving figures seemed to quicken to a more natural pace, until, as Erringer opened the door, and Kopeksky and Milliken followed him through, everything became normal. Around them people were hurrying about, yelling, waving, running up and down the stairwell. On one side of them, a soldier wearing a headset was turning knobs on a communications box set up on the reception desk, from which a voice was gabbling unintelligibly, sounding like one of the Chipmunks. Beside him, another soldier was talking into a hand mike. "Slow it down, slow it down, for chrissakes! We can't make out what you're talkin' 'bout, in here." Kopeksky stopped and looked back the way they had come. Now everything in the street outside looked strangely cold and blue. And the people out there were strutting about with stiff, jerky movements in a way reminiscent of old-time movies. Kopeksky shook his head, then turned to follow after the others.

They used the stairs to go down, since the elevators were either out of commission or shut down as a precaution. The basement area presented a repeat of the experience upstairs, appearing reddened as they came out from the stairway, then changing to normal coloring as they moved into it. The place was typical of the larger computer setups that Kopeksky had seen, although glitzier and more elaborate than most: rows of metal cubicles with consoles and lights; lots of screens and keyboards; thick carpeting and glass-walled offices. Erringer went over to talk to some technicians who had opened the up several of the cubicles and were probing inside with tools and test instruments, manuals lying open on the floor and countertops around them. The insides of the units they were working on, Kopeksky could see, were noticeably red. That meant red with respect to the normal-looking room that they were in, which he already knew was itself red to the world outside. He gave up trying to visualize what it all meant. Maybe it was time to move to Wyoming.

In another area, by a door leading through to another part of the installation, several of the electronics units had been pushed back against a wall, and a part of the false floor taken up to expose the tangles of cables beneath. Two men were examining the concrete beams and steel ties of the underlying structure, and cutting off pieces of the floor supports.

"Those have to be your guys," Kopeksky said, turning to Milliken. "What kind of problems are you finding, exactly?"

The engineer waved toward one of the cabinets that had been moved back. "Damndest thing. The floor gave way underneath a heavy mass-storage unit, right there. There just isn't any way that should be able to happen. The metal under it just gave out. It's crazy. This building's practically brand new."

"Did it use any new kind of material or some new wonder technique?" Kopeksky asked.

"Nope. It's all the same as everybody's been using for years. Doesn't make a scrap of sense."

"What about upstairs, where the red fuzz is inside the windows? Is there anything up there too?"

"There's a measurable sag in a couple of the floors, all right. That's why we moved most of the people out. If the foundations are affected too, we could be in real trouble." Milliken nodded to indicate the two men working under the floor. "Let's go see how Bill and Rick are doing." Kopeksky followed him over. "What's the news on the floor pillars?" Milliken inquired.

One of the two held up a piece of metal tube about eighteen inches long. It was buckled and misshapen, the material itself being at the same time swollen in a strange kind of way that didn't happen with metals. "If it was wood, I'd say we had a bad case of dry rot," the man said. "It's got no strength. We'll take some samples for testing, but it looks to me like the whole grain structure is disrupted." Kopeksky took the piece out of curiosity and examined it. It reminded him of bomb fragments that he had seen from time to time.

"What could cause it, Rick?" Milliken asked the other engineer.

"Beats the hell outta me."

"What about the foundation structure?"

The first engineer, who had to be Bill, selected a piece from a collection of concrete samples detached by drilling and chiseling, and showed it. "This doesn't feel right, Chuck," he said. "Here, try for yourself. Too grainy. It's like it was mixed with too high a sand content."

"But that's not true. It was top quality," Milliken objected.

"I know that. But something's changed it since. It has to be whatever's corroding the steel here too, but don't ask me what."

"If you asked me I'd say it was mice," Rick said. "Except mice don't eat that kind of cheese."

Milliken passed the sample to Kopeksky, at the same time talking to Bill. "Is the integrity of the whole structure threatened? Does this mean a total evacuation?"

"I don't know. Could be. We need to go down farther and do some checks at the parking level. But it doesn't look good to me."

Kopeksky saw that Erringer was looking around to see where he had gone. "I'd better get back to the doc," he told Milliken. "Can I keep these?" He showed the samples that he was holding.

"Who's he?" Bill asked Milliken.

"Police. He's with one of the scientists who works here—the tall guy over there with the yellow hair." Milliken nodded to Kopeksky. "Go ahead. We've got plenty more of it around here." He looked around and picked up an empty plastic bag that was lying on top of some boxes. "You can put them in this."

"Thanks."

"Nice talking to ya."

Kopeksky crossed between a graphics plotter and line printer to where Erringer was standing with the computer technicians. Erringer saw him approaching and gestured toward the opened cubicle. It was filled with stacks of the green fiberglass boards packed with things that looked like rectangular cockroaches that could have contained voodoo for all Kopeksky really understood about them. The redness that he had seen from across the room was just "there." It didn't seem to emanate from any discernible source, but permeated the innards of the unit as a diffuse reddening of the light from without, and hence everything that it fell on.

Erringer saw Kopeksky looking at it. "It was more pronounced earlier," he said. "Apparently it's eased off since they shut this machine down."

"Like at the airports, Kopeksky said.

"Quite."

"It quits when the switching stops."

"So it seems . . . after a while, anyhow. And there's this." Erringer showed him a piece of precision-made, rotary machinery, consisting of a shaft mounted in a bearing assembly, with supporting plate and bearings. But it was no longer so precise. The once-gleaming metal surfaces had lost their sheen and become buckled and distorted. Parts that should have turned freely were locked solid. "From one of the disk units," Erringer said. "Totally seized up. It's the same with the cooling fans and motors too, and the printers. All the mechanical peripherals are wrecked. That's going to cost hundreds of thousands alone."

There were other parts taken from different units, and some printed circuit cards from the worst-affected electronics cabinets, which were apparently also nonfunctional. The cards showed the kind of deformation that Kopeksky would have expected to see had they been in a fire, but without any scorching. Odd, he decided, and added a couple of them to his collection of items to take back.

Then two men whom Kopeksky recognized from the managers that Erringer had talked to on the sidewalk outside appeared from the stairwell, which now had a bluish tint, and drew Erringer aside. Kopeksky heard some talk about a pier cracking on the second floor, and then they called Milliken over, who came across with the engineer who was called Bill. Meanwhile, a police officer with lots of braid and several lieutenants came out from the stairway and stood hovering. Kopeksky decided that this wasn't the time to be hanging around waiting to ask theoretical questions. He caught Erringer's attention long enough to say that he would be on his way, and for Erringer to let him know the news when he had a chance. Then he left via the blue-tinted stairs to the lobby and exited into the blue-tinted street that suddenly reverted to normal daylight again.

Kopeksky found a pay phone in a coffee shop along the street, but was unable to get through to the Bureau since the exchanges were having more than the usual amount of trouble. He went back to one of the police cruisers to try via the radio, but the channels had all drifted way out of tune. If this was typical of what was happening city-wide, they weren't far away from a complete breakdown, he thought to himself. He thrust his hands deep in his overcoat pockets and stood staring back across the street at the facade of the Scicomp building. More people were being brought out onto the street, drifting lazily through the pink light inside the lobby and then snapping into life as they came through the doors.

Mice, one of the engineers had said. Except that mice don't eat machinery, or steel and concrete from the inside until a building suddenly starts to fall down. If it had been wood, the other had said, they would have had a bad case of dry rot. Kopeksky turned the words over in his head. Mice. Buildings. Wood. Wooden buildings. Wooden buildings falling down. . . .

Termites.

"It's bugs, ye should be looking for," Moynihan had told them. What did bugs that ate buildings have to do with time? Kopeksky frowned and went over the question again, trying to ask himself what, exactly, he meant by it. He wasn't sure, but an instinct told him that there was a convoluted connection somewhere. Who to talk to? Erringer was unavailable for the time being, and there didn't seem to be a way to contact anyone at the Bureau. Which left only one person.

Kopeksky walked over to the cruiser again and opened the front passenger-side door. "I need a ride to the Lower East Side," he told the driver. "It's a church near the Manhattan Bridge. I'll give you directions when we get down there." He climbed in and showed the plastic bag containing the samples that he had collected. "And after you drop me off, I want you to take these to the materials lab at City Bureau HQ. Ask for a guy called Jack Orelli. Tell him we need a report on the internal condition of this stuff. It's from the place where we've had the worst time lag so far, which means they drop whatever else they're doing and give it priority. Okay? Let's move."

9

The basement room of the presbytery at St. Vitus in The Fields was brightly lit with fluorescent tubes and whitewashed brick walls. A laboratory-type bench with sink, burner, and microscope ran along one side beneath shelves carrying an assortment of chemical glassware, jars, and bottles, and a biological specimen cabinet with glass doors took up most of the other. On a solidly built table in the corner opposite the door was a glass-walled tank three-quarters full of sandy soil with pieces of wood and wet cardboard scattered on the surface. Inside it, hundreds of orange bodied, waxy-looking insects were scurrying in and out and about an egg-shaped structure of what looked like cemented clay, partly exposed to reveal its extraordinarily intricate construction. It was about the size of a pineapple standing on end, and made up from top to bottom of rows of galleries and openings leading through to the inside, arranged in regular tiers like the floors of a building.

First fish, now bugs, Kopeksky thought to himself as he watched. "It looks like Grand Central at five-thirty," he commented.

"This is a species from the genus *Apicotermes,* found mainly in the Congo basin," Father Moynihan informed him. "The nests of termites include some remarkably complex structures that are without parallel in the animal kingdom. This particular kind is strictly subterranean. But as you're probably aware, there are others that build mounds above ground, sometimes to amazing heights. Some in Australia can top twenty feet. That would be about the same as ourselves putting up a building over a mile high."

"They don't have to worry about the elevators going out," Kopeksky said, peering closely through the tank wall. The termites appeared soft bodied, with no trace of a hard outer shell. "I always thought of them as kinda like ants. They don't look like ants."

"At one time they were popularly referred to as white ants, but the term is incorrect," Moynihan said. "They're a completely separate order that evolved from an ancestral stock resembling modern roaches: the order Isoptera—as opposed to Hymenoptera, which are the bees, wasps, and ants."

"So are there lots of different kinds?"

"More than you'll find freckles on an Irish boy scout troop."

"What makes up an order? Different species?" Kopeksky asked.

Moynihan nodded. "There are estimated to be somewhere between two and three thousand of them. As a rule they exist in more rigidly structured societies than other social insects—necessary for food sharing to exchange the bacteria and symbiotic microorganisms that they have to have to digest the cellulose they live on." He leaned forward to peer into the tank alongside Kopeksky and pointed. "See those. They're some of the soldiers, which are interesting. Their heads and bodies are so thoroughly modified into weapons that they can neither feed themselves nor reproduce. A bit like some Irishmen that I've known in me time."

Kopeksky straightened up. "And these are the guys who can eat your house away until it falls down, right?"

"Well, not this particular variety," Moynihan said. "All of them eat wood, true, but most of the damage to property is caused by what are called the *Kalotermitidae*, or dry-wood family."

"Whatever," Kopeksky said. "They chew up a bit at a time from here, from there, all spread out so you don't notice at first. And then one day all that stuff that you thought you had under you isn't there any more, and holes start appearing all over your house."

Moynihan moved back from the tank and recited:
"*Some primal termite knocked on wood*
And tasted it and found it good,
And that is why your cousin May
Fell through the parlour floor today."

"You write poems about them too?" Kopeksky sounded surprised.

"Ogden Nash."

"Oh. Okay. . . . Anyhow, what we think of as a solid building material, they see as food."

Moynihan scratched the side of his nose, unsure why Kopeksky was dwelling on this. "Yes, I suppose you could put it like that," he agreed. "A rather odd way to think of it, if you don't mind me saying. I have the suspicion, now, that you're leading up to something."

Kopeksky turned fully to face him. "Father, how much do you know about these universes that are supposed to exist in other dimensions, like these scientists keep talking about?"

"And why would you be asking me that, now?"

"Would something in this universe—the one we're in—still look like the same kind of . . . 'substance' to somebody in one of the other universes?" Kopeksky rapped the top of the bench with a knuckle. "This, for instance. To us it's real stuff. Hard and solid. Could it look like a 'hole,' say, to one of these aliens—not something solid at all? . . . Or maybe something that's completely different from substance: something that doesn't take up any room at all, empty or solid?"

"This is a fine riddle you're getting me into now," Moynihan said, wrinkling his face and trying to follow.

Kopeksky came to the point that had been forming in his mind ever since he left Scicomp. "When you were at the Bureau yesterday, you said that what we oughta be looking for is bugs." He waved vaguely at the glass tank beside them. "Now this might sound crazy, I know, but I figure you're pretty used to it. Could you have a situation where something that's solid stuff in one of these other universes comes across like time in ours? See what I mean? Then if they had some kind of bugs that ate it, then it would be just food to them, but making holes all over the place in our time—just like with the species that eat houses."

Moynihan stared at him in astonishment. "Bugs? Bugs that eat time?" he repeated.

Kopeksky shrugged and showed his palms. "I listened to what you said and to what the doc said, and I look at what's been going on. It's the only thing I can think of that fits with what we've got."

As Kopeksky had expected, Moynihan did not ridicule the suggestion out of hand, but paused to give it some thought. "That's an unbelievable thing that you're asking me to believe now," he said at last.

"I'm not saying it's true," Kopeksky said. "I'm just asking if you think it's possible."

"Well, stranger things have happened under heaven than either you or I are capable of imagining," Moynihan answered.

"So it isn't impossible?"

"I'd be the last one to tell you that it was."

Kopeksky felt suitably encouraged and went on, "The part of it that I still don't get is the building starting to fall apart at Scicomp. Maybe the story gets more complicated, and some of what these bugs eat *does* still look like solid stuff in our universe. What do you think?"

Moynihan held up a warning hand. "Wait a second, now. Don't you be putting me in the position of venturing an opinion. This is your own theory, not mine. It's the scientists that we should be putting this kind of a question to."

"We?"

Moynihan looked mildly indignant. "Well of course, 'we.' Now that you've got me curiosity roused, you don't think you're going to keep me away from finding out what the answers are, do you?"

Kopeksky had no problem with that. He nodded. "That's fine by me."

Moynihan went on, "I'd suggest talking to that fella Erringer. He struck me as one of the few that you meet who's prepared to listen more than he wants to talk."

The first thing would be to see what kind of reception this got back at the Bureau, Kopeksky decided. If the things he'd seen so far were a preview of what the rest of the city was in for, they were going to need as much start as they could get— assuming that somebody came up with a way of doing anything about the situation.

"Communications are shaky all over, so we probably won't be able to get in touch with him that way," he said. "Can you go to Scicomp up at Fifty Ninth and drag him out if you have to, then get him over to Bureau HQ? I'll go on there and brief whoever I can get ahold of that's around. I'll meet you there in an hour. Ask for Ellis Wade's office. He's my chief there. And his boss is a guy called Langlon. I'll be with one of them."

"Very good."

They left the basement and went up to the hallway leading to the front door. "An hour," Moynihan repeated as they put on their coats. "What time do you have now, just to be sure?"

Kopeksky pulled out his silver watch and compared it with the old grandfather clock ticking sedately by the hat stand. To his surprise the pocket watch was reading six minutes behind. He showed it and looked at Moynihan inquiringly. The priest raised his eyebrows and shrugged in a way that said Kopeksky could make anything of it that he wanted. Kopeksky hesitated, then adjusted his watch to conform to

Moynihan's clock. They left and walked together to the end of the block, then parted to head for their respective destinations.

By the time Kopeksky got back to the Bureau, reports were pouring in of mounting chaos everywhere. The phones were practically all out, since timeshift reddenings had begun appearing in the exchanges, and the operators were refusing to work there. Staff were walking out at a number of other large computer sites for the same reason, and several more buildings had been evacuated because of structural deterioration. Two—a data services center on the West Side and a clearing house for one of the major banks off lower Broadway—had actually started falling down inside. Thousands of people were quitting the city, and the tunnels and bridges exiting Manhattan were jammed.

Kopeksky checked that the samples he had sent from Scicomp had reached the lab and were being worked on, then went up to his office on the twelfth floor. Deena had recruited the help of one of the electrical specialists from Technical Services to complete the wall chart, and they were examining the results when Kopeksky joined them. The tech was new to the department. Kopeksky had seen him around but not gotten to know him. His name was Hasley, and he looked all engineer: crew cut and wearing a short-sleeved shirt with its pocket stuffed with pens, rule, and a calculator.

"It's mainly large computer sites, but there are other focuses as well," he said when Kopeksky questioned him. "The time dilation seems to correlate with some combination of fast, regular, electrical switching activity and local power density. Without a lot of detailed investigations and measurements, I couldn't be more specific than that."

"Pretty much what Graham guessed," Deena said.

Hasley nodded. "I'd say he was right."

"That's good enough for now," Kopeksky said. "I think we may have a new angle on it." He went on to summarize the theory that he had put to Moynihan, and Moynihan's reaction to it. He concluded, "Don't tell me it's straight outta the Far Side, because I already know that. Does anyone have anything better?"

Deena hadn't. "Well, it's different. I'll give it that," was all she could offer just for the moment.

Hasley shook his head in bafflement. "Bugs in another dimension, eating time? Hell, I don't know. I'm just an electrical engineer, not a witchdoctor."

"I think we should talk to Graham," Deena said.

"Definitely," Hasley agreed.

"Moynihan's gone to Scicomp to bring him over," Kopeksky told them. "They should be here any time. Meanwhile we need to fill in Ellis, before they show up."

"Oh-oh," Deena said ominously.

"What's up?" Kopeksky asked, sensing a problem.

"Grauss is back. Apparently there was a hell of a row with those scientists that he went to see up in Chicago. They seem to think he's crazy. Ellis and the rest of the suits are tearing about all over the place upstairs. I don't think you're gonna get sense out of anybody up there today."

"We'll see," Kopeksky replied.

10

Arriving at Wade's office on the fifteenth floor, they found Ruth valiantly holding a roomful of people all gabbling at once and waving their arms in the air, and with a Christmas tree of lights flashing on her desk. Kopeksky managed to extract that Wade had fled to yet higher ramparts of the building, muttered a few words of encouragement to Ruth, and left again with Deena and Hasley.

Wade and Grauss had holed up in the office of Wade's boss, David Langlon, on the sixteenth. Langlon had been academy-trained to believe in delegation and usually left it to Wade to handle awkward visitors. Hence, his secretary was less experienced than Ruth in protecting the inner sanctum, and no match for an old hand, like Kopeksky, at getting into places where he wasn't wanted.

Langlon was sitting behind his desk, and Wade was in a visitor's chair on the other side, both looking equally glassy-eyed, while Grauss stood facing them from the wall opposite, in front of a whiteboard covered in diagrams and mathematical hieroglyphics. The departmental procedure manuals had nothing to say about this kind of situation, and Langlon was too dazed to offer any resistance to Kopeksky's intrusion. Wade started to go through the motions of checking his subordinate, but Kopeksky circumvented him with practiced ease and went on to repeat his story.

A stupefied silence settled on the room like a fog blanket when Kopeksky had finished. Langlon and Wade looked at each other helplessly, and then, as if with one mind, turned their heads toward the scientist for salvation. Grauss was still standing motionless before the whiteboard, a red marker pen in one hand and his eyes popping like poached eggs behind his Coke-bottle lenses.

"*Pugs!*" he managed to choke at last. "Serious issues are ve concerned mit on der breakthrough fringe porderlands of science, unt of pugs you are talkink us? Vass iss mit pugs? Vere kommen from, zese pugs?"

"He says you're a nut," Wade interpreted.

"Why am I a nut any more than him?" Kopeksky demanded indignantly. "What is there that says somebody has to be stealing anything deliberately? Look, downstairs we've charted all the data. Come and see it for yourselves. The pattern isn't the way a hoist ring operates. It *is* the way that bugs spread diseases. There's an expert on his way here who can tell you about it."

Grauss waved his hands in small circles like a Mississippi sidewheeler stranded on a mudbank. "But mit der aliens, ve haff ze *motive*, ja? Der time do zey vant to live easy, pecause der technology zey haff to take. But pugs? Vy der time do zese pugs vant?" He gestured toward Kopeksky. "Iss fir essen, he says? To eat? How eat zey der time?" He turned his hand upward and shrugged scornfully. "Vat nutritional value iss der time? How many calories iss vun hour?"

Kopeksky shook his head. "I'm not saying they eat time—"

"Vat ziss?" Grauss interrupted, throwing out a hand. "Virst he say der pugs, zey do eat der time. Now zey don't eat der time. Iss makink up der mind you should be, not vastink vat time iss left dat der aliens haff not taken."

"To *them* it's not time," Kopeksky persisted. "In their universe, they eat some kind of food, sure. But what I'm saying is that with all these dimensions and stuff, maybe it gets altered somehow and looks like time to us."

"They could convert one to another," Deena interjected in an effort to clarify. "Maybe in the same kind of way that energy and mass are interconvertible within our universe. . . . Or space and time between Einsteinian reference frames."

Grauss blinked. Wade stared at her in astonishment. Hasley nodded.

"I think there might be grounds here for a basic policy review for the entire investigation," Langlon said in a tone that sounded as if that wrapped the whole thing up, right there. Nobody took any notice.

"How zis food unt der time, zey transform?" Grauss challenged. But at the same time, he was twiddling uncomfortably with the marker pen and sounding less sure of his ground.

"I dunno," Kopeksky answered. "That's your department. But instead of saying they can't, and putting the brakes on everything before you've even started, why not say maybe they do, and try working backward? Then see where that gets you."

"Inductive, not deductive," Deena pointed out, being helpful in case anyone had missed it.

"It could form a complete transform group," Hasley murmured, more to himself.

"How did we ever get into this shit?" Wade groaned, looking perplexedly around the room from one to another.

The intercom on Langlon's desk buzzed. He stared at it with the paralyzed expression of a human cannonball watching the net go sailing by below. "Better answer it," Wade suggested.

Langlon reached out and pressed a button. "Yes, Betty?"

His secretary's voice replied from the outer office. "I'm sorry to interrupt again Mr. Langlon, but there are two gentlemen here wanting to see Mr. Kopeksky and Mr. Wade. I told them you're in conference, but they are being most insistent. One of them is a priest, and the man with him—"

"They're the guys I'm expecting," Kopeksky said. Langlon shot Wade an inquiring look. Wade nodded resignedly in a way that said this couldn't get any worse.

"Show them in, please," Langlon said to the intercom and clicked it off.

The door opened and Moynihan came in, followed by Erringer. "You're taking your life in your hands crossing the street out there, and that's for sure," Moynihan said. "It's like Lansdowne Road in Dublin when Ireland beats the Brits at rugby."

Betty hovered guiltily in the doorway behind them,

looking like a embarrassed beaver whose dam had fallen down. "I'm sorry, Mr. Langlon, but they were most insistent. . . ." Langlon nodded that it was okay and waved a hand. Betty left, closing the door.

Kopeksky introduced everybody. Erringer's news was that the Scicomp building had been declared unsafe and evacuated, and city engineers were now examining the Queensboro Bridge adjacent to it, which had apparently contracted similar problems. He had heard the gist of Kopeksky's idea from Moynihan on the way across town and was intrigued. "Well, whatever else, it sure fits," was the only judgment he was prepared to pass at this stage, however.

Grauss wasn't prepared to let another scientist onto the territory without some show of credentials. "Vy zen zese patches do ve see all over der city? Vy zese pugs, zey eat time from here unt from here, but not eat it from zere unt from zere?" he queried, waving an arm first on one side, then the other. "Vy der Pell Telephone's time zey eat, unt der JFK time zey eat, but der time from der Park unt der footpall stadiums unt der churches zey don't eat? Vass iss difference? Time iss time, nein? Vere iss sense? Makes no sense."

Wade looked at Erringer curiously. Erringer just shrugged.

There was a short silence. Then Deena said, "I wonder what Eskimos would say if they knew we had all kinds of different words for construction material."

Wade shook his head as if to clear it. "What?"

"Well, you know, maybe this is like with Eskimos. . . . To us it's just snow, but they've got I don't know how many different words for it, because to them it has all kinds of different functions." She looked around quickly, as if seeking moral support. The others returned expressions totally devoid of encouragement or comprehension. She went on, anyway. "Time could work the same way with these bugs that we're talking about. For us it's just . . ." she made clutching motions in the air as if groping for a word, then gave up, " 'time,'—it's all the same. But for them there might be different kinds of time." She nodded to herself as if finally getting straight in her head what she wanted to say. "What I mean is, they could see it as different kinds of . . . whatever it is they eat—but it all looks like the same 'time' to us. Or I guess you could say that they see different kinds of time, where we don't. So the reason why they eat it from some places and not others is that different kinds of time, somehow . . . 'taste' better."

"Taste better?" Wade repeated the words, thought about them, shook his head and looked at Langlon. Grauss stood hunched like some scrawny bird of prey, his fingers curled around the marker like talons.

"If it's a total transform group, who knows what might happen?" Hasley said at last, still distantly. "If matter in their universe can transform into something as apparently unrelated as time in ours, who's to say what variations there might be about time that make it as different as chalk from cheese to these bugs?"

"Or granite from wood," Moynihan said, taking the point and nodding. "Tastes different to them, eh? My word, there's thought enough for a few wet Sundays in all this."

"Something qualitatively different about different kinds of time that gives it a different . . . flavor," Hasley completed. He spread his hands to show that that was as far as he could take it.

Everyone seemed to be waiting on everyone else for an inspiration. Erringer paced slowly over to the window and looked out. The others watched but said nothing.

"Why not?" he announced finally, and turned to face them. "Deena said that time looks all the same to us, but does it really? I know that the instruments we physicists measure time with don't distinguish one kind from another. But isn't it true that we, as beings that are far more cognitive than any instrument, are well aware that time comes in all manner of brands and flavors?" He paused and looked around invitingly. Then he indicated the priest with a nod. "Father Moynihan here just said it. We all know the difference between how time drags on a wet Sunday and flies when you're enjoying yourself at a party; or a morning spent waiting for an appointment with the dentist and one rushing to an airport. See what I mean? We all *know* that different kinds of time feel different. They even seem to run at different rates. Well, conceivably the differences in time in our universe that correspond to whatever these bugs base their preferences on in theirs, have to do with just that: what's *happening in it!*"

Now it was Deena's turn to look confused. "You mean different things happening in what we see as time? That's what gives it a different flavor to them?"

"Right," Erringer said.

Moynihan pinched his nose dubiously. "What's happening in it?" he repeated. "Are you telling us that day-to-day affairs of living that would only have meaning to men and their maker could be of significance to microbes? Ah, now, that's too much for me to be swallowing. I don't think I could go along with that at all, at all, at all."

Erringer shook his head. "No, I didn't mean that they're sensitive to events that are meaningful only at the subjective human level. That was just to illustrate the point. But quantities that are objectively measurable, such as rates of change of various physical variables, do give different intervals of time distinctly different characteristics, which might equate to properties that the bugs in the other universe can distinguish between."

"All right, I'm with you now," Moynihan said, giving the notion his blessing.

"Such as rate of change of electric field!" Hasley exclaimed. "Especially when in regular patterns, and with overall power density figuring in somehow as a secondary variable. Which is what we've already said characterizes the worst-affected sites."

"I think you've got it," Erringer said, moving back from the window.

Hasley nodded rapidly as a lot more pieces of the picture fell into place. "It would explain the whole pattern that we've been seeing," he said. "Not only why it happens most at places like computer sites or TV centers, but also why things improve when they shut down: the bugs lose their appetite and go feed someplace else."

"And why the effect is smaller at less active installations, such as smaller computer sites, nighttime telephone exchanges, and even individual electronic appliances," Erringer said.

Kopeksky held his hands up and looked in amazement at the two watches he was still wearing, one on each wrist. "You mean that's why this piece of digital junk falls behind the windup? There's bugs actually being attracted to the electronics . . . that are eating the time there?"

"Exactly," Erringer said.

"Jeez!" Kopeksky breathed, staring fixedly at his chronometer as if he half expected to see them buzzing around it.

"And why there was nothing at all at St. Vitus," Moynihan said. "Everything of ours is clockwork, the way God intended."

Kopeksky frowned. "But wait a minute. If that's so, then how come my windup watch was behind yours when I was there earlier?"

"You'd just come from Scicomp," Erringer said. Kopeksky failed to look any the wiser. Erringer explained, "The time loss is worst at the innards of equipment that produces the conditions that the bugs find tastiest—in other words at the cores of the busiest parts of the machines, where there are more of them consuming it and presumably reproducing."

That made sense. Kopeksky nodded. "So that's why the red haze started in places like that," he guessed.

"Yes. Let's call that the 'core time.' So the depletion begins at the core, and hence in the early stages you get electronics running slow and all the effects that we observed, but outside the cabinets and in the immediate surroundings you don't see anything abnormal. But if I'm correct, this depletion at the core creates something like a 'time hole,' which causes time to fall into it, as it were, from the surrounding vicinity, and eventually the loss becomes perceptible in the room outside and the region around in general."

"And I'd spent some time in a place that was affected like that. So the watch I was carrying registered it. Okay." Kopeksky nodded to say that he was prepared to buy that much.

Erringer went on, "And if the parallel in our universe is anything to go by, the bug population increases, and the effect continues to spread outward from there."

And what after that? Kopeksky wondered. It *was* like a termite attack. Things appeared normal until a state of imminent collapse was reached, and then suddenly everything started falling in at once.

"And that is why your cousin May,
Fell through the parlor floor today," Moynihan murmured absently to himself. Evidently he had arrived at the same conclusion.

"From the measurements I saw at Scicomp, the local time outside the machine cabinets was slipping by about twenty percent," Erringer said. "That's just about the figure you'd need to shift the normal spectrum of visible wavelengths into the red. And again, that's just what was observed."

Kopeksky gave Wade a satisfied look. Whatever that meant, it sounded as if it confirmed his theory. "See," he said, making his voice sound as if it should have been obvious all along.

Wade and Langlon exchanged questioning looks. The others waited, having said all there really was to say. "What do you think?" Wade asked finally.

"I don't know. It's . . . I guess it's just about the craziest thing I ever heard."

Wade nodded. "Me too. In fact, it's just crazy enough that it might be true." He shrugged, as if excusing himself for stating the obvious. "But you get to expect that with Joe." Kopeksky grunted and raised his eyebrows at Deena.

Grauss was looking uncertainly from Erringer to Hasley to Kopeksky and then back again. For a moment he seemed to be tottering on the edge of reconsidering, but then he rallied and pounced on the point that was still unanswered. "Unt vy, zen, now der puildings zey fall down? Iss it der pugs now der city are consumink? Eizer zey eat der time or zey eat New York. Now iss both? Iss dat vat ve are now to believe, you are askink us?"

"That's the part I'm not too clear on either," Kopeksky admitted.

"Of course, I shall expect a full report on all this," Langlon said, having duly considered his options. His desk intercom buzzed. He answered it. "Yes?"

This time Betty didn't bother apologizing, but answered in an unquestioning tone that sounded resigned to accepting that everyone in the building would eventually end up in Langlon's office. "Jack Orelli from the materials lab. He's got the results of some tests they've been doing down there, that Mr. Kopeksky said can't wait."

"Send him in," Langlon said without asking.

A broad-chested, swarthy-skinned man in white shirtsleeves came in, carrying a wad of handwritten notes and figures, and a folder. He singled out Kopeksky and opened the folder to reveal x-ray pictures and micrographs. "I'll tell you one thing, Joe, right up front, and that's that nobody downstairs has seen anything like these before," he said.

Kopeksky indicated Erringer with a motion of his head. "I'm just the mailman for this one, Jack. That's who you should tell it to—Dr. Erringer, from an outfit called Scicomp, which is where the stuff came from. And this is Father Moynihan, who's helping us out. I guess you know everyone else."

Orelli selected some of the pictures and addressed Erringer. "There aren't any signs of what you'd call normal material deterioration. In cases of metallic corrosion or decomposition of concrete, you expect to find evidence of chemical activity and decay products. But here we don't have any. No signs of chemical changes. The materials are all of regular composition, but they're deformed. In every case the microstructure is altered in a way that I've never heard of before."

"No chemical reactions?" Erringer repeated. "So you're saying there's no actual material deficit? What accounts for the loss of mechanical strength, then?"

"That's exactly it." Orelli spread some of the plates out on Langlon's desk. "There's no loss of mass. But the density is reduced. It's as if all those materials—the steel tubes there, one of the bearings here, a sample of the concrete in this one—have been turned into microscopic styrofoam somehow. They're full of holes."

"You mean like sponge, Jack?" Deena said, looking puzzled. So did everyone else.

"On a much smaller scale," Orelli replied. "I'm talking about way, way smaller than that—as I said, microscopic." He picked out another micrograph and pointed. "Look there. In that piece of metal the interstices occur between the crystal grains, which have all been displaced. So what was an internally cohesive material turns into popcorn. That's where all its strength went."

Wade told himself that he might as well stick a toe in the water with all this scientific stuff too. What the hell? Everyone else was trying it. "Then it sounds as if what we said earlier was wrong," he ventured. "These bugs *are* eating the buildings as well, after all. Like with the termites."

But Orelli shook his head. "No. The holes aren't there because of anything that's been eating the material away. It's more as if the holes were *added* to what was already there." He looked up, showed his palms, and shook he head as a disclaimer. "It's as if tiny volumes of space had been *created* somehow, all the way through the material. That causes the mass to expand and distort, which is why all your bearings and motors started seizing up."

"Let me get this straight," Kopeksky said. "You're saying that there's holes in there, but not because anything got eaten away. All the stuff that was there before is still there now. But the holes just started appearing . . . like outta nowhere?"

Orelli threw his hands out. "That's exactly it, Joe. What else can I tell ya? It's got us beat."

"And it's spreading out from the primary sites and affecting nearby structures like the Queensboro Bridge," Erringer said distantly. "Where do the holes come from? Where does the time go?" For once he seemed at a loss. He focused back inside the room and turned questioningly toward Moynihan, but the priest was looking equally baffled.

"What happens to the wood that termites eat, anyhow?" Kopeksky asked, more to fill the void than with any constructive thought in mind.

"They metabolize it into gas, mostly," Moynihan replied. "Mainly carbon dioxide."

"Hm."

And then Grauss, who had gone quiet while absorbing it all like a crossbow slowly bending under tension, suddenly had his moment of conversion. *"Ja! Mein gott, ja!"* he exclaimed, springing upright and startling everyone else in the room. "At vonce der complete picture do I see. In der other-dimensional universe, vat ve haff as time unt space, zey are convertible. Unt der pugs, zey metabolize der vun into der other. As der time it iss input, but turned into space it outputs. Unt der space is diffused like mit der termite gases." He looked proudly at Erringer. "Ja? Nein? Vat off dat, Dr. Erringer, you zink?"

"What's he saying?" Wade asked, mystified.

Erringer could only shake his head incredulously. "That the bugs eat time and excrete space," he replied. "The way that things project into our universe, their metabolic process converts one into the other. It's the craziest thing I've heard all day. And this has been some day."

Grauss threw his arms up in exasperation. "Vy you say iss crazy?" he objected. "Everypody I listen to today iss crazy. Der zings vat you say, too, dey are crazy, unt vat he says, unt vat she says, unt vat he says. So vy not I can be crazy? But all together ve make sense. See. . . ." He turned back to the white-board and cleaned it with a series of rapid sweeps of the eraser pad.

"Didn't I say something like this?" Deena said to the room, but everyone was watching Grauss too intently to hear her.

Grauss put down the eraser and turned to gaze at the blank board. "Virst ve assume der governing equation to be off similar form to der Einstein relationship for der space unt der time, like so," he said, scrawling the familiar $E=m.c^2$ at the top. "So, ve take space, vich iss volume, or length cubed, equated to der light-velocity squared." He added a further line of symbols, looked at them, and shook his head. "But in dimensions ve see zat der two sides do not balance. Vor completeness ve must insert here der factor havink dimensions off length multiplied by time." He carried on, swiftly adding more lines with calculus operators. "Unt here, from der velocity expression, ve see zat der factor iss identical mit der time-integral of distance. Unt now ve ask, vat quantity it iss ve know dat hass such dimensions?" He looked around expectantly like a professor in a lecture room, as if answers should already be pouring back from all directions.

"He needs a factor to balance the equation," Erringer informed the others. "And it has to have the dimensions of length times time. From basic mechanics you can express it as the time-integral of distance. Or to put it in English, what is it that increases with time when nothing's happening?"

"Boredom," Deena answered automatically, without really thinking.

Langlon's intercom buzzed again. "The chief commissioner is on the line," Betty announced. "He's got the mayor on the line, who's got the state governor on his line, who's got the President on hold. Queensboro Bridge has been closed and could collapse at any moment. One of the towers of the Trade Center is starting to lean. Seven more buildings have been evacuated in the last half hour, and the streets around twelve city blocks have been closed. They want to know what you're going to do about it." Langlon stared at the unit with an expression that would have won a fish on a slab a an animation prize. "What do I tell them?" Betty's voice asked. Her tone was flat and deadpan, as if she were preparing for someone else to reply that Langlon had jumped out of the window. A morgue-like stillness enveloped the room.

"Well, what do you do to get rid of bugs?" Wade asked at last, more because somebody had to say something. He lifted a hand half heartedly. "What can you do? . . . You can spray them, poison them. What else? . . ."

"Take out the nests," Kopeksky tried. "Find something else that eats them. . . ." He shook his head. "Nah." Nothing like that was going to get them anywhere, and they all knew it.

And then Hasley said, "Look I don't know if this makes any sense, but if these bugs . . . or whatever they are . . . like to eat time that's got electrical activity going on in it, then maybe time without anything electrical happening in is . . ." he shrugged, "non-nutritional."

Erringer looked up sharply and stared at him. "What are you saying? That we might be able to starve them?"

Hasley nodded. "Something like that." He shrugged again and looked around. If everyone else was into crazy things today, then that was his nickel's worth.

Erringer looked at Langlon, who was still sitting with a finger on a button of the silently waiting intercom. "It's a thought," Erringer said. "At least it gives us something to say to them. And who knows? It might even work."

11

But it didn't.

Kopeksky stood with Erringer and Deena in the main control room of Con Edison's Energy Control Center on the West Side of Manhattan. This was the nerve center that directed the switching and routing of power from thirteen generating plants in the New York area and coordinated their operation with the six other utilities that formed the statewide New York Power Pool. The same center also supervised the distribution of natural gas across the area, as well as controlling the supply of piped process steam to over two thousand customers.

The panel above them in the series of huge mimic displays overlooking the floor of control desks and monitor consoles showed the part of the power supply grid covering Union and Essex counties, New Jersey. In the center of the sector, Newark International Airport and its immediate environs, which had been selected for the experiment, lay cut off from all power, isolated. The hope had been that if all electrical activity in the vicinity ceased, the mysterious alien "chronovores," as the scientists had now dubbed them, would famish and die out, or else migrate elsewhere in whatever peculiar realm they inhabited. But the reports from the scientists ringing the area with crystal-controlled timers and frequency standards locked to transmissions from outside showed that the bugs were simply migrating outward from Newark in search of new forage. The measures were not only failing to eradicate the plague, but actually spreading it faster.

"Well, it might have worked," Erringer said. He was feeling particularly glum just then. On the other side of town, the Scicomp building had collapsed that morning. Wall Street was missing a few teeth, and only the Triborough and George Washington bridges were still operating, both of them down to single lanes.

Hasley turned from a table with a large map spread out on top, where a group of scientists and city engineers were plotting the information coming in from the measuring stations set up across the river. Coordinating with the external world was a feat in itself, since the core dilation of the systems inside the Con Edison Center was averaging around sixty percent. It meant that everything in the outside world was running over half again as fast, and they were constantly having to reset their clocks to catch up.

"They're latching onto whatever they encounter," Hasley announced. "Some trucks have been stopped carrying them down the Turnpike with their CBs. In other places it's personal computers and TVs, even portable radios. If this goes on it'll turn into a national epidemic. We'll be sending carriers all over the country."

The director in charge of operations took stock of the situation from his seat in the center of a master desk on a raised dais overlooking the room. "Abort the whole thing," he instructed. "We're just making a big fan and throwing shovelfuls at it. This way it'll be in California by tomorrow."

"What do we do about the test sector?" one of the aides beside him asked, meaning the airport and its surroundings.

"Turn everything back on. It'll give 'em something to chew on. At least that way we'll know where they are until somebody figures out what to try next."

Deena looked unhopefully at Kopeksky. "Any thoughts what to try next?" she asked.

"Go find a hot-dog stand or something," Kopeksky growled. "All this talk about starving bugs has made me hungry."

"A drop o' the dew of Tullamore," Father Moynihan said. Kopeksky watched from one of the armchairs in the priest's study as Moynihan leaned over the side table between them and poured two glasses of Irish whiskey. He motioned at a jug beside the glasses "You can add water to suit your taste. I just take a splash meself."

Kopeksky decided to try it straight. It was warm and mellow, a lot smoother than he had expected. Didn't hit the back of the throat with diesel fumes, like scotch. He suspected that Moynihan might have pulled off another conversion.

"I, ah, take it that it's all right?" Moynihan said,

pausing as he lifted his own glass and looking up. "Ye being on duty and that, I mean."

Kopeksky heaved his shoulders and sighed. "What the hell? The way things are going, there won't be much more duty in this city to be worrying about for very much longer." He took another sip. "How about you? On duty it's okay?"

Moynihan smiled. "Ah well, now, in our line of work we're on duty, as it were, all the time. Therefore we have to be, what one might call, a little more pragmatic about these matters."

"And to fit in back home, right?" Kopeksky offered, to give Moynihan an even broader excuse.

"Ah, now don't ye be so quick at slagging us," Moynihan said. "We're a very devout and holy breed, I'll have you know. Why, doesn't every Irishman try to model his life on that of Christ?"

"How'd you figure that?"

"Ye've only got to look at them. They're still living at home at the age of thirty. All with twelve good drinking buddies, faithful and true. And there isn't a one where both he and his mother doesn't think that he's God. . . . Anyhow, it isn't the best of news that ye've brought, I gather. The experiment they tried at Newark didn't work?"

"It made things even worse." Kopeksky went on to summarize what had happened. He ended, tossing out a hand wearily, "So they had to call it off. It was all ready to take off across the state."

Moynihan, who had been listening intently, nodded over his still quarter-full glass. "That's just what it was by the sound of it. The microbes were finding carriers. We should have guessed, if we'd thought about it, from the way those two watches that you carry get out of step. It's only a small difference, I know, but it means that the electronic one manages to draw a few of them to itself. That would be enough to grow into a large population again, as soon as they found a larger source of food."

"You mean they could follow a person's watch?" Kopeksky looked horrified. "Maybe hitch a ride on a plane someplace, like rats on a ship? And then start breeding again when they got to a big IBM center or somewhere? It works like that?"

"That's the way it's beginning to sound to me, all right. A classic case of carrier transmission."

Kopeksky shook his head protestingly. "Well . . . hell. What do you do about it?"

"Quarantine is the first step, of course. Strict quarantine. Thank God the airports closed when they did, or else it might have been everywhere by now. But you have to stop those people who are moving out of the city and into the state and elsewhere from taking anything electronic with them. Call in all the radios, TV's, calculators, everything. And keep a strict watch for outbreaks in other places they might have taken it to already, and contain them too."

"That doesn't sound too easy," Kopeksky said uneasily.

"I never said it would be."

"Okay, suppose we manage it. Then what?"

Moynihan shrugged. "You apply any measures you know of to kill it . . ."

"We don't."

". . . in which case you can only wait for it to die out."

"What if it doesn't?"

"It has to eventually. Every organism depends on some source of nourishment. If you cut that source off, it stands to reason that the infection must terminate."

"I thought you said the Irish didn't always care too much about what stands to reason."

"They don't. But fortunately with reality it's a different matter."

Kopeksky watched the flames in the fireplace and considered the proposition. It didn't sound very encouraging. "We could end up sending the whole world back to the Stone Age before we're through," he murmured.

"Then maybe we'll make a better job of getting out of it the second time round," Moynihan said.

Kopeksky stared at the fire. "You might even end up with fields around again. . . . So there's not a lot else. Nothing more, sorta . . . positive?" He looked back across the room, sensing that Moynihan wasn't listening. The priest was lost in thought, staring through the hearth rug. "Hello?" Kopeksky tried cautiously.

"Rats," Moynihan said, still with a faraway expression.

"What?"

Moynihan returned part of the way. "You compared them to rats a minute ago. I'd never thought of that. I've always had this vision of them in me mind as insects."

"So?"

Moynihan came back fully and turned in his chair. "Maybe there is something better that we can do," he said. "If these creatures that we're talking about find time with electrical activity going on in it to be so tasty, then perhaps we can arrange a really irresistible morsel or two that will enable us to send them away somewhere else." His eyes glittered in the firelight. "I'm sure you've heard the story about a fella known as the Pied Piper from a long time ago, in a little place they called Hamlin. . . ."

12

It was possibly the most outlandish cavalcade ever to have trundled its way along a U.S. public highway. In the middle, an Army field tractor hauled one of the enormous flatbed trailers designed for transporting the M1 Abrahams Main Battle Tank. On it, surrounded by the now familiar reddish haze, were mounted a double line of steel cabinets containing a collection of some of the most powerful computer hardware available, obtained from sites all over the New York metropolitan area. A mobile generating system coupled behind supplied power, while trucks ahead, behind, and on the flanks carried teams of scientists with equipment to measure fluctuations of time dilation in the immediate vicinity.

Kopeksky was back in Con Edison's control center, watching as the situation around Newark was reconstructed on one of the mural displays above the lines of control desks. Once again the power to the area centered upon the airport had been switched off, and the chronovores had moved outward to its periphery to form localized clusters around small computer setups, neon signs, telephone switchboards, hi-fi stores—anything that offered something to nibble on until their next opportunity for a hearty meal. "Sweeper One," as the mobile installation on the flatbed trailer had been designated, was just passing an automated bottling plant south of the airport, where one of the centers of localized time dilation had been detected.

"Flank Right is reporting a dip. I think we've got it. Looks like they might be moving," a controller at one of the monitors sang out. A tense expectancy rose around the room. On the dais the operations director and his staff sat motionless, waiting.

"Station Seventeen reporting now," another voice called. That was the measuring post inside the bottling plant. "Their lag is reducing already, slipping back to EST . . . oh, fast, fast!" The swarm had caught the scent of the passing meal wagon and were pouring out after it.

"Trail has a dip. They're following."

A voice high with surprise: "Seventeen's heading for zero. This is incredible? It can work that fast?"

"Andy, get a second check on that reading from Seventeen and report." The director's voice this time.

A pause. Then, "Yep, they're clean there. No question about it."

Kopeksky turned toward where Moynihan was standing next to him. "Do you hear what I hear?" he muttered disbelievingly. "I'm starting to think that this crazy idea of yours might really work."

"Ah, what are ye talking about? 'Twas a grand idea, to be sure, to be sure."

For the rest of the day Sweeper One lumbered around the periphery of the airport area, adding more chronovore swarms to its catch. And all along its route the digital watches, clock-radios, and other devices that had been showing minor time lags all ceased misbehaving, which seemed to indicate that, as everyone had hoped but none had dare predict, the strays along the way were being swept up too.

By nightfall all of the measuring posts around the quarantined zone were reporting null results, and Sweeper One had crossed the Pike and traversed the industrial parks and railroad sidings of Jersey City to the west bank of the Hudson. From there, moving with agonizing slowness in its own cocoon of fifty-percent-retarded time, the convoy led its strange following through the Holland Tunnel and back into Manhattan. By next morning all readings were still showing the Jersey side to be clean.

In the Con Edison Energy Control Center, the operations director sat back at his desk up on the dais and looked satisfied. "It looks as if we're good on the test run," he told his lieutenants sitting on either side. "Okay, let's try for the big one while we've still got some of this city left. Alert all zone controllers and copy the governor's office. We're going straight to EXTERMINATOR right now. Get the activation plan up on the screens."

13

New York lay wrapped in an unheard of stillness. Its towers stood empty and silent like the stones of a gigantic, forgotten graveyard. Every window of the stores and office blocks was unlit; not a neon sign flickered; nor did a traffic light wink, an elevator move, or a motor hum, anywhere. The entire electrical supply to the city had been shut off and the use of battery-powered devices of any kind banned. The hospitals had been evacuated, the businesses closed, and most of the residents had left for surroundings that offered at least some vestige of the comforts and conveniences that they were accustomed to. Detachments of police and Guard patrolled the streets to enforce the emergency regulations and protect property from looting. Scientists had set up a network of stations to record the vicissitudes of local times, and engineers were maintaining a constant watch for further instances of failing structures. But apart from them, only a few, through curiosity, obstinacy, or simply the elevated feeling that some people experience from being different, remained to wander through the parks or along the deserted avenues, reveling in the solitude, feasting on the silence, or stopping occasionally to take in the spectacle of sagging floors exposed by the collapsed side of a skyscraper, or a street filled with the rubble of what had yesterday been a whole building.

Wearing a nylon overjacket on top of his coat and a headset plugged into a socket by his seat, Joe Kopeksky sat in a NYCPD helicopter circling above the East River, just off the southern tip of Roosevelt Island. Moynihan was next to him, with Erringer and Deena in the two seats across the narrow center aisle. Wade and Grauss, along with several other scientific people and a couple of officials from Washington, filled the rear section of the cabin.

Below them, a short distance to the north, what looked like a deep red cloud lay on the Manhattan shoreline, just opposite the rear of what was left of the Scicomp building, below the ruined west end of the Queensboro Bridge. The cloud enveloped a pair of huge barges lashed together and moored alongside FDR Drive. A flotilla of tugboats stood a short distance out on the fringe of the cloud, trailing towing lines back to the barges.

One of the barges was loaded with diesel engines, electrical generating equipment, and a pumping system to circulate cooling water. From it, a tangle of cables and hoses connected across to the other barge, which was fitted with a canvas canopy supported by posts. Beneath the canopy was a super version of the lure that had been tested as Sweeper One: an array of several hundred electronics cabinets jammed side by side in rows and stacked several tiers deep. The assortment included the supercomputers from Scicomp's basement, which had survived the collapse of the building; giant machines from the banks and Wall Street; heavy peripheral drivers from service bureaus and commercial sites; and processor-bound number crunchers from engineering centers, research institutes, and colleges. There were no disks drives or anything else mechanical to break down—just cubicles containing pure electronics, which would take days to deteriorate to the point of becoming nonfunctional. They didn't have to do anything that would normally be considered productive; only to run programs that would drive every piece of circuitry to its utmost.

Hence, at just this one spot in the entire New York area, there existed a concentration of millions of the fastest electronic circuit chips that had ever been produced, switching tightly regimented patterns of data at a local power intensity that one of the engineers had described to Kopeksky as being like, "half of IBM and Con Edison put on the Staten Island ferry."

The decks of the barges and the quay alongside them were scenes of hectic activity. At least, the observers in the swarm of helicopters overhead and on the boats dotted about the river were assured that what was going on down there was hectic activity. But through binoculars, the figures moving among the bundles of cables snaking all over the decks, waving direction from the tugs, or going up and down the gangplanks to the shore all seemed to drift about their tasks with a strange, dreamlike lethargy—an impression which at first sight seemed all the more objectionable on account of their being volunteers on a thousand dollars an hour. In fact, the time dilation in the vicinity of the barges was now running in excess of 25%, while the circuits at the core of the operating electronics were losing no less than forty-five minutes out of every hour.

In terms of sheer space-concentration of electrical activity, it was the equivalent of an island of rain forest in the center of the Sahara, or a single supernova pouring out light into the intergalactic void. As a source of chronovore food, New York had been turned into a desert; and to entice its locust swarms away from whatever scraps and remnants they might have found across the metropolitan wilderness, a feast had been prepared in the midst of the famine.

And it seemed to have worked. For days now, the scientists across the city had been measuring time returning to normal everywhere and a halt in the appearance of new cases of structural decay. As had happened with the trial scheme at Newark, some localized pockets had remained along the fringe of the area, and a fleet of lumbering "Sweeper" units had been going out, back and forth, all day long, bringing them back into the common pound. By now, no time losses were being reported from anywhere else, and the dilation around the barges had escalated to the highest that had been encountered. The Pied Piper had rounded up his catch. Now it was time to take them away.

A red dot appeared on the shoreline across the river from the barges, on the Queens side. It grew to become more distinct, and then rose slowly to hang a couple of hundred feet above the command post that had been set up to coordinate the river part of the operation. The balloon was a signal that the final phase had received its go-ahead.

"There it is, folks," the pilot's voice announced over the intercom.

"Ja, see now. Ve haff der palloon," Grauss's voice said excitedly on the circuit.

Deena craned forward in her seat until she could pick it out herself over the rooftops. "That's it? So everything's clear now down there?"

"Let's hope so, anyhow," Erringer muttered next to her.

"Want me to go down and check it out," the pilot asked.

"Do that," Wade's voice said.

The helicopter banked into a turn and dipped toward the east shore. As it came closer, the observer up front with the pilot used binoculars to read the signal being run up on flag masts below. The helicopter was under strict radio silence, no use of radar allowed, no computers, no navigational electronics. Strictly seat-of-the-pants stuff, the way real flying used to be. And ditto, especially, for ground control and the other operations going on below, where communications were restricted to dispatch riders, semaphore, Morse lamps, and a minimum of rudimentary field telephones.

"*All clocks reporting in synch,*" the observer

decoded. *"Final traces infestation appear eliminated. Proceeding Phase Green."*

"Did ye hear that? The saints be praised!" Moynihan exclaimed. A burst of cheering and hand-clapping erupted from the rest of the cabin. Erringer turned and gave Deena a hug. Wade pounded the armrest of his seat solidly in satisfaction.

"Vy iss saints all off sudden?" Grauss asked, looking at Erringer. "Vat dey do to stop der pugs? Ve haff something to do mit also, a little, ja?"

"Ah, you know how it is with these PR guys," Kopeksky told them, indicating Moynihan with a jerk of his thumb.

The chopper climbed again and moved back toward the red cloud hanging over the barges on the Manhattan side. Already, the gangplanks to the shore were being lifted back. In the eerie shroud of red fading to smoky purple at the center, the figures on the decks moved in slow motion, hauling in lines, securing cables, and making last-minute checks and adjustments. Then the water at the sterns of the waiting tugs churned into orange foam—they were inside the fringe of the optically affected zone—and one by one the tugs began straining forward to take up the slack in the lines. Slowly, slowly from the viewpoint of those watching from overhead, the vessels formed into two fans of tugboats ahead of and pulling the pair of heavily laden barges. Still surrounded by the red cloud, which slowly detached itself from the shoreline, the strange armada moved out to the center of the East River and set course downstream. It passed under the Brooklyn Bridge, and moved out into Upper New York Bay.

There it lay moored a mile out from the shore, bathed in its red aura, for a full week. During this period several chronovore swarms that had been missed were found on shore, lured away, and brought out to the barges by a floating version of the Sweepers. Finally, every test that could be devised failed to find any remaining trace of the affliction anywhere in Manhattan or its surrounding boroughs.

It was time for the final act. A freighter that had been specially prepared in south Brooklyn docks was brought out to the barges—a 20,000 ton container ship whose holds had been reinforced and made watertight, and then fitted out with more banks of high-power computing hardware. The hardware aboard the barges, which by now was just about at the end of its span and had begun giving out, was shut down, and, exactly as planned, the accumulated swarm moved to the new concentration running flat-out in the freighter. The freighter was then towed to a point a thousand miles out above the North Atlantic deep, and sunk. Five miles down, in the lightless, lifeless desert of the abyssal plain, everything switched off.

Utter stillness reigned. Utter silence. Nothing moving, nothing changing. Time eternal. Time with nothing happening in it. Bland time. Insipid time. Tasteless time. Nutritionless time.

And there the chronovores starved.

All but a few, that is. In a separate compartment of the vessel, a personal computer was left running at a low activity level to keep a small, controlled population alive. Instruments would automatically adjust the running program to keep the numbers in check and report the situation periodically via a surface buoy satellite-linked to shore.

For as Erringer had pointed out, if such creatures existed, they posed a constant threat to any civilization that hoped to advance itself further. Hence there could well be a need to develop permanent means of monitoring and pest control to add to mankind's armory of weaponry to maintain his well being. Hence, a few samples for future research would be worth preserving.

14

The traffic was flowing again—and snarling up, and hooting and honking—in New York City. It sounded good. There was still a lot of rubble to be shoveled up and some rebuilding to do, but on the whole, when it came to demonstrating its capacity for getting back to business as usual with alacrity, humanity had excelled itself.

Kopeksky was just in the process of putting the last pages in his file to wrap up the case, when a call came from the Day Room to say that Moynihan was downstairs, asking to see him. "Yeah, sure. Send him up," Kopeksky said. "For him it's any time, okay?"

"Who's that?" Deena asked from across the office as he put down the phone. The latest assignment from Wade was to look into the problem of a new kind of computer virus loose in the networks, that was causing dire fundamentalist religious warnings to pop up without warning on screens everywhere. She and her purse were sandbagged behind piles of books on programming and communications, and a layer of manufacturers' catalogs and phone company literature had been added to the stratifications on her desk. She also, Kopeksky had noticed but not gone out of his way to mention, had turned up in a new, nicely balanced two-piece of beige and white trim, shoes that matched, and had coaxed her hair into an attractive ponytail.

"Moynihan," Kopeksky answered. "Maybe we're due for another delivery of tea."

"We're still only halfway through the first batch. Do you think I should heat up some water?"

"I wouldn't bother. It's almost lunchtime." Kopeksky looked over and nodded to indicate the semicircle of precariously balanced confusion at arm's length around Deena's chair. "How's it going with that stuff?"

"It's fascinating. By some definitions you could

argue that these things are really alive. It makes me wonder if you could base a prosecution on sending live animals through the mail."

"Don't tell Grauss about it. He'd have everybody looking for a whole zoo." The last they'd heard, Grauss was busy following up a speculation of his that there might also exist bugs that operated on the inverse metabolism of feeding on empty space and turning it into time. If so, it might prove possible to harness them as the basis of a means for life extension and staving off old age.

"Shall I go and get him?" Deena offered.

"I think he knows his way by now. Anyway, isn't it supposed to be kind of a sign of hospitality with the Irish to tell people to walk right in?"

As if on cue, there was a light tap on the door, and Moynihan entered. He was once again in a black raincoat and carrying an umbrella. "Just on me rounds and passing this way," he greeted. "And a grand morning it is that I've brought ye. Ah, 'tis great to see the city itself again, the way God intended. You're both very busy, I see, so I won't be keeping you. I was wondering if you were done with the books that I left here. . . . They wouldn't have been a lot of use to you, I suspect, with the way things turned out."

"I think Deena just about went through every one," Kopeksky replied.

"They were interesting," Deena said. She got up, knocking over some of the books stacked by her chair, and began sorting Moynihan's out from among more folders and papers piled on a table in a corner. "I think I could use the extra space though. Here, these are all yours, I think. Will they be okay in this?"

Moynihan took the plastic bag that she produced from somewhere in her purse and helped her put the books into it. "That will do just fine. . . . What is it they've got ye's into now, if you don't mind my asking?"

"More bugs," Deena told him.

"Ah, no, you're pulling me leg."

"But strictly in this universe this time. Some people are being a nuisance with computer viruses."

"Is that a fact?"

"There's no rush. We were just about to break for lunch," Kopeksky said. "Care to join us? Where would be a good place to go?"

"Well now, there does happen to be a place not far from here that has the best lamb this side of the water, and the Guinness could be from St. James's Gate in Dublin itself."

Kopeksky nodded. "Sounds good to me." He cocked an inquiring eye at Deena. "Wanna give it a try?"

Deena flushed and began sorting, totally unnecessarily, through papers that were lying on her desk. "Oh, that would be nice. But as it happens I'm already having lunch with Graham, if he stops by. . . . I mean, I know he is stopping by, but just in case nothing happens that means he can't . . . if you know what I mean."

"Ah yes," Moynihan said, taking the bag of books and nodding.

"We'll come down with you as far as the door, anyhow," Kopeksky said.

They took the elevator down and came out into the main lobby of the building just as Erringer appeared from the street. He was wearing a crisp white shirt with diagonal stripe college tie and navy blazer, creased gabardines, and carrying a white raincoat folded over one arm. "Uh-huh," Kopeksky murmured to himself.

Erringer grinned a shade self-consciously to acknowledge the presence of Kopeksky and Moynihan. "It's good to see the city back together again," he said.

"With all of it keeping in time, too," Kopeksky agreed.

"I'm borrowing this partner of yours for an hour or so," Erringer said, indicating Deena as they went out onto the street.

"That could be a problem," Kopeksky replied. "I think the department has a regulation that says you have to put in a requisition for something like that."

"What? Even for one of your consultants? I just helped you solve one of your most important cases."

"In that case, maybe you're exempt."

"Just as well. I was never much good at filling out forms, anyway."

"Get out of here," Kopeksky told them.

Erringer offered his arm. Deena slipped hers through, and they disappeared around the corner of the block.

"I guess that just leaves you and me," Kopeksky said to Moynihan. "Now were you saying about that place with the Guinness?"

"I thought you were on duty," Moynihan answered.

"Well, there are days when I qualify for an exemption too. I just decided this is one of them. Hey, you've got the umbrella. Let me carry that bag."

The policeman and the priest walked away together and were lost among the avenue's midday crowd.

JAMES P. HOGAN
Real SF

Bug Park (HC) 0-671-87773-9 $22.00 ☐
(PB) 0-671-87874-3 $6.99 ☐
All it takes to change the world is one visionary—and a
team of people to keep him alive.

Paths to Otherwhere (HC) 0-671-87710-0 $22.00 ☐
(PB) 0-671-87767-4 $5.99 ☐
"Readers awed by explorations of either inner or outer space
will want to sign up for this ride." —*Publishers Weekly*

The Two Faces of Tomorrow 0-671-87848-4 $6.99 ☐
The ultimate AI—logical but not reasonable.

Endgame Enigma 0-671-87796-8 $5.99 ☐
A shining city in space—or tyranny's ultimate weapon?

The Proteus Operation 0-671-87757-7 $5.99 ☐
The victorious facists had conquered nearly all of the
world—freedom's only hope was a counterstrike back
through time!

If not available at your local bookstore, fill out this coupon and send a
check or money order for the cover price(s) plus $1.50 s/h to Baen Books,
Dept. BA, P.O. Box 1403, Riverdale, NY 10471. Delivery can take up to ten
weeks.

NAME: _____

ADDRESS: _____

_____

I have enclosed a check or money order in the amount of $ _____

THE SHIP WHO SANG IS NOT ALONE!

Anne McCaffrey, with Margaret Ball, Mercedes Lackey, S.M. Stirling, and Jody Lynn Nye, explores the universe she created with her ground-breaking novel, The Ship Who Sang.

PARTNERSHIP
by Anne McCaffrey & Margaret Ball

"[*PartnerShip*] captures the spirit of *The Ship Who Sang*...a single, solid plot full of creative nastiness and the sort of egocentric villains you love to hate."

—Carolyn Cushman, *Locus*

THE SHIP WHO SEARCHED
by Anne McCaffrey & Mercedes Lackey

Tia, a bright and spunky seven-year-old accompanying her exo-archaeologist parents on a dig, is afflicted by a paralyzing alien virus. Tia won't be satisfied to glide through life like a ghost in a machine. Like her predecessor Helva, *The Ship Who Sang*, she would rather strap on a spaceship!

THE CITY WHO FOUGHT
by Anne McCaffrey & S.M. Stirling

Simeon was the "brain" running a peaceful space station—but when the invaders arrived, his only hope of protecting his crew and himself was to become *The City Who Fought*.

THE SHIP WHO WON
by Anne McCaffrey & Jody Lynn Nye

"Oodles of fun."   —*Locus*
"Fast, furious and fun."   —*Chicago Sun-Times*

ANNE McCAFFREY:
QUEEN OF THE SPACEWAYS

"Readers will find themselves riveted by the nonstop action adventure that constantly surpasses even the most jaded reader's expectations, and by a relationship as beautiful as it is indestructible."

—*Affaire de Coeur*

PARTNERSHIP ☐
by Anne McCaffrey & Margaret Ball
0-671-72109-7 ◆ 336 pages ◆ $5.99

THE SHIP WHO SEARCHED ☐
by Anne McCaffrey & Mercedes Lackey
0-671-72129-1 ◆ 320 pages ◆ $5.99

THE CITY WHO FOUGHT ☐
by Anne McCaffrey & S.M. Stirling
0-671-72166-6 ◆ 432 pages ◆ HC $19.00 ◆ PB $5.99 ◆ 87599-X

THE SHIP WHO WON ☐
by Anne McCaffrey & Jody Lynn Nye
0-671-87595-7 ◆ HC $21.00 ◆ PB $5.99 ◆ 87657-0

And don't miss:
THE PLANET PIRATES ☐
by Anne McCaffrey,
with Elizabeth Moon & Jody Lynn Nye
3-in-1 trade paperback edition
0-671-72187-9 ◆ 864 pages ◆ $12.00

If not available through your local bookstore send this coupon and a check or money order for the cover price(s) to Baen Books, Dept. BA, P.O. Box 1403, Riverdale, NY 10471. Delivery can take up to ten weeks.

NAME: _____

ADDRESS: _____

_____

I have enclosed a check or money order in the amount of $ _____